BLOOD OF
CAIN

ALSO BY TOM LOWE

A False Dawn
The 24th Letter
The Butterfly Forest
The Black Bullet
Blood of Cain

BLOOD OF
CAIN

A Sean O'Brien Mystery/Thriller

TOM LOWE

K

Kingsbridge Entertainment

Blood of Cain – Copyright © 2013 by Tom Lowe. All rights reserved. No part of this book may be reproduced, scanned, stored in a retrieval system, or transmitted in any form or by any means, electronic, photocopying, Internet, recording or otherwise without written permission from the author. Please do not participate or encourage piracy of copyrighted materials in violation of the author's rights. Published in The United States of America. For information, address Kingsbridge Entertainment, P.O. Box 340, Windermere, FL 34786

Library of Congress Cataloging in–Publication Data. Lowe, Tom 1952-

Blood of Cain by Tom Lowe – 1st edition

1. Cain and Abel—Fiction. 2. The Prophet—Fiction. 3. Carnival, County Fair—Fiction. 4. Ocala National Forest—Fiction. 5. Ireland—Fiction Title: *Blood of Cain*.

Blood of Cain is distributed in ebook and print editions. Printed books available from Amazon Inc. and bookstores.

Cover design by Damonza

Formatting and digital conversion services by CreateSpace

ISBN-10: 1494496194
ISBN-13: 9781494496197

First Edition: December 2013. Published in the U.S.A. by Kingsbridge Entertainment.

"I've learned a lot about good and evil. They are not always what they appear to be."

—Charles Van Doren

ACKNOWLEDGMENTS

A fter I write *"The End,"* I get to tell how it began. This page of the novel is where I have the opportunity to thank those who've helped me. Although *Blood of Cain* is a work of fiction, some of the material related to experiments into government covert human mind control is based upon information gathered from declassified documents related to CIA experiments and testing during the 1960s. A special thank you to Todd Garner, Ph.D. Thanks to John Wortman for his consultation on guns and ballistics. Thumbs up to Tom Greenberg and Greg Houtteman of EO MediaWorks for the design of my website, tomlowebooks.com.

A big shout out and thanks to my daughter, Cassie, my first beta reader. To readers John Buonpane and Helen Christensen. To Damonza for cover design; to Carina, Lauren and Kandis with CreateSpace for ebook and print formatting. I want to thank my family for their strong support for each novel that I write. This includes Natalie, Cassie, Christopher, and Ashley. A drum roll and special thank you to my wife, Keri. I'm grateful for her spot-on suggestions, listening skills, patience, smile, and sense of humor. Keri, you are my inspiration and truly the wind in my sails.

In memoriam: to Sadie, a little bit of her lives on in the character of "Max." We miss you.

And now to you, the reader. If you've read other books in the Sean O'Brien series, here's a toast to you. Welcome back! If this is your first venture into the journey, I hope you enjoy *Blood of Cain.*

For Cassie

PROLOGUE

COUNTY KERRY, IRELAND - 1970

Kate Flanagan was glad that the confessional booth would keep her from looking the priest in the eye. Father Thomas Garvey's sapphire blue eyes had a strange power, she thought. It was a power not of this world. But he was a priest, someone who walked a straighter path under God's direction. *He was a man of God.*

Then why was she so physically attracted to him?

It had begun six months ago when Father Garvey first moved to the parish and started delivering mass at St. Vincent's Church. Kate had sat in the pew with her husband and listened to Father Garvey speaking in a soft, yet deep voice when he led the service. His angular face was movie-star handsome. He had thick, dark eyebrows and combed his black hair straight back. Although the priest would be scanning the congregation as he spoke, she felt that his eyes sought hers, connecting, even if only for a few seconds at a time. He was somehow linking with her deepest most personal thoughts, her soul. She could feel it. Kate would catch herself fantasizing about him, her face flushing, the damp warmth smoldering under her Sunday dress. Then she would silently pray to God to forgive her for sinful thinking, and of all places, in our Lord's house.

She tried to put that out of her thoughts as she entered the confessional booth. Before she left her home, she had spent extra time fixing her dark, shoulder-length hair, and applying blush and lipstick to her oval face and full lips. Now, she waited. How long had it been since her last confession? Was she the first to speak or was it supposed to be the priest? *Think*. She waited a half a minute. She could hear a farmer's tractor, the diesel straining, pulling a load up the road outside the rural church. She looked at her watch. Too early for her husband Peter to be picking her up. She heard a sheep cry, its bleating coming from a field behind the church. Then there was the long, confident stride of someone approaching. Kate felt her breathing quicken. She heard Father Garvey take his seat. She could *feel* his physical presence just beyond the thin wall. She looked at the lattice grid and cleared her throat. Her heart beat faster, and she dropped down on her knees, making the sign of the cross. "Forgive me Father, for I have sinned."

Father Garvey said nothing.

Kate folded her hands in prayer, waiting. "Forgive me Father, for I have sinned."

"When was your last confession?"

"I can't remember, Father."

"Our Lord, Jesus, remembers."

"Yes, Father. I'm sorry."

"What is it you wish to confess?"

Kate paused a moment, her hand rubbing the rosary beads she carried. "Father, I confess that I haven't been completely honest with my husband."

"You have lied?"

"Yes, I haven't been completely truthful with Peter."

"In what way?"

"We have been married for three years. The last two years I have been trying to become pregnant. The Lord hasn't blessed us with a child yet, and I believe it is my fault."

"Why do you feel this way?"

"I think God is punishing me because I have unclean thoughts, thoughts of others."

"Other men?"

"Yes, Father. I am so ashamed. I love my husband. I really do, but there is something happening to me that I don't understand, these feelings inside me. He can tell that all is not right. He asks, but I lie to him and pretend all is fine. Over and over I lie. He is a good man. I seek absolution…penance, Father."

"That's why our Lord brought you here, Kate."

She held her fingers to her lips. "How do you know who I…"

"Our Lord knows all."

"But you're not…"

"Not what? You haven't been chaste in thought and word, have you, Kate?"

"No, Father."

"You haven't used sex for its sole purpose of procreation. It has been self-gratification, hasn't it?"

"Yes."

"That violates the Word."

"Yes, Father."

"And you seek absolution? Yes? You desire to be fruitful under God's command?"

"Yes, and I'm sorry for being deceptive to Peter. Am I forgiven, Father? What is my penance?" She closed her eyes and stroked the rosary beads.

The door to the confessional flew open. Kate, still on her knees, looked up at Father Garvey in the open doorway. He said, "I am your penance. God, has sent you to me."

"What?"

"Stand up."

Kate slowly stood. He entered the booth and stepped next to her. He smelled of testosterone and lilac soap. His dark blue eyes fiery. Intense. His lips were moist. Square jaw-line as hard as granite. He placed his big hand on her shoulder, his fingers massaging her, working his way down to the small of her back.

"Please, Father…"

He leaned closer and whispered. "Sex is for procreation. God has delivered you here for a reason, Kate. Sometimes we fail to understand His plan. You cannot deny divine providence." He stroked her face gently, the tips of his long fingers moving over her cheek, lips, and down to her breasts. He leaned in to kiss her, slowly, his lips soft, his mouth warm and hungry for her.

She broke away for air. "I can't!"

"You can! And you will because God has a greater plan for you, Kate. You can atone. Impure thoughts can be absolved." Father Garvey skillfully forced his right hand up her dress. His hand was wide and strong, fingers

TOM LOWE

firm as he stroked her inner thighs. He kissed her again. This time Kate felt her lips part, his tongue touching hers, his fingers arousing heat and wetness inside her. She wanted him, wanted him to take her. Suddenly, he lifted her out of the confessional, carrying her like a child in his powerful arms. She felt fragile and yet sheltered.

He walked by the front pews, through the open door in his office, and set her down on a large wooden desk, spilling papers onto the floor. He cupped her face in both of his large hands as he kissed her. She moaned, her tongue meeting his. His hand was under her dress, fingers entering her. She gasped, leaning her head back, eyes closed, her heart racing.

'Dear God!' she thought, glancing out the window as a car pulled into the parking lot. *It's Peter.* Kate made a move to get off the table.

"No!" shouted Father Garvey.

"My husband's outside. I must go to him."

"And you will, Kate. This won't take long. God works miracles. Your husband didn't get out of his car. He's being delayed for a reason. Don't you see the bigger picture, Kate?" He pushed her back down, one strong arm holding her shoulders, the other ripping off her panties. His finger moving inside her wetness.

Kate looked over her shoulder and could see her husband patiently waiting for her, the car window up, Peter listening to music. She was frightened, a dark sadness filling her pores, her eyes burning. "Please let me up. My husband's here."

Father Garvey pulled her to the edge of the table and pushed open her legs. She slammed her fists against his chest. "No! Please," she begged, biting her lower lip. Within seconds he had penetrated her. The pain was intense. Hot tears streamed down her face. Father Garvey reached for her chin, holding it with one hand and turning her head toward him.

"Look at me, Kate. Look into my eyes as I enter you." She looked at him, his face twisted, eyes fiery, nostrils wide. He pushed back and forth inside her, each stroke penetrating deeper. The priest said, "He who comes to the sacred table of the Lord without faith, communicates only in the sacrament and does not receive the substance of the sacrament whence comes life." He drove deeper into her, his penis throbbing, ejaculating.

Kate screamed. "No! Dear God, no." She looked over her shoulder and could see a small statue of the Virgin Mary. A painting on the wall of the Last Supper. Through the office door, across the sanctuary, was a stained glass window depicting Christ ascending to heaven. The room was spinning. She was nauseous, vomit rising in her throat. She looked out the other window into the parking lot. She could see the sky growing dark. Peter stepped from the car and walked around to the trunk. He got an umbrella for Kate, like he always did. She watched him and wept. "Peter, dear Peter," she whispered. The clouds opened into a hard rain, engulfing the old church with the roar of a waterfall. Lightning cracked and thunder rolled, smothering the final grunts of Father Thomas Garvey.

ONE

CENTRAL FLORIDA,
NEAR DAYTONA BEACH, PRESENT DAY

Of all the rides in the carnival, Courtney Burke felt safest on the ride that scared many people. She liked the double Ferris wheel the best. She loved to ride it at night, wind in her face, hair blowing, and the lights of the town like stars twinkling in the valley. She rode after the crowds had gone back to their cozy homes, gone back to warm places where beds had real pillows. On the double Ferris wheel, she was free. It was as if she had wings, flying high above the evil that crawled across the ground like the rattlesnake slithering on its belly. As a girl, she remembered almost stepping on a rattler behind her uncle's barn, the same barn where bad things had happened. But that was in another world, a world that couldn't hurt her again. Now, at age nineteen, she was free, free to travel the country with the carnival, free to ride the Big Wheel.

Courtney lowered the safety bar in the seat, pinned her long raven hair into a ponytail, and turned toward the ride operator. He was cute, she thought. Maybe two years older than her. She smiled, the dimples showing, her blue-green eyes wide, catching light like the crest of a breaking wave on a moonlit tropical beach. "Just a quick ride, okay, Lonnie?"

"I don't know, Courtney. We're gonna get caught one of these nights, sneaking back to turn on this wheel."

"Where's your sense of adventure, huh? C'mon let's ride a wheel that turns but never takes you anywhere, unless you let it. Pretty please, Lonnie."

1

Lonnie Ebert lifted his baseball cap and ran his hand though dirty blond hair that hadn't been washed in two weeks. He glanced around the carnival grounds, his lean face unshaven, eyes searching for a sign of movement. Most of the carnies were asleep, stoned on weed, or in honky-tonks knocking back cheap whisky chased by cheaper beer. He licked his dry lips and looked at Courtney, her smile the brightest thing in the shadows of the midway. "I do things for you that I wouldn't do for no other girl."

Courtney smiled. "I know, and I don't take it for granted. Okay? Press the button."

"All right, but we gotta make it quick. If Big John catches my ass he'd fire me, or worse."

"He's gone to town. I saw him leave. C'mon, start this thing. I wanna feel the rush."

"Five minutes. Tops." He pressed the green start button, the black dirt under his thumbnail visible as the lights popped on and the Big Wheel lurched into motion.

She grinned. "Thank you! Can you stop it at the top on the second time around for a minute? I love the feeling of being that far up. I've never been in a jet plane. But up there I'm on top of the world."

Lonnie blew out a pent-up breath, ran his tongue on the inside of his cheek, and looked to his right, down the midway. "Just for a few seconds, and one time only."

Courtney gripped the safety bar, electricity surging through the motors, gears groaning, metal popping, the Big Wheel defying gravity and lifting the double wheels higher into the night sky. She rose above the lingering smells of the midway, the spilled beer and half-eaten corndogs and cotton candy stomped into the sea of damp sawdust, the stench quickly replaced with a cool night breeze of wild honeysuckles as the Big Wheel turned skyward in the warm summer night.

She sat in the center of the seat and glanced up at the harvest moon. It seemed so close, so big and bright. The wind whipped her hair as she raised her arms. *Tonight, I'm a bird, a dove flying high above the world.* She looked down. Lonnie smoked a cigarette and paced near the operator's stand, the tiny orange glow the only movement on the ground. Up here the wind caressed her face under a big yellow moon, and the stars seemed almost within her reach. She held her breath as a meteor streaked across the deep purple with a welder's spark of fire that sliced a fleeting crack into the heart of the heavens.

The Ferris wheel lifted her higher, almost to the summit of its cycle, the wind picking up. As the Big Wheel crested at the top, it descended quickly, going through its spinning cycle. She held her hands up and made a contorted, funny face at Lonnie, zipping by him on her way back to the top. "Yeeeeessss! I'm a bird," she sang the words.

At the top of the cycle, the Big Wheel came to a sudden stop. Courtney looked down and blew a kiss to Lonnie, who removed his baseball cap and grinned. The night was suddenly very quiet. She raised her eyes up and felt as if she could see for a hundred miles in any direction. There was the night-glow of Gainesville, Florida, at the edge of the horizon. She saw the headlights of cars creeping down dark back roads in the distance. A flicker of heat lightning hung in the outlying clouds for a beat no longer than the blush of a firefly's belly.

The seat, attached by two metal pins as wide as her little finger, rocked back and forth at the top of the Ferris wheel. Courtney couldn't help but smile. She closed her eyes for a moment and felt the breeze on her skin, her mind in sharp focus, the world now smaller, her troubles and past seemed far beyond the horizon. She watched a plane flying low in the distance, climbing higher as it gained altitude after leaving an airport. *One day I'll catch a jet plane to fly to some far away, romantic place. But right now this is the best seat in the whole world. My rockin' chair with a view that goes forever.*

She glanced down. Lonnie was smoking a cigarette, looking across the darkened midway. A movement caught her eye. Someone in the shadows. A man wearing a hooded sweatshirt. He was standing between the RV's, campers and trailers, someone staring up at her. Even from the distance, she felt there was something wrong with the way the man was looking at her. The fairgrounds suddenly darkened. Courtney looked to the sky as a cloud shadow-danced over the face of the moon, and she thought of her grandmother. Her Irish grandma, someone who spoke Gaelic and Irish cant, was believed by many to be a psychic. She used to say that Courtney's ability to see things, to get a feeling that something or someone was not right -- that something was about to happen, was a gift from a higher power. "It skips a generation, baby girl," Grandma told her one spring night on the steps of her grandmother's small home in South Boston. "Your mother never got it. But you sure did."

She remembered looking into her grandmother's sea-green eyes, eyes that smiled with insight and absolute love. "Use your gift wisely, Courtney." People, mostly from the clan, the Irish travelers—the gypsies, called the old woman a mystic, and they'd consult her for all kinds of things. Some wanted to know about the future. Others wanted to know how to hide their past to protect their future. A few wanted to reach out to dead relatives. Most things, Courtney figured, based on the conversations she overheard between Grandma and her clients, had to do with sex. The lack of it. Too much of it. Men chasin' it, and women fakin' it. It's all crap, really.

Courtney looked down at Lonnie, her seat rocking slightly as she leaned over the safety bar. He waved and started the wheel again. Courtney closed her eyes as she descended, the wind in her face, her thoughts over the horizon. As she rotated closer to the ground, she looked toward the operator's stand.

The horror hit her in the gut.

Please, God, no. She held her hand to her mouth and screamed, her lower lip trembling. She felt sick. She looked down a second time. Maybe Lonnie would stand up and say he was joking. But she knew the way he was lying in the sawdust he was hurt, maybe killed, his left leg twisted behind him.

Courtney knew that Lonnie Ebert wasn't going to stand up.

And she knew the man in the hooded sweatshirt was the killer.

But she didn't know why.

TWO

The image could have been a hallucination. I was that tired, physically and mentally exhausted. I flashed on my high beams. A ground fog was building in the night, and the high beams did nothing to help me see what I believed was a girl walking on the shoulder of the road. Nothing there. *Maybe a deer.* I stuck my head out the open window of my Jeep driving down County Road 314 through the heart of the Ocala National Forest. Max, my ten-pound dachshund, was curled on the passenger seat, fast asleep. It was near midnight, and I was glad there was no other traffic on what was undoubtedly one of the darkest highways in the nation.

The road twisted through canopies of ancient live oaks, thick branches stretching high over the highway and blocking out what little light was coming from the moon. I'd spent all day sanding and repainting the bottom of *Jupiter*, my vintage 38-foot Bayliner at Ponce Marina near Daytona Beach. I would have stayed overnight on the boat if it weren't hauled into the yard, propped up with jack-stands and blocks. Tomorrow, *Jupiter* would take her place back at slip L-17. Now I was heading home to my old house on the St. Johns River.

The image returned, ghostlike through the fog. A young woman, maybe a teenager, definitely walking on the side of the road. She wore jeans and a blue T-shirt, walking slowly, too near the pavement to be safe. Not that it was safe walking down a rural stretch of highway late at night through the heart of a national forest known as much for its body count as its beauty. It was the same forest where convicted serial killer Aileen Wuornos had left some

5

of her victims. And it had a history of murder and bloodshed dating back to the Spaniards slaughter of the native people.

The girl didn't stop walking when I slowed down and pulled up beside her. Max awoke and stood on her hind legs, bracing to peer out the open window. I asked, "Can I give you a ride to wherever you're going? This is not the safest place in the nation to be taking an evening stroll."

No response. The girl kept walking, hugging her arms in the humid night air, the chant of cicadas echoing through the dark forest. She swatted a mosquito. I drove slowly, keeping pace with her. "The mosquitoes will eat you alive out here. Look, I'm not trying to do anything but help you."

Max barked. The girl stopped and turned toward us. She said, "I don't need your help. Please, just go away. Leave me alone, okay?"

She looked at Max and the girl's agitated face softened for a second, a tiny smile at one side of her mouth. She bit her top lip and started walking. I could tell she'd been crying for a while. Eyes swollen, red blotches on her face, hair tangled like she'd been running before walking, running away from something or running to something. Even through the mosquito welts, through the confused and hurt face, she was a pretty young woman. And she was someone who might be zipped into a body bag if she walked this road all night.

The T-shirt had two dark stains across her waist, like she'd wiped blood on her shirt. Something had caused her world to come crashing down, at least from her perspective something bad had happened. Right now the only thing that mattered was her safety. She was somebody's daughter, and she was all alone in a dark and dangerous place where no one should be alone.

I said, "You're hurting Max's feelings."

She stopped again, looked at us, leaned closer to the window and said, "Excuse me?"

I smiled and Max cocked her head. Then Max did her little half bark. Sort of her way of asking, "What's up?" The girl smiled. It was a natural, beautiful smile. Her eyes, even from the spill light of my dashboard, were mesmerizing. They were wide, the striking look of the irises was even more pronounced because of the dark circles wrapped around the color. They were the shade of golden light through emeralds, and they were very frightened eyes.

She inhaled deeply through her nose, and looked back down the long, dark highway. An owl called out from one of the live oaks, the grunt of bullfrogs coming from the swamp. I could smell smoke from a hunter's camp somewhere in the deep woods. I said, "Please, get in the Jeep. I'll take you into DeLand. It's about twenty miles away. Are you a student at Stetson?"

"I've never been to college. Look, I appreciate your generosity. I can tell you're a nice guy. But I'm gonna be okay. I just need some space away from people. Your dog's cute."

"I can understand how you need space, but there are better places to find quiet time. I'm Sean O'Brien. What's your name?"

"Courtney Burke."

"Nice to meet you Courtney. I live near here in an old house by the river. I've been sanding, painting, and working in a boatyard at Ponce Marina all day. Let me take you into town. There's a Waffle House open all night. Do you need money to catch a bus?"

She rolled her eyes, crossed her arms, and said, "No thanks." She coughed, reached into her pocket and removed an asthma inhaler—taking a long hit from it.

"Are you okay?"

She nodded, breathing deeply now through her nose, her eyes moist. "Yes."

"Look, Courtney, I'm too tired to hang out here on a dark road about five miles from where police found a body last month, less than fifty feet off the highway. A runaway teenage girl. She'd been dumped like trash. Now, please, get in the Jeep."

She leaned closer to the open window and looked at me, studying my face for a long moment, a small gold Celtic cross hanging from her long neck. "You said your name's Sean O'Brien, right?"

"Yes, why?"

"No reason. You lived here all your life?"

"Part of my life. The important part. Why?"

"It's nothing. Look, I…"

Light raked across the left side of her face. I glanced into my rearview mirror and saw headlights approaching. I said, "Car's coming. Step back, I'm pulling off the road." I turned the Jeep's emergency flashers on and eased off the road directly behind the girl. Within seconds we were passed by a pickup truck. And three seconds later I saw the brake lights pop on.

Not a good sign.

THREE

I thought about my Glock. Thought about how I'd left it in the house after cleaning and oiling the pistol when I took it out of the Jeep two days ago. I glanced down at Max. Since she couldn't see over the dashboard, she followed the movement of the truck with her head and ears. And then she growled. Another bad sign.

The truck slowly backed up, coming parallel to my Jeep. Two men inside. There was enough light from their dashboard and the ambient glow from my Jeep to see their faces. Both wore cut-off black T-shirts. Tats on beefy forearms. Hard faces with a week's growth of whiskers. The man on the passenger side had hooded, red-rimmed eyes that didn't blink, like a drunk at a bar staring at condensation rolling down his beer bottle. He wore a baseball hat turned backwards. The driver locked his thin lips on a bottle of Crown Royal in a wrinkled paper bag, turned it up, and took one long gulp, his face shining from sweat, cheeks blooming a shade of crimson. He stared at me through moist eyes and said, "Ya'll look like you need some help."

I could smell diesel fumes mixed with burning weed. I said, "Thanks for stopping. Everything's okay. She just got carsick. She wanted to get some fresh air."

The man closest to me said, "Ya'll got all your windows down. Plenty of air in a Jeep. Maybe you and your girlfriend got into a ruckus. Maybe she don't want you no more and she's lookin' to hitch a ride."

I said nothing. Max growled again.

The man looked at Max, grinned, and turned to the driver. "He's got a fuckin' muskrat on the seat next to him. One of 'em wiener dogs."

"No wonder the bitch walked." They laughed and then the guy on the passenger side gazed at the girl, like he was seeing her for the first time. He said, "Hey, sweet thing. That right? This dude botherin' you? We can make him go away. You just say the word."

"C'mon darlin,' get in the truck and we'll take you home."

The girl said, "No thanks."

The man sneered and touched the tip of his nose with a thick finger. The driver gunned the truck and quickly pulled off the road in front of my Jeep. "Get in!" I yelled to the girl. She hesitated a moment and then reached for the door handle.

Too late. The man on the passenger side moved fast, not even waiting for the truck to stop before flinging open the door and running toward the girl. He grabbed her by the forearm.

"Don't touch me!" she shouted. The man laughed and wrapped his arms, fur, ink, and muscle around her.

"She's a fighter!" he shouted, dragging her toward the truck. "This bitch got some spunk. She's gonna be real good."

The driver, carrying a Billy club, approached me. I got out of the Jeep. He grinned, slapped the wood in the palm of his big bear paw hand and said, "Weiner dog dude, you ready for the whoppin' your daddy shoulda done years ago?" His belly hung over a belt that I couldn't see because of the girth. I guessed he was more than 290 pounds of muscles and fat, mostly fat. Plus he was stoned, very stoned. Each body movement was telegraphed before it happened.

I waited for him, never taking my eyes off of his. He raised his huge right arm and swung at my head. I easily dodged it, the Billy club missing my forehead by a few inches. The kinetic energy, the torque of the swing, threw him off balance for a half second. That's all the time I needed. I grabbed his right wrist, pulling his arm behind his back and forcing his hand up to his neck. The pop of tendons and bones separating was like the sound of eggs cracking.

He screamed and went down on his knees the same time I brought up my knee hard into his nose. He fell backwards, out cold.

The other man had abandoned the girl and was reaching for a shotgun cradled in the window behind the truck seats. His hand was touching the stock when I slammed the truck's door into his legs. He yelled louder than his sleeping partner had screamed, and he tried to turn around—again an opponent losing equilibrium. It gave me a moment to draw far back and deliver a hard hit with my fist into the center of his mouth. I felt my knuckles plow through lips, front teeth and nose. I knew his jaw had dislocated. He stared at me through incredulous dull eyes, now glazed and rolling upward in his small skull. His lips were macerated, blood pouring from what was left of his mouth and nose. He smelled of weed, sour beer, and bacon fat. He tumbled forward, falling into the undergrowth, less than five feet from a canal.

I looked in the truck and lifted a cell phone from the seat and punched three digits.

The dispatcher said, "Nine-one-one, what is your emergency?"

"Looks like two men got in a fight. Severe injuries. County road 314. About halfway into the Ocala National Forest. Their Ford pickup is pulled over on the side of the road. Send an ambulance."

"Are the men breathing?"

"Yes."

"What is your name, sir?"

I disconnected and threw the phone into the center of the canal.

Then I looked for the girl, the fog growing thicker, rising through the light from the Jeep's headlights, the bellow of bullfrogs coming from the canal. "Are you okay?" I called out to the girl, hoping she would be standing in the shadows. "Courtney!" I felt fatigue growing behind my eyes as I walked back to my Jeep. Little Max stuck her head out the side window and made a slight whimpering sound. "She ran away, Max. The girl's gone."

FOUR

The next morning I awoke at sunrise, poured a cup of coffee, and walked onto my screened porch to feed Max. The porch overlooked the St. Johns River, a 310-mile river of history that meandered north from Vero Beach, spilling its heart into the Atlantic Ocean east of Jacksonville. My old cabin, built in the 1930's from cypress, pine, and red oak, sat at the mid-way point of the river. My nearest neighbor was a mile away. The Ocala National Forest, with its primordial beauty, bordered the far side of the St. Johns.

I sipped coffee and watched the match-flare of dawn smolder in the horizon behind live oaks and cabbage palms. The sunrise cast the trees in silhouette, their leafy heads and shoulders stitched in the golden threads of morning light. At the base of the old oaks, and deep in the ancient forest, secrets lie buried in folklore and fauna like the watery graves of mastodon skeletons discovered at the bottom of the forest's gin-clear springs.

I thought of the girl I'd found last night, Courtney Burke. I hoped she was on a bus heading to someplace safer than where she came. My thoughts were interrupted by a cardinal, tossing back his head and singing to the new day.

A breeze danced across the river and brought the scent of wood smoke and honeysuckles. A fisherman puttered down the center of the river in a dark green Boston Whaler, a V formation from the boat's wake pitching the surface into a sea of copper pennies winking in the sunlight.

Max barked once. "Patience, little lady," I said, pouring some food into her bowl. I watched her eat for a few seconds and then looked at the framed picture of my wife, Sherri, which I kept on a small end table next to a rocking chair on the porch. Sherri died a few years ago from ovarian cancer, but her spirit still lived with us, Max and me. When I worked as a homicide detective with Miami-Dade PD, Sherri bought Max when I was on an extended criminal surveillance. She'd named her Maxine, but with the little dachshund's feisty brown eyes and fearless heart of a lion in a ten-pound body, she took on the swagger of a Max.

She swallowed her last bite and stepped to the screened door, glancing over her shoulder at me with the look that asked, *what are you waiting for?* We walked toward the dock, under the limbs of live oaks. Spanish moss, streaked and damp with dew, hung from the limbs like gray lamb's wool left in the rain. From the top of a huge cypress tree near the shore, a curlew called out to the rising sun. The bird's river song echoed across the St. Johns in a haunting tune of rhythmic chants. Its symphony skipped over the water with the beat of smooth stones cast in the alluring harmony of sad and sweet notes long ago sung by the Sirens of Homer's Greece.

As we walked toward my dock on the river, my thoughts again drifted to the brave but frightened face of Courtney Burke. Even though I was exhausted when I first saw her, I remembered seeing a cue in her eyes that alluded to something long ago lost, maybe partially buried. What was it?

"You lived here all your life?"

"Part of my life. The important part. Why?"

"It's nothing. Look, I…"

I sat on one of two Adirondack chairs at the end of my dock, the girl's face, the blood on her T-shirt, her compelling and scared eyes swirling in my mind like moths circling a light source. Her eyes, with their sea green-golden irises enclosed in dark circles around the mesmerizing color, reminded me of the iconic picture of a young Afghan girl captured years ago by a National Geographic photographer. It was the eyes, the haunting image of the girl seen and felt around the world. I hoped Courtney Burke didn't make the morning news. I reached for my cell to check local news sources, but paused, not wanting to confirm that she'd become a runaway statistic.

Max leaned over the edge of the dock. She watched an eight-foot alligator swimming from dark water surrounding knobby cypress knees protruding out of the river less than thirty feet from where Max stood. She growled.

The gator stopped moving, its yellow eyes and snout visible from our perch above the river. Max lifted her front foot, like a little hunting dog, a pointer. The gator dropped below the surface, and Max whined, looking over her shoulder at me. I said, "Leave well enough alone, kiddo."

Watching the river dress in the colors of the morning, I tried to remove the girl's face from my thoughts. An osprey dropped straight down out of the hard blue sky, plunging into the center of the river and hooking something in its talons. Within seconds, the bird was beating its massive wings, gaining altitude, its claws deep in the back of a wriggling bass.

My cell buzzed. I pulled it out of my pocket and read the text message. It was from an old friend, Dave Collins.

I just heard your voice on the morning TV news report, at least I think it was you. Police released a recording from someone who called 911 to report a fight last night. The caller used the phone of the guys he beat up to call 911. Could be mistaken, but the voice on the phone…it remotely sounded like you, Sean.

Are you OK? What's going on?

FIVE

By noon, I'd made the half-hour drive from my place on the river to Ponce Marina south of Daytona Beach. I'd called the marina boatyard before I left, and they'd begun the process of lowering *Jupiter* back into her slip. Max and I pulled into the gravel and oyster shell parking lot, the popcorn crack of shells snapping under the tires. The teasing smells of blackened grouper, garlic shrimp, and mesquite greeted us from the Tiki Bar, an open-air restaurant adjacent to the marina office. Max's eyes ignited. She was now more Pavlov's dog than mine, her eyes wide, pacing in her seat, her nostrils sucking in molecules of food scents. She uttered one of her half barks, now more of a command.

"Chill," I said, lifting Max up, tucking her under one arm and carrying a bag of groceries in the other arm. "You mind your manners in the restaurant. No begging. If not, the board of health will hunt you down, the county will pass anti-dog laws, and it'll be plain dog food forevermore." She glanced up at me, her brown eyes suspicious.

I was being generous referring to the Tiki Bar as a restaurant. They served food, but it was a secondary item on a menu that featured thirty different craft beers and twenty brands of rum, along with all the other adult beverages.

The restaurant was somewhere between rustic and rundown, but it had character. The rough-hewn wooden floors, made with railroad crossties, and long-since worn into a smooth finish, were stained with twenty-five years of bar graffiti, mixed from a palette of spilled beer, blood, sweat, and a few tears. The Tiki Bar was built on stilts, fifteen feet above the harbor water at high tide.

It had no real windows. Most of the year its plastic isinglass siding was rolled up and tied off. The result was a cross-breeze that kept the flies to a minimum and allowed a maximum opportunity for the scent of grilled seafood to drift over a marina community of at least two hundred boats. That's marketing using all the senses. And it worked because the place was usually packed.

Max and I walked around a sunburned family of four standing at the entrance, debating items listed on a plastic menu stapled to a six-by-six beam, their Jersey shore accents getting as hot as their scorched skin. "Try the grilled pompano," I said, smiling and stepping around them.

"Hey Miss Maxie!" said Kim Davis, the Tiki Bar day manager. She came out from behind the bar and greeted us, taking Max into her arms and cuddling her, Max licking Kim's brown cheeks. "Gimme kisses, sweetheart." Kim was radiant, caramel-colored eyes animated. She was in her early forties, genuine smile, shoulder-length chestnut-brown hair, and flawless skin to match. She wore tight, faded jeans that accentuated her curvaceous hips, and a T-shirt with a graphic image of a doe-eyed, blushing oyster that read:

Eat 'em Raw at the Tiki Bar
Ponce Inlet, Florida

She said, "I saw Bobby and his crew putting your boat back in the water." She glanced through the open isinglass and smiled. "Looks like *Jupiter's* still floating. Nick, whether they wanted his help or not, assisted or rather insisted on helping." She set Max on the wooden floor and handed her a piece of cheese.

I said, "You're one of the reasons she's turning her nose up at dog food."

Kim smiled. "That's because she knows she's not a dog. She's a princess."

"She's spoiled."

"A girl needs to be spoiled from time to time. Makes her feel special." Kim held her brown eyes on mine for a moment, a perfect eyebrow raised slightly over her right eye.

I nodded. "What can I say, Kimberly?"

"Sean, you know what a woman really wants. It's some--"

"Hey Kim, turn up the TV, will you?" A grizzled, retired charter boat captain, face whiskered and scarred from sun cancer surgeries, his forearms

15

the color of saddle leather, sipped from a can of Bud and pointed to the television above the bar. "They got something on the TV 'bout that killin' at the carnival."

Kim picked the remote control off the bar and pressed the button for sound. The images were of a county fairground, parked police cruisers, flashing blue lights, emergency medics moving with no sense of urgency, carnies standing in the background, smoking and hiding their faces from cameras as the coroner loaded the body into a white van. The body was covered with a sheet, a baseball-sized dark red color in the chest area.

The picture cut to a TV reporter. "Police are saying that the man, whose identity is being withheld until his family is notified, was found dead with an ice pick in his chest. An autopsy will be performed. They say that no witnesses have come forth; however, one of the carnival workers said the deceased man was last seen with a young woman who also works for the carnival as a ticket taker." A picture of a woman cut to the screen. The reporter continued, "Police are looking for nineteen-year-old Courtney Burke, who they say apparently left the scene sometime after the man was stabbed to death. They are not calling the young woman a suspect; they simply say she's a person of interest and are trying to find her for questioning. Authorities say the murder is the third in six months near carnival sites. So the question right now is this: do police have a serial killer, a carny killer, somewhere out there? And is nineteenyear-old Courtney Burke part of the equation? From the Volusia County Fairgrounds, Todd Guskin, Channel Two News."

I stared at the screen, my mind flashing through every second of the dialogue I had with Courtney Burke, the blood on her T-shirt, Celtic necklace she wore, the way she pushed her dark hair behind her ears, and those compelling and frightened eyes. Even in the picture of her on the television screen, her eyes drew you in to them. Kim looked at me, lifting her eyebrows, her face filled with questions. "Sean, do you know her, the girl they're looking for in connection with that murder or murders?"

"I don't really know her."

"Oh my God. But you've *met* her?"

"Yes."

"Where? What happened? Maybe I don't want to know."

SIX

The sun had been up from more than an hour when an African-American woman, on her way to teach school, saw Courtney Burke walking on the side of the road through the Ocala National Forest. She slowed to a near stop, looked at the girl through the open passenger-side window and said, "Sweetheart, you okay? Can I give you a ride somewhere?"

During the long night, Courtney had walked more than twenty miles, staying off the road when she saw headlights in the distance, reappearing and walking on the shoulder of the highway after the car or truck had passed. Exhausted, she had fought with mosquitoes and almost stepped on a cottonmouth water moccasin at daybreak when she stopped to pee behind the brush within a few feet of the river that ran along part of the highway. Courtney stopped walking, looked at the woman behind the wheel and said, "I'm fine, thank you."

The woman, early fifties, touch of gray in her hair, took in Courtney from head to toe. "I don't believe you're fine. I believe you could use some help right about now. You're a sad looking site, girl. Now get in the car before you make me late to teach my third grade class."

Courtney nodded, bit her lower lip for a moment, and got into the car.

The woman said, "Sweet Jesus, looks like the bugs had a field day with you. Maybe I ought to take you to the DeLand Medic Clinic. You can get something to help with the swelling."

"I've been mosquito bit before. I'll survive."

"I don't doubt that. Looks like you have been walking all night. What happened? Did you get in a fight with your boyfriend and jump out of the car in the middle of nowhere?"

"No."

"Well then, you picked a fine place for a walk. This forest has a history, and it's not too good."

"That's what I heard."

"Then why on earth are you way out here, child?"

"Tryin' to find somebody."

"Who's that?"

"Just somebody from my past."

"I understand." The woman drove in silence, driving under boughs of live oak branches stretching across the highway, sunlight poured through the limbs and thick leaves in funnels of gold. A white-tailed deer, a doe, less than twenty feet off the highway, stood and stared. Then the doe ran through a shaft of light, like an apparition caught in the burst from the flash of a camera.

The woman smiled and said, "I see that mama deer at least twice a week. I know it's the same deer 'cause of the diamond-shaped white patch on her throat. I feel sorry for the poor thing. Her baby, a spotted fawn, was hit by a car a couple of months ago right back there. I think that young mama is still in mourning for her baby." She glanced over at Courtney. "Tell me, child, where's your family, where's your mama?"

Courtney folded her arms and stared out the front windshield, her face filled with masked thoughts, the mottled sunlight capturing the vivid color changes in her eyes. "She's dead."

"How about the rest of your family, do they know where you are?"

"I always wanted a real family, but that never happened. The only one who ever gave a shit about me was my grandmother."

"Does she know you're here?"

"No. She's pretty sick."

"Call her. Let her know you're alive and you're okay."

"I left my cell back at—" Courtney paused and turned to the woman. "Why do you care? I don't mean to come across rude, but I don't see much hope in people."

"I care because you're hurting. It's plain as the skeeter bites on your cheeks. There's a lot of hope, lot of love in people. You'll see it if you look for it."

"What I see in many people is dark stuff. Mean stuff. They try to hide it, but it's there, right under their skin, flowin' in their blood."

"Who hurt you so bad?"

Courtney was silent

The woman nodded. "What's so heavy on your mind? I don't want to sound forward, baby, but are you pregnant?"

"No, and I'm not a baby."

"And you're not all grown up either. My name's Lois. What's your name?"

"Courtney."

Lois stopped at a crossroads, turned right, and headed toward DeLand. She said, "Are you hungry, Courtney?"

"Not really."

"Do you have any money?"

"A little."

"I have an idea." They entered the town of DeLand, turning onto New York Street. Lois slowed her car down in front of a red brick building and said, "I have twenty five third graders waiting for me about five blocks from here, and I'm late. I have to get to class." She gestured toward the old building, green ivy heavy on one side. "This is the Good Samaritan Clinic. You can get help in there. My friend, Carla, runs it. Tell her Lois Timbers sent you. They're great, caring people. You can get anything from a shower to a hot meal, even a bed. Okay?"

Courtney placed her hand on the door handle, started to get out of the car, and watched a police cruiser drive slowly down the street. She turned back to Lois and managed to smile. "I'm feeling a little sick now." Courtney lowered her head down.

The woman glanced from Courtney to the police cruiser that had turned right at the next street. She asked, "What happened to you? The police are looking for you, right? Why?"

SEVEN

Lois Timber's cell rang in her purse. She reached for it and answered. After a few seconds, she said to the caller, "I'm sorry I'm running late. I had to give a friend a ride to town. Yes, I'll be at the school in a few minutes. Please see if Carol can watch my class until them." She looked at Courtney. "Whatever's happened to you, you need to go to the authorities and tell them. Don't run."

Courtney nodded and blew out a breath. "You wanted me to call my grandmother. Do you have a phone I can use for a second?"

"Absolutely. This is worth me being tardy to my own class." She lifted a cell phone from her purse.

Courtney took it, opened the car door, and said, "I won't take long. Just need to make the call in private."

"I understand."

She stepped out of the car and into the shade of a large pine tree next to the sidewalk. She punched numbers and waited. The morning turned warm, a mockingbird called out from the tree, the smell of fresh-cut grass in the air. The voice of an older woman said,

"Hello."

"Grandma…"

"Courtney, I've been so worried about you. Where are you?"

"Something bad has happened."

"What honey? What happened?" The woman coughed.

"A man's been killed. He was stabbed to death. It was horrible. I tried to help him, tried to stop the bleeding. But I couldn't. I didn't know what to do, so I just ran. I had to get out of there." "Courtney, where are you?"

"Florida. I think the town's called DeLand. I was trying to find the Celtic torc he stole from you. I heard he was workin' the carnival circuit. I was getting closer. Then all this happened."

"I told you to stay away from him. He's more evil than you can understand." She coughed into the phone. "Courtney, listen to me. You have to go to the police. Tell them what happened. Then you come on back home. You understand?"

"I can't go back there. You know why." Courtney saw a police cruiser slowly coming down the street in her direction. She turned her back to the cruiser. "Grandma, I gotta go."

"Courtney! Courtney, come home."

"I love you. I'll call you."

"I love you too, sweetheart."

Courtney disconnected, opened the car door, leaned in and said, "Thank you for the ride. I really appreciate you stopping." She cut her eyes to the right and watched the police cruiser continue down the street, slowing in front of a Dairy Queen restaurant and turning around in the parking lot.

Lois said, "I hope you're gonna be okay. The women in the clinic will help you."

Courtney nodded. "I appreciate what you did, stopping for me. Bye." She closed the car door, turned her back toward the cruiser and walked to the front entrance. From the reflection on the dark glass doors, she could see the police car pulling up to the curb.

Courtney entered the clinic. A receptionist looked up from the magazine she was reading behind the desk. "May I help you?"

"Yes, I'm here to see Carla."

"Do you have an appointment?"

"No, Lois Timbers sent me."

"Please, have a seat. I'll see if Mrs. Flowers is available."

Courtney looked through the front glass. Two officers were getting out of the car, one speaking into a radio microphone clipped to his sleeve. "Where's the ladies' room?"

The receptionist pointed to her left. "Through that door. It'll be on your right."

Courtney smiled. She walked in the direction she was given, but turned down a hallway that led the opposite way from the front door. She stepped quickly over the polished tile floor, ignoring a nurse who asked if she could help her. Courtney found the rear exit and bolted out the door. She ran down a long alleyway. A frightened black cat jumped from a garbage can, the aluminum lid falling to the concrete. The sound of Courtney's hard soles echoed off the old walls between the buildings and the rattle of dripping air conditioners. Drops of warm water hit her in the face. She ran harder, turning the corner at the end of the alley.

A city bus was pulling away from a stop at the corner. Courtney banged on the bus door. The startled driver opened the door and Courtney paid the fare, taking a seat in the back. She noticed many of the passengers were about her age, college students. She rode for more than ten minutes, and when the students began getting off the bus, she followed suit. She found herself on the campus of Stetson University.

The campus was set in acres of well-manicured grass. Caladiums and oleanders were planted behind rows of border grass. Squirrels hopped between stately old oaks, the blooming jonquils and azaleas like perfume to Courtney. The red brick buildings were majestic, reminding her of Old South plantation mansions she'd seen in part of South Carolina. She watched students walk by talking and laughing about some event they shared together earlier. Some rode skateboards, iPods in ears, backpacks slung over their shoulders. Two male students tossed a Frisbee.

Courtney sat on a park bench beneath an oak tree and watched them for a minute. She could hear church bells in the distance. The smell of grilling barbeque chicken was in the breeze. Suddenly she felt a deep sense of sorrow, as if she was an absolute stranger in a strange world and was just passing through, never belonging, never achieving. Never becoming, only witnessing from afar. And she felt so alone.

An acorn fell from the oak, bouncing off the wooden bench to within inches of her shoe. She watched a squirrel coming closer to her, the squirrel's eyes on the prize. Courtney leaned over to pick up the acorn. It was hidden in a patch of grass that had somehow missed the mower's blades. Next to the acorn grew a tall, perfect clover in the speckled sunlight through the branches. She picked the clover and held it in front of her, rotating the four leaves in her hand.

Maybe this is a good sign. She touched each of the leaves and remembered a conversation she'd had with her grandmother about the Irish shamrock. Courtney would continue. She had no choice. She smiled, reached for the acorn and said, "Come here little fella." She gently tossed it to the squirrel, the animal scampering like an outfielder chasing a groundball. The squirrel sat back on its haunches, looking directly at her and gnawed the heart out of the nut, its cheeks puffing out.

Courtney Burke smiled, glanced down at the four-leaf clover in her hand, and she no longer felt so alone.

EIGHT

Jupiter was home. She was docked, back in her stationary course less than eighty yards from the Tiki Bar in the small universe of Ponce Marina, slip L-17. Seeing my old boat at her place secured to the docks, floating on a rising tide, was like seeing an old friend back in the game of life. Max and I walked down the long pier, *Jupiter* near the end. The breeze across the harbor brought the smell of a receding tide, barnacles drying in the sun, mangrove roots, and grilled shrimp. Three brown pelicans flew just above the masts of the sailboats. The birds cut a sharp right and alighted near a fish-cleaning station as a charter boat arrived. Fresh meat.

After watching the newsflash on the television hanging above the bar, I told Kim Davis that I'd seen the young woman, Courtney Burke, walking along Highway 314 last night. The girl refused my offer to drive her to town, or anywhere for that matter. But that's all I told Kim. No need to mention the two gents who tried to drag the girl into their pickup truck or what had happened after their attempt. I thought about the message Dave had left on my cell phone after recognizing my voice on the 911 call.

Max stopped, ears rising, nostrils testing the breeze, her eyes like heat-seeking missiles locking on smoke drifting from the *St. Michael.* The boat was forty feet in length with a much longer lineage connected to ancient mariners who sailed the Sea of Galilee two-thousand years ago. *St. Michael* was designed with an Old World style bow that could take high waves. The wheelhouse looked like it was lifted from a small tugboat and plopped near the bow. The large, open transom was intended for commercial fishing, and its captain, Nick Cronus, was one of the best in the business.

Nick stepped from the salon door, lifted the hood on his small grill perched in the center of his cockpit, and turned over a piece of fish. The smell of garlic, lemon, olive oil, and grilled fish filled the air. The smoke rose like a ghost beckoning Max. That's all it took. She barked once and darted down the dock toward *St. Michael*. Nick spun around, greeting her with a wide smile and open arms. "Hot Dog!" he bellowed. "Come see Uncle Nicky." Max trotted to the boat; Nick, leaning over the side of *St Michael*, scooped her up in one hand and stepped to the grill, Max's tail wagging in overdrive.

Nick, born in Greece, made a living from the sea, and he looked it. Wide shoulders, forearms like hams, olive skin, thick moustache, black eyes that smiled, and a mop of dark, curly hair styled from sun, surf, and salt. We'd become close after I pulled two bikers off Nick late one night. They'd accused him of making a pass at one of their women, and they jumped him from behind in the parking lot after the Tiki Bar closed. They were using a tire iron on his wrists and knees, and were about to split his skull when I pulled up and caught them in my high beams. I'd stepped out of my Jeep, Glock extended. Show over. I'll always remember Nick looking up at me through swollen eyes, teeth red with blood, broken jaw, a shattered wrist, and grinning wide. "There's a special bond when a man saves another man's life," he said later. "I got your back forever."

That was about three years ago. I stepped from the dock onto the cockpit of *St. Michael* and Nick said, "I'll toss some more grouper on the grill. Wanna beer?"

"Little early for me. Stopped at McDonalds for breakfast."

"Sean, you feed Max fast food and you'll clog her little arteries. That stuff's not chicken of the sea." Nick used his fingers to break off a small piece of fish from the grill and hand-fed it to Max. "That's better, hot dog. No more chicken nuggets for you."

"Kim told me you helped Bobby and his crew put *Jupiter* back in the water. Thanks."

"No problem. New props looked good. Everything is jam up and jelly tight. After they lowered her from the sling, I just helped the boys dock her.

Bilge is purring. *Jupiter's* lookin' damn sexy." He took a long pull from a sweating can of Miller, his eyes animated, face hot. He gently lowered Max to the cockpit, looked over my shoulder, and said, "Here comes Dave. He had to go get a newspaper. Still likes reading them rather than using his tablet, phone, or computer. But he has to drive farther and farther to find a place that sells papers anymore."

Dave Collins, dressed in shorts, flip-flops, Hawaiian print shirt hanging loose, carried a large Styrofoam cup of coffee, a small brown bag, and a folded newspaper. For a man in his late sixties he stayed in good shape, wide chest, thick wrists, white hair, beard neatly trimmed. His ruddy face was lined from a career in covert intelligence, the creases intersected with laugh lines around his mouth. His penetrating blue eyes were filled with wisdom and humor. He smiled and said, "Smells good, Nick. Sean and little Maxine, welcome back."

Nick said, "Want some grouper? Gonna pile it into pita bread. Made a quart of my special sauce last night."

Dave held up the bag. "Éclairs. The French lady at the Inlet Bakery is a goddess."

Nick shook his head and glanced down at Max. "Pay no attention to Dave. Between him and Sean you'd go from hot dog to chunky monkey."

Dave smiled and sipped his coffee. He said, "Save some for me. Sean, did you get my message? That may not have been your voice on that 911 call I heard during the newscast, but if it's not, then it's someone who sounds a lot like you."

Nick looked at Dave through the smoke from the grill. "What 911 call? Something happen, Sean?"

I glanced across the marina and watched a fifty-two-foot Beneteau motor out into the Halifax River. Within seconds, the spinnaker was unfolding in the light breeze. I said, "Nothing really happened. I tried to prevent something from happening."

Dave held his hand up. "Whoa. This I have to hear. I'm coming aboard, claiming one of the canvas chairs, and will enjoy a fresh-baked éclair while listening."

Nick used a large two-prong fork to lift the fish from the grill, stuffed it inside pita bread with sliced onions, tomatoes, and chopped lettuce drenched in an olive oil concoction. He took a bite as Dave settled into the chair. Max cocked her head, waiting for a sliver of food to fall from Nick's sandwich.

I said, "Dave, what you heard was me. I found a teenage girl walking on State Road 314 through the Ocala National Forest past midnight. I stopped to see if I could help her or give her a lift somewhere. That's when two good ol' boys decided to pull their truck in front of my Jeep, get out, and do some serious damage to me before forcing the girl into their truck."

"Oh, shit," Nick said, food bulging under his left cheek. He glanced at my right hand. "Looks like you got a few bruised knuckles."

I told them what happened. They both listened without interruption, Nick chewing, speechless, his eyes filled with amazement, as if I said I'd stumbled upon an alien in the forest. Dave propped his feet on the transom and used a paper towel to wipe chocolate from his fingers.

Max uttered a growl as Joe, a large cat with calico markings, strolled down the dock, head in the air, not giving Max a second thought. I said, "Be smart Max. You're outweighed by at least five pounds."

Nick grunted. "Sean, how in God's great universe does this stuff happen to you? Forrest Gump was talkin' about guys like you when he said 'shit happens.' I wonder where the girl went. What the hell was she doing out there?"

Dave cleared his throat. "This morning the lovely French baker said it better than Forrest Gump. When I asked her why she no longer sold my favorite buttery croissants, she said 'c'est la vie,' it is what it is, my inference was that more people bought the éclairs." Dave glanced down at the newspaper in his lap. He said, "If the news is accurate, the girl Sean found walking in the woods is a little more than a typical runaway. She's a suspect, or at least a person of interest, in a murder."

"Murder?" Nick crushed the empty beer can with one hand. "What murder?"

Dave said, "A carny worker was stabbed through the heart with an ice pick."

Nick sat in one of the deck chairs. He scratched Max behind the ears. "Sean, you think the girl did it?"

"I don't know."

"What'd she tell you?"

"Just what I told you and Dave. She was scared. A deer in the headlights. And then the guys in the truck showed up, half stoned, half drunk, and in full-bore rape mode."

I watched Dave look over my shoulder, his eyes following movement on the dock. Nick looked in the same direction. Dave said, "Sean, describe the girl. What'd she look like?"

"About a hundred ten pounds, five-five maybe, shoulder-length dark hair, high cheekbones and eyes that drew you into them."

When I saw Nick shake his head and purse his lips, I didn't want to turn around. Dave shifted in his seat and said, "Can't see her eyes from here, but everything else you described is spot on."

I turned in my chair and saw Courtney Burke coming our way. Over my shoulder I heard Nick say, "I don't care what your French baker said, Dave. When it comes to Sean, my man Forrest Gump said it best, shit happens."

NINE

Courtney Burke was still wearing the same clothes she had on when I found her. She approached *St. Michael* with trepidation, her body language communicating before she spoke. She used her right hand to pull a strand of her hair behind one ear, licked her bottom lip, and looked back toward the marina for a second. She said, "You'd told me about your boat when we met, said you did work on it at this marina. The woman at the bar said I could find you here."

I nodded. "Hello, Courtney." Max cocked her head and wagged her tail. "These are my friends, Dave Collins and Nick Cronus."

"Pleased to me you," Dave said.

Nick grinned and wiped his hands on a white towel. "Come aboard. I'll fix you my special grouper sandwich."

She blew air from her cheeks. "Thanks, but I can't stay long." She cut her piercing eyes at me. "Mr. O'Brien, I didn't get a chance to thank you for what you did."

"You didn't stick around long enough to, but I'm glad you're safe."

She crossed her arms. "I don't mean to intrude, but can I talk to you in private?"

"*Jupiter's* two boats down. We can chat there. Mind if Max tags along?"

She smiled for a second and looked at Max. "Sure. She's sweet."

"So am I," Nick said with open arms. "But only in an Uncle Nick kind of way."

Something moved over her eyes like black ice. Nick lowered his arms, grinned, cleared his throat and said, "I'm gonna make you a take-out meal. 'Cause if I don't, Dave will give you a chocolate éclair and maybe send your blood sugar so high you fall off the dock." He grinned.

The glacier melted from her eyes. She nodded. "That would be good, thank you."

I lifted Max up and walked with Courtney to *Jupiter*. The boat wore its fresh colors well, the slight smell of paint and varnish in the air, the mid-day sun licking the back of my neck. "I'll open the salon doors and let *Jupiter* breathe some. She's just been re-painted. We can talk up on the fly bridge. It'll give you a nice view of the marina. You can see for miles in any direction."

She nodded and we climbed the steps to the bridge. "Sit anywhere you'd like," I said, unzipping the isinglass and setting Max on the deck where she promptly began investigating the nooks and corners for new smells. Courtney sat on the long bench seat, and I lowered into the captain's chair. She looked around the marina, from the lighthouse a half mile away, to the parking lot in front of the Tiki Bar. A gentle cross-breeze delivered the smell of blooming mangroves and the salty soul of the sea.

"How old is your dog?" she asked.

"Max won't tell her exact age, but I know she's three, which makes her about your age in dog years."

Courtney smiled, eyes following Max. "I'm nineteen." She blew air from her cheeks, her thoughts now far away. I let her take her time. Then she said, "Mr. O'Brien-"

"Sean."

"Sean…anybody ever tell you that you look like that actor Gerard Butler?"

"Not yet today."

Courtney smiled and said, "I came here because you seemed like you really gave a shit when you found me. I'm sorry I hid from you and ran. When you saw me walking on the road I was running away from something really bad that happened."

"What was that?"

"My friend was killed. He was stabbed to death at the carnival where we both work. It was late. Lonnie was a ride operator. I talked him into letting me take a midnight ride on the Big Wheel. I feel so terrible, but there was nothing that I could do." "Courtney, take it from the beginning. Leave nothing out. What happened?"

She nodded and stared at the lighthouse a moment before looking back at me. She took a deep breath and began telling me everything that happened in her life during the last twenty-four hours. She said, "I know I shouldn't have run off, but I didn't know what to do. I had Lonnie's blood on my hands and shirt. I've had some trouble before with the police in my life…I just didn't want to go there. I got scared and ran."

"What kind of trouble?"

"I've had to become pretty independent. My childhood turned to shit, so as I grew older I made up my mind that no one would hurt me again."

"Why would the killer attack your friend, Lonnie, in the middle of the night? Was it a mugging gone very badly, or was it some kind of revenge killing?"

"I don't know."

"Did he have enemies? Someone he owed money to, maybe? Deal in drugs?"

"I don't know that either."

"And you never got a good look at the killer's face, right?"

"He wore a hoodie. It was too dark."

"Why were you working at the carnival?"

"I grew up in an Irish-American gypsy family. I'm used to being on the road. But we…or they, don't call themselves gypsies. The name used is travelers."

"So did you begin working in a carnival because you like to travel?"

"That's part of it. The other part is because I'm looking for somebody."

"Who's that?"

"The man who…who hurt me, murdered my mother and father, and stole something from my grandmother, something my grandfather had given her a long time ago." Her nostrils flared slightly, eyes forceful.

"Who is this man you're trying to find?"

"My uncle."

I thought about Nick's *'Uncle Nick'* comment earlier to her. "I'm sorry to hear that. Does this man work at that carnival?"

"I was hoping he did, but I guess I was wrong. A friend of mine told me he thought he'd seen my uncle working at a county fair that came through Charleston, South Carolina. That isn't too far from where I'd lived. So I went there. My friend said this guy was working as a weight and age guesser. That sounded like something my uncle would do."

"Was he good at it?"

"Yeah, he was. As a traveler, working the summer circuit, he would sell senior citizens a new roof when they didn't need one. He'd convince people their driveway needed paving, whatever. He worked with a three-man crew, did crappy work, and like basically conned his way throughout the South. They stayed one step away from the sheriff."

"When was the last time you saw him?"

"It's been a little more than four years."

"Why try to find him on your own? Maybe you should turn it over to the police."

"They couldn't ever find him. It's a cold case. My grandmother's scared shitless of him. I can't prove he raped me from the time I was twelve 'till I could hold a butcher knife in my hand. Before he was spotted working at a carnival, we'd heard he was a preacher in some Kentucky mountain town. He's mentally a sicko, but he can charm people, especially women. He knows hypnosis, too. We heard he settled there, Kentucky. Somebody supposedly started calling him a prophet. He stole every dollar the little church had."

"How do you know this?"

"FBI. They came around when a man fitting my uncle's description robbed a bank in South Boston. And he did it without a gun. The teller said she couldn't remember anything, even giving the money to him. It was like she'd been hypnotized. My uncle's picture was on the bank's security tapes. My grandmother identified him."

"Is the FBI still actively looking for your uncle?"

"I think so."

"What would you do if you found him?"

She was silent for a few seconds, her eyes drifting across the marina, fingers gripping her knees, knuckles cotton-white. She swallowed dryly and whispered, "I don't know."

"Could this man have killed Lonnie?"

"Maybe. If he was somehow there. He could be anywhere."

I watched her staring at my hands, her thoughts remote. Then she raised her riveting eyes up at me like she was looking through me. She lowered her eyes to the pendant that hung from a chain around my neck. "What is it, Courtney?"

"The pendant you're wearing…can I ask where you got it?"

"It was a gift from my mother. The last thing she gave me before she and my father were killed in the same year, and that's been many years ago."

"It's great that you still wear it."

"I've worn it so long I don't even think about it."

She was quiet, her eyes narrowing and falling to just above my heart. I said, "When I offered to help you, it was to give you a ride into town. You really need to take all this to the police. Tell them what you saw when your friend was killed at the carnival. If you run, it'll look very suspicious in the eyes of a county prosecutor. Tell them what you know."

"I don't know anything, especially like who killed Lonnie. You did more than offer to give me a ride to town, you saved my life. Those two men would have killed me. I do know that. Maybe it's some kind of weird destiny thing, but I don't believe you just happened by last night."

"What do you believe?"

"That sometimes, in some places, stuff happens 'cause it was supposed to happen. I believe there was a reason we met on the road in that forest. I don't know what it is, but I think the reason might be bigger than you pulling those men off me."

I was silent, watching her body language, fingernails bitten down, red nail polish chipped. She looked up as a white pelican alighted on the canvas top of an adjacent boat. I could see the frightened young girl's face in the pretense of the bold disguise she tried to wear.

She said, "But I don't know the reason I'm here. Maybe it's because I have no place else to go. Maybe it's because you might be the only one who believes I didn't kill Lonnie, and somewhere inside of me something tells me that you might help find who did. Lonnie, was a carny, so the cops won't do much, except say I did it." She bit her lower lip for moment. "You found me in the forest walking in the dead of night. Maybe you can help me find my uncle. He took something from me, but he took something from my grandmother, too. I'll never replace what he stole from me, but I might get back what he took from her, the gold Celtic torc she wore all her life. I feel so freakin' self-conscious even coming here. I'm sorry."

"I wish I could help you, but I'm not a police officer. I'm not a private detective. I'm just a guy teaching part-time at a local college."

"What do you teach?"

I started to change the subject, and then said, "Criminal justice."

"Were you a cop?"

"Once."

"My instincts were right." I said nothing.

"I'll pay you. I don't have much money now, but I have strong principles and work ethic. I'll pay you for your time." Max jumped up next to Courtney and rested her chin in the girl's lap. She scratched Max behind the ears and said, "This little dog is smart. I wish I'd had a dog when I was a girl. I'm sorry, I shouldn't have come here. I apologize for wasting your time." She stood to leave.

"Just sit still a minute," I said, looking to her left, down the dock toward the Tiki Bar parking lot. Two police cruisers and an unmarked car pulled into the lot. "Sit back down, Courtney."

"Why?"

"Unless you can swim across the bay, there's no place for you to run. The police just got here. And they're coming this way."

"I don't know what to do?"

"Yes you do. Tell them the truth."

TEN

Two Volusia County sheriff's deputies walked down the dock next to a detective. As the three men approached *Jupiter*, Courtney and I were standing in the cockpit waiting for them.

"Here, Courtney, take this."

"What is it?"

"My business card." I handed it to her. "It says Sean O'Brien…fishing charters. I'm not very good at it, that's why I teach part-time. Job changed, but the phone number's the same."

"Thank you." She slid the card in the back pocket of her jeans.

The police officers were coming closer. I recognized the detective. Dan Grant, skin the color of coffee with a shot of cream, mid-forties, wide shoulders, dressed in a tan sports coat, pressed jeans, and no tie. He walked with a straightforward pace, hands slipping into his jean pockets and shaking his head when he stepped up to *Jupiter's* stern.

"Well, well," he said. "Why am I not surprised to see Sean O'Brien standing here with a person wanted for questioning in a murder?"

"Hello, Dan. It's been a while."

"I'm sure you both have great explanations as to why we're all gathered here today. But let's start with the basics." He cut his eyes to Courtney and stepped closer. Max wagged her tail. "Are you Courtney Burke?" Grant asked.

She nodded her head. "Yes."

"Miss Burke, we'd like to talk to you about your relationship with Lonnie Ebert."

"Okay."

"But before we do, I'd want to hear how you got to this marina and this boat." He sighed and took out a small notepad. "Sean, let's start with you. How'd she get on your boat?"

I told him how I found her and added, "That's when we were visited by two gents with a lot of fur and gang rape on their dull minds. That would have happened to her after they split my skull."

Grant slid the pencil behind his ear. He looked over to a charter boat that was coming into the marina, the whiff of diesel exhaust in the wind. "So, that was you who did some damage. Those bad boys are gonna be out of work for a long time." He turned toward Courtney. "And that's how you got here. Sort of took your time hitchhiking through the Ocala National Forest after leaving a murder scene. Why'd you leave in such a hurry?"

"I was scared. I didn't kill Lonnie. You gotta believe me."

Grant studied her a few seconds in silence, probably trying to read eyes that were unreadable. Two sea gulls flew above the masts of moored sailboats, their staccato cries like mocking laughter across the harbor. Grant said, "Miss Burke, I'm going to take you downtown to talk about this murder. At any time you can have an attorney present."

"Am I under arrest?"

"No, but we need to talk. I want to hear your story." He nodded to the two deputies who boarded *Jupiter*. "These officers will escort you to their patrol car. We'll all reconvene in a little while. Sean, if you can think of anything else you may have seen or heard, you know where to find me. Let's go."

Max barked once and followed Courtney to the steps leading over the transom to the dock. A deputy sheriff walked on either side of her. As they took her away, she turned toward me, her eyes wide, frightened, and now pleading, terrified eyes that would forever be padlocked deep in my mind.

— • —

FOUR HOURS LATER, Dave Collins ambled across the dock and boarded *Jupiter*. He stuck his head in the open salon and said, "Well, the arrest of that young woman is the talk of the marina, especially down at the Tiki Bar, and you're nowhere to be seen."

I looked up from the bilge housing where I was storing some new belts and filters I'd bought. "She wasn't arrested, Dave. They took her in for questioning." I stood, closed the hatch, and used paper towels to wipe some oil from my hands. "How'd they track Courtney here? You're probably the only one who picked out my voice on that 911 call."

"I walked down to the Tiki Bar for ice. Kim said she recognized Courtney when the girl stopped in and asked for directions to your boat."

"Did Kim call the police?"

"No. She said Captain Bill, you know the guy, retired charter captain with too much time on his hands, overheard the conversation and dialed 911." Dave stepped to the small bar that divided the salon from the galley. He sat and blew out a deep breath, his forehead creased in thought. "So what do you think, Sean? Did the girl murder that guy? Is she a killer?"

"A killer? I don't know, maybe. Did she kill the man found dead at the carnival? I don't believe she did." I told Dave everything Courtney had said to me and added, "Dan Grant is a good detective. He'll be fair with her. Unfortunately, fairness, integrity, and circumstantial evidence don't always balance the scale of justice. It'll depend on the physical evidence, apparent motive, and whether the prosecutor thinks he has enough on her to get a conviction." I walked to the galley, pulled two very cold Coronas from the refrigerator, sliced fresh limes for each one, and handed a bottle to Dave.

"Thanks," he said, taking a short sip and setting the bottle on the bar. "I've never seen eyes on anyone quite like the eye color I saw in Courtney's eyes. I saw something else, too."

"What's that?"

"I don't know, exactly. But for a kid like her, it's the oxymoronic combination of a saddened wisdom of the ages, and an old, recycled soul, if you will—cluttered with the outlying hope of real trust. It's as if she's a war refugee, a young woman with normal dreams buried inside some Old World culture."

"When anyone's raped, especially a kid, the physical pain will fade with the passage of time. The torment of the spirit never completely heals. That will give a child an old soul before her time. It's horrible and a damned shame."

Dave started to respond as my phone buzzed from where I'd set it on the table. It was Detective Dan Grant on the line. He said, "Sean, we cut the girl loose a couple of hours ago."

"Good."

"Maybe not so good."

"What do you mean?"

"I'm telling you this for two reasons: one is because we have a history together. You helped with a couple of cases. But then I remember why you helped. It was because, in one way or the other, you either knew the victim, or as a former detective, you'd crossed paths with the perps."

"I told you why she came to see me at the marina."

"Back away from this one, Sean. I'm still gathering information, but I have enough to push my suspicion meter way up. Courtney Burke is a nut case. I've got a report that tells me she's been in two different mental institutions, diagnosed as a paranoid schizophrenic."

I said nothing, watching the condensation roll down the Corona bottle.

Dan said, "The FBI will be checking into this one, no doubt."

"Why?"

"The murder at the carnival's on their radar because it's apparently not isolated. Feds are reporting the deaths of two other people, all men in their mid-twenties. All carny workers who were killed in the last six months. Each victim worked at a different carnival. If the perp is Courtney Burke, the county has a serious problem on its hands."

For a brief moment, I remembered the look on Courtney's face when the two men in the pickup truck rolled their windows down. I saw chipped red polish on her fingernails, her cotton white knuckles, her eyes looking back at me as she was led away by the deputies. I said, "She may have issues, but I don't believe she's a serial killer."

"Maybe not. But I'm betting the dried blood on her T-shirt will match the vic's blood. And I know she claims she got it on her hands trying to help the vic. But then she fled the scene and did nothing to call help, no dialing 911. The carnival is at the county fairgrounds for a week. I'd wager I'll have a confession from her before the week's up."

"And I'm betting there is another reason why you're telling me this. You think she's coming back to the marina, don't you?"

"She came to you once. She might return. Female serial killers are rare, but not rare enough for me. If she contacts you, let me know everything she says. I'd hate for you to wind up with an ice pick through your heart."

ELEVEN

It was a half hour past sunset when Courtney Burke arrived back at the Bandini Brothers Amusement Carnival, the noise of the thrill rides like simulated thunder in the cool night air, the earth trembling beneath coasters and big wheels built to challenge gravity. As she weaved her way through the crowds, she was hoping the throngs of people would provide some degree of concealment walking down the midway. But the lights, screams, and roar of motors and hydraulics captured her every move in slices of bright surrealism. The air was heavy with the scent of sizzling Italian sausages, grilled onions, peppers, and funnel cakes, thick as the dust kicked up by thousands of shoes.

With suspicion following her like harsh shadows, there was no anonymity in a sea of strangers. The carnies watched her from behind the games of chance. Their eyes veiled under the sweat-stained baseball caps, eyes long ago blinded from lack of empathy and focused on near constant distrust. The hooded eyes tracked her every move as she made her way down the bright midway to the Bandini trailer.

She looked straight ahead, ignoring the stares as she thought about the events of the day—the time she spent on Sean O'Brien's boat and the interrogation at the police station. She liked Sean. He had a calm way about him. She tried to remember the last time she trusted anyone, especially a man. Maybe she couldn't trust him either. But something pulled at heartstrings she knew long ago had been cut and cauterized by bad people. *What is it about him?* Why did she feel she could trust him? *What was the connection? Was there even a connection?* She fought back the rise of hope in her heart, covered it with doubt and buried it beneath the frost of uncertainty. *Forget him. I'm innocent. Police will have to see that.*

She knew the Detective Dan Grant didn't believe her story. She felt that the carnies weren't the only ones watching her. Plainclothes police could be mixing in with the crowd. She glanced over her shoulder, to her left, then to her right. *Who was the man in the open sports coat? Did he avert his eyes from mine?* Her head hurt. She looked away, folded her arms across her breasts for a few seconds, and then walked on, moving faster, the music from the rides loud, piercing, and bouncing around inside her skull like a .22 bullet.

The reverberating layers of noise grew louder. She placed the palms of both hands over her ears, the lights of the midway like a freight train barreling down the tracks of her mind. She saw Lonnie's eyes staring up at the full moon behind her. She looked at her hands, the blood wet and sticky between her fingers. "No!" she shouted.

Two teenage boys shooting hoops, trying to win plush animals for their girlfriends, turned and stared at Courtney. One said, "Maybe her meds wore off." He turned around and tossed the small basketball, sinking the shot. One of the teen girls shrieked and popped a bubblegum bubble.

Courtney turned and ran, ran hard down the midway, knocking a box of popcorn from an overweight woman who stepped in front of her. "Hey! What the—?" the woman said to her thin husband. Courtney darted past the swarms of people, around the Zipper, Tilt-A-Whirl, and cut between the House of Mirrors and the Lost Mine, slipping into the shadows beyond the midway. She stopped walking behind the House of Mirrors and looked up at a cracked full-length mirror propped against a metal garbage can. She stared at her reflection in the damaged glass, her face flushed and glistening in the light. She lowered her eyes to her hands, expecting to see Lonnie's blood on them. Nothing. Nothing but broken fingernails, and a tiny ruby in a gold setting, a ring from her grandmother on Courtney's sixteenth birthday.

There was a sound from behind her. She looked into the mirror and saw the image of a little man, a dwarf. He was dressed in a red and purple Hawaiian-print shirt, shorts, and flip-flops. His dirty blond hair was combed straight back. His tanned faced creased with laugh lines set in the cheeks, dimples the size of dimes, and he wore a gold hoop earring in one ear.

Courtney turned around and smiled. "Hi, Isaac. You're a sight for really sore eyes, a hurting brain, and other things."

"Glad you're back, kiddo. The police were looking for you."

"They found me."

"What happened?"

"They questioned me for hours. Tried to get me to change my story, like to say stuff that isn't true. They truly believe I killed Lonnie. No matter what I said, they've got their minds made up. Lonnie was dead when I got to him, after a man knifed him. To get to Lonnie, I had to jump from the Big Wheel when it swept close to the ground, but I was too late."

"Are you okay?"

"No...no, I'm not okay. Lonnie was lying in a pool of blood fighting for his life. I tried to pull that ice pick outta his chest, but I was too late. He just looked up at me, then looked beyond my head like he was staring at the moon and he stopped breathing. I felt like I was gonna vomit. I just ran. And I didn't stop running until I was so far away I couldn't see the lights from the carnival. I spent the last three hours telling the same story over and over to the police. Nobody believes me."

"I believe you. Looks like you could use a hug." Isaac walked to her and held out his short arms, a wide smile spreading across his face. Courtney leaned down, and he hugged her. At three and a half feet, Isaac Solminski had a line-of-sight most people didn't possess. He could read people, could see into situations, spot trouble, and avoid it if possible. After twenty years on the road, he had no illusions about anything. But he did have faith and hope.

He had befriended Courtney Burke when she started working at the carnival three months earlier. Isaac believed Courtney was a special young woman who would never fit in as a carny. She was put on this earth for something else. He could feel it in his heart. And he could see farther than most men twice his height. Tonight he didn't like what he saw. He said, "My precious Courtney. I'm surprised you came back."

"Where am I gonna go? I need the work. I need to feel I'm getting closer to what I came for, too. Besides, if I run again, the cops will think I'm running from all this. I'm innocent."

"Come with me. I'll make us some tea. There's something I want to tell you."

She nodded and followed the little man as he stepped over a garden hose and waddled around pitched tents, campers, and motorhomes, many covered with grime and years' worth of travel dents and dings in the body paint. Diesels hummed. Air conditions rattled. Courtney could see the blue lights from a TV screen flickering through the dirty window of a trailer. The night air carried the odor of diesel fumes.

Isaac climbed the two wooden steps to his small camper, opened the door and turned on the lights. Courtney had been in the small camper once before. It was a morning he'd made her breakfast after a drunken carny had slapped her across the mouth because she refused to go to McDonald's with him for breakfast.

"Have a seat at the table. I'll heat the water. Are you hungry?"

"Not really."

"I'll take that as a yes." He sliced a wedge of carrot cake, placed it on a paper plate, and set it in front of her on the table. "With this cake, you'll get your veggies, too."

Courtney smiled and used a plastic fork to take a bite. "It's so good. Thank you."

"You're welcome." Isaac placed tea bags in two steaming cups and sat across from Courtney. He pushed a cup near her plate. "Courtney, you don't belong here. Find something else."

"I don't have anywhere else to go. I needed the work. And I haven't finished what I set out to do."

"What if you don't find him?"

"I'll find him. If not here, some other carnival, fair, or circus."

"You've been working this circuit for three months. The season's usually six to eight months. Where are you going to go after that?"

"I guess I'll find work at some other carnival."

"It's a rough life, kiddo. You get in this game and it changes you. Since I've come to know you, I don't believe you're put on this earth to work the carny circuit. Some people come here 'cause they're running from something. Others are running to something. It's a human train, a vagabond life, picking up and moving on like migrant workers comin' to a new field to pick the marks, empty their pockets after they cash their Friday paychecks. That's not you, not who you are."

"Why do you stay, Isaac?"

"Look at me. I'm three and a half feet tall. Where am I gonna earn a living? But you don't have to. You have your whole life ahead of you. This guy you're looking for, why's it so important to find him?"

"Because he took something from a person I love very much, my grandmother."

"What if you don't find him?"

"I can go to my grave knowing I tried."

"You're a little young to talk about end-of-life scenarios. You once told me the man you're hunting for is a hypnotist,

someone who can get others to do stuff."

"Yeah, he's good at it, too. Scary good."

"At any one time in the summer, there are more than two hundred carnivals touring the states. I've worked a bunch of 'em. Seen some excellent hypnotists, some not so great, and a few that used magic and hypnotism for no good. Saw it more years and years ago, back when little people like me were called freaks. Back in the days of touring with the bearded lady, the three-headed cow, and a whole bunch of people and critters that looked like long-distance ancestors who were rejects from Noah's ark."

"You're not a freak. You're a sweet and caring man."

Isaac nodded and looked at her, his olive-green eyes filled with compassion. "Courtney, what you don't know is that Lonnie was a dealer for Tony Bandini and his older brother Carlos."

"What?"

"He moved meth, pills, coke. Somewhere between Boston, Buffalo, and here in Florida, the accounting didn't jibe. I'd heard that Lonnie was into the Bandini brothers for five grand. Carlos Bandini runs five carnivals. He's here from time to time. Neither he nor Tony offer many repayment plans."

"Did Tony Bandini or his brother kill Lonnie?"

"I doubt it. But Tony would just as soon take him out as not. Probably ordered it done. Cops won't trace it back to him unless they can find the actual hit man. The Bandinis have a network of roustabouts. It sends a message to other dealers—the house gets paid first. Tony Bandini doesn't care if you take the fall, he probably planned it that way."

Courtney pushed the plate away, her eyes burning. "I gotta go."

"Go where?"

"Bandini's office. I need to—"

"Listen to me, Courtney. Play it cool. You walk in there and you'll walk into a hornet's nest. You don't know this guy. He's about as dangerous as they come."

She stood. "I've seen a lot of dangerous people in my life. I'll start by asking him if I still work here. I guess we'll see where it goes from there. Can I borrow your phone for a minute?"

"Yes, but stay away from Bandini's office tonight. Promise me?"

"I can't make a promise that I know I won't keep."

He shook his head and handed her his phone. "Are you calling your grandmother?"

"Yes, and then I'm calling the man who picked me up on the side of the road at night. If he's not there...if anything happens to me, if for some reason I vanish, I want you to ask him a question for me. His name is Sean O'Brien."

TWELVE

I was getting ready to lock *Jupiter* and head back to my cabin on the river when Dave Collins leaned in through the open sliding glass doors from the cockpit to the salon. "Sean, is your phone working?"

"Last I checked."

"Knowing you, that could have been a month ago."

I lifted my phone off the bar in the salon. "I'd set it to vibrate. Looks like there are three missed calls, and two voice messages. One's from Nick's phone and one from a number I don't recognize."

Dave shook his head of thick silver-white hair and stepped inside. "Nick's been trying to reach you. He's at the Tiki Bar. Said he overheard, and I'm quoting here—two shit-faced carny types talking about the killing at the county fair. He said one guy, a fella who'd partaken in a wee bit more Miller beer than he should have, was telling the other guy that the word on the street, so to speak, is the death of the worker was a contract killing."

"Are these two men still there?"

"I don't know. Nick called me after trying your phone for the last half hour or so."

I said nothing, the only sound coming from halyards clanking against a sailboat mast in the warm night breeze.

"What are you thinking about, Sean?"

"Dan Grant said he found some records indicating Courtney Burke has spent some time in a psych ward. I don't know the details."

"Could have been by court order. Her family could have institutionalized her. Regardless, it indicates some kind of mental instability."

"Not always. Why was she locked in an asylum? We know the effect, but what was the cause. You were trained in understanding human breaking points, how to accelerate reaching them. Sometimes it's physical. Sometimes it's mental. It's still pain, in the case of repeated sexual assaults, it's layered pain. In my book, years of sexual abuse is physical and mental. It's encrusted like a hot branding iron on different sections of the victim's soul. The pain may dull, but the mark to your psyche is like a bad tattoo that blurs through time."

"Let's take a walk down the dock." I turned to Max who napped on the salon sofa. "Hold down the fort. If ole Joe the cat comes near, try not to be too inhospitable."

I COULD HEAR the Friday night entertainment at the Tiki Bar before Dave and I reached the end of L dock and opened the locked gate leading away from the boats. We walked around a deserted fish-cleaning station that featured a weathered and knife-scarred wooden table, stainless steel sink, and a thatched roof made from dried palm fronds tarnished in splashes of black and white pelican poop. The smell of fish scales and dried blood mixed with the drifting scent of deep-fried hushpuppies and blackened grouper coming from the bar grill.

The Tiki Bar was filling up with salty regulars and sunburned tourists, a combination that created a culture club of opposites. A solo singer wearing a Panama hat and a surfer's shirt sat on a stool in a corner, guitar in one hand, the crowd in the other as he led them in a rousing chorus of Irish ballads and Jimmy Buffett songs. After a few drinks and sing-along songs, the drawbridges of class distinctions lowered and the yellow brick road to Margaritaville, by way of Dublin, became a festive group journey. The fishing captains swapped stories of great catches and beating storms in open waters. One middle-aged vacationer grinned and admitted how he'd love to trade places away from the predictable, the office politics—the mundane, to fish for a life of adventure. "We have half-day and full-day rates to get you started," bellowed a gray-bearded charter captain, lifting a bottle of beer in a toast to the promise of a personal quest.

The entertainer told the crowd he was taking a short break. Kim Davis finished pouring a tall glass of dark beer and handed it to a shiny, red-faced customer wearing a Mickey Mouse T-shirt. Kim turned toward Dave as we sat down at the only two open bar stools. "Dave, did you have to round up a posse to find Sean? Nick has been 'more anxious than I've seen him in a long time." Dave grunted. "Sean had his phone turned down." "Where's Nick?" I asked.

She glanced over my right shoulder. "Looks like he's returning from a bathroom break."

Nick approached the bar, shaking his head, his dark eyes animated. "Kim, can you send a Corona my way?" He turned to me. "Sean, man, I'm glad Dave found you. I was sitting at a table in the corner, doing my monthly accounting, when I overheard these two half-drunk dudes at another table, talkin' about someone dying—a murder." Nick took a long pull from an icy bottle, his face blooming in color, the center of his moustache wet from beer foam.

"Are they still here?" I asked.

"No. They left when the music started."

"Describe them."

"Hell, Sean, they looked like most of the deck hands around here. Like they'd been sleepin' in their clothes. Kinda like I look after I have been at sea for a couple of weeks. One guy was about twenty, I guess. Blond. Tryin' to grow whiskers. Wore a Yankees' hat backwards and a blue Orlando Magic jersey. The other due was older, maybe forty. Heavyset fella. He was wearin' a black T-shirt with the words Harley-Davidson on the front. He had a tattoo of a naked mermaid on his arm. Big damn tits—" He cut his eyes over to Kim. "Sorry, Kimberly." She smiled and Nick said, "Both left with barbecue sauce in the corners of their mouths 'cause they must have eaten a few dozen wings between them. The older guy called the younger one Smitty."

Dave nodded. "Your powers of observation are improving.

Maybe it's because you've spent quality time with Sean." "Nick, what exactly did you hear?" I asked.

"They were goin' through a few pitchers of Miller Beer during the happy hour. Before they left, I overheard some crazy shit. Stuff like how the dead guy at the fair got what was comin' to him 'cause he was markin' the deck."

"What's that supposed to mean?" Kim asked. "A payback for cheating a poker bet?"

"Could mean just about anything," I said. "Sounds like he was taking a cut of some kind of action."

Dave nodded. "Carnivals can be a backdrop, true moveable feasts, for crime and those who commit crimes."

Nick looked around the bar for a moment. "Sean, maybe this means the girl didn't kill the guy, unless she does hits for hire."

"It means that the police need to question these two. I'll put in a call to Detective Grant. Nick, tell him what you told us. Describe the men to him." I punched in Grant's number. Nick flexed both hands into fists, relieving tension. Thirty seconds later, Grant answered. "Sean O'Brien. I'm glad you called. Did the girl,

Courtney Burke, happen to return to your boat?"

"No, why?"

"Because now a warrant's been issued for her arrest. Forensics matched. Blood. Prints on ice pick. Her story of a hooded assailant is iffy at best. A witness came forth and said he'd heard them arguing. Seems like Ms. Burke is the jealous type. Sounds like a typical case of hell has no fury like—"

"Sounds like supposition to me, Dan. Listen, I'm standing here at the Tiki Bar at the marina. A friend of mine overheard two men talking. Carnival workers, most likely. They were drinking heavily, and one was telling the other that the murder was a hit—a payback or revenge killing for something."

"Can your friend ID these men?"

"Yes."

"Okay, but before I speak with your friend, unless the men he overheard were eye witnesses to a murder, most likely they'll deny having said anything in the bar, and it'll be circumstantial at best."

"Dan, just listen to what Nick has to say."

I handed the phone to Nick, who took a long swallow from the bottle, blew out a breath and said, "Hello." He placed one hand over his open ear and stepped out on the dock to tell his story.

I turned toward Kim. "Can you remember what these men looked like?"

"Nothing beyond what Nick said. Judy was the server. She left as the night servers came to work."

"How'd they pay the bill, cash or credit?"

"Hold on, I'll look at Judy's tickets." Kim licked her thumb and leafed through a few dozen receipts. "Looks like this is it. Three platters of wings and four pitchers of beer, table fourteen. Paid half with a credit card, the other half in cash."

"What's the guy's name on the card?"

"Randal Barnes."

Nick returned. He handed the phone to me. "He wants to speak to you."

Detective Grant said, "Sean, I'm heading back to the fair. If you hear from Ms. Burke, let me know. Three killings at three fairs, that spells serial."

"Can you place her at each of the carnivals?"

"Don't know yet. Shouldn't be hard to find out."

"Dan, I have a name for one of the carnies who Nick overheard. The name on the charge receipt is Randal Barnes."

"Why doesn't it surprise me that you'd find that quickly? Maybe you still have cop in your DNA, or maybe you just give a damn more than most do."

"Good luck, Dan." I disconnected.

Nick said, "Detective Grant didn't sound too promising to me. Said he'd question the dudes if he could find them." "Well, now he has a name," Dave said.

Kim leaned her elbows on the bar, the lights from a car in the lot sweeping across her face. She said, "I just met the girl briefly when she stopped in here asking directions to your boat, but I got the feeling that Courtney isn't what she appears."

"What do you mean?" Dave asked, sipping a vodka over ice.

"I can't put my finger on it. Working a bar, you develop a pretty good feel for people. I call it the bullshit meter. She seemed real, but somehow cloaked in...I don't know exactly...she has a mysterious presence about her. Like she's out of sync with people around here, and so saddened by something."

"Murder can have that influence on people," Nick said.

Dave nodded. "The carnival is at the county fairgrounds through Sunday. Maybe Grant will find one or both of them before the carnival pulls out."

Kim sighed. "I wonder where the girl is right now." "Probably returned to the carnival," I said.

Nick shook his head and reached for the Corona. "Why the hell would she go back there? Back to a place where evil rides the merry-go-round."

I remembered the look in the girl's eye as the police officers escorted her away. "She returned because she didn't kill that guy, but she might know who did…she's just not certain of that yet.

Nick, when was the last time you were at a carnival?"

"Been years, man. Why?"

"Let's see what Detective Dan Grant and his colleagues can find. They have Randal Barnes' name. That's a good start."

"What if they go on and arrest the girl for murder?"

"If that happens, we can take in a night at the carnival and play a few games of chance."

Nick sipped his beer and said, "Oh boy. I wonder if any shrimpers are here tonight."

"Why?" Dave asked.

"Because, as my man Forrest Bubba Gump said—shit's about to happen."

Dave said, "I don't recall that exact line."

"Close enough," Nick said, draining the last of his beer and looking straight at me.

THIRTEEN

The Bandini Brother's Amusement office was in a million dollar, custom-made bus. It was parked less than one hundred yards from the midway, in a gravel lot, generators purring, the smell of diesel fumes acrid in the night air. Light spilled from all of the windows, venetian blinds pulled down behind the glass.

Courtney stood at the door marked *Office*, took a deep breath and knocked on the burnished aluminum. She could hear someone moving inside, a monotone conversation, and then the door opened wide. A man who went by the name of Johnny Johnson, someone Courtney had only seen a few times, stood in the light. He was more than six and a half feet tall, hair in a ponytail, heavy forehead, and flat nose with a faded pink scar across the bridge, shoulders and chest like a hammered armor under a black T-shirt. He wore a gold chain around his wide neck. He grunted. "What do you want?"

"To speak with Mr. Bandini."

"He's busy. Go away." The man started to close the door, but paused, his leaden black eyes studying Courtney's face in the light. "Wait a sec. You're the chick who took an ice pick to my ride op,

Lonnie Ebert. I heard you were arrested."

"I wasn't arrested because I didn't do it."

"Go on. Get the hell outta here."

"I'm not going anywhere until I see Mr. Bandini. He hired me. If I'm fired, he needs to be the one who tells me that, too."

TOM LOWE

"What's going on?" came a question from behind the man blocking the door.

"Nothing, Mr. Bandini. Girl's just leaving."

"What girl?" Tony Bandini asked, stepping to the door. He was a foot shorter than the other man, head shaved, glossy with perspiration, lidless snake eyes that didn't seem to blink. His narrow face was pastel, the color of old bones. He looked down and nodded when he recognized Courtney. "What do you want?"

"To talk about my job." "Johnny, check her." "Arms out," Johnny said.

Courtney lifted her arms as he slowly patted her down, his breath reeking of marijuana and tuna. He felt around her breasts, down her waist to her buttocks, his hands moving like a serpent to her inner thighs.

Courtney looked directly in his eyes and said, "You move your hands any closer and I'll kick in your teeth."

"This one's got some piss and vinegar." Johnny grinned, his hands inching closer.

Bandini said, "That's good enough. If she can hide a bug in there, she's got some talent. Johnny, take a walk. Go get some smokes."

"Sure, Boss, but you got a nut job standing here."

Bandini gestured with his head. The man grumbled and walked away. Bandini looked at Courtney from head to toe in an appraising glance. "What do you want?"

"To talk with you."

"About what, your job?"

"I don't want to lose it. And I wanted a chance to explain to you what happened."

"All I know is I got a dead worker and cops believe you stuck him. I'm gonna miss Lonnie. The kid had potential. Sounds like a hellava love fight between you two."

"Maybe it was between you and Lonnie."

Bandini didn't blink. Face empty. "Didn't know him that well. So you want to stay on here, huh?"

"Yes, I really need this job."

He studied her for a few seconds, moistened his wet lips and said, "Never hurts to talk. Come on back to my office."

From the shadows between the trailers, Isaac saw Courtney enter the office. As the door closed, he watched the custom bus. He could hear the screams from the townspeople riding the coasters. Then his eyes followed two bats in aerial acrobatics, flying in and out of light cast from a streetlamp. Isaac felt his scalp tighten, his skin taut as a drum across his wide forehead. He whispered a silent prayer and made the sign of the cross.

FOURTEEN

As Dave, Nick and I walked back down L dock toward our boats, I played a missed call voice message on my phone. "Sean, this is Courtney Burke. I don't want to bother you, but when you gave me your card you said call if…look, you'd asked me if Lonnie was dealin' drugs. A friend of mine here at the carnival says he was. Said Lonnie was a mule for Tony and Carlos Bandini, the owners of the carnival. He said Bandini may have been the one who killed Lonnie 'cause Lonnie owned him money. Maybe you could like tell that detective, the one who knows you, Detective Grant, maybe you could tell him for me. Thank you…something else…do you have…never mind, it's not important. Bye."

I put my phone on speaker and replayed the message for Dave and Nick. When it concluded, Nick said, "Sounds like life is really turning to shit for the girl."

"Maybe not," Dave said, his eyes following a sixty-foot yacht, diesels humming, making the turn from the marina into the Halifax River, heading for Ponce Inlet and the Atlantic Ocean. "Maybe this will take the heat off Courtney and give police investigators a look into the real core of evil, the guy who slammed an icepick into the heart of the murder victim."

I said, "She mentioned 'something else' and then disconnected. What was the 'something else' and why didn't she leave it in her message?"

Nick shrugged. "Probably wasn't that important."

Dave said, "Someone could have walked into the room and she didn't want them to hear what she was going to tell you."

I watched the rotation of the light coming from the Ponce Lighthouse. "Maybe. I think she called me from the carnival because she said *'here at the carnival.'* What else did she start to say?"

Dave leaned against a wooden dock pilling, the slight smell of fresh creosote coming from near the waterline. "Leave it alone, Sean. The police have probably already arrested her. If she's innocent, it's up to the legal system to prove her guilt. At this point in time, I spotted a grey goose flying over the marina. Alas, the bird thought it was an artic penguin and took up refuge in my freezer where it resides. Let's have a drink and toast to American jurisprudence."

"You guys go without me."

"What are you gonna do?" Nick asked.

"I'm going to hit the redial button on my phone and see who picks up from the number Courtney Burke used to call me."

— • —

COURTNEY FOLLOWED TONY Bandini into the office decorated in dark woods and leathers, antique framed carnival posters on the walls. He took a seat behind a desk, stacks of banded money, checks, and a calculator placed neatly on the desk, a dark cigar smoldering in a tarnished ashtray, a half empty glass of scotch on the rocks, sweating. A two-inch line of cocaine on the desk. A Beretta was on the far right side. Bandini said, "I got a dilemma on my hands. Murder at a carnival isn't good for business, at least in the same town. The beauty of this life is we move on, move past obstacles, head towards new opportunities. Maybe I could have a few opportunities with a filly like you in my stable, but I can't have you killin' the clients."

"Clients? I'm a ticket taker—that's it. I didn't kill Lonnie. I was on a ride when he was stabbed. A man in a hooded jacket did it.

I need this job. Do I still have it?"

He grinned out of one corner of his mouth. "Everything is negotiable. Come here."

Courtney stepped closer to the desk. "Thank you."

He shook his head. "No. Come around here."

She stepped behind the desk, within a few feet of Bandini.

He said, "You wanna get high?"

"No."

He grinned, stroking her body with his eyes. "Now, it's negotiation time. Depending how good you are, purely based on performance, you can have your job back…. And other jobs, too. Now, get down on your knees and open your mouth." Bandini started to unzip his fly.

"No! That's not gonna happen." Courtney held up one hand.

Bandini rubbed his crotch and grinned. "Shut up! I say what does and does not happen in this carnival. Now get down on your knees and open your fuckin' mouth." He reached out and grabbed her left wrist, pulling hard, gripping her hair with his other hand and dragging her down to his open zipper. She could smell the odor of dried sweat, testosterone, and cigar smoke on his clothes.

She fought back, trying to stand. He slapped her hard across the mouth, splitting her lower lip, blood running down her chin. He tore open her shirt and reached for her breasts, laughing, his breath smelling of scotch and garlic. She drew back, then slammed her right fist into his testicles.

"You fuckin' bitch!" He reached to his right, trying to grab the pistol on the desk.

Courtney scrambled, kneeing him a second time between his legs as she grabbed the gun. She pointed the Beretta directly between Bandini's eyes and shouted, "Stand back!"

He sneered, eyes fierce. "You won't shoot me!"

She backed away a few feet, reached down and picked up four one-hundred bills from a stack. "This is what you owe me in salary and the cost of replacing my shirt you just ripped open. I'll take another hundred for what you owed Lonnie. I'm sure he'd want that. And I'm telling the cops you had Lonnie killed."

Bandini pushed back in his chair and stood. "You're crazy! Take that money and you won't live to spend it." He stepped closer.

"Put the gun down and we'll talk."

Courtney backed up. "Stay where you are!" Bandini grinned and stepped a little closer.

Courtney raised the pistol in her hand. "Stop!"

"Or what! You don't have what it takes to kill a man. Your hands are shakin' like a little girl." He took another step.

Courtney backed up against the closed door. "Don't make me do this."

"Do what?" He grinned, moved a toothpick from one side of his mouth to the other. "Gimme the fuckin' gun. Johnny's gonna be back here in a second. He's a big boy. Hung like a mule. He'll literally tear you up so bad you'll wear a diaper for a month."

"No! No, he won't. Stop! I swear I'll do it."

"Get real, bitch. You never took the safety off the gun."

Courtney glanced down at the Beretta, searching for the safety. Bandini jumped, reaching for the pistol. "No!" she screamed as he tried to wrestle the gun from her hands. She squeezed the trigger, the bullet hitting Bandini in his throat, severing the spinal column in the back of his neck. He fell to the floor, eyes wide—disbelieving, head trembling. He died with the toothpick still in the right side on his mouth.

Courtney placed the gun in her purse and ran has hard as she could, running by motorhomes tucked in the long shadows, hidden from the lights of the midway, sequestered from the crowds. She could hear the contrived narrative from a reality TV show coming from the open windows of one trailer, heard the bark of a pit bull chained to the steps of a motorhome.

Someone stepped from the dark into the soft light.

She stopped, tried to catch her breath, eyes wide and frightened.

Isaac Solminski said, "Courtney, follow me. Hurry!"

She nodded and followed the dwarf between the tents, campers, and motorhomes. He snatched open the door to a camper and said, "Come on!" He closed the door behind Courtney and led her to a couch and two chairs. He gestured for her to sit on the couch and said, "I saw you go into Bandini's office. What happened to your mouth? Hold on, let me get some ice for that." He opened the door on a small refrigerator, removed two ice cubes, wrapped them in the center of a clean, white washcloth, and stepped back to Courtney. He reached out and tenderly touched the cool cloth to her lips. "What'd Bandini do to you, or was it Johnson who did this?"

"It was Bandini. He tried to force himself on me. I fought back as hard as I could. He'd left a gun on his desk. I got to it before he could. He kept coming for me. I warned him."

"Is he dead?"

"I don't know…I think so."

"Look, it was self-defense. You had no choice."

"Nobody's going to believe me."

"I believe you. Just tell the cops what happened."

"They're convinced I killed Lonnie. I have to leave. I have to think."

"I have a friend who lives south of Tampa in a little town called Gibsonton. It's a carny town. The place where circus workers and carnies live in the winter during the off season. My friend's name is Boots Langley. He recently retired from the business, and he knows just about everyone in it. He rents out cottages. Stay as long as you need. Tell Boots to put it on my account. I'll write his address down for you. He's a quirky kind of fella, but once you get to know him, you can overlook his…uniqueness. Also, he knows a lot of people in the business. Maybe he can point you in the right direction, help you find who you're looking for."

"Thank you." She stood up to leave, walking to the door.

"Wait!" Isaac climbed down from the chair and stepped to the door. He slowly opened it and peeked outside. He watched Johnny Johnson and two other men as they pounded on camper doors, spoke into the crackle of walkie-talkies, and shined flashlights into the dimly lit areas backstage from the midway. "I'm gonna go out there and stall them best I can. Courtney, leave through the side door. Cut between the Himalayan and the Zipper. The taxis are out there. Head for the bus station. Go see Boots Langley."

She leaned down and hugged Isaac. "Thank you for being here…for helping me. I won't forget you."

There was a loud knock at the door. Johnny Johnson bellowed. "Open up! Ten seconds and we rip the damn door off."

"Gettin' my pants on. Hold on a sec." He turned back to Courtney and whispered, "Go now. If they find you, God help you. Go!"

Courtney nodded and slipped out the back door moments before Johnny Johnson stepped inside, flashlights igniting the entire camper in a blaze of white.

FIFTEEN

When I stepped over the ladder onto *Jupiter's* cockpit, Max was there to greet me. "Hi, little lady. Were you the captain of this ol' boat while I was ashore?" She sat and cocked her head, brown eyes bright. "Kim sent a piece of pompano for you." I held up the Ziploc baggie with the small piece of cooked fish and Max moved her tail like a maestro's baton. She followed me inside the salon where I set the warm fish in her bowl. Three gulps, gone. "Let's head to the bridge to catch some air."

I tucked Max under one arm and climbed the steps to the fly bridge. I sat in the captain's chair and thought about the call I was about to make. I thought more about the message Courtney Burke left. *'Maybe you could like tell that detective, the one who knows you, Detective Grant, maybe you could tell him for me. Thank you...something else...never mind, it's not important. Bye.'*

I hit the dial button to Detective Dan Grant. As he answered, I could hear the heightened communications coming from police radios and the blare of carnival music in the background. "Dan, Courtney Burke left a message on my phone. She said a guy by the name of Bandini ordered the hit on the victim. I don't know who he is, but—"

"Was."

"What?"

"He's dead."

"How?"

"Shot through the neck. Witnesses say Courtney Burke was seen going into Tony Bandini's trailer just before the shooting."

"Where is she?"

"I'll tell you where she's not, that's here at the carnival. Gone, baby, gone. But somebody who just arrived is Carlos Bandini, brother of deceased. I hope we find Burke before he does."

"What if Courtney is taking the fall for a hit?"

"Her prints are on the murder weapon."

"That means she was at the crime scene. But it doesn't prove she shoved the ice pick into the vic's heart"

"Look, Sean, now I have another murder to investigate. Gotta go. But I want to leave you with a piece of advice: this crazy chick's a serial killer. And now she's on the run, packin' a pistol and a hard-on for any man who gets in her way. That would include you. If she shows up again at your boat or cabin, let's hope you're faster than she is, pal. This is gonna be one fuckin' long damn night around here." He disconnected.

I looked at Max, who sat on the bench seat behind the captain's chair. She watched the boat traffic in Ponce Marina, her dark eyes reflecting the lights from the mast of a sailboat entering the harbor. The tide was rising, *Jupiter* rocking slightly, the ropes groaning like a nautical snore. I glanced down at the phone in my hand, scrolled to Courtney's message, and hit the redial button. It rang five times before a beep came on indicating the call had entered voice-message mode. No instructions to leave a message after the beep. Just the beep. "This is Sean O'Brien trying to reach Courtney Burke. Courtney called me earlier tonight from this number, and I wanted to return her call. Thank you." I disconnected and wondered whose phone I'd left the message on, and whether Detective Dan Grant was right about Courtney Burke.

"Sean, how about a nightcap?" Dave Collins crossed the dock from his boat, *Gibraltar* and stood near *Jupiter's* cockpit holding two glass mugs in his one hand. He stepped over the transom steps and looked up at me.

"Maybe later. Max and I are just enjoying the night air."

"Hells bells, you might want a cocktail now. I just saw a live TV news report from the county fairgrounds. Place looks like a circus, no pun intended. There's been a shooting. It's Courtney Burke, Sean. Police believe she shot a guy through the neck. Another damn murder."

"Maybe it was self-defense."

Dave climbed the steps to the bridge, petted Max, lowered his big frame onto the bench-seat and set one mug on the small table. He released a heavy sigh and said, "It certainly could have been self-defense, but according to the news, she didn't stick around long enough to tell that to the police."

"Detective Dan Grant feels the same way."

"You spoke with him?"

"Just a couple of minutes ago. He said witnesses saw her going into the office, the trailer of the guy who owns or co-owns the carnival with his brother. Their last name is Bandini."

Dave nodded and sipped from a sweating mug, the ice tinkling against the glass. "I saw video of the surviving brother. The guy looks more like he's Tony Soprano's brother. In his sound bite he said if the police can't find the killer of his brother, he will. The news reports are saying that the girl is MIA. If it was self-defense, why run?"

"Maybe she panicked."

"She was composed enough to not leave the weapon behind. According to the news reports, police haven't found the gun. That didn't happen in the first murder."

I said nothing, the only sounds coming from the lapping of water around the dock pilings and a sailing halyard tapping against the mast of a sailboat.

Dave sipped his cocktail. "What are you thinking? I've seen that look on your face too many times. Leave it be, Sean. Police are focusing heavy on this one. It has serial killer written on it like graffiti on a wall of shame."

"Dan Grant said a report indicates that Courtney Burke spent time in a mental institution. More than once."

"I assume she didn't self-commit, so it begs the question:

who wanted her locked up and why? Was it ordered by a judge—maybe from recommendations by child services or foster care? Or was it her family? What did she do?"

"What if she didn't do anything? Maybe that was part of the problem. She could have been helpless and victimized. Or traumatized from witnessing something horrific as a child."

"Reached her breaking point?"

"For a child who has been sexually abused, it's often a layered breaking point. Created from a series of horrendous layers of physical damage to the body coupled by the most painful—emotional damage to the human spirit. It's the scar left from a branding iron to the soul, and the mark doesn't fade like a cheap tattoo. What kind of therapy completely erases the fallout from that? Did she get help in an asylum…or did locking her up in a psych ward add more layers?"

Dave scratched Max behind her ears. "Maybe all of your speculation is true. But we don't know that. We do know that since you found that young woman walking near a remote highway in the dead of night, there's been a second murder—"

"There's been a second killing. Murder isn't an act of self-defense."

"Do you really believe that, Sean? Or are you trying to come to grips with the sad fact that a pretty young woman can be a lethal killer?"

As I started to answer Dave's question, my cell rang, the call coming from the same number Courtney had used to call me. I answered and a falsetto voice of a man said, "Mr. O'Brien, my name is Isaac Solminski. It was my phone that you called."

"Who are you?"

"Courtney's friend."

"Where is she?"

"I don't know."

"Are you calling from the carnival?"

"Yes, and she's gone. Police are here."

"Do you know what happened? Why'd she run?"

"Feared for her life. Courtney was about to be raped. She told me that she took the money owed to her after Tony Bandini tried to force himself on her. They wrestled for the gun. It went off and he was killed."

"Did you tell that to the police?"

"Yes, but I'm not sure they're buying the story. I'm just a carny, in their eyes not very credible. Since there was no eyewitness, it looks to me like they believe she stole money from Bandini and killed him."

"Did they tell you that?"

"No, but I overheard the cops talking right outside my trailer."

"Speak with Detective Dan Grant. He's African-American, probably the lead detective. Tell him what Courtney told you."

"I did. He's a better listener than the others, but I can tell he's just as skeptical. Mr. O'Brien, Courtney said if you called to give you a message."

"What message?"

"She wants to know if you have a birthmark on your left shoulder."

I said nothing. I knew I was wearing a shirt each time I spoke with Courtney, the night I found her, and then on *Jupiter*. My heart beat faster.

"Are you there, Mr. O'Brien?"

"Yes."

"She said she believes you might have a small birthmark on your left shoulder that resembles a four-leaf clover, or an Irish shamrock. Do you, Mr. O'Brien?"

For a long moment I didn't want to answer, the question too invasive. My personal space in some way now violated. I knew the girl hadn't seen my shoulder. How did she know? Who'd she know that knew me that well? *Think.*

"Mr. O'Brien, are you there?"

"Yes."

"I assume Courtney was right, you have a small birthmark resembling the shamrock?"

"Yes."

"She said one other thing…if you do have this mark on your left shoulder, you are related to her. She didn't say how. Could you be her father?"

SIXTEEN

After I disconnected from the man with the falsetto voice, I turned to Dave. He said, "You look like someone just said that you have three months to live."

I said nothing, my thoughts racing.

"Who was on the line, Sean? What happened?"

"A man who goes by the name of Isaac Solminski. He works at the carnival. It was his phone that Courtney used when she called me."

"What'd he say?"

"He told me that Courtney said I might have a small birthmark in the shape of an Irish shamrock on my left shoulder. Dave, there is no way that she could have seen it. I didn't mention it, and very few people even know it's there."

"I've known you for five years, see you working on your boat many times in nothing but your swim trunks, and without my glasses I'd never see it."

"It's not much larger than a postage stamp. But the birthmark looks like a clover or a shamrock. Sherri used to call it God's perfect little tattoo on my shoulder. How in the hell did Courtney know it was there? Solminski said she told him it meant that she was related to me."

"Did she say how, as in a niece or a long lost daughter?" Dave grinned.

"For Christ sakes. You sound like the guy on the phone. I have no living family. Sherri was an only child. My parents died when I was in my last year of high school. I had no siblings. I lived with my uncle until age eighteen when I left for college and then joined the military. My uncle had no children when he and my aunt died. So I'm it—the last of the bunch. It's just Max and me." I reached in the topside cooler and lifted out a Corona, popped the top, and took a long pull from the bottle. "Now I know what Courtney meant in her voice message when she said there was 'something else.'"

Dave nodded. "It's a hell of a something else. What if she'd been stalking you from the beginning?"

"What do you mean?"

"What if all of this is some kind of an elaborate ploy to get you involved in her bizarre world, a place where the Mad Hatter holds the keys to her Wonderland?"

"But why? That doesn't make any sense."

"It's not supposed to make sense in the playground of a psychopath."

"But we don't know that's what she is, do we?"

Dave grunted and sipped his drink. "My friend, Sean O'Brien, the time-less optimist, the man who sees good where evil hides in the shadows."

"Evil couldn't exist without the presence of good. I like to believe that good is a little more predominant and a lot more appreciated because of evil."

Dave laughed and lifted Max onto his lap. "Maxine and the other critters don't operate in either camp, it's just us free-willed, vertical-walking mortals. So now that Courtney Burke has laid a bomb under your mental hood, what are you going to do?"

"I want to know how she knew about the birthmark."

"Maybe some things in life should remain a mystery. Once the genie's out of the bottle, it might become Pandora's Wonderland."

"Dave, at this point, I can't think of anyone alive who knows that I have a tiny birthmark on my shoulder. Someone would have to get close to me without my shirt on, and then be looking for it. Otherwise it's not that obvi-ous. Who knows it's there? Who could have told Courtney and why? Since Sherri's death, I've only been with a few women. Two of them are dead, too."

"Maybe a look at your birthmark is like looking into the face of Medusa, fatal, or dangerously rocky at best. Perhaps you'll recall that Medusa was a mere mortal, too. I'll remind you to keep your shirt on." Dave smiled and sipped his drink.

"Something's very strange here. I want to pay a visit to the guy who was just on the phone, the man with the falsetto voice."

"Why?"

"He may know where Courtney can be found."

Dave shook his head. "Let Detective Grant, the FBI, and whoever the hell else might be following this young woman, let them track her down."

"You and Grant both mentioned Bandini's brother, Carlos. What if he finds her before the police do? If he's the real bad ass in the bunch, what would he do to her? If she vanishes, I may never know how she was aware of my birthmark."

"Then let it go. Plan A is hoping the cops find her first."

"What's Plan B?"

Dave sipped his drink, watched the rotation of the light from the lighthouse sweep high above the tops of the sailboat masts and challenge the dark over the Atlantic Ocean. He lowered his eyes to meet mine. "Plan B, unfortunately, Sean, is when somebody's Plan A didn't work out for them and you get involved."

"Too bad I can't design Plan B, only answer it. Maybe I'll have a better answer when they arrest Courtney."

SEVENTEEN

A taxi pulled up to the curb in front of the Greyhound Bus station in Daytona Beach and slowed to a stop. The dark-skinned driver wore a Cardinals' baseball cap and a diamond stud in one ear, the earring winking from the passing headlights on Ridgewood Avenue. He cut his black eyes up to the rearview mirror and looked at Courtney Burke in the back seat. "This is the place. Do you know what time you catch your bus?"

She didn't answer, her eyes following a police car that entered the parking lot from a road behind the building. "Drive on, please."

"What?"

"Now! Just go."

The taxi driver nodded, put the car in gear, and pulled back into the night traffic. "So where'd you want to go?"

"Where's the closest truck stop?"

"Less than three miles."

"Take me there."

The driver sighed, accelerated and changed lanes. He glanced back in the mirror at the girl. "You in some kind of trouble?"

"No."

"When you saw that cop car, you got an instant case of the hee-bee-jee-bees. Know what I'm sayin'? Hey, I've been there. Why are the cops lookin' for you?"

"I didn't say they're looking for me. I just don't feel like hanging around a creepy bus station half the night."

"So you're gonna hang around a creepier truck stop? C'mon, that don't take a hellava lot of smarts."

"Please, just take me there, okay? I don't feel like talking either."

The driver was quiet for a minute. Then he said, "Look up ahead. Lots of blue lights. Either a wreck or the cops are runnin' a sobriety check stop."

"Turn around!"

"I can't do a U-turn here."

"Let me out!"

"What? In the middle of the damn road?"

Courtney opened the passenger door a few inches. "Slow down!"

"Hey! Wait a second, okay? There's a side street up ahead about fifty yards. I can turn to the right and by-pass all that shit up there."

"Okay."

The driver cut through two lanes of traffic, horns blasting, drivers swearing. He made a sharp right turn and zoomed down a darker road, the staccato pockets of light from the streetlamps popping like overhead fireworks bursting. "Damn, girl. You know how to get the adrenaline pumping."

"Thank you for doing that."

"No problem. Long as I don't see flashing blue lights in the next thirty seconds, we're good to go. Why the hell are the cops lookin' for you?"

"I don't want to go into it."

"All right. Probably best I don't know. Don't want to be called an accessory to some friggin' crime, especially one I didn't do."

A few minutes passed in silence, and then the driver pulled into a large, well-lighted parking lot half filled with semi-trucks, neglected palm trees, and steel trash barrels overflowing with garbage. Beyond the rows of fuel pumps was a single-story brick building with a blue neon sign that read: *Open 24 Hours*. Many of the big rigs were parked with running lights on, diesels idling, drivers climbing in and out of the cabs.

Courtney watched a middle-aged woman open the passenger side door of a parked truck. She took a moment to adjust her short skirt as she stood on the top rung in spike heels, and then stepped down to the parking lot.

The taxi driver stopped near the building and turned back toward Courtney. "You sure you wanna get out here?"

"I'm sure."

"That'll be twelve even."

Courtney handed him a ten and five. "Keep the change."

"Be careful. Most of these drivers are hard working stiffs like me. Good guys. But some are real degenerates. They can use their mobility to do a lot of rough shit and never get it pinned on them 'cause they're here one hour and gone the next." He looked around the three-acre lot. "Big place. I'm glad they have surveillance cameras out here. But it just makes some of them more careful."

Courtney got out of the taxi. She paused and leaned in the front side window. "Thank you."

"No problem. You take care of yourself. Shit, I don't want to read that they found your body in a dumpster or some other God-awful place."

Courtney smiled and then turned, stepping into the jumble of lights and sounds, the cranking of diesel engines as a country song blared from outdoor speakers. She walked around two truckers sipping black coffee from paper cups, steam rising in the cool night air. Their eyes met her as she walked through the odor of fuel, fry grease, bacon, and cinnamon buns, leading to the truck stop entrance drenched in the blue glow of a neon sign that read: *PRIVATE SHOWERS*.

EIGHTEEN

Two hours after Dave had walked back to *Gibraltar*, I still sat in *Jupiter's* fly bridge as the midnight hour approached. A warm breeze blew across the marina from the east, carrying the scent of the sea and night-blooming jasmine. Max slept curled up in a ball on the bench seat, an occasional dream-induced whimper escaping from her throat. I could hear a woman's laughter coming from the Tiki Bar at the far end of the dock, the sound of Harleys cranking and pulling out of the parking lot. I was exhausted, tired but yet too wired to go down to the master berth for the delusion of real sleep. I had been sitting in the same spot for two hours thinking about the message the man with the falsetto voice had left with me. *"She said one other thing…if you do have this mark on your left shoulder, you are related to her. She didn't say how. Could you be her father?"*

Courtney Burke said she was nineteen maybe close to twenty. Doing the math and trying to fit it in with the time-line of my life, I thought about the women I'd known—the women I'd taken to bed. I pictured Courtney's face, the slight cleft in her chin, the texture of her hair, the slant of her cheekbones, and even the way she carried herself—straight, shoulders back, her strong sense of presence. Who might have resembled Courtney twenty years ago? I tried to superimpose images of former girlfriends over Courtney's face. I struggled to match a gene pool that tonight had an opaque surface hiding the passage of time and people in my life. Most of the images were faded, blurred in a scrapbook that I rarely opened for all the reasons that they were part of the past.

I closed my eyes and attempted to run a movie trailer of my life from two decades ago through the film gate of my mind. Some of the women I'd known were there in full color, captured in slow-motion angles—the way they'd turned their heads, the way they'd smiled, their physical features still vivid. Other faces were harder to see through the lens of the past, the landscape of their appearances now more distant on the horizon, and the closer I tried to focus, the more stonewashed the faces became. It was like trying to replay a dream I'd made a mental note to remember, but couldn't.

One picture stopped. It became a freeze-frame when I remembered her eyes.

Like the image of an old National Geographic cover.

Like Courtney's eyes.

Her name was Andrea Hart. A woman destined for better things than what I could bring to the table after college graduation. She wanted no part of a possible "military life," hop-scotch jumping from base-to-base if I wanted to climb the ladder while, at the same time, searching for purpose in what I would do. In retrospect, after we went our separate ways, I probably have Andrea to thank for my determination to get through Delta Force training and the Special Activities Division. The experience forever changed me—the good, bad, and ugly, scars and all.

Where was Andrea Hart tonight, twenty something years later? Could she be Courtney Burke's mother? Could I be her father? *No way.* I touched the cleft in my chin and pictured her face. I stood from the captain's chair, my back muscles in knots, a slight headache forming over my left eye, my scalp tight. "Come on, Max. Let's go down. I need to use the computer to track a ghost from my past. If not, the image of Courtney and what she might represent, will haunt me for the rest of my life."

— —

SHE KNEW HE was looking at her. Even from behind her, Courtney could feel his eyes on her like a breath. She was stirring cream and sugar into her black coffee when the man approached.

She sat at the café counter inside the truck stop and sipped from a cup of coffee in front of her. She'd felt the man staring at her twice, both times when he'd walked past her, once heading from the restrooms, the second time when he pretended to be looking at magazines in the rack.

The man moved and sat on one of the stools beside her where he waited for the waitress to return from the kitchen. He glanced at Courtney, his face ruddy and chapped, lips cracked, eyes dancing like flames across her face. He said, "This place has the best coffee of all the truck stops in Florida."

Courtney nodded. "It's pretty good."

"Ought to be real good. I hear the nightshift manager, gal's name is Flo, puts on a fresh pot ever' half hour."

"Really?"

"Hell yeah. But this time of night they'll go through a few pots ever' hour anyhow."

Courtney sipped her coffee.

"What brings a girl like you in here? Can't imagine you drivin' a rig."

"I'm not. I hitched this far. The trucker was going toward Miami. I didn't want to go down there."

The man ran his tongue over his front teeth and swallowed.

"Where do you want to go?"

"Which way are you headed?"

"It for damn sure ain't Miami. You almost need a passport to drive through the city. Try askin' for directions if you don't speak Spanish." He grinned, a small crack in his bottom lip strawberry red. Courtney finished her coffee and turned toward the man. "Where'd you say you were going?"

"Anywhere you want to go, sugar." He grinned, his breath smelling of beer and beef jerky. "C'mon girl, let's jump in the truck. My rig's fueled up and good to go all night long, if you know what I mean."

"Yeah, I know what you mean." Courtney followed the man out the door, keeping her back to the three security cameras she'd spotted earlier. She unzipped her purse as she walked, her fingers touching the Beretta, her thoughts touching the face of her grandmother so far away.

— ▪ —

THEY WERE IN the cab of the big-rig less than a minute when he made his move. The trucker reach behind his seat and pulled out two cans of Budweiser from a small cooler. "How 'bout a cold one?"

"No thanks. Never got used to how beer tastes."

"I wonder how you'd taste." He popped the top on the can and took a long pull, his Adam's apple moving like a piston.

Courtney rested her hand on the Beretta in her open purse between her right leg and the cab door.

The man used the back of his left hand to wipe his mouth, his lips wet with beer foam and saliva. He grinned. "Best way to learn to like the taste of beer is to slip me some tongue. That way you can get the flavor little doses at a time. You got some damn pretty eyes, girl."

"Please, just drive."

He laughed and snorted, his eyes lowering from her face to her lap. "If you won't slip me some tongue, I'll slip you some. Take your pants off."

"I'm on my period."

"Take your panties off."

"What if I took your head off?" She raised the Beretta and aimed right between his eyes. "Oh shit! Put the gun down!" "Drive! "Huh?"

"Drive the truck! Head to Tampa."

He held both hands up, a nerve below his right eye twitching like a beetle was crawling under his skin. "I ain't goin' that way."

"You are now."

"Listen, I'm supposed to have this load to New Orleans in a day. This truck's got GPS on it, which means dispatch knows where it's at twenty-four-seven."

"You should've thought about that before you tried to force yourself on me." She used her thumb to flip the safety off. "Drive."

He cranked the diesel, his ruddy face now shiny with perspiration. He checked both side mirrors, put the truck in gear, and eased out of the parking lot. "You gonna keep that gun on me the whole way?"

"Yes."

"You shoot me out there on the highway doin' seventy, this rig will jack-knife, roll over and you'll die, too."

"But you'll die first. Don't talk to me again until we're there."

— —

ALTHOUGH I HADN'T seen Andrea Hart in two decades, it didn't take long to track her down. If I cared more about politics, I wouldn't have had to use a combination of data-finding search engines, social media sites, and sites that accessed public records. I learned as much as I could about the woman I'd known as Andrea Hart.

She was now Andrea Logan, wife of U.S. senator, Lloyd Logan, a three-term member of the senate and chairman of the Appropriations Committee. More than that, he was a front-runner in the pack of candidates vying for the Republican presidential nomination. I would have known about her status earlier had I watched cable news the last few months.

They lived in Grand Rapids, Michigan where she worked as director of development for a large conservative think tank guised as a foundation. I couldn't find anything indicating Andrea had a daughter or any other children. No birth records. No school records. Any adoption records were probably sealed.

I stared at a picture of Andrea. Her eyes were still just as beautiful as the morning I'd first met her in a coffee shop twenty years earlier. I remembered walking in the crowded shop, and after waiting in line to order coffee at the counter, it appeared as if every table in the place was taken. From across the shop I first saw Andrea's eyes, and then her smile. I stepped to her and she offered me the vacant chair across from her. We spent the entire morning talking. A week later to the day, a Sunday morning, she awoke next to me in bed, and in the soft morning light coming through the window, she traced her finger over my birthmark and said, "That is really beautiful. It's like art." *So damned long ago.*

As the image of Andrea stared at me from my computer screen, I enlarged the picture then envisioned Courtney Burke's eyes. Although Andrea's eyes had a captivating command to them, they didn't have the mesmerizing power and depth I'd seen in Courtney's eyes. What would a geneticist say about the probability of Courtney's iris color having come from the cobalt blue in my eyes and the hazel green in Andrea's eyes?

Tomorrow I would do my best to find out.

NINETEEN

The next morning, as the sun rose over the Atlantic, I jogged along the beach at Ponce Inlet. I ran between the gentle roll of waves breaking, the surge of water yawning and stretching on the cool hard-packed sand under my bare feet. I pictured Andrea Logan's face, then ran harder for a short burst, the sea foam scattering in the breeze like confetti defying the laws of gravity. The old lighthouse was behind me, Daytona Beach ten miles to the north, my thoughts not in either place. A gull flew over my head, flapped its wings twice, sailing in the cross-breeze and squawking a wake-up call over the crash of waves. I was shirtless, the morning sea breeze already warm across my chest. I glanced at the shamrock-shaped birthmark on my upper left arm and thought of Courtney Burke.

Max followed me at a trot. Twenty feet behind, the tip of her pink tongue visible in her open mouth, panting, short legs moving in a dachshund dash, her eyes bright with the potential discovery of what a new morning by the sea might bring. She stopped to inspect a starfish stranded on the beach. I spun around toward her. "Max, what do you say we return this little fella to the sea?" She cocked her head and stared up at me as I lifted the starfish from the wet sand, walked into the swell of waves lapping over my knees, and lowered the starfish back into the ocean.

I jogged a final fifty yards, Max doing her best to impersonate a greyhound loping along the beach. We stopped and sat on a park bench under a canopy of palm trees. I thought about what I'd say to Andrea when I found her—what I hoped not to hear in return. Then I thought about

Courtney again, a girl on the run, a suspect in at least two killings, possible cold-blooded murders.

Where was she at this very moment as the sun peaked over the edge of the world and painted the ocean in rippling brushstrokes of red wine and dark honey? Did it shine light at the end of her dark path? I stared out into the enormity of a crimson sea and felt no larger than little Max resting beside me. I watched the surface of the ocean turn the color of a new penny and I tried to picture what was waiting just beyond the horizon.

— —

THE TRUCK DRIVER glanced at the Beretta once again as he slowed the big rig and exited from I-75. He said, "Okay, we're here. I done what you asked. What the hell else you want?"

Courtney rested her gun hand on her raised left knee, the Beretta still aimed at the driver's head. "I want you to turn right at the light. Pull into the Shell station."

The driver went through the gears, and entered the parking lot of a Shell gasoline station and eased to a stop. "What now?"

"Give me your phone."

"What? Why?"

"Give it to me!"

"All right. Hell, you weren't jokin' when you said you were on your period."

"And I wasn't joking when I said I'd kill you. The phone. Now."

He slid the phone across the seat. "You *are* crazy."

"Maybe. Now, you listen to me, you pervert. You're gonna turn this truck around, drive up the interstate to New Orleans or wherever you're supposed to be heading, and you're not going to tell anybody about our little road trip. Because if you do, then I get to tell them you tried to fuck a teenage girl, me. Your wife will be the first to know."

"How'd you know I'm married?"

"I didn't. But most of you creeps are, I just feel very sorry for the wives." Courtney scooped the phone from the seat, opened the door, and climbed down from the cab, slipping the pistol into her bag.

▄ ▄

I CLOSED THE sliding glass door to *Jupiter's* salon and sat on the couch with my laptop looking up Senator Lloyd Logan's campaign tour, his fund-raising events. There were a half dozen here in Florida, one was very soon and not far away. A place called The Villages about an hour north of Orlando.

I'd heard about The Villages. It wasn't a retirement community, but rather a retirement city. High average net worth of its residents. Golf for life. Defibrillators on most corners. A donor pit-stop in every presidential race. Mitt Romney was the last to refuel there. And now it was Senator Lloyd Logan's turn at the wheel.

All I wanted was a few minutes with his wife, a few minutes to take me back two decades. Maybe it was politically incorrect, but I had to go there, had to go into the past for the sake of a girl whose future was looking very dark.

TWENTY

took a small can of dog food from the galley and picked up the leash. Max cocked her head, knowing change was in the air. "Come on, kiddo. I have to hit the road for a few hours. Let's see if Dave or Nick can hang out with you until I get back." I locked *Jupiter* and stepped onto the dock, Max trotting in front of me, her nose lifting in the air. Smoke signals were coming from Nick's boat. Dave Collins and Nick Cronus were sitting in deck chairs on *St. Michael*, a Hibachi behind Nick puffing white smoke, the scent of cooking grouper, garlic, lemon, onion, and red pepper in the air. Max stopped in her tracks and headed for *St. Michael*. Dave had a GPS device in his lap, bifocals at the tip of his nose, and a small jeweler's screwdriver in his large fingers as he opened the back panel.

"Hot Dog!" Nick bellowed, standing to turn the cooking fish. "Where you been, huh? You supposed to help Uncle Nicky in the kitchen." Max trotted over the transom and stepped down onto the cockpit, squatting in full attention next to Nick. "Sean, you and Hot Dog come eat. Grouper and snapper's on the grill. Got some bread, cheese, and Greek wine is in the icebox."

I stepped aboard as Dave looked up. "Nick has an ailing GPS. I'm trying to re-set its clock, so to speak."

Nick used a fork to break off a small piece of fish for Max. "My GPS is more than ailing; it's a sick puppy. Not like you, Hot Dog. I was in my boat half a mile off the rocks last week. Had to use my Greek sailor's sixth sense to find a school of snapper." He squeezed a ripe lemon over the sizzling fish and closed the Hibachi lid.

Dave grunted as he removed the back panel. "GPS is a wonderful thing, when it works—which is most of the time. And speaking of time, a global positioning system is really all about timing. Anywhere on the planet, at any given moment, at least four satellites with overlapping radio signals can pinpoint your GPS location within a few meters. It gives weight to Einstein's Theory of Relativity. Time moves differently the farther you are from earth and the faster you're moving. This means that astronauts coming back from the International Space Station actually age less than babies born on the earth at the same time that the astronauts were in space. But it's all relative." He looked over his bifocals and grinned, then dropped his smile. "What's the latest on the girl and the killing?"

Nick glanced down at my hands. He said, "You're holding a leash for Max. You don't ever do that unless you want one of us to watch Hot Dog for a while. Where you heading, Sean?"

"A place called The Villages."

Nick smiled. "I've heard of it. Heard the V might as well stand for Viagra. Lots of baby-boomers doin' the big boom. Gotta blame it on those seeking medical attention or some kinda attention for those four-hour erections." Nick grinned, his moustache rising. Black eyes vibrant, squinting in the noon sunlight. He bent down and picked up an icy bottle of Corona next to his deck chair.

"Why are you going up there?" Dave asked.

"Because a girlfriend I knew twenty years ago is visiting her mother there. She happens to be with her husband, Senator Lloyd Logan who's making a fundraising stop. I'd like to ask her a question."

Dave pushed his glasses up to the top of his head. "Wait a minute, Sean. Your ex-girlfriend is the wife of a presidential candidate?"

I smiled. "That's assuming he wins the Republication nomination." I told them the story of my relationship with the former Andrea Hart.

Dave exhaled and nodded. "I'd rather contemplate Einstein's theory than yours. You may have, unknown to you, impregnated this former girlfriend, Andrea Hart, now Andrea Logan, the wife of a powerful U.S. senator, a man vying for a presidential bid. She gives the baby up for adoption nineteen years ago, and then almost two decades later, you find a young woman walking on a remote road in the heart of a national forest. You prevent two Neanderthals from attacking her. Later, she shows up here at the marina in the aftermath of a murder. A man with a Munchkin voice tells you that she told him about a shamrock-shaped birthmark on your upper left arm. And if you bore this mark, then you may be related to her. But she didn't say how. Why wouldn't she say how she believes you're related if this girl was your daughter? Why the mystery?"

"I don't know. And I don't know how she knew about my birthmark."

Dave crossed his thick arms. "What happens if you go waltzing back into Andrea Logan's life and somehow find out that Courtney Burke is your daughter? And to extrapolate this theory, what happens if it's later proven that Courtney is in fact a serial killer and the biological daughter of a woman who could be the next first lady in the White House, should her husband, the esteemed Senator Lloyd Logan win the Republican nomination?"

I said nothing for a moment, listening to the slap of water against *St. Michael*, the sound of a siren in the distance, the flapping of a pirate's flag on a trawler tied up behind us. "I didn't seek this intersection at this point in my life. I can go left, right, turn around, go straight, or go nowhere."

Nick wiped his hands on a white towel. "Sean, Forrest Gump may be a spot-on philosopher as movie characters go, but this is the real deal, brother. Shit doesn't always have to happen if you don't make it happen. Man, just walk away from this one. The only place this can go is the dark side."

"What would you do if she was your daughter, Nick? I couldn't give a rat's ass about some politician's desire to become president and what, if anything, this could or couldn't do to his campaign. What I care about is the girl, what's happened to her and what might happen to her."

Nick lifted Max to his lap and said, "But if she's a killer, all positive bets are off, and if she's your daughter, how would you deal with that? What if she drew down on you, had you in her sights...would you take her down? Could you?"

TWENTY-ONE

Senator Lloyd Logan lifted the wireless microphone from the podium, surveyed the people, smiled, and said, "This is my kind of crowd! Hello good people of The Villages!" I watched as the audience of more than three-thousand cheered. Logan, tall, a touch of gray in his dark, neatly parted hair, looked like he was sent from a casting office to play the part of a presidential contender. His smile beamed as he worked the spectators into rousing bursts of applause, saying all the well-rehearsed lines he knew they expected to hear.

He spoke to them from a raised platform in the center of the town square, American flags and red, white, and blue balloons were everywhere. The town square that could easily be a facade for a film set. The perfect blend of eateries, coffee shops, trendy bars, and a movie theater all around the city center dotted with majestic oaks draped with Spanish moss.

Many of the over age fifty-five residents sat in customized golf carts, resembling miniature classic cars, holding bottles of water in their hands and high hopes in their hearts that Senator Logan was there for them. He was a man who told them he could change Washington into a streamlined system of efficiency.

I stood as far to the right side of the podium as possible in order to get a good look at the first few rows of people standing, wearing sunglasses, ball caps, and big grins on their faces. I didn't watch Logan. I watched for his wife.

And there she was.

Andrea looked stunning. She wore a blue summer dress, brown hair to her shoulders, and a strand of pearls around her long, slender neck. She stood next to a man in a sports coat, pale blue shirt open at the collar, no tie, dark glasses, and a flesh-colored receiver in his left ear. I knew he wasn't listening to music.

I thought about Dave's reference to "Plan B." Maybe I could come up with a Plan C when dealing with the Secret Service. If the guy to her immediate right was visible to me and everyone else, the other members of his team were not. What I didn't know was why Lloyd Logan would warrant government agent protection at this stage of the race. He hadn't won the nomination yet. He certainly wasn't a minority or an obvious threat to hate groups. There were six other Republican hopefuls hitched to the dream-wagon as well. Did they all have a federal posse in tow?

Maybe these guys were the newbies. Maybe not.

Plan C.

I worked my way through the crowd, careful not to move too quickly, keeping my hands open and visible. I knew their first responsibility was the guy on the stage, the candidate, not the candidate's wife. These meet-and-greets were more casual, geared to press the flesh, to solicit campaign contributions, to convince voters to buy into future visions. All I wanted was a look into the past. And I wanted to look into Andrea's eyes when I asked the question that gnawed at my gut and now, my heart. I stepped next to her, the opposite side from where the Secret Service agent stood, and I said, "You must be very proud of him."

She turned to me and smiled. "I am. The country needs Lloyd right now."

"What do you need, Andrea?"

Her eyes opened wider, mouth forming a slight O, removing her sunglasses, the carotid artery in the side of her neck pulsating. "Sean…Sean O'Brien. Oh my God! It's been so long." Her eyes moistened. She didn't know whether to shake my hand or give me a hug. She just stood there and looked at me like a ghost just tapped her on the shoulder.

The agent turned to me and nodded, face suspicious. He looked at Andrea. "Is everything all right, Ms. Logan?"

"Yes, everything is fine, Robert. Sean is an old friend of mine."

The agent looked at me again, his body language taut, lower jaw muscles rigid. I could tell he was listening to a voice in his earpiece. The agent nodded and turned from us, whispering something into his sleeve.

I looked into Andrea's eyes, eyes as lovely as the first day I saw them across the coffee shop. "If you can sneak away for a quick break, I'd love to buy you a cup of coffee. There's a Starbucks across the street. As I remember from that first day we met, you liked your coffee with a touch of cream, no sugar."

She smiled. "I still do. Sean, I can't believe you're standing right here. How *are* you? Do you live here in Florida?"

"I'm good. And even better now. I do live in Florida, but not here. I don't meet the age criteria. I have an old cabin on the St.

Johns River, and I'm restoring a boat in a marina."

"You always loved boats. You loved anything nautical."

"Andrea, I need to talk with you."

She bit her full bottom lip for a second, glanced at her husband on the stage, and turned back to me. "We'll have to make it quick. Lloyd will wrap up in a few minutes. He'll do some Q and A, and then we're off to Tampa for another fundraiser."

"I'll have you back before he finishes."

She inhaled deeply through her nostrils, turned to the agent and said, "Robert, I'm going to have a cup of coffee with my friend, Sean. We'll be back in a minute."

"Absolutely, Ms. Logan. May I ask, what's your friend's last name?"

"O'Brien, Sean O'Brien."

I smiled at the agent as I walked away with Andrea, glancing up at the platform and into the eyes of Senator Lloyd Logan. I knew now that they had my last name, probably my image on face-recognition data banks, the searches were moving at the speed of light through the government's computers. And I knew it was just a matter of a time before more than one agent would enter the coffee shop.

TWENTY-TWO

Only one customer was in the Starbucks, a man sitting in one corner. He had an iPhone on the table, as well as a tablet and small keyboard. Everyone else was outside, listening to Senator Logan speak. Andrea and I ordered coffee and sat at a table in the opposite corner. I took a chair where I could see the front door. "Your husband's an eloquent speaker."

"He's passionate about what he's saying as it relates to the betterment of the nation."

I smiled. "I wish him the best. Why the federal agents at this point in the horse race?"

"The Secret Service offers protection where they think it's needed the most. Lloyd is a front-runner, doing great in the polls. That means he has his share of detractors, people who would rather harm him than try to beat him at the ballot box."

I looked over her shoulder and spotted the agent, Robert, standing outside the large front window. "Andrea, do you and I have a daughter?"

Her eyes opened a little more. Nostrils widening. "What? A daughter? Sean, what the hell's going on? Is this some kind of a joke? Why are you showing up twenty years after we said goodbye, coming out of nowhere to pop up at my *husband's* campaign appearance?"

"Because a young woman's life might hinge on what you tell me."

"What are you saying?"

"I'm saying that a girl, maybe twenty years old, walked into my life. She knew that I had a shamrock-shaped birthmark on my left arm. And there's no way she could know that unless someone told her. You always said you loved that birthmark, loved touching it because you said it gave you good luck. This girl said because of it—the birthmark, she *knew* that she was related to me. But she didn't say how. She didn't get a chance, really. She was running from the scene of a killing. Police believe she murdered a man, maybe more than one."

Andrea shuddered, her eyes on the cup of coffee in her hands. "Dear God," she whispered.

"I have my doubts that she's the killer. But right now I need to know if you were pregnant when we separated."

Andrea lifted her eyes to mine. She started to speak when the front door opened wide and two men walked inside. The agent, Robert, remained outside. The two coming into Starbucks were older, wearing suits. Splashes of gray in one man's hair. The other was balding. A straightforward walk. Wingtip shoes loud against the tile floor.

"Tell me, Andrea, were you pregnant?"

"Sean...this can't be happening. Maybe one of Lloyd's opponents is doing something to try to destroy the campaign."

As the men walked toward us, I glanced at my phone on the table and discreetly pressed the video record button. The taller of the two, a man with a shave so close the pores on his face seemed threadbare, stepped closest. He said, "Excuse me, Ms. Logan. We need to have a word with this man."

Andrea looked up from the table. "This man is a friend of mind. Everything's fine, Andy."

The agent nodded. "We understand. However, we still need to ask him a few questions."

"Okay, but I want to be present to hear his answers, too."

The agent scratched his clean-shaven face with one finger.

He looked at me. "Mr. O'Brien, why are you at this rally today?"

I smiled. "Last time I checked it was a free country, and people could attend political rallies. What if I came to hear what the senator has to say?"

His chest swelled. The second agent stepped closer to the table. The sentinel at the window touched his earpiece.

Andrea said, "Sean, please. They're just trying to do their jobs." She looked at both agents and added, "Sean and I go way back. We're simply catching up. That's all."

"Well, Ms. Logan, you're catching up with a man who was in the middle of shootout a while back involving a radical Islamic group, Russian arms dealers, and weapons-grade uranium found in an old German U-boat. Mr. O'Brien has quite a history. Delta Force, serving in the Middle East. And a checkered past that's either buried and sealed due to the nature of it, or he simply vanished off the radar for almost two years." He looked down at me, his face well within the wide-angle lens of the phone. "So, Mr. O'Brien, we'd like to know why you're here, and what's the nature of this conversation?"

I looked him dead in the eye. "I'm here because I have a right to be here. And the nature of what Andrea and I are talking about is private. None of your business."

"All right, stand up. We'll have the discussion elsewhere."

I reached for my phone, video recorder still capturing the moment. "I have done nothing wrong, and I'm not going anywhere with you unless it's to a cable news station, where they can broadcast the video I just recorded of your little inquisition, and we can take calls from viewers who'd be happy to ask you questions about First Amendment rights. How do you think that would flatter the campaign of Senator Lloyd Logan?"

His face smoldered for a brief moment, the tops of his ears red. He started to reach for my phone when Andrea raised her hand. "Gentlemen, we know you're just doing your job. Please, leave us. Sean is one of the most honest, patriotic men I've ever known. And he's right; what we're discussing is private. Please, respect that. We'll be done soon."

I smiled at the agents as they checked their egos, exhaled tension, turned around, and left us alone in the coffee shop. Andrea raised an eyebrow and asked, "I remember hearing about that big takedown. News reports said it stemmed from the recovery of nuclear material on a German U-boat off the coast of Florida and involved Russian arms dealers and a radical Islamic sect. So you were in the middle of that?"

"By default. I was just a team member."

She smiled. "I'm almost afraid to ask what other career choices you've made these last twenty years."

"Andrea, if we had a daughter, if you had to give her up for adoption, I understand. I'm not here to judge, to do anything that might have an impact on your life or your husband's political aspirations. I only want the truth. If we had a child together, she or he would be about the same age as this girl. Sometimes to help someone in the present, to shape the future, you have to know the past—to understand how the puzzle pieces interconnect."

Andrea looked away, her face filling with two decades of sequestered thoughts. She blinked back tears, a red rash spreading on her throat.

Now, I knew. But I wanted to hear it from her.

"Sean, I'm so sorry. I should have told you. I owed that much to you. My parents were so unforgiving at the time, Dad especially. I think he took it to his grave. I literally went into hiding, and I gave the baby up for adoption the week that she was born."

"So the baby was a girl?"

"Yes. And hardly a day goes by that I don't think about her. Wonder what she's like, what's she's doing, whether she's happy. I've prayed for her."

Her eyes seem to burst in tears. Two decades of hidden thoughts, emotions, breaking through the dam she's built to hold it all back. She stood and simply hugged me, her tears soaking into my shirt.

"It's okay, Andrea. You did what you felt was right. Did you ever see the child again?" I reached in my coat pocket and handed her a clean, white handkerchief.

After she dried her tears she said, "No. Adoption records were sealed. And I thought not interfering would be the best thing for the child and the family that adopted her. So I didn't try to meet the adoptive parents."

"If you never saw her, you never told her about my birthmark, correct?"

"Yes, there's no way. And I've never mentioned your birthmark to anyone else, either. No reason to."

"Then how would Courtney know? It doesn't make sense."

"Courtney, that's a lovely name. Please describe her to me?"

"Her eyes are mesmerizing, like yours. She has dark hair, and she's about your height. Very independent. I think she's been through a lot in her life." I could see Andrea's eyes beginning to well with tears again.

"Is she charged with murdering someone?"

"She's wanted in connection with at least one death, possibly two."

"I feel so…so disconnected. I never got pregnant again, and I've often thought it was God's way of punishing me for giving away a gift he gave. What are you going to do now?"

"I don't know."

She stood from the table, her face troubled. "I best be getting back. I hope you can help this girl, especially if somehow she is our daughter. If she is…tell her…tell Courtney how much her mother loved her and how hard it was to give her to someone else."

I stood and Andrea hugged me again, her arms holding onto my shoulders for a long moment. "Goodbye, Sean. Stay safe." She looked up at me through moist eyes and kissed my cheek just as Senator Lloyd Logan walked through the door with the news media snapping pictures.

TWENTY-THREE

A U.S. Senator, in the throes of a presidential campaign, doesn't simply enter a room, he or she tries to decorate a room with their presence. Senator Lloyd Logan along with his entourage of handlers and advisors, poured into the coffee shop with three TV news crews and an assortment of media types, their flash-photography like strobe lights and hand-held devices uploading sights, sounds and opinions to blogs, social media, and news media sites.

I was glad the cameras were to Logan's back when he saw us. Even with the swagger of a politician's ego, Logan looked like he'd burped up a bad pepperoni. His shark's smile was more lopsided than predatory. He stepped up to us and extended his hand.

"Hi, I'm Lloyd Logan."

I smiled. "Sean O'Brien. It's nice to meet you."

"It's mutual. I see that you and Andrea know each other. I'm glad you're here for the rally, Sean. I do hope we can count on your support. Andrea, we have a plane to catch."

"Lloyd, Sean and I were good friends in college. He came out to hear your message. We were just catching up. It's been at least twenty years."

Logan lowered his voice, his legislator's smile returning. "How much of my message could he hear if you've been in Starbucks?" He slapped me on my back. "Good meeting you Sean. I do hope you heard enough of my agenda for the country to take personal stock in it." With that, they turned and streamed out of the coffee shop, mustering even more fanfare than the entourage did entering. I watched Andrea walking hand-in-hand with the candidate under the wide oaks, she moved slightly out-of-step, her former unbridled gait, her free spirit, now more like a compulsory march.

I felt a stab of sadness for the woman I'd once known, for what might have been had we persevered. And now the knowledge of a child, *my child*—a daughter, accentuated a kind of remorse I'd never known before. I watched the media pack stalk them and thought of Courtney. Was she my daughter? Our daughter? If so, and even if she had killed in self-defense, what would that mean for the campaign of Senator Lloyd Logan if it became public? And what would it mean for Courtney Burke?

I walked out of the Starbucks and placed a call to the mobile phone of Detective Dan Grant. He answered and said, "Talk to me. Did Courtney Burke try to contact you?"

"No. Look, Dan, since you and I go way back, there's something I need to tell you about Courtney." "I'm listening."

"She knew something about me that very few people know. I'm trying to make sense of it, but I don't have enough to go on."

"What are you telling me, Sean? I'm almost afraid to even ask that question."

"I might be related to her."

"You mean as in *family*?"

"Maybe."

"Oh shit. What a damn modern family that would be. Don't tell me she's your daughter."

"I don't know…she knew about a small birthmark on my arm. And she said if it was there, then we're related."

"Did she actually tell you this?"

"She told a guy at the fair, and he told me."

"Who's this guy?"

"Said his name's Isaac Solminski."

"The dwarf?"

"Don't know what he looks like. Spoke with him on the phone. High voice."

"I interviewed him. He's like most carnies, always holding their cards close to their chests, only revealing what they want to reveal. Cooperation with the cops isn't their thing."

"Did you speak with Randal Barnes, one of the two guys who Nick overheard talking in the bar?"

"We found him. He wanted to deny ever being in the Tiki Bar. I told him credit card records don't lie when somebody fitting his description, mermaid tattoo and all, was there with a guy named Smitty. Barnes finally admitted he was there, but denied ever talking about the killing of Lonnie Ebert. He said the guy called Smitty was someone he met at the bar."

"He's lying, Dan."

"I know that, but we couldn't find this Smitty character. Probably walked away from the carnival. So all of this isn't even good circumstantial evidence. The carnival is pulling out earlier than the full week schedule. Seems murder is bad for business. One other thing, forensics found a partial print on the ice pick that wasn't Courtney Burke's print. Looks like a thumb. This wasn't left in blood, but it was there. No match anywhere, yet."

"Thanks, Dan—"

"Quick word of advice: I don't care if you think this chick is your niece or a daughter you never knew you had, stay away from it, Sean. You're a former homicide cop. In my book, she's a serial killer. Man, that's a bad damn mix. We'll find her because she's good at leaving a trail of bodies."

He disconnected as I stood next to my Jeep, watching the entourage of Senator Lloyd Logan load into limos, the Secret Service in a black SUV, the convoy circling the town square for a final pass, waving to the crowd and smiling, before driving to the airport and boarding a private jet. Andrea Logan was sitting in the back seat of the black Lincoln, going through the motions of the dutiful wife of a career politician. But as the car passed me, as she looked my way, I could see a distant mourning in her eyes that would follow her far beyond the White House.

TWENTY-FOUR

The taxi driver looked up in the rearview mirror and said, "This is it. Gibsonton. Know where you wanna go?"

Courtney nodded. "Just let me out at the corner."

"You have family here?"

"No."

"Okay. The corner seems like as good a place as any in Gibtown. I don't get too many customers comin' out here. They got some funky zoning laws in this town. They call it residential business zoning, which means you can keep a freakin' elephant in your yard. The town's made up of mostly all carny and circus people, retirees and whatnot. Used to be a hellava lot of 'em back in the fifties. At one time, the fire chief of Gibtown was an eight-foot giant, and the police chief was a three-foot midget. My old man once told me he pulled up to a traffic light here, and in the lane next to him was the Bearded Woman behind the handle bars of a motorcycle and sitting in the sidecar next to her was the Lobster Boy."

The taxi eased to a stop at the corner of Maggie Street and Alice Avenue. Courtney paid the fare and got out. She walked west through a neighborhood of 1950's-style ranch homes, some with remnants of Dodge-'em cars and rusting animal cages in the front yards—yards filled with crabgrass, weeds, and decomposing monuments to the sideshows of a departed era in America.

Within three blocks, she was standing at the entrance to ShowTown Fish Camp. She walked down a dirt and gravel road, pockets of dark shade cast from thick oaks and long-leaf pine trees, green acorns scattered underfoot.

There were about a dozen 1950's vintage Airstream trailers, their shiny humpback exteriors smudged from age and tree sap. Cicadas hummed in the branches, and a mockingbird darted through the dappled light and low-hanging limbs, following Courtney with a series of vigilant screeches, each one sounding different.

The office was a small, free-standing cinderblock building, Army-green paint peeling from the blocks, large sunflowers on either side of the screened front door. A bumblebee hovered above one flower, the drone from its wings as loud as the cicadas in the trees. A dog barked somewhere behind the building. Courtney entered the dimly lit office, the smell of cigarettes and bug spray in the room. The walls were made from shellacked board cypress, adorned with carnival posters and old black and white framed photos of carny icons, the world's smallest woman, Samantha, and the Siamese twins.

A television was on in the back room. Courtney rang the bell on the front-desk counter.

"Behind you," came a man's voice.

Courtney turned around and saw a dwarf with a snake draped over his shoulders. The little man had a bulbous red nose, a bald head dotted with age spots the color and size of pennies, and thick arched eyebrows over sorcerous dark eyes. He wore a purple and gold vest, Bermuda shorts, and no shoes. His long toenails resembled the talons of a hawk, curled and the shade of mustard. The dwarf stroked the snake's yellow and white skin, its black tongue coiling in and out of its mouth, eyes like red pearls. The man and said, "Welcome to Gibtown, the best-kept secret on Florida's west coast."

"Are you the manager?

"At your service, Courtney."

"How'd you know my name?"

"I knew of your description from my dear friend Isaac. I figured you have to be Courtney Burke. I'm Boots Langley. Don't let my size trick you. Although I don't have Samson's girth or prowess, I do have his inner strength, or so I've been told."

"What kind of snake is that?"

"A ball python. She's an albino. That's why her eyes are red as rubies. I was just about to feed Sheba a fat rat. Would you like to watch? Most people do like to watch, you know. They say they don't, but in reality they enjoy seeing the life literally squeezed from vermin. Maybe it's the shrieks from the dying rat, too. Would the same sentiment prevail if the dinner was…umm…a cat, the natural-born adversary of the mouse?"

"I hope not. I love cats."

"But do cats love you? Is the feline brain capable of emotional attachment, let alone love? We humans perform janitorial work for cats, and what is their reciprocity, beyond sitting atop a piano and refusing to socialize unless it's caused by a culinary bribe.

ALF was one of my favorite TV shows."

"Isaac said you were a little different?" "I'll take that as a compliment." Courtney smiled.

"Isaac told me what happened. How does a young woman like you get in the middle of not one, but two killings? You seem like a dove. Are you a hawk at heart?"

"I didn't kill anybody."

Boots studied her for a moment, his eyes impish. "One of the former police chiefs in Gibtown used to say *'sometimes some people needed a good killing.'* He kept the peace quite efficiently, I do recall. And he was shorter than me." Boots' tongue flickered once through his pursed lips like the snake around his shoulders.

Courtney blew out a breath. "Maybe I should go someplace else."

"Butterfly, where are you going to go? As long as you weren't followed, this is a great place to hide out. And you will, by no means, be the first seeking refuge here from the long arm of the law. Isaac told me Carlos Bandini is looking for you, too. I'd be more concerned about him than the police. Come, child. And since I'm older than dinosaur dirt, I can say that. I'll show you your castle, not by the sea. But by a place known as Bullfrog Creek."

Boots led Courtney through a curtain of multi-colored beads hanging in a doorway. They walked down a short hallway and onto a screened-in back porch overlooking a wide creek at the end of a long, sloping yard. Inside the enclosure was a rattan table and two chairs. Blooming petunias grew from three hanging baskets. A television, tuned to CNN, sat on a small wicker table in front of a brown rattan couch. In one corner, a large white cockatoo perched on a T-stand dropped a strawberry, and started barking like a dog.

Courtney smiled. "That bird…I heard barking just like that when I was walking up to the door. I thought it was a big dog. That's amazing."

Boots smiled, his eyes playful. "Shhh, don't let her hear that she's not a dog. I had a Rottweiler for six years. Clementine, up there on her perch, sounds identical to my sweet Eve before her untimely death."

Courtney looked at the snake, its eyes trained on the cockatoo rocking back and forth on the stand. "What happened to your dog?"

"The serpent got to her."

"What? Your snake?"

"No, not Sheba, of course. It was a moccasin down by the creek. The serpent struck Eve on her chest. It was sort of a debauched homecoming in a post-Eden kind of way, I suppose." He stroked the snake's head. "I worked circuses, carnivals, and sideshows for fifty years. I bought this property in 1975 with the intent to retire here, rent out a few trailers, fish, and watch sunsets over the Gulf of Mexico." He pointed to an Airstream trailer down by the creek. "That trailer is yours. It's the most remote one I have. Sits less than twenty feet from the creek. Stay as long as you want.

Isaac vouches for you, and that's more than good enough for me."

"Thank you."

"Just be mindful of water moccasins. Especially at night."

As they turned to walk out the door, a news anchor on CNN said, "In Florida, police have a manhunt underway for a young woman who is a suspect in two murder cases. Both are involving carnival workers who were killed. Police are searching for nineteen-year-old Courtney Burke, last seen at the county fairgrounds not far from Daytona Beach. Investigators haven't officially confirmed whether she's also a suspect in the deaths of two more carnival workers earlier this year. If so, she would be one of the youngest female serial killers in the nation's history."

Courtney stared at the TV screen. "Oh my God! That's so wrong. I can't believe this is happening to me."

"Come, I need to hear your story. You'll be safe for a while here. But people talk. Stay in your trailer as much as possible. Another thing, if you ever hear Clementine barking real fast, consider that a warning. She has a slow bark which you heard when you were arriving. Her fast bark is when danger is closer. She may be able to imitate sounds, but in her tiny bird brain she has a sixth sense about real threats. Heed her warning."

TWENTY-FIVE

*T*wo hours after I left The Villages, I was pulling in the Ponce Marina parking lot. I shut off the Jeep's engine and could smell the coming of rain in the humid air. The entire drive I'd thought about what Andrea Logan told me. A daughter.

My daughter, maybe.

Now a grown woman. My gut was churning. After the deaths of my parents, there was no biological family left. Period. My wife, Sherri, and I had talked about children. When she began her long fight with ovarian cancer, it was never discussed again. And now…and now what? How could I miss someone I never knew existed? Maybe it was the absolute knowledge of a daughter's physical being—her life, the absence of shared experiences, the total emptiness of a cancelled twenty-year flight to the moon and back with a little girl who I never knew lived in the same universe. How could I sit here in my Jeep, listening to the ticking of the cooling engine, and feel a coldness in my heart for circumstances that were truly beyond my control?

Fat raindrops began to flatten across the Jeep's window, and then a hard rain fell. I watched the water sluice from the leaves of banana plants growing near the Tiki Bar, puddles rising in low spots across the parking lot. How did the void of an unknown father-daughter relationship cause me to feel pain from a wound that was never self-inflicted? Until now. It wasn't physical. Purely a wound of the heart, a mourning for the lost years, the hugs, butterfly kisses, ball games, school plays, the unconditional bond between a father and daughter that has no expiration date.

As a homicide detective, I learned to look closely at patterns, patterns of human behavior, and patterns of physical and forensic evidence. Very few things in the nature of crime were coincidental. Human influence always creates spin on the cue ball of fate. Was it a coincidence that Courtney Burke popped into my life? Was it a coincidence that I found out about Andrea's pregnancy?

Was Courtney Burke my daughter?

I didn't know. But I did know that come hell or high water, I'd find out. And then what would I do in view of the circumstances of late? I had no idea. Slay one dragon at a time, unless they come in pairs.

There was a tap against the Jeep's side window. Kim Davis stood there under a large black umbrella. I opened the door and she said, "Hi, Sean. Thought I'd come rescue you. Saw your Jeep pull up a while ago."

I got out and ducked under the umbrella. "Thank you. Looks like the storm is sitting right on top of us."

She smiled, the mist from the blowing rain wetting her chestnut hair. She pulled a dark strand behind her right ear and looked up at me as I wrapped my hand around hers to steady the umbrella in the wind and rain. "C'mon, Sean, let's go jump in the puddles." She put her left hand in the small of my back and playfully nudged me toward a large puddle, the thump of rain hard against the umbrella.

I stopped a moment. "Tell you what, let's jump over the puddle instead of jumping into it."

Kim grinned and said, "Okay, on your mark...get set...go!" We ran and jumped over the puddle like two school kids caught in the rain. She laughed. "If I didn't have any customers, we could play in the rain."

We huddled under the umbrella and walked inside the Tiki Bar. A retired charter boat captain who resembled Willie Nelson, perched on a stool with his back to the bar, watching us and grinning through salt and pepper whiskers. He said, "Ya'll don't have 'nough sense to come outta the pouring rain." He chuckled and shook his head, reaching for a can of Miller, draining the last few sips. "Ya'll look like dizzy ducks out there. When I was a young man, I did that stuff. One more for the road, Miss Kimberly." He turned around and stared at his reflection in the smoked-glass mirror behind the bar, his thoughts in the lost-and-found box of his youth.

Kim walked behind the bar and reached for two white towels, tossing one to me. She dried her arms and face, her skin looking fresh-scrubbed, hair damp, smile radiant. "Sean, you want something to eat or drink?"

I started to answer when the retired captain asked, "Kim, where's your remote control for the TV? The news has a story on about Senator Logan's visit to Florida." Kim lifted the remote from the center of the bar and turned up the sound.

A reporter stood in The Villages town square and said, "Republican front-runner, Senator Lloyd Logan seemed to make quite an impression on the crowd here today. He spoke of reigning in government spending and his five-point plan to balance the federal budget in three years." The video cut to a sound bite with Senator Logan emphasizing his approach to fiscal spending, and then cut back to the reporter. "Senator Logan, of course, came to The Villages seeking support and a large campaign contribution. It's believed that he received both. However, the Senator got something he wasn't expecting. Apparently, almost the entire time Logan spoke and worked the crowd, his wife, Andrea Logan, was inside a nearby coffee shop working out something with an unidentified man. Video shot by a customer on his iPhone, video that's going viral on the Internet, shows Andrea Logan crying as she's talking with the man at a table. She reaches out and holds his hand for about thirty seconds, and then upon leaving, she is seen touching his cheek, kissing him on the cheek, and embracing him in a long hug just before her husband enters the coffee shop."

As the reporter talked, the story cut to video of Andrea and me at the table. Innocent as it was, the visuals, with no narration, looked suspicious at best, and at worst, it was like former lovers meeting and returning to a place and time where it all went away.

The reporter concluded by saying, "No one in the Logan camp is saying what the coffee shop incident was all about. The mysterious tall man, with what one spectator called 'movie star good looks,' remains unidentified, something Logan's Republican opponents for the nomination would, no doubt, like to know. From The Villages, this is Chris Bellum, Channel Three News."

Kim turned to me, eyes wide, face confused, disbelieving. "Sean, what was that? You're in a Starbucks with the wife of Senator Logan bawling her eyes out and hanging onto you like you were her old boyfriend."

"I was."

"What?"

"It's a long story, Kim." I glanced toward the captain at the bar, his mouth partially open, a can of Miller dripping condensation from his large, weather-scarred hand. "And it's a private story."

"Private? Sean, it's all over the news. The reporter said the video is going viral. You just got yourself in the middle of a nasty political campaign. For what? Senator Logan's wife was your old girlfriend...wow."

I said nothing, the sound of rain beating against the palm fronds outside.

She said, "Look, I'm sorry. It's none of my business. It's just so weird, so unexpected."

"I'd better go find Max." I started for the door leading to the docks.

"Sean..."

I didn't turn around. As I opened the door, I heard the old captain say, "Bet you don't dance with him in the puddles again."

I stepped out into a soft rain, the marina drenched in a subdued bluish-gray world, the tops of sailboat masts lost in the mist. I turned my collar up and walked down the dock, watching the raindrops splatter off the creosote-stained wooden planks. The bowlines on the boats moaned, protesting the slow lift on the shoulders of a rising tide. I stepped through the cold rain toward *Jupiter*, which now felt a hundred miles away.

TWENTY-SIX

By the time it took me to walk to the end of Dock L, the rain was slacking. I stepped onto Nick's boat, *St. Michael*, and tapped on the sliding-glass door between the cockpit and the salon. Nick opened the door, Max at his feet. "Sean, you picked a great time to take a stroll through the marina. C'mon inside. Lemme get you a towel."

Max sniffed my damp shoes, stared at me and cocked her head with a look that said: *Don't you have enough sense to get out of the rain?* Then her tail danced. Nick tossed a towel to me. "You just gettin' back from The Villages?"

"I drove slowly. Had a lot to think about." I dried off as my phone rang.

Dave Collins said, "I saw an aberration board Nick's boat. It looked a little bit like you, Sean. I just watched the story on Channel Three, hell it's on the cable news networks, too. Stay put. If you feel up to talking about it, I'll be right over."

"There's not much to say."

"Then I won't stay long."

Dave disconnected and I dropped my phone back in my pocket, bent down and picked up Max. She licked one side of my face and then stared through the glass door, watching Dave amble across the dock, an umbrella in one hand, a bottle of Jameson in the other.

I set Max down and handed Nick the towel. He asked, "Want some dry clothes? You're taller than me, but I got some sweats that ought to fit you."

"I appreciate the offer, but I'll be heading over to *Jupiter* in a few minutes."

Dave opened the door, closed the umbrella, and said, "Welcome back from the big V." He stepped over to the salon bar and settled on one of the three stools. "Nick, can I trouble you for three glasses and some ice? I believe Sean could use a drink, and after he tells us why his meeting with the wife of Senator Lloyd Logan set her off into tears, followed by hugs and kisses, we might need a drink, too."

Nick reached for glasses and ice. "What are you talkin' about?"

"The latest YouTube video to go viral, starring our good friend, Sean O'Brien. Sean, what the hell happened? You went to a political rally and caused a political firestorm."

Dave and Nick sipped the Irish whiskey as I told them the story. Neither saying a word until I had finished. Dave swirled the ice in his glass, looked out the window at the rain falling over the marina, and then cut his eyes to mine. "You think this daughter you conceived with the woman who might be the next first lady is Courtney Burke?"

"I don't know."

Nick blew out a long breath. "Maybe Pandora's Box won't get completely opened and this'll all blow over."

Dave said, "Pandora's Box is open, and there's no getting that prophetic genie back in the bottle. Sean, we're your marina mates and the closest thing you have to a band of brothers, let's assess the situation. Hypothetically, if Andrea tells her husband how she and you are connected, if they believe there is the possibility of Courtney Burke's identity being related back to Andrea, there will be trouble, no doubt about it. Although Courtney is innocent until proven guilty, this is a presidential election year, and all bets are off the table of due process. Your background alone, even without the premise of a daughter between you and Andrea Logan, would be fodder for the media and Logan's opponents. You have enough surreptitious baggage to keep Fox News and CNN speculating for days."

"Thanks, Dave."

He grunted. "This unfortunate chain of events might play out very poorly for Courtney. She's hiding somewhere in a house of cards, and all it takes is some investigative reporter to connect the dots. What we know now is four people working in the carnival business have been killed. We don't know if Courtney was in close proximity to the first two killings. She was definitely at the scene and may have been the source of the last two deaths, certainly the shooting of Tony Bandini. The FBI will intensify their investigation, should Courtney be connected to the Logans. The Secret Service will join the posse. In the meantime, local police are searching, and members of the Bandini family may be looking, too. By now, there might be a hit placed on the girl. And if, by sowing of the seeds of fate, Courtney is your daughter, Sean…even with your considerable skills and tenacity, how in the hell can you protect her?"

"The best I can."

Dave nodded. "Fair enough."

"But I don't know that she's my daughter. Until a few hours ago, I didn't know that I had a daughter. Adoption records were sealed. Andrea says she never knew the adoptive parents nor wanted to interfere with their parenting of the child. Right now the only tangible connection, the common familiarity, I have with Courtney is her awareness of my birthmark. How'd she know about it? How'd she know its symmetry to a four-leaf shamrock if Andrea didn't tell her? If she didn't, then who did?"

Nick stood from his stool. "The only way to find that out is to track her down and ask her."

"And that's what I'll do."

"You will?" Nick's dark eyebrows arched.

"Yes, and I'll need your help to start. I figure if I go to the carnival before it pulls out, I might find those guys you overheard talking in the bar. If you come with me, you can point them out.

Saves time. Makes it simpler."

Nick grinned, his thick moustache lifting. "Sounds good. I'll be your back-up."

"I hope it doesn't get to that."

Dave crushed a piece of ice with his back teeth and said, "If it was a simple case of a run-away, and you're just trying to help someone—no problem. But this case is far from simple. It's now national. A missing girl wanted in connection with serial murders, a missing girl who may be biologically linked to the wife of a powerful U.S. Senator who is spending millions to occupy the White House, a missing girl who's killed a member of the Bandini family…

and last but certainly not least, a missing girl who might be your daughter. Now, Sean. How the hell are you going to simplify that?" Dave poured himself a second shot of Jameson.

And I had no answer.

TWENTY-SEVEN

It was a few minutes past 10:30 in the morning when Nick and I arrived at the Volusia County Fairgrounds, Nick nursing a slight hangover and holding his third cup of dark-roast Greek coffee in his hand. He sipped and then said, "You never told me what we're gonna do if or when we find these dudes."

"Right now it's questions only."

He grunted. "And what if they don't want to give us any answers? You're not a detective anymore, so you can't question them in some police room, strap these guys up to a lie detector."

"I don't need a lie detector."

"How so?"

"A lot of it's in the way you ask the questions. I'm not looking always for the oral responses. I'll assume most of that will be lies based on what Detective Dan Grant heard when he interviewed Randal Barnes. I'm looking for the physical responses, or lack of them, the silent signals that most people don't realize they give when they're lying. When you catch them there, that's when the real interrogation begins."

Nick sat a little straighter on his side of the Jeep, draining the remains of his coffee. He gestured with his hand. "It's still kinda early. The lot isn't filled yet. But since this is a Saturday, figured more people would be here in spite of the fact two carnies died. This is the last day, huh?"

"Yeah, I heard that they shortened their contract with the county in view of circumstances, and they're leaving tomorrow."

I pulled into the sawdust parking lot next to an empty school bus, paid the fee, and Nick and I entered the fairgrounds. Many of the venues were just opening, carnies extending attached awnings, restocking food and plush animals, the smell of damp sawdust and cotton candy in the warm air. School kids, chaperones, and dozens of teens roamed the midway. Off-duty sheriff's deputies, in uniform, strolled the grounds, dispatch radios crackling under the music from the rides and outdoor speakers.

"One shot to win your girl a cupie doll. How 'bout a doll for your doll?" Shouted a carny barker, teasing some of the teenagers, enticing them into games of chance—the *Knock 'Em Down, Water-gun Horse Races, Balloon Pop, Free-Throw* and dozens more.

I glanced at Nick. "Do any of those men working the venues and the carnival rides look like either of the two guys you saw that night in the Tiki Bar?"

"Nothin' is jumping out at me."

"Let's keep moving. When you see one or both of them, say the word."

We walked about another fifty yards, past the Tilt-A-Whirl to where the double Ferris-Wheel stood. More than a dozen people were in the queue line to ride the Big Wheel, the smell of funnel cakes in the breeze. Nick lifted his hand and pointed to the ride operator, "There's one of the guys. He has the tattoo of the mermaid on his right arm."

I replayed some of what Courtney told me that day on Jupiter. *Lonnie was a ride operator. I talked him into letting me take a midnight ride on the Big Wheel.*

The ride op was at least six feet tall, thick chest, beer belly, a sweat-stained bandana on his head, tanned face, two hoop earrings and wrap-around dark glasses. He worked with a partner, a skinny man with jeans an inch below the crack in his butt, arms covered in ink, unlit cigarette parked behind his left ear. He was lowering the safety bars as each rider took his or her seat on the Big Wheel. "How about the guy locking the riders in, Nick, recognize him?"

"No, different dude."

I stopped walking and watched. Within a few seconds, the riders were all strapped in, anticipation on their faces. The ride op slapped a button at his stand and the Big Wheel began moving, rock music blasting. "Let's go, Nick."

We approached the ride op as he lit an unfiltered cigarette, borrowing a lighter from his helper. I smiled and said, "I used to love this ride."

He nodded and spit a piece of tobacco from the tip of his tongue. I could see myself in his dark glasses. He said, "Three minutes pal, you and your BFF can catch a ride on the Big Wheel."

"I imagine this was right about the spot where Lonnie Ebert was standing when he was murdered."

He said nothing, cupping the cigarette in the palm of his hand, the letters E-V-I-L tattooed on each of the fingers holding the burning cigarette. He blew a slow stream of smoke out of one side of his mouth. He looked away, down the midway.

"Where's Smitty today?"

He turned back to me. "Don't know nobody called Smitty. You two cops? You need to check in with the office. I'm just a hired hand."

"We're not cops."

"Then take a hike." He inhaled a mouthful of cotton-white smoke. His skinny partner, an acne-faced older teenager, stepped over to the control console.

I said, "You know, it's good that we're not cops. Cops, detectives, the whole shebang, they ask a lot of questions, poke around, come back, and ask more questions. Then they drag you into court as a witness. I imagine it wouldn't be fun to testify against the Bandini brothers, seeing how you work for the family." I raised the palms of my hands. "Now with us, it's different. No cops. No cuffs.

No court."

"No shit."

"I'm going to ask you direct questions that I think will result in direct answers and lead us away from you and Smitty. The girl didn't do it, you and Smitty said as much."

"Told you, don't know anybody named Smitty."

"Why was Lonnie killed?"

"I heard it was that crazy bitch that done it."

"Is that what you've been told to say?"

"Go fuck yourself."

"You and Smitty were overheard saying Lonnie was taken out to send a message. He was dealing for the Bandinis and probably skimming. Now all we want from you is a name. Who did the hit? You damn well know the girl didn't do it. You tell us who did, and we never see you again. We buy some funnel cake and go far away."

He grinned, a tooth missing in his lower jaw. "Maybe the music is impacting your hearing. Fuck off."

Nick looked over at me. He said, "Hey, mermaid man. I overheard you and your BFF Smitty talking, so the denial can end here."

Randal Barnes took off his sunglasses, his eyes taking in Nick like a picky eater inspecting a meal. He said, "Then you need to get your hearing checked. You didn't hear shit."

I nodded. "Is that what you told Detective Dan Grant? He has your credit card receipt from the Tiki Bar. Witnesses saw you with the other guy, let's call him Smitty because that's what you were calling him on the night of the twelfth...right before your VISA card receipt was printed and signed by you."

Randal Barnes turned to his assistant and said, "I gotta take a shit, Bobby. It's my break anyway. When you unload, tell Carl to help 'till I get back." He stepped off the ride operator's platform, crushed the cigarette under his tennis shoe, brushed by me, and walked through the crowd, vanishing between the Tilt-A-Whirl and the Zipper.

Nick turned to me. "What do we do now?"

"I mentioned the silent signals to you. Randy Barnes is speaking volumes. Now is where the real interrogation begins. Let's follow him and see where he takes the bait."

TWENTY-EIGHT

Boots Langley packed a .410 shotgun in his customized golf cart and drove down a gravel path toward Bullfrog Creek. In the small wagon he pulled behind the golf cart, he had secured four bags of groceries. He took his foot off the gas pedal and coasted up to the small Airstream trailer, shotgun cradled in his arms, and tapped on the door, using the tip of the barrel to knock.

Courtney Burke peeked out between the venetian blinds, pulled her bag to her right shoulder, her hand touching the Beretta. She stepped to the door, dust swirling in the sunlight pouring into the dark trailer. Boots read her face and said, "I've had this sweet little thing for longer than you've been on earth."

"Why do you carry it?"

"I'll show you. Follow me."

Courtney set her bag on a chair, walked outside, and followed the little man as he shuffled to the edge of the wide creek. The surface water was dark and smooth, the shade of a ripe avocado. The creek was more like a river, wide and lined with cypress, bamboo, and weeping willow trees. An osprey cried out skimming over the water. Boots stood near a gnarled cypress tree, his eyes scanning the trunk and branches swathed in Spanish moss. He grinned, flame-blue eyes igniting, a smile working in one corner of his small mouth. He raised the shotgun barrel and fired. A snake dropped from the branches and hit the ground with a thud. At mid-length, the snake's heavy, olive-green body was as thick a man's forearm. A piece of meat the size of a billiard ball was blown from the mid-section. The snake pitched and convulsed, its body turning in a half circle, hissing, opening its cotton-white mouth, biting air.

Boots looked at Courtney without moving his head. He snorted. "That's why I carry this little shotgun. It's a moccasin killer. That serpent has enough poison in its bite to kill a horse. Imagine the slow death, the pain my poor Eve felt when she was struck in the chest, less than a few inches from her heart, by an even bigger serpent than what you see there."

"But you didn't have to shoot it."

"It's insurance, Courtney. One less water moccasin means your odds down here on Bullfrog Creek are even better. Ever notice the word sin in moccasin?"

"No."

"Look around you. Look at all the blooming bougainvillea, the orange and tangerine trees filled with ripe fruit, the wild flowers, and the creek. It's a little slice of paradise. If the first sin took place in the Garden of Eden, where will the last sin take place?"

"Never thought about it. I don't know."

"Nobody does. This is my paradise. Maybe it's an acre sliced from Heaven, but I'm the caretaker. And I take that responsibility seriously. That serpent lying dead before you will be replaced by a dozen more. It's an on-going clash." He gestured to the golf cart. "I brought you some food and a few things you'll need while you're here."

"You didn't have to do that, thank you."

"You're welcome, and yes, I did. Your angel face is all over the news. You'd be spotted in any grocery store you entered. Come, let's put the provisions away. I need to learn more about your plight, your search, and journey. Isaac could only enlighten me so much, and now the rest falls in your court."

— • —

NICK AND I followed Randal Barnes as he wormed his way between the carnival attractions, the noise from the rides and the blare of piped-in rock music covering the sounds we made following him. We darted behind the Himalaya Run and the House of Mirrors, keeping Barnes in our sight, yet trying not to send signals to the other carnies working the food-stands, rides, or standing around and smoking in the artificial alleys leading off the midway to the back lots away from the public areas.

Nick pointed. "He's going inside that tricked out, million dollar bus."

"That can mean that he's reporting our presence to Bandini because he's involved in the illicit activities they operate. The second option might be he's looking for brownie points and simply telling them that we're here, and that we're asking questions about Lonnie Ebert's murder, not about the drug connection to the Bandini family."

"What the hell do we do now?"

"Play it by ear."

"Sean, I never was a cop. I don't know how to play this shit by ear."

I watched a man wearing a Yankees cap and an Orlando Magic jersey stop to open a door to a free-standing toilet. "Speaking of shit…didn't you say the guy named Smitty was wearing a Yankees cap and a blue Magic jersey the night you saw him?"

"Yeah, why?"

"See those porta-potties over there?" I pointed to a half dozen free-standing portable toilets about one hundred feet beyond the trailers and parked campers.

"Yeah, I see them."

"A guy just went in the one to the far right. And you know what Nick? He matched your description of Smitty to a T. You'd think these guys would take some time to hit the laundromats. Let's see what Smitty has to say."

"How the hell do you notice stuff like that from a distance?"

"Sometimes I wish I didn't notice. Let's go."

As we approached the porta-potty, I whispered to Nick.

"Stand back some. I don't know if the guy has a weapon." "You don't have one."

I reached behind under my shirt to the small of my back and pulled out my Glock, keeping the gun out of sight from the campers and trailers behind us.

Nick's eyes went wide. "Oh shit. I didn't know you'd brought your pistol."

"Stand to the right, Nick. This interrogation will be real quick." I could read the United Rental sign on the light blue door to the John. Also, I could see that the occupant failed to lock the door. Bad mistake. I held the Glock in my right hand. With my left hand, I jerked the door open. There was Smitty, pants down around his ankles, sitting on the seat, best friend in his hand, looking down the barrel of the Glock. His face melted. I said, "Didn't your daddy tell you to lock the bathroom door? Don't even think of lying to me! If you do, they'll find you dead on the shitter. Understand?" He nodded, his voice caught in his throat. "Courtney Burke didn't kill Lonnie Ebert, right?" He nodded, his face bright red.

"Who killed Lonnie?"

"Don't know! I swear!"

"Did Bandini order it?"

"That's what the word on the street is, yeah."

"Why?"

"I heard it was on account Lonnie was double-dipping."

"How'd you hear that?"

"From Lonnie. He was my friend. He told me Tony Bandini had actually shorted him two G's so he was taking it back in installments. I don't know how Bandini or his guys caught him. But Lonnie knew they were on to him. He was makin' plans to get out of town with that chick, Courtney. But he waited one night too long."

I pulled a business card from my shirt pocket and tossed it to Smitty. "The number on that card is to Detective Dan Grant of the Volusia County Sheriff's Office. Here's what you're going to do. You're going to pull your pants up, and then you're going to call the detective and tell him what you told me."

"You don't know the Bandini family."

"And you don't know me. I won't let an innocent girl take the fall. If you even think about running, I'll hunt you down. And guess what?"

"What?"

"I will find you."

I slammed the door and walked away. Nick followed me and said, "That guy's balls shrank to the size of two peas. You believe he's telling the truth?"

"He didn't have time to lie."

"You think he'll call that detective?"

"Don't know. But I will, and I'll tell him where he can find Smitty." I looked across the back parking lot to where the customized Bandini bus sat, diesels purring, Randal Barnes, no doubt, conveying everything I'd asked him. Worse yet, what Nick had told him. I walked to a spot where a large camper blocked the line-of-sight from Nick and me to the bus. "You made a mistake back there."

"What mistake?"

"Nick, you told Barnes that you overheard the conservation between Smitty and him. They were probably drinking so much they don't remember exactly what they said about the murder, the hit on Lonnie. But now they know that you know, and that makes you a potential liability to these guys."

"You think they could come after me?"

"Maybe."

"They take one step on my boat and I'll put what's left of 'em in my crab traps."

"Let's head back to the marina."

As we walked through the midway, I was now worried for two people, a girl who might be my daughter, and a man who was like my brother.

TWENTY-NINE

It was on our walk back to the parking lot when I heard a voice that stopped me in my tracks. "Lemme guess your age and weight," said the man. "Nobody can beat the Guesser. How about you, young lady? Bet I can guess your weight to within one pound and your age to the exact year."

I could hear some teenagers laughing, the conversation fun, challenging each other. "Nick, let's see what's on the other side of the Shoot-O-Rama, I heard a familiar voice."

We walked around the arcade and watched as a dwarf sat on a three-legged stool, wireless microphone in one hand, a large weighing scale to the right of his stool. A half dozen high school students stood near him, watching as he sized up a large man and said, "Sir, I bet you are two hundred five pounds, including the weight of those brogan boots you're wearing, and they haven't gone out of style since their introduction in the Civil War."

The man laughed, and looked at his girlfriend next to him. He turned back to the dwarf and said, "You're good."

The little man leaned forward in a short bow. "Okay, pilgrim, stand on the great revealer called a scale."

The man stepped on the scale and the needle swept past the two-hundred mark for a second, and then pointed to 206. The man shook his head and smiled. "All right, how old do you think I am?"

"Old enough to know better." The dwarf held his hands like he was looking into an invisible window. "I can see back to your birth. You were born thirty-seven years ago."

The man's mouth dropped, eyebrows arching. "That's damn good."

"Tell the crowd your age?"

"I'm thirty-seven, turning thirty-eight next week."

"But that doesn't count right now. Thank you, sir. Next person for the Guesser, step right up here."

The man grinned and pulled a baseball cap back on his head and walked away with his girlfriend, both laughing. The teenagers drifted off, chasing toward the Toboggan Run ride. The dwarf turned to Nick and me. "Aren't you a tall one? Bet I can guess your weight, height and age."

"I bet I can guess your name...Isaac Solminski."

He looked at me, eyes widening, smile growing. He tilted his head. "That's impressive." His falsetto voice rose slightly. "However, I recognize your voice, too, Mr. O'Brien. And your friend is..."

"I'm Nick. You'll never guess my age 'cause Greeks age differently than most of the world. I'm a two-thousand-year old optical illusion."

"I like your friend, Mr. O'Brien. He doesn't look a day over forty-four."

Nick grinned. "Something's wrong here. Nobody ever gets my age on the nose. Either I've aged a hellava lot in the last two days, or you're really good."

"It's the latter."

I watched Solminski click off the switch on the microphone. I said, "Courtney trusted you enough to tell you about my birthmark. Did she tell you how she knew, who told her? Your answer is very important."

"She told me exactly what I relayed to you on the phone."

"Where is she?"

"I couldn't say for sure."

"You're a good guesser but a bad liar. I'm the only one looking for her who actually believes she's not a killer. I need to find her first."

"I wish I could help you, but to help you would only hurt Courtney. But I can say..." He paused and looked beyond my left shoulder, his eyes cautious, locking on to something behind me. He set the microphone on a corner of his stool. "If I were to venture another guess about you both, I'd say you're being watched, no you're being followed."

I looked up at a slight reflection off the round glass face on the scale. I could see two men standing in the midway, their body language in surveillance mode, standing out in a crowd of moving people. "Is it Carlos Bandini?"

"No. It's some guys who work for him. Why are they tailing you two?"

"You know a guy named Randal Barnes and one called Smitty?"

"Smitty is Tyler Smith. Barnes works directly for Bandini."

"Barnes and Smitty were drinking in a bar, someone overheard them saying Lonnie was a drug mule for the Bandini family. I wanted to give Barnes the opportunity to tell me how Courtney wasn't involved."

"Why would he do that?"

"Because if he wasn't involved in the Bandini drug enterprise, he might be willing to tell me just enough to take any potential heat off him. But now I know his job description is beyond only working as a ride operator. Smitty was Lonnie's friend. I strongly encouraged him to call the same detective who spoke with you the day you called me, Detective Grant. Smitty can vouch that Courtney Burke had nothing to do with Lonnie's murder."

"But will he? I've worked carnivals, circuses, and sideshows when it was politically correct to pay money to point, stare, and laugh at what were called freaks of nature. The real freaks aren't created by nature. Greed is the mother of most spiritual mutants. Evil is their father. Mr. O'Brien, the Bandinis aren't freaks of nature, they're products of gluttony. After you and Nick leave, I will be questioned by them. When this season ends, I'm hanging it up.

You'd best be going now."

"Before I leave, tell me, do you know where I can find Courtney?"

"No."

I watched him for a moment. "I think you know. And you believe that by not telling me, she will be better for it. She won't. That's no guess. It's a fact. You have my number. If you change your mind, call me. If you hear from Courtney, have her call me."

Nick and I left and walked toward the midway, the two men following us trying to blend into the crowd. I glanced at the House of Mirrors and caught a quick reflection of the Guesser still sitting on his stool, watching us leave. For an instant, he resembled a character from a Lewis Carroll book, Tweedledee or was it Tweedledum? All I could remember from *Through the Looking Glass* was something about how a large black crow swooped down on the little men.

Even through the noise from the midway, somewhere near the vanishing point of my perception, I thought I heard the mocking cries of a crow.

THIRTY

From the west side of the midway to the lot where I'd parked my Jeep, it happened. The two guys tailing us disappeared. Maybe they thought we'd spotted them. Maybe they'd decided to ask Isaac Solminski what we'd chatted about. He was a savvy carny. A survivor. Smart. He'd tell them what he wanted Bandini to know.

The parking lot was nearly filled. My Jeep was parked between two yellow school buses, almost invisible from any passersby. Nick glanced over his shoulder and said, "Looks like the dudes are gone. You think that guesser guy really doesn't know where to find Courtney?"

"I believe he knows, but until he trusts us, he's keeping his cards close to his red vest. In the meantime, the feds and police will tighten the dragnet for her."

Walking across the lot, my phone rang in my jeans pocket. Dave Collins said, "Sean, you and Nick had better get back here. This thing with Senator Logan's wife is gaining traction. The video with you and her in the coffee shop has more than two million views on YouTube. Kim Davis told me that a TV news satellite truck drove up a little while ago and parked in front of the Tiki Bar. Looks like something's going down. The final Republican primary debate is tomorrow night. I have a feeling your former relationship with the senator's wife might be part of the agenda."

I listened to Dave as I unlocked the Jeep, Nick walking around to the passenger side. From the reflection on the Jeep's side window, I noticed a slight movement inside the school bus behind me. Maybe a student. Maybe the driver. Maybe not.

The bus door flew open and Randal Barnes stood on the step with a .357 pointed at me. "Hands up asshole!"

I dropped my phone and lifted my arms as a second man came from behind Barnes. "You too!" he yelled at Nick. Nick's hands shot straight up. Both men stepped out of the school bus, Barnes first, followed by the guy who wasn't showing a pistol. He seemed to be the leader. He was tall, hawk faced with dirty blond hair pulled back in a ponytail. He wore a tank top, steroid biceps, Australian bush hat, and an alligator-tooth necklace. A knife protruded from a sheath on his hip. Gatorman looked at Nick, "Move! Stand beside your pal."

Nick's jawline popped. His dark eyes narrowed. He rolled his shoulders and walked around the Jeep and stood to my left, closest to the Jeep.

Gatorman said, "We really don't need the silencer. So much noise at the carnival, nobody would ever hear us pop you dudes. You with the Hawaiian shirt on, turn around and put your hands on the top of the Jeep."

I complied and he lifted my shirttail, pulling the Glock out of my belt.

He held my Glock and said, "Turn around and stand next to your pal."

Nick and I stood beside each other. Gatorman slipped my Glock beneath his belt next to his right pants pocket.

Barnes moved to my right, gun pointed at my chest. He said,

"You fucked up when you pulled a gun on Smitty."

I smiled. "Thought you didn't know anybody called Smitty." "Shut up!"

Gatorman stepped next to Barnes and sneered, his predator teeth small, lips thin. "Nobody walks into Mr. Bandini's sandbox and pulls a pistol on one of his employees. Sends the wrong message."

"Why doesn't Carlos tell me that?"

"That's what he's doin.' We're just delivering the message."

I watched Gatorman. His first mistake was sliding the Glock under his belt. So the immediate plan was to remove the cocked gun from Barnes' right hand, the same hand where the tattoo on top of his fingers spelled E-V- I- L.

Gatorman pursed his thin lips, looked away for a second, and then cut his red-rimmed eyes to me. He shook his head like a disapproving parent. I knew he'd say something mild, nonthreatening, before he made his move. Keep the prey off-guard. In that moment, I wished I could warn Nick. Gatorman said, "Maybe you boys can promise to never come back to our sandbox and we can all do what we do without gettin' in each other's ways. Follow what I'm sayin'?

Nick nodded and glanced at me. That one second was the green light. Gatorman slammed his fist into Nick's mouth. Barnes aimed the pistol at my head. The tattooed E on his trigger finger less than three feet from my face. *Come a little closer,* I hoped. As Nick wobbled, holding onto the Jeep's hood, blood spurting from his mouth, I pressed the emergency button on the key remote in my left hand. Barnes whirled around toward the Jeep. Green light in my lane. I hit him hard as I could on the left jaw. He fell to his knees like he was hit with a Taser. He dropped the pistol on his way to the sawdust. I scooped it up and had the barrel pointed at Gatorman before he could pull the Glock out of his belt.

I nodded. "Nick, get my gun."

Nick held his left hand to his bleeding mouth and pulled the Glock from Gatorman's belt. As soon as Nick stepped back, Gatorman said, "You have no fuckin' idea what you're doing."

"You're wrong. I have more than an idea, I have a plan. Let's call it a business plan. Here's bullet point number one." I fired a shot, the bullet making a thump in the sawdust next to his left foot.

"You're fuckin' crazy!" His eyes jutted, a string of saliva hanging from his lower lip.

"You're probably right about that. Bullet point number two will be through the top of your foot if you think of lying to me. What and how much is Bandini running?"

He glared at me, a vein moving like an earthworm under his right eye. I pointed the pistol at his shoe.

"Okay! Fuck! He's runnin' coke, crystal meth, and heroin. Used to sell a lotta weed 'til they started making the shit legal in some states. And then the medical marijuana crap hurt business real bad."

"How much is the family running?"

"What?"

"Quantities? How much do the Bandinis move?"

"I don't know that. A shitload. They got six carnivals. They're all over the country, which means their drug operation is all over the nation. Movin' from one city to the next."

I kept the gun leveled at him as I bent down and picked up my phone. I hit the speakerphone button and said, "Jimmy, did you hear all of that?"

Dave cleared his throat. "Yes. Loud and clear."

Gatorman looked like he'd pulled a herniated disc. I said, "The other bullet points will hurt more than a bullet through your foot because they'll send you to prison. These points include three witnesses who will swear in a court of law what we heard you say. Could be painful for you to testify against the family. Here's the last bullet point." I raised the gun.

"No dude!" he yelped.

"The last point is the most important. I'd share it with Bandini if he had the balls to stand here. But since he doesn't, I have to rely on you and sleeping beauty to deliver it. Listen closely, Crocodile Dundee. You tell Carlos Bandini I'm here for one reason, and that's Courtney Burke, the girl who Bandini's brother, Tony, tried to rape. She shot him in self-defense. So tell Carlos to back off; leave her alone. If he doesn't, if he tries to harm her, the DEA, FBI, and local cops will be at each of Bandini's carnivals with search and arrest warrants. Now, do you get that point?"

He shook his head. "Yeah."

Nick spit blood and stared. I said, "Come on, Nick." I used the tip of the barrel to motion for Gatorman to step out of the way.

He stood a moment too long. Nick backhanded him with his wide right hand. The blow spun Gatorman around.

We got in the Jeep, and as I started to pull away, I held the pistol through the open driver's side window. Gatorman watched me, his eyes burning. I said, "I'll keep this souvenir from the county fair. A Beretta sure beats a Teddy bear."

I drove off, glancing up in the rearview mirror just as Barnes was coming to, standing on wobbly legs. They watched us drive away, Gatorman sticking his middle finger high in the air, then punching the buttons on his phone. I wondered what he was going to tell Carlos Bandini.

THIRTY-ONE

On the way back to Ponce Marina, I dialed Detective Dan Grant. "Dan, the second guy in the Tiki Bar that night Nick overheard their conversation, his name is Tyler Smith. Goes by Smitty. I ran into him at the fair and gave him your card. He was talkative, admitted that the Bandini's are big players in the distribution of stolen meds, crystal meth, coke, and heroin. He said Lonnie Ebert was a friend of his and Lonnie told him Tony Bandini had threatened him. This is the motive, something Courtney Burke didn't have."

"Psychopaths don't need a motive. Desire works for them."

"I doubt Smitty will pick up the phone and call you. But you can find him working as a ride op on the Tilt-A-Whirl."

"You said you ran into him." Dan sighed. "Leave it alone, Sean. What'd you do, use a water-board to torture the guy before he'd admit that stuff?"

"No, actually I opened the door to a toilet he and his best friend were using. In all the confusion and embarrassment, he starting talking. Couldn't shut him up, really. Smitty's pal at the bar, Randy Barnes, also admitted the Bandini family is using the carnival circuit as a drug route."

"I'll pay another visit to the carnival before they pull out. The fact is, though, this guy Smitty and his friend Barnes can say whatever they want. The physical evidence established Courtney Burke was there—her prints on the ice pick in the vic's heart. She's a scorned lover. And she fled from a murder scene. One other thing, the deaths of the two other carnies earlier this year, the murders were two months apart. Both happened near a carnival owned by Bandini Amusements. At the time of each murder, Courtney Burke was working at that specific carnival. Even you, Sean, can't believe that was a coincidence. Are you chasing this thing because she mentioned the birthmark and you still think she might be related to you?"

"Maybe."

"Does this have anything to do with all this stuff about you and Senator Logan's wife? It's all over the news."

"I don't know."

He was silent a moment. "Sean, don't fucking tell me the kid that the media are talking about, the one that you and the senator's wife supposedly had, is this girl...Courtney Burke?"

"Let me know if you find Smitty. Got to go, Dan."

◂ ▬

WHEN NICK AND I drove onto the Ponce Marina parking lot, trouble had beat us there. Two television news satellite trucks, a few SUVs painted in TV station logos and displaying slogans such as: *Your 24-Hour News Source*, and *Eyewitness News First*.

"Wonder what's going on?" Nick mumbled. "You think this is because of what happened at the fair?" "It's not that."

"What is it then? Oh shit. I recognize that dude from CNN. Sean, they're walking toward us."

I slid the two pistols under the seat. Within half a minute, a squad of reporters was encircling the Jeep. "Nick, don't say anything to them."

"I got nothin' to say. Plus my lip's busted."

"We have to get you some ice."

"Let's walk through the Tiki Bar and then onto the docks. It's private property and gated. That'll slow them down."

We stepped out and were surrounded by reporters, cameras, microphones, iPads, lights, and then the shot-gunning of questions started. "Is it true that you conceived a child with Andrea Logan?" I said nothing.

A second reporter said, "How long had you two dated?"

A third barked, "Were you ever given the chance to see the baby?"

A fourth asked, "Why didn't you seek custody?"

The FOX News correspondent said, "Mr. O'Brien, can we sit down for an interview?"

"Not right now," I said, working my way through the pack.

"Okay. Let me ask you this then, do you think your involvement in the take-down of the terrorist group last year in Jacksonville will come into play during this presidential election?"

I stared hard at the guy, so hard, he looked away, fumbling with his notes. Another reporter asked, "Any comments before tomorrow night's final Republican presidential primary debates? Polls indicate Senator Logan, the front-runner, is less than five percentage points ahead of Governor Les Connors. The fact that you and Mrs. Logan had a child together is of a lot of interest to many Americans. Your thoughts on the circumstances in view of the upcoming presidential election?"

"My thoughts have to do with walking my dog. Now, excuse me." I stepped through the mob. Ignoring more questions, Nick making a bee-line for the Tiki Bar entrance. I followed right behind him, the horde after us.

As we waked across the restaurant, Kim looked up from behind the bar, her full mouth forming an O. Two charter boat deckhands almost spilled their mugs of beer, turning on their barstools, watching the entourage. I smiled at Kim, her face still locked in disbelief.

Nick and I stepped out on the public dock and then quickly dialed the combination lock and entered L Dock, slamming the gate behind us with loud bang. The sign on the gate read:

PRIVATE DOCK - BOAT OWNERS ONLY
See Dock-Master in Office

We walked toward our boats. I could see Dave standing in *Gibraltar's* cockpit, Max standing in one of the deck chairs, her nose pointed in our direction. I whispered to Nick, "Don't look back. No need sending distress signals to the media."

"No problem. Eyes straight ahead." He smiled, immediately turning his head toward an attractive brunette, dark glasses, white bikini, white smile, lounging on the foredeck of a sixty-foot Hatteras, a pink cocktail in her manicured hand.

"What a time to have a fat lip. I hang with you, Sean, all this hoopla chasing us, and the ladies think I'm a knight, even the married gals."

"We have more than hoopla chasing us. Let's lie low for the afternoon. You step back out there and they'll pepper you with questions."

"I can't go on TV looking like this. Plus, I have nothing to say."

"I told you and Dave about my past with Andrea, that's enough for them to ask you things that can get twisted. You heard them in the parking lot."

Dave met us on the dock next to his boat. He shook his head and cut his eyes to the end of L Dock where reporters stood, setting up to do live shots. He said, "I take it you didn't hit your mouth on the roller-coaster safety bar. Nick, what the hell happened to you?"

I said, "We'll tell you when we get out of sight of the media mob."

"By default, you're putting Ponce Marina on the national map. Next thing you know, after the theme parks, the Space Center, and the beaches, tourists buses will pull through this marina and the driver's will point out that this is where Sean O'Brien spent weekends on his old boat coming up with ways to take out presidential contenders."

"It all started when I saw Courtney Burke walking down a long and dangerous road."

"And look where that road's led you. Come aboard, gents. The proverbial defecation is hitting the fan."

We followed Dave onto *Gibraltar*, and into the large salon, the boat's tinted windows sure to prevent eyes and cameras from snooping. I sat in a canvas deck chair, Dave on his leather couch. Nick stood at the bar, an ice cube wrapped in a paper towel and pressed against his mouth, dark eyes filled with thoughts.

Dave said, "I'm not sure where to start. We have a media gang at the gate, all now aware that you fathered a child with the woman who might be the next first lady, and you and Nick come back bloodied after visiting Bandini's camp. So, what happened?"

I filled him in on the events at the carnival, who the players were, and the message I sent to Bandini.

"You think Carlos Bandini will leave Courtney Burke alone?"

"Maybe. He could be looking to even the score for his brother's death. Before Tony Bandini died, if he told his brother what Courtney said to him about how much she knew of the family's operation, Carlos might try to silence her. Since they know Nick was the one who overheard Smitty and Barnes admit Lonnie was the victim of a Bandini hit, I wanted to try to diffuse that. So that's why I put you on speakerphone and called you Jimmy. Harder to kill three people than one."

Nick wrapped a fresh ice cube in another paper towel and applied it to his lip. He said, "I've seen some pretty fast guys in my life, but none quicker than my man, Sean. He touched the emergency button on his key remote and the second that Barnes looked away, Sean hit him so hard he fell like he'd been struck by lightning. Before his pistol could fall to the ground, Sean grabbed it and drew down on gator guy. The whole thing was over in three seconds."

Dave shook his head. "It's not over. It's just beginning. Ranging from a carnival mob family to what may be the next first family. Sean, how'd the news media find out that you and Andrea had a child together?"

"I don't know."

Nick said, "It's a damn good bet she never said anything to anybody."

Dave nodded. "Not after twenty years of keeping it a secret. Logan's opponents are making a lot of political hay out of this thing. It'll be a hot topic in tomorrow night's debates, too. Have you heard from Andrea?"

"No, and I doubt that I will. Outside of her parents, someone else must have known...someone who she trusted. When the video of Andrea and me hit YouTube, a ghost had to have come out of the woodwork."

Dave said, "Somebody looking for fifteen minutes of fame."

"Or a pile of money," Nick said. "Sean, can you think of a close friend of Andrea's at the time, somebody she might have confided in?"

"Yes. Twenty years ago her name was Susan Lehman. Dave, turn on one of the cable networks."

THIRTY-TWO

Dave lifted the remote off the coffee table and pointed it at his 42-inch flat screen behind the bar. CNN was in the midst of a newscast. The anchorman finished a story about Syria and said, "Turning to news here at home, the uproar continues in the Republic Presidential Primary debates as front-runner, Senator Lloyd Logan, faces questions about his wife's past, with new revelations coming forth that she had a daughter out of wedlock. Logan, a staunch opponent of abortion, told reporters that he defends his wife's decision to give the baby up for adoption almost twenty years ago. In the meantime, Andrea Logan has had nothing to say publically about the situation. However, a woman who says she knew Andrea when she became pregnant, Susan Cohen, said that the former Andrea Hart never told her boyfriend at the time, a man by the name of Sean O'Brien, that she was carrying his child. It was O'Brien seen on the YouTube video with Mrs. Logan, deeply sobbing in a Starbucks, while her husband raised five-million dollars in contributions outside the door."

The video cut to an interview. The lower third of the screen flashed her name: *Susan Cohen*, the former Susan Lehman. Blonde, early forties, owl eyes that seldom blinked. She said, "I knew Sean, and I knew Andrea. They were the perfect couple, really. After Andrea broke off the relationship with him, she was almost three months pregnant at the time, she never told him about the baby. When I asked her why, she just said it would make things more complicated. But in my heart-of-hearts, I believe Sean would have raised the baby by himself if he'd known about the child. It really wasn't fair to him or the child."

The images on screen cut to the Ponce Marina parking lot.

"Oh shit," said Nick as he watched us get out of the Jeep.

The narrative connected with the video. "Sean O'Brien is a former homicide detective with the Miami-Dade Police Department. It's reported he spent time in the first Gulf War, and he was the sharpshooter who was involved in taking out the al Qaeda sect in Jacksonville last year. So, how all of this will play out in Senator Logan's bid for the White House, nobody knows. When asked for a comment, O'Brien had little to say."

The image cut to a close-up of me with a microphone in my face when I said, "My thoughts have do with walking my dog. Now, excuse me."

The news anchorman added, "If Sean O'Brien is a good caregiver for his dog, can it be assumed he would have been a good father had he known that his former girlfriend, the current wife of Senator Lloyd Logan, was pregnant twenty years ago?"

I looked at Dave, "Shut it off."

Nick ran his tongue across his front teeth and said, "Lookin' at the pictures of Andrea Logan on television, and lookin' at you now Sean, I can see a resemblance in Courtney Burke's face." I said nothing.

Dave clicked the button and the screen went to black. He said, "I wish I could turn all this media frenzy down. You said it all started when you found Courtney Burke walking down that dark road. If she's your daughter…the daughter of Andrea Logan, too, and Courtney is arrested on murder charges…and it's found out, the media frenzy is going to hit unimaginable heights. And then Senator Logan's bid to become the next president of the United States comes to a screeching halt."

I stood from the deck chair and stepped to one of the salon windows facing the main public dock. I could see the dock master shaking his head, arms crossed, speaking with reporters. He was trying to keep them off private property. How long would that last? I turned back to Dave and Nick. "There's only one way to know if Courtney Burke is my daughter, and whether Andrea Logan is her biological mother. I need DNA samples from both. And I need to have mine analyzed."

Dave looked at me over the glasses at the end on his nose. "There's no way in hell that Logan's people are going to let you within a city block of Andrea."

"I don't need to get to her; I already have it."

"What?" Nick's eyebrows arched, like two dark crescent moons. "I'm almost afraid to ask how you got it."

"I was wearing a sports coat the day I met Andrea. There were no napkins at the table in the Starbucks. Inside the front pocket of my jacket was a clean, white handkerchief. When Andrea started crying, I handed her the handkerchief. She used it to wipe her eyes and nose. I remember seeing a smudge of her red lipstick on it, too." "Where is it?" Dave asked.

"In a Ziploc bag in the pocket of my jacket, and that's hanging in the closet on *Jupiter*."

Dave shook his head. "That little plastic bag and its contents could prove to be a Pandora's Box for Senator Lloyd Logan and his two-hundred million dollar campaign to become the next president of the United States."

Nick said, "But to get Courtney's DNA, you got to find her. That's not gonna be easy. In the meantime, Bandini may have put a price on her head."

Dave said, "Carlos Bandini will be small potatoes compared to Senator Logan's camp if this thing swirls out of the box or plastic bag. If the connection is ever close to being made that Courtney Burke is his wife's biological child, a 'love child' who may have grown into a killing monster, what would they do to keep it from becoming public?"

I leaned down, picked up Max, and thought of something Courtney said on my boat, *"This little dog is smart. I wish I'd had a dog when I was a little girl."*

THIRTY-THREE

Courtney Burke stood next to a window in the Airstream trailer and watched as the moon climbed above the dark waters of Bullfrog Creek. She listened to the chorus of frogs along the creek bank, their frenetic bellowing in the night taking Courtney back to her childhood. She remembered the time her gypsy parents parked their Volkswagen camper-bus on the bank of the Edisto River in South Carolina's Low Country.

They were there for three days, living off the land, eating river mussels, rabbit, and fried squirrel. Her father spent a dollar to buy a half-dozen catfish and shrimp from a black man who sold them from a Styrofoam cooler on the side of the road, the yellow-bellied catfish and shrimp covered in shaved ice. Her mother fried them in a cast-iron skillet on a campfire her father built. After each meal, mama rinsed the grease out of the pan, usually in the river, and stored the pan in two crumpled brown paper bags she kept in the back of the camper bus.

Courtney blinked at the rising moon and buried her memories. She reached for a flashlight on a small table near the window, opened the screened-door, and stepped outside. The humid air smelled of moss and blooming orange blossoms. She thought of Boots' warning about water moccasins and turned on the flashlight, its narrow beam shining over the dark water. There were more than a dozen sets of red eyes, some moving on the surface, others simply staring toward the light. *Alligators.* She could make out the head of one large gator, its red eyes spaced at least a foot apart. The gator swam slowly, blinking once, and coming to within twenty feet of the creek bank before sinking beneath the murky surface.

A dog barked. Courtney whirled around, looking up the long, sloping yard toward Boots Langley's old 1950's-style ranch house. Somewhere inside the screened back area, the large cockatoo, Clementine, sat on her perch barking like a dog. Courtney smiled, the slow, loud bark coming from the small throat of the bird and giving the frogs a run for their money.

Courtney swatted at a mosquito hovering around her face. She took a step toward the wrought iron bench seat under an old oak. She stopped walking, shining the light on the empty bench. Was a water moccasin lying on a low-hanging limb ready to slither down around her shoulders? She thought of the snake that Boots carried around on his shoulders, the snake's cool skin touching the back of the little man's thick neck.

The screened door slammed. Courtney looked up toward the house. Boots Langley stepped from the porch and shuffled down the yard, flashlight in one hand, a can of insect repellent in the other. He walked up to Courtney. "Saw your flashlight. Thought I'd bring you some mosquito spray. You stay out here long enough and you'll be a quart low. If you don't believe in vampires, watch a mosquito feeding on a human. They'll gorge themselves on blood, increasing their body mass by fifty percent in one feeding. They're such gluttons, sometimes they can't even fly away." He handed her the repellent.

"Thank you." She sprayed it on her exposed arms, legs and neck. She closed her eyes and sprayed some quickly across her face. "I don't know what's worse, the bug bites or the junk in the spray."

"Often the art of life is about rotating our poisons to prevent buildup."

"I was gonna sit on the bench, but I didn't want one of those moccasins falling from the tree."

Boots grinned, a diamond stud in his left ear catching the moonlight across the wide creek. "Those cottonmouth moccasins would rather bite a fish or frog than you. At night, most of them are out hunting. Don't worry about one being in the trees, just watch where you step."

"Okay."

"Let's sit down." They sat on the park bench, Boot's feet a foot above the grass, the rising moon reflecting off the black water, the bearded profiles of Spanish moss like toothed shadows hanging from the tree limbs. "Now, Courtney, you want to tell me a little about what Isaac mentioned? He said you're in search of something. Sounds like a person, and maybe that person took something of yours, correct?"

Courtney looked out across the flowing creek, her face drenched in the soft moonlight. She turned toward Boots and said,

"You and Isaac are related. I can tell."

"Did he tell you?"

"No."

"How did you know? Is it because those hauntingly beautiful eyes of yours see what most others can't?"

"It's more of a feeling than anything. Who's the oldest?"

"Me, by seven minutes. We're fraternal twins. I like to think of myself as the older, and wiser brother."

Courtney smiled and Boots said, "You have a lovely smile. It's the first time in two days that I've seen you smile."

"I haven't had a lot to smile about lately."

"I believe it'll get better. I'm impressed that you knew Isaac and I are brothers. Except for our size, there are no similar features. Although he's the Guesser, you dear, are not to be outdone. My brother tells me you're looking for someone who took something. Who is it and what is it?"

"Boots, you've been kind to me. Allowing me to stay here. They'd arrest you, too, if they thought you were helping somebody like me."

He smiled. "I'm not helping somebody like you. I'm helping you, and I'm not so sure there's another quite like you. And that's good because you're unique."

"Thank you. I'm looking for someone who owes my family something. He's a little bit of a magician, hypnotist, and country preacher. He's my uncle, and he's pure evil."

The sound of a dog barking fast came from the screen-enclosed porch behind Boots' house. "That's Clementine. And that bark is not the good bark."

"You said it's a warning. What does it mean?"

"It means someone or something is coming."

"What do we do?"

"Shhh, keep your voice down. My gun is in the house."

"I have one in my bag."

"Now's the time to get it."

THIRTY-FOUR

They kept the flashlights off. As Courtney opened the screen door on the Airstream, Boots said, "Don't turn on the lights. Just hand me the pistol. I may have to hold it in two hands, but I know how to use it."

"Okay."

He waited by the door. The fast barking from the cockatoo suddenly stopped, the chants of frogs and cicadas mixing in the night air. Courtney handed him the Beretta and said, "Be careful."

"Hide over there, behind the canoes. Here are the keys to the old red Toyota truck in my drive. If something happens, get away.

Take the truck and go."

"Boots, I can't just—"

"Shhh. I'm going to check around the house and perimeter of the property." He turned and vanished in the night, carrying a flashlight and the Beretta. Courtney stepped closer to the seawall that separated the property from the broad creek. She tried not to think about the water moccasins as she squatted between two canoes turned upside down and propped off the ground on cinderblocks. She could see Boots walking around the house, staying away from the direct light cast from floodlights on each side of the home.

Within a few minutes, Boots returned. He said, "Courtney, you can come out."

She stood and walked back to the edge of the trailer, where Boots was waiting in the shadows. "What was it?"

He smiled. "It's something that's very scary to Clementine on her perch inside the screen. There's a bobcat, probably weights forty pounds, and it caught some chickens in my neighbor's yard last week. I saw fresh bobcat tracks in the wet dirt near my garage. Can't get grass to grow there because it's always in the shade. Clementine knew the bobcat was very near her. Poor thing. Come, let's sit and talk. I'm intrigued by this hypnotist—magician—uncle of yours and what that thing is he owes your family. I've known a few magician and hypnotist types in my career. I want to hear more."

They sat back down on the bench and Courtney said, "The thing taken is an Irish torc, a bracelet. It was my grandmother's. My grandfather found it in a bog in Ireland many years ago. It was made during the time of the ancient Celtics. My grandmother wore it on special occasions, like their anniversary. She kept it aside in a safe place because of its value."

"Is it worth a lot of money?"

"The value I'm talking about doesn't come from money. It comes from the power of the bracelet, the power within the torc."

"What kind of power?"

"Grandma said it truly brought guidance and wisdom to its rightful owner. Since my grandfather found it, after its original owner was dead for centuries, and because he gave it to my grandmother, she was the rightful owner. A thief is not the owner. Grandma said it also brought a little bit of luck, along with the guidance. Something I could use a lot of right now."

"Is that why you seek this torc—guidance and good fortune?"

"No, it's not mine. I want to return it to my grandmother."

"Who took it?"

"My uncle from hell. He killed my mother and father. She was his sister, and he left with the torc."

"And police can't find him?"

"The FBI was even looking for him at one time. He's like a chameleon; he can blend in anywhere."

"Do you think he sold it?"

"No, because it would be worth more to him wearing it on one of his wrists than it would be for him to sell it." Courtney watched as two fireflies rose out of the grass and flew up into the boughs of the old oak, the light like small blinking lanterns in and around the leaves.

"This uncle of yours, did he work the carnival circuit?"

"Yes. He's been spotted working as a hypnotist. He's real good at taking volunteers out of the audience and hypnotizing them into doing stupid stuff, you know, making them strut like a chicken and crow like a rooster. People think it's funny. I think it can be dangerous."

"How so?"

"Because he's a dangerous person…no…he's an evil man. He'd think nothing about using his skills at hypnosis to make people do stuff that would benefit him."

"What kind of stuff?"

"Who knows? Maybe even rob banks for him."

Boots slapped at a mosquito that alighted on his big toe, near the yellowed and curled toenail. "The human subconscious mind is a destination with a landscape as different as that person's character and his or her hidden thoughts. Many in the business say people under hypnosis won't do something that violates their code of ethics, such as commit a crime. Do you believe that?"

"No, not with somebody as immoral as my uncle. I believe he has the power to prey on the weak, to persuade them to do things they wouldn't ever do under normal circumstances."

"When's the last time you saw your uncle?"

"It's been more than four years. Between carnival gigs, he was a con-man preacher in a few backwater churches. He's the opposite of Robin Hood. Rather than take from the rich and give to the poor, he takes from the poor and gives to himself."

"What's he look like?"

"Women like him, unfortunately. He's got dark hair and handsome features. I think he's about forty-four, maybe forty-five. He has thick eyebrows and eyes the color of a blue sky. Wears his hair combed straight back."

Boots snatched a firefly from the air in his right hand, then cupped the firefly in both hands, the broken light seeping out between his short fingers. "This creature possesses the secret to cold light. The properties of light create heat, but not in this being." He leaned closer to his hands, the light from the trapped insect caught in his eyes.

Courtney said, "Don't hurt it. Let it go."

"I shall. It will journey through the dark with its own light. You must travel through a dark world with an internal light, one from your heart. I think I know your uncle. Before I retired, I worked a summer circuit with Sun Amusements. They were looking for a new act. He showed up, as if from nowhere. He called himself the *Illusionist*. He drew in the crowds, night after night. Hypnotizing people from the audience with lightning fast speed. Even some of the carnies thought he worked with plants in the crowds. Not so. He was fired after he was found having sex with underage girls, girls he'd culled from the audiences and enticed them back to his trailer."

"Why wasn't he arrested?"

"Because none of the girls could actually remember having sex or being raped by him. His powers of hypnosis were that good. The carnival boss got rid of him to prevent big lawsuits and horrendous publicity. He left carnivals and began posing as an itinerant evangelist, traveling the country and calling himself the Prophet."

"How do you know this?"

"Because a woman he left with, Mariah Danford, is a friend of mine. She traveled with him for a few weeks before escaping."

"Escaping?"

"He'd held her against her will and started picking up other women, marrying them in some make-believe fashion, and either brainwashing them or keeping them under his control by hypnosis. He sells the women over and over as prostitutes. The Prophet was really the pimp."

"Where is Mariah Danford?"

"New Orleans. I'll give you her address and number. No guarantee that she'll know where the Prophet is today, but she might.

If she does know, what will you do?"

"I'll find him."

"Be very careful, Courtney. You stay in touch with me. This thing will work itself out, okay?"

Courtney smiled and kissed Boots on his cheek. "Okay."

Boots opened his cupped hands, the firefly in the center of his palm. "Go little one," he said. "Because you travel at night, darkness surrounds you. Don't be afraid of the dark." He turned to Courtney. "Be vigilant. Your journey will be most difficult. When will you go?"

"Soon." Courtney watched the firefly crawl to the tip of Boots' short index finger, open its wings and fly toward the creek. It flew over the sets of fiery red eyes on the surface, and then rose higher, flying with the guidance from a bright moon so far away, like a lighthouse on the edge of a dark sea.

THIRTY-FIVE

It was after midnight when the news media filed their last salacious reports of the day, pulled out of Ponce Marina, and went to roost wherever vultures go at night. After the last satellite truck left, I walked Max across the marina and down an oyster-shell road leading to the beach. We could hear the breakers rolling across the dunes and beyond the sea oats, a high tide rising under the bright moonlight. I wondered where Courtney Burke was at this very moment. Was she in a safe place? If Isaac Solminski, the 'Guesser,' knew where she was, did Carlos Bandini believe Solminski could tell him? Would Bandini force him to talk?

Earlier in the evening, I'd looked in my coat pocket and found the handkerchief that I'd let Andrea Logan use to wipe her eyes. In the morning, I planned to call Detective Dan Grant to see if he'd run DNA tests on the samples in the handkerchief and my DNA, too. But now the immediate job was finding Courtney and getting a sample from her.

What if she is my daughter? I have no living family. The little dog walking at my feet is my sole dependent. I thought about what Nick said, his reference to Courtney resembling Andrea and me. And then I considered the message that Courtney had asked Isaac Solminski to give me. Did he get it right? Did he leave something out? If Andrea Logan was truthful, if she never had contact with the child after the adoption, how would Courtney know about the birthmark? What was the missing puzzle piece? How close was I to finding it? If I did find it, would it be in time to help a girl who might be my own flesh and blood?

I scooped Max up and walked over to one of the larger sand dunes facing the Atlantic Ocean. We sat and watched the breakers roll ashore across a deserted beach in the moonlight. The breeze blew in from the east, bringing the scent of saltwater and schooling fish leaping through the crashing waves.

Max uttered a low growl. Moments later, a sea turtle crawled from the rolling surf and slowly made her way up the beach, beyond the high tide line. "Shhh, it's okay, Max. No barking." We sat on the dune and watched the large turtle crawl to less than twenty-five feet from us.

She began using her back flippers to dig a hole in the soft sand. I knew she'd lay close to one hundred eggs, cover them up, and trudge back to the sea, never seeing her young. Maybe two or three turtles would survive out of the entire hatch to make it to adulthood. And if at least one was a surviving female, she'd eventually return home, to this exact same beach years later to lay her eggs.

Courtney Burke was a survivor. But what did she have to return to? What warm memories did she have of her home? Were her parents adoptive or biological? Were they attentive or indifferent? If they were attentive, then how was she subjected to abuse? Or had one of them been the abuser? If Detective Dan Grant is right, if she's a cold-blooded killer, when was the seed planted? And could I be partly to blame?

Enough.

Max and I watched as the green sea turtle began laying her eggs, her head turned toward the sea. I could see where the digging had flung loose sand against her head and face. Under the bright moonlight, it looked as if she was crying as she laid her eggs. I attributed the wet streaks coming from her eyes to the sand on her face, possibly in her eyes. Maybe I was wrong. All I knew at the moment was that Max and I shared a small plot of beach with a sea turtle, and perhaps, just somehow on this windswept, empty beach, we shared a link that was without biological boundaries.

— —

TWENTY MINUTES LATER, Max and I walked down the oyster-shell road and returned to the marina parking lot. I noticed a motorcycle in the lot that wasn't there when we'd started our walk. Kim Davis' white Honda was still parked, as was a second car I recognized, a Chevy owned by the Tiki Bar cook. But the Harley-Davidson wasn't there at midnight. Now it was near 1:00 am. I made a mental note of the license plate number and the blue gas tank with a skull and crossbones painted on it.

The Tiki Bar door was locked, so I looked through the glass door and saw Kim doing paperwork at the bar, the cook sitting and nursing a cup of coffee. All the customers were gone. I tapped on the door. Kim looked up, smiled, and walked over to open the door. Her hair was pulled back in a ponytail, her caramel eyes still animated after the end of a shift. "Did Max find you or did you find her, or are you both out for a midnight stroll?" She grinned and let us inside.

We followed her to the bar where the cook sat, shoulders slouched, his eyes heavy, white T-shirt blotched with food stains. He looked up at Kim and said, "I'm heading out. See you tomorrow night."

"Goodnight, Bobby." Kim turned to Max as the cook left and said, "Sorry, Miss Max, all the food's gone for the night. Will you take a rain check?" Max sat on the wooden floor near a barstool and cocked her head, her nostrils in seek 'n eat mode. "So, Sean, what brings you here a half-hour beyond closing time?" Kim reached in the cooler and popped the tops on two bottles of Corona, setting one in front of me, the other she held up and said, "To you Sean, you helped the Tiki Bar have its best business day ever. Those reporters eat as much as they talk."

"I'm not so sure that bringing that business to the Tiki Bar is something I'd want to raise a glass to, but I will take the beer. Thank you. We couldn't sleep, so Max and I went for a walk along the beach."

"You have every right to be sleepless in Daytona. Your face is all over the news. Those so-called reporters are saying you and the wife of Senator Lloyd Logan had a child together. The whole Republican presidential primary election is turning upside down. Can imagine you'd have some restless nights. Sean, we have a history together and you know I'd never do anything to violate your privacy, but tonight it looks like you could use a friend." I smiled and sipped the cold beer.

She said, "I feel really bad for you. It has nothing to do with Senator Logan's presidential campaign. It has to do with the daughter you never knew you had. It wasn't fair to you."

"Who's to say what wasn't fair? I don't blame Andrea Logan. We were both kids, twenty-something. She was scared. She could have aborted, but she chose not to. And I know it wasn't easy for her to give the baby up."

She was quiet a moment. I heard the motorcycle in the lot start and pull away. "Sean, I don't want to pry, but that girl, the one who came into the Tiki Bar and asked me for directions to your boat, the girl police are hunting for… is she your daughter?"

"I don't know. She was walking on County Road 314 late at night when I found her. So it's not as if she was looking for me. She wasn't some kid trying to reconnect with a father she never knew. Maybe it's purely by chance."

"I remember you telling me, when you were a detective, you didn't believe in coincidences."

"When it came to crime, I didn't. In the cycles of life, maybe."

"But we're talking about crime here, too, right? She's wanted for killing those men at the fairgrounds."

"She's wanted for questioning in their deaths."

"But you don't think she did it, right? Is it because of what Nick overheard from those two drunk carny workers that night?"

"That's part of it. It's also the way Courtney Burke responded from the first night I saw her until the last time I saw her.

Just a feeling in my gut."

"Or maybe your heart."

"Maybe. She knew about a tiny birthmark on my shoulder. It looks like an Irish shamrock, a four-leaf clover. Andrea used to call it God's tattoo. But how did Courtney know?"

"Someone told her."

"No doubt, but who? It's not common knowledge even among my friends."

She smiled and sipped her beer. "I've seen you without your shirt, at least from a distance, as you worked on your boat. I've never seen your birthmark up close. Are you going to find the girl?"

"I'll try."

"If anybody can, it's you."

"Thanks for the beer, Kim."

She reached across the bar and touched the top of my hand. "Hey, I'm here, Sean. Anytime, okay? Get some sleep. If Courtney is your daughter, I'm sure it'll all work out. I need to get going. My dog, Thor, has been home alone for almost ten hours."

"I'll walk you to your car."

139

"You don't have to do that."

"Yes I do."

She smiled and titled her head slightly, pulling a strand of hair behind her left ear. "Okay, that'd be nice."

She turned the lights off behind the bar and the three of us walked to the entrance door, Max following at our heels. After locking the door, we walked across the crushed oyster shell parking lot to her car. She used her remote key to unlock the car door. She turned back to me, the moonlight falling softly on her hair, the sound of the breakers in the distance. "Thank you, Sean, for the escort. Maybe one day Max can meet Thor."

"That sounds like fun."

"I think they'd get along well."

"I bet they would."

She watched the light rotate from Ponce Inlet Lighthouse, its beam touching the edge of the Atlantic. Then she looked up at me, her brown eyes elusive, inviting. "Can I give you a hug before I leave?"

I leaned down and she hugged me, Kim's hands flat against my back, their warmth penetrating my shirt. She leaned in, kissed me on the cheek and said, "You're a good man, Sean O'Brien. I hope all of this you're going through works out, and I believe it will."

"Thank you. Goodnight, Kim."

She smiled and turned to get in her car. Max and I stood there, watching the red taillights fade into the darkness.

━ ━

WE WALKED DOWN L Dock, Max sniffing the nocturnal smells, the glow from the security lamps chasing moving shadows between the tied-down boats rocking in the changing tide and soft breeze. From the next dock, I could hear the slap of a halyard against a metal sailboat mast, bowlines groaning in the night air.

Then there was a moan not produced by straining ropes pulling against a tide. It was human. Painful. And it was coming from *St. Michael.* Nick's boat.

THIRTY-SIX

My mind made the mental leap before I could physically get to him. *Be alive.* Nick was lying in *St. Michael's* cockpit, his back leaning against the exterior wall of the salon. One arm was pulled near his slumped head, his hand somehow propped on the wall. I ran hard and jumped from the dock into the center of the cockpit.

Be alive. I looked at his face, bleeding from the nose, right eye swollen shut. He was unconscious. His left hand was cocked at an awkward angle, just above his head. An icepick was through his palm, the icepick embedded into the marine plywood. Blood trickled down the white exterior marine board, running over his neck and seeing into his white T-shirt. I felt for a pulse. It was there. Slow. Strong.

"Nick, hold on buddy." No response. I reached for the icepick and pulled it out of the wood. I held Nick's hand higher than his heart, checking for signs of other wounds, looking for additional bleeding. Nothing. I wiped blood out of his right eye. He groaned, tried to open the eye. "It's okay, Nick. Stay still. I'll call paramedics."

"No," he coughed. "Gonna be okay." Another raspy cough. "It's just my head and hand. No broken bones or busted ribs. Let's keep the police outta this one." He looked up at me, forced a smile, his teeth red from blood, the white of his swollen eye the color of ripe strawberries.

"You need medical attention. You need a tetanus shot."

"I need to lie down. You worry too much, Sean."

I reached for my phone and called Dave. Max paced the dock, a slight whimper in her throat. Three rings, no answer. On the seventh ring his voice grumbled through the comatose vocal cords.

"Sean...what's going on?"

"Nick's been hurt."

"What? Where?"

"His boat."

"Be right there."

Within a half minute, Dave sprinted across the dock from his boat. His T-shirt was on backwards, his face filled with worry. "What the hell happened? How bad is he?"

"No indication of broken bones. Looks like his face took the brunt of the beating. Whoever did it impaled that icepick through Nick's hand and pinned it to the wall."

"The bastards...who did this?" Dave knelt down and braced Nick's face in his hands. "We need to get you to an emergency room, Nicky."

"No...I'll survive. I'm a little behind on my health insurance payments."

I said, "Got you covered. No sweat. Let's get you checked out."

He tried to stand. Dave and I grabbed his big arms and steadied him. He said, "Lemme go in. I have one hellava headache."

"Lean on us," I said. We led Nick inside *St. Michael's* salon and eased him down on the couch, Max following quietly.

Dave said, "I'm wrapping your hand in some clean towels, and then I'm coming back with my first-aid kit. We'll get you fixed up, Nick. We need to flush out that hand and sterilize the area around the cuts and bruises." Dave walked into the galley and pulled a wad of paper towels off the shelf. He returned and wrapped a few towels around Nick's bleeding hand. "Hold your hand up, okay? You must keep it elevated above your heart. We need to stop the bleeding. I don't think it needs a stitch, but it's a hell of a puncture wound. Through one side, out the other."

"Tell me about it," Nick said, leaning his head back on the leather couch, holding his arm up. Dave left and I got a pillow for Nick and brought it to him, gently putting it behind his head.

"Who did this to you?"

"Don't know his name." He coughed and closed his eyes.

"Was it Bandini's guys, the two who jumped us at the carnival?"

"No, a different dude. Workin' for Bandini. He made the other two look like Mutt and Jeff. This guy was taller than you.

Probably six-five, two-hundred-sixty maybe."

"What happened?"

Dave arrived and pulled up a chair, opening the first-aid kit, applying antiseptic and gauze to Nick's wounds. He said, "Hang in there, Nick. All of this will burn some. Especially around your eye."

"Doctor Dave, do your thing."

I asked, "What happened?"

"I thought I heard ol' Joe the cat on the transom looking for a grouper I had left for him in the bucket. But I couldn't remember if I'd taken the top off the bucket. I cover it up to keep the pelicans from stealin' Joe's food. I was sleepy, just woke up. I opened the door to step outside and somebody hit me from behind. Bam! The guy had a crowbar in his hand. I fell and he started kickin' me in the face and ribs. He had on steel-toed boots. I broke a long marine flashlight over his knee before he pulled a pistol and stuck it under my chin and said, *This is payback. Don't ever come lookin' again.'* Then he said, *'Tell your asshole friend he's next. Now it's your turn to get the point.'* He skewered an icepick through my hand and kicked me in the head. Lights out. When I came to, you were leaning in my face, Sean. For a split second, I thought you were God, and that scared the shit outta me."

Dave smiled and said, "In the morning I'm taking you to the medic-clinic for a tetanus shot."

I said, "You were jumped from behind...wonder how your attacker knew this was your boat. Describe him."

"Like I said, was a big mother, six-five, two-fifty or sixty. Lots of tats. Hoop earring. Wore one of those pirate bandanas around his head. I remember seeing him swingin' the tire iron, and he wore black leather gloves."

Dave nodded. "Probably no fingerprints. He's a professional knee-breaker."

I took a step back and gave Dave room to work on Nick. He'd mend in time, the hole in his hand would fill leaving a small scar, but the partial act of crucifixion, impaling Nick to his boat, would forever burn in his heart. He was a proud man, a good man, and Bandini's soldier had nailed a portion of Nick's spirit to a wall and left him for dead.

I thought about the Harley that pulled out of the lot when I was talking with Kim inside the Tiki Bar. I played back the license plate number and then filed it in a dark place in my mind that I didn't like to enter, the attic of the aberrant. It was where I stored old case files from my days as a detective, the profiles of killers I'd hunted. Their faces frozen in time, usually the moment a jury returned a guilty-as-charged verdict. Those images are now like glassy-eyed trophies long-since covered in dust and cobwebs, hanging on the dark inside of my skull, relics of the criminal mind. These were faces I didn't want to remember but couldn't forget. It was a shadowy mental hard-drive of stored experiences that taught me how good people can live honorable lives, but evil people exist by cannibalizing the soul of human virtue.

It was time to meet Carlos Bandini.

THIRTY-SEVEN

I left *Jupiter* an hour before sunrise just as a TV news satellite truck was rolling into the marina parking lot. Dave, who was keeping an eye on Nick and Max, was going to drive Nick to a medical clinic for a tetanus shot later in the morning. They'd planned to take a motorized rubber zodiac from Dave's boat, cross the marina to the lot away from the news media, get into Dave's car and leave. If the reporters hadn't seen Nick entering the marina with me earlier, he'd remain anonymous.

Somebody in Carlos Bandini's camp probably saw our faces on the national news and knew where to find us. And I had a good idea where to find Bandini. Maybe I could locate his hired gun first. He might be in the customized million-dollar bus, sleeping soundly after ambushing Nick. He could be just crawling into bed after drinking and celebrating the pounding he gave Nick and the warning he left for me. Maybe he was no longer in the area, shipped out to another Bandini Amusement playground, imposing the will of the family among its extended clan of thieves.

It didn't matter. It's hard to hide when you impersonate the hulk. As Kermit sang so eloquently, 'It's not easy being green.' And it wouldn't be easy for a knuckle-dragger the size of Nick's attacker to disappear, even in a carnival with hordes of people and the macabre facade of the shows along the midway.

I drove another mile and turned right into the parking lot of a Denny's Restaurant. As I drove across the lot, a black Ford SUV with tinted windows entered. I made a splint-second decision to park on the left side of the building, near the delivery entrance. I got out, walked toward the front entrance and went inside. The SUV was parking in the front.

I ordered breakfast from a nineteen-year-old college kid who said he was working here to earn money for the fall semester. He took my order and quickly brought back a plate with three scrambled eggs, turkey sausage, rye toast, potatoes, and a quart of black coffee. As I ate, I caught one man sitting at the counter staring at me, trying hard to place my face. He looked the other way.

I didn't know whether Detective Dan Grant started his day before 7:00 am, so I sent him a text rather than calling: *Dan – can we meet today? Urgent. Something's come up. I'm at the Denny's on Palmetto Blvd. - Sean*

He responded within seconds: *Five blocks away. Be there soon. Order coffee for me.*

I was pouring my second cup of coffee when he walked through the door. He slid onto the bench seat across from me and shook his head. "Morning, Sean. I feel like I just saw you. As a matter of fact, I did. Caught a few minutes of Good Morning America, and I see your face, the face of Senator Logan's wife, and all the commentators are talking about is this 'love child,' a daughter you two supposedly had together. One anonymous source offered a million bucks to anyone who knows her whereabouts, or the money goes to the girl herself if she can prove she's the daughter."

"That's one of the reasons I wanted to see you."

"What do you mean?" He poured coffee from the plastic thermos pot the server had left on the table.

I pulled out two Ziploc bags and pushed them toward him.

"What the hell's that?"

"The bag with the cotton swab has my DNA in it. The one with the folded handkerchief has Andrea Logan's DNA in it."

"How'd you get something that usually takes a court order to get?"

"She provided it."

"Provided it?"

"Look, Dan, Andrea is being vilified by the cable news channels. She's done nothing wrong. She's not the first mother who's given a child up for adoption. She shouldn't be penalized, nor should her husband, for a decision

146

she made two decades ago that she felt was the best thing for the child. I really need your help. Can you test the samples?"

He looked at me a long moment, sipping his coffee, his face filled with contemplation. "You placed two DNA samples on the table. Where's the trump card, the DNA of Courtney Burke?"

"I don't have it."

"Then you have nothing to match these to."

"I'll get it."

"If you get it, Sean, this'll mean you've come in contact with a woman wanted in connection with the deaths of two men, and a suspect in the deaths of two others. If you find her, and only bring back a DNA sample, if she continues running, you could be charged with aiding and abetting a murder suspect."

"And I'm hoping that you can prove she didn't kill anyone."

"The proof is in the physical evidence."

"Not always. People are set up to take falls, you know that, Dan. And when did self-defense become a prosecutable offense?" "We don't know that she shot Tony Bandini in self-defense. That's what she told the dwarf, but she didn't want to stick around to tell the police. So what the hell does that tell you?"

"That she's a scared kid. Someone who trusts no one."

"Let's speak hypothetically for a moment. If we're talking in 'what ifs,' what if you do stumble upon a DNA sample for Courtney Burke. And what if that DNA test is a match, a scientific guarantee that she's the daughter of you and Andrea Logan? And if Courtney's arrested and charged with multiple murders, what's that going to do when you've connected the Republican presidential nominee's wife to a serial killer?"

"But if this girl's innocent, to keep her off death row, I'm willing to make whatever valid connection I have to."

"This thing has snowballed into a national, no, an international obsession in the last twenty-four hours. Your coffee shop video's gone through the roof. Who the hell shot that?"

"Must have been the only other customer in the store. I saw his phone on the table when we walked in, I just never saw him pick it up because I was trying hard to comfort Andrea." I pulled out a pen and wrote across a paper napkin.

Dan stirred sugar into his coffee. "What's that, lotto numbers?"

"The tag number to the guy who ambushed, beat up, and left an icepick through the hand of a good friend of mine."

"What?"

I told Dan what happened to Nick, and he shook his head. "How much does this have to do with you and your pal questioning Bandini's guys after I did?"

"Some. The prime reason we dropped by the carnival was to see if Smitty was still working there. You told me your team couldn't find him, and Randal Barnes, of course, denied even knowing him. So we went only after you'd been there. We just happened to see Smitty walk into a porta-potty. Figured it was a fairly small place for a conference, so we made it quick."

Dan fought a smile at the corner of his mouth. "Sometimes I don't believe you retired from Miami-Dade PD."

"I didn't retire. I quit before I turned completely numb to our species."

"I can relate."

"I don't think the real reason Bandini sent his boy to nail Nick to the cross has that much to do with our visit to the carnival. I believe it had more to do with leaving a warning in Nick's psyche. His message was simple: don't be a witness or say anything about the conversation you overheard in the bar and we won't come back."

"Is Nick going to press charges?"

"I think he will if you find the guy. But because the attacker never actually mentioned Carlo's Bandini's name, only implied as much, Nick can't prove the connection. Since this guy's so good with icepicks, maybe he's the one who slammed one into the heart of Lonnie Ebert."

I slid the napkin with the tag number to Dan. "This is the license plate number on the motorcycle he parked in the marina lot. Harley. New model. Skull and crossbones on the gas tank. He may be walking with a limp. Nick managed to crack a heavy-duty flashlight across the guy's shin."

"All right. I'll see what I can find. And because I'm conducting a murder investigation, I can do DNA tests on the other stuff, too. I just need Courtney Burke's DNA, which we will get sooner or later. All of this will prove one way or the other whether this girl is the biological daughter of you and Andrea Logan. It won't prove her innocence. If she is the alleged love child the media keep yammering about, it should make one hell of a presidential election year because I will find her and I will arrest her, Sean. If she's your kid, too bad you never had a chance to have an influence on her. Thanks for the coffee."

He got up to leave and walked across the lot. As I watched him get into his unmarked police cruiser, I noticed the same Ford SUV parked in the corner of the lot. The men never got out. I knew I was now being followed, and I was fairly sure it wasn't Carlos Bandini's men. If I was right, these guys reported to men who would make Bandini look like a Boy Scout leader.

THIRTY-EIGHT

The college kid asked me if there was anything else he could bring me. I said, "Maybe. What are you studying in college?"

He grinned. "I want to get into film. I took some visual arts and video classes in high school and loved it. Plus, I've always like acting, and I think I'd be a good director one day. I even shot a short film on my iPhone this summer. It has the eight millimeter app, shoots great stuff."

"I bet it does. Here's a chance for you to practice your acting and earn some money for college, too"

"What do you mean?"

"I have a friend in the black Ford SUV in the lot. He wants a large Coke with lots of ice. I have to make a phone call." I reached in my wallet and whipped out four twenties. "This is yours if you deliver it to him. Might as well make it two large Cokes because he's got a friend with him. Your job is to tap on his window and deliver the Cokes. But since you'll have them on a tray, you're going to spill one or both in his lap, and you'll act like it was an accident. Offer to pay for the dry-cleaning, okay? They won't take your offer because they have their own dry-cleaning service. But here's an extra twenty if they do."

"Man, I don't know...I could sure use the money, but—"

"You're not spilling hot coffee, only a soda. Not that big of a deal, and if you're as good of an actor as I think you are, piece of cake. It's just a dress rehearsal for a scene you might use later as a director." I smiled.

"Okay, what the heck. Long as it doesn't get me fired."

I gave him the money and watched as he filled two large cups with ice and soda, put them on a tray and walked out the front door.

I stood and headed for the kitchen, quickly walking through it, smiling at a sweating Mexican cook with a maroon bandana on his head, spatula in one hand. I left through the back delivery door, stood in the sago palms for a second, and looked around the edge of the restaurant. I watched the tinted glass window slide down on the SUV, the college kid saying something, and then spilling the sodas through the window. I jumped in my Jeep and left through the rear exit of the lot, pulled out onto a back street, and headed straight for the carnival.

— —

COURTNEY BURKE OPENED the windows in the small Airstream trailer, the cross-breeze puffed the curtains on the window facing Bullfrog Creek. She could smell the blooming lilac and tangerine blossoms in the morning air. She looked out the window and watched a blue jay hop between limbs on an oak tree, the bird squawking a morning melody. The blue jay was one of her grandmother's favorite birds. Her favorite was the puffin. Courtney thought about her grandmother and had the overwhelming urge to call her.

Then she heard the steady, non-excited sound of a dog barking. *Clementine.* She smiled and thought how unreal it was for the cockatoo to bark so much like a dog. She turned to make a cup of tea when there was a knock at the door. Courtney felt her pulse rise. She stood to a far right angle to the front window and saw Boots standing at the door.

"Courtney, it's just me."

She opened the door. "Hi, come in."

"I can't. Heading into town. What can I bring you?"

"You've been so kind to me already. I'm fine."

BOOTS NODDED. HE wore a purple tank top, red shorts, flip-flops and a yellow fedora with a white feather stuck under the band. "I spoke with my brother, Isaac. He tells me you like carrot cake. I'll bring some."

"Thank you."

"Another thing he just told me over the phone…there's a man looking for you. He said he came to the carnival and asked about you."

"What man?"

"Said his name was Sean O'Brien."

"What'd he want to know?"

"Where to find you."

"Did he tell him?"

"No, of course not. Do you know him?"

"Yes. He stopped two drunken men from attacking me." She looked away, her eyes following a blue jay in the cypress trees.

Boots watched her for a moment. "I sense he did more than that, although that is quite a noble feat. Is there something else about this man you want to tell me, something you want to talk about?"

"No."

"Okay. Isaac did say this gent, O'Brien, seemed to be searching for you independent of any police. Maybe he's a private detective. Why would he be interested in you? Is it because he pulled those men off you?"

"I guess so. I don't know." She bit her lower lip.

"My brother told me something else. He said Carlos Bandini questioned him about the extent of his relationship with you. Isaac said he knows Bandini won't stop until he avenges his brother's death."

"I had no choice. Tony Bandini had his fist wrapped around my hair, and was reaching for the gun on the table."

"I understand. But Carlos Bandini knows only one way, an eye for an eye. If this man, Sean O'Brien, if he's more than a good Samaritan, just maybe he's the person who might intervene on your behalf. Is he more than a good Samaritan, Courtney?"

She looked down at Boots and said, "No."

THIRTY-NINE

Dozens of brown-skinned men, many already with their shirts off, bare backs glistening, were rolling up huge canvass tents, dismantling rides as massive as the double Ferris wheel. Semi-trucks and large flat-beds were being loaded as the Bandini Amusement Company prepared to move to another town, delivering its brand of entertainment to another county fairground.

I pulled my Jeep to a stop near a closed *Daugs 'n Franks* stand, turned off the engine, and got out. I tried to stay inconspicuous, staying out of the open, blending in with the workers, county fair employees, and the dozens of truck drivers. The air was filled with dust and the sky a hard blue. I heard the crackle of a walkie-talkie and looked in that direction. The man speaking into the radio was tall. He wore wrap-around dark glasses, had wide shoulders, a narrow waist, dirty blond hair pulled back in a ponytail. He stood under the shade of a tree and barked orders to others, when he wasn't speaking into the walkie-talkie.

Was this the man who hung Nick out to dry? I watched him for a minute. He walked over to a black worker and said something. No limp. I moved on.

I walked around dozens of trailers and motors homes, carnival workers packing, the smell of diesel fumes and fried bacon in the breeze, rock music blaring from a set of outdoor speakers. I saw the dwarf, Isaac Solminski, stepping down from a Winnebago, holding a phone to his ear, talking with someone. He walked to a white bulldog chained under a shade tree. The little man put fresh water in the dog's bowl as he continued talking. He turned back around towards the Winnebago and saw me. He abruptly ended his conversation, setting the phone down on a card table next to a sweating can of Mountain Dew, a paper plate with crackers, purple grapes and cheese. Two black flies crawled across the white cheese.

He said, "You're back. And we move on."

"Before you go, maybe you can tell me where Carlos Bandini would be about now."

"Probably getting ready to attend the funeral of his brother."

"Where's the funeral?"

"I hear it's supposed to be held in Zephyrhills, small town outside of Tampa."

"Have you heard from Courtney?"

"No. Don't expect I will either."

I said nothing, watching the bulldog eyeing a squirrel.

Solminski raised his shoulders in a shrug. "This thing really has you, doesn't it?"

"What thing?"

"That birthmark on your shoulder. You're going plain crazy trying to figure out how Courtney knew, I can tell. I guess more than age and weight."

"Sure, I'd like to find out how she knew about it. But more importantly, I'd like to find her before Carlos Bandini does. And you don't have to guess why. I think you care about Courtney, the question is this: how much do you care?"

"He won't be able to find her."

"You hire the right people, throw enough money at it, and you can find anybody anywhere." I watched the bulldog jump up and charge the squirrel, snapping the chain.

"Winston!" shouted Solminski. He darted after the runaway bulldog. I reached down and lifted his phone off the table and looked at his recent call history. Could Courtney's number be at the top of the list? I memorized the number I saw most frequently called in the last two days. Then I set the phone back exactly as I'd found it.

Within thirty seconds the little man had caught the big bulldog, both breathing heavily as Solminski held what was left of the chain, now shorter than a leash. "Winston's been acting weird. He usually doesn't open an eye at a squirrel. Now, he's trying to kill them. Look, no offense, but could you just leave? It's not healthy to be seen with you."

"He's here, isn't he?"

"Who?"

"Where's Bandini? I didn't see the bus."

"That's because it's parked near the county office by the livestock area. I don't know if he's there or en route to the funeral. But the bus is there. Now get outta here, okay?"

"One last thing. You guessed the age of my Greek friend Nick Cronus. Made his day. One of Bandini's goons almost killed Nick. Whoever did it rides a Harley with a skull and crossbones symbol painted on the side of the gas tank. Where can I find this guy?"

"That question implies that I know the answer. Maybe you should ask Bandini?"

"I'm asking you."

"Don't know his name. He's one of a dozen motorcycle gang members Bandini uses from time to time. I saw the dude yesterday. Big fella. He rides a motorcycle. Lots of chrome. One of the carnies said the guy spends time at a biker bar outside of Daytona called the Lone Wolf Saloon. Every town or county we play, there's always a work-for-hire person the Bandini family has on call. The Daytona area seems to have more than its fair share of talent."

"Thanks. If you have contact with Courtney, please tell her to call me."

Isaac Solminski sat in a metal fold-out chair next to the card table, the panting fat bulldog drooling saliva beneath his feet. He popped a purple grape in his mouth and said, "Good luck to you, Mr.

O'Brien. Your face is all over the news, by the way."

"So I hear."

I headed in the direction of the livestock arena, a large white compound that smelled of cow manure and sawdust. Red, white, and blue banners hung from the main entrance near signs that welcomed the FFA and 4-H students. Bandini's customized bus was parked in front of a sign that read: *Volusia County Fair Office.* I watched as smiling kids and their parents left with prize-winning cows, pigs, goats, chickens and rabbits, all packed into pickup trucks or animal trailers hitched to pickup trucks.

I put on dark glasses, pulled a baseball cap down to my eyebrows, and walked past the office window. Even from the rear, I recognized Carlos Bandini from his image I'd seen when the news media interviewed him about the death of his brother. He looked like a younger version of Al Pacino, short, maybe five-seven. He stood with two of his employees, the guys who'd stopped Nick and me in the parking lot when they popped out of the bus.

And now I was going to do the same, but from a different vantage point.

FORTY

I stood under a cottonwood tree and watched the customized luxury motor coach for a moment. The door opened and a driver stepped outside. He had the build of a gym rat, defined forearms, beefy wide shoulders, black T-shirt stretched over his muscular chest. He lit a cigarette and stood in the shade of the livestock building. He glanced down at the gold watch on his thick wrist and inhaled a lungful of smoke, exhaling out of his nostrils. Ten seconds later, he dropped the cigarette, crushed it beneath the heel of his boot, and ducked into the restroom.

I adjusted the Glock under my belt in the small of my back, shirt hanging around my waist. I walked quickly to the bus, looking up into its wide side-view mirrors to see behind me, to see if Bandini and company were leaving the office. Clear. Was anyone else on the bus? I didn't know. I took a deep breath and stepped up and into the cool, dimly lit interior.

The sound system was tuned to a classic rock satellite channel, Bob Seger's *Night Moves* pulsating through the Bose speakers. The interior could have been a luxury mansion on wheels, polished woods, designer furnishings, sixty-inch flat-screen TV, liquor in hand-cut crystal decanters.

I walked down the hallway, the slight hiss of the cool air blowing through the vents onto the back of my neck, wine-colored carpet thick beneath my shoes. The door to an office was partially opened. I instinctively touched the Glock and pushed the door open. No one. I did a fast walk-through of the entire bus. No one. I went back into Bandini's office and looked out the tinted window. Bandini was leaving the fairground office with his two associates. They were joined by the driver. I watched them point toward an approaching taxi that pulled up behind the bus.

A blonde woman wearing a miniskirt, stiletto heels, dark glasses, and a low-cut blouse revealing ample cleavage, stepped from the taxi. Bandini walked over to the cab, smiled, tossed money through the open window to the driver, and then placed his hand on the center of the woman's back, escorting her to the bus. I could see they were entering a side door, his men boarding from the front entrance.

I quickly relocated to the large master bedroom in the rear of the bus. Elvis Presley's designer could have created this haunt, round bed with a purple and gold bedspread, mirrored ceiling and walls, mini-bar, with inlaid white holiday lights. A lime green alligator was propped next to the purple pillows.

I heard the side door open. As much as I hated the idea of popping out from a closet, I had no choice. I stepped in and closed the door behind me, the odor of leather, shoes, and starched shirts encircled me. Within seconds, Bandini and the woman were in the bedroom.

She said, "Pretty fancy place you got here. This is like a mansion on wheels."

"You got that right, Susan."

"It's Suzy."

"Whatever. Look, I got to ride across the state to attend a funeral, and I need you to take my mind off stuff. Depression isn't for me. God rest my baby brother."

"I'm sorry for your loss. What do you want me to do?"

"We're gonna do it all, and then some."

I heard Bandini walk around the room, to the far side of the bed and press a button, a white noise filled the room. Then someone said, "Yes sir."

"Let's roll."

"Headin' out, boss."

I could feel the transmission being put into gear, the bus move a few feet, and then start off slowly, building speed as it moved around the parking circle in front of the livestock arena.

Bandini said, "All right, Suzy. You can ditch the clothes."

"You mind if I freshen up a bit? I just got off my shift at the club. Been dancin' most of the night. Where's the bathroom?"

"This bus has three Johns. The master is the door to the left. By the way, when I'm done with you, I want you to take care of the troops. But not in here. You can fuck 'em in the middle bedroom down the hall to the left."

"Hold on. I didn't agree to some kind of multiple sex thing. I screw one person. That's it. That's what I agreed to."

"Take it up with your boss when we ship your used ass back. I paid a grand for you, bitch. I plan to get my money's worth, which includes watching the boys do you, too."

"No! I'm getting off this bus."

Bandini laughed. "Take your fuckin' clothes off or I'll rip 'em off."

"Go to hell. Stop this bus!"

"You're not going anywhere."

I heard him slap her hard, then the sound of clothes tearing. I pushed open the door just as Bandini had his pants down to his knees. The girl was recoiling on the floor, blood running from her mouth. I raised the pistol and said, "Back off."

He looked at me as if a ghost had entered his bedroom. "You're a dead man!"

"And you're wearing your britches a little low to be a bad ass." He fumbled under one of the purple pillow cases for a pistol. I kicked him in the center of his bare butt, the gun falling to the floor. He picked up a glass ashtray and threw it at my head. I ducked and drove my right fist into his jaw. The sound was like a dog biting into a drumstick. He tried to stand, his eyes rolling, blood seeping out of his lips. I grabbed his collar and pulled him to within a foot of me and said, "Listen very closely because I'm telling this to your face one time only. I hear you left a message for me. Bad idea not to deliver it in person. Makes me agitated. You sent your gorilla to ambush a friend of mine. You had him beaten up. Ice pick through the hand. Another bad idea." I brought my knee up into his groin.

The blow lifted him off the carpet.

He coughed blood and muttered, "Fuck you."

I backhanded him hard across the bed, the stuffed lime-green alligator falling to the floor near the girl. I grabbed his bare feet and pulled him across the purple and gold bedspread, slamming his head against a dresser. "Bandini, you're not listening. Here's the deal. You touch Nick Cronus again and the crabs will be eating what's left of you. If you send your knee-breakers out to hurt Courtney Burke, I'm coming back for you. Guess what...I'll find you. I got on this bus. I can get to you anywhere. Is that clear?"

He stared at me through half closed, cold eyes, blood pouring from his loose teeth. "Is that clear?"

He nodded and spit blood. I said, "Now press the intercom and tell your driver to return to the main parking lot at the fairground." I stepped back and picked up the Glock, pointing it between his eyes. "Now!"

He leaned over to pull his pants up, and walked to the speaker, looking back at me once more. "Don't make me spray your brains across this lovely bed."

He pressed the speaker button and said, "Eddie, head back to the fairground, main parking lot. I forgot something."

"No problem, boss."

I turned to the woman still on the floor, holding her ripped shirt over her breasts. I reached down and helped her up. "Come on,

this is where you're getting off the bus, too." "Thank you," she said, standing.

The bus rolled to a stop. I kept the Glock in my hand, looked one final time into the burning eyes of Carlos Bandini, then I led the woman through the back of the bus to the exit door. I pushed it open and we got off. "Come on," I said. We have to get out of here."

We jogged through the parking lot, the sound of a helicopter in the distance. I heard the bus pull away. I turned to the girl and said, "You're lucky. You might not have lived through what they'd planned to do to you."

"Thank you. I've never had a man stand up and defend me."

"You're welcome. I have a couple of safety pins in my Jeep. It'll help you keep your shirt closed. Looks like Bandini ripped most of the buttons off of it."

I glanced over to where three carny workers stood in the shade, taking a break, smoking, drinking sodas and staring at us. "Let me give you a ride. Where's home?"

"I can't let you take me there. My husband's home. Just drop me off at Big Lots down the street. I'll buy a blouse and take a cab."

I walked her to my Jeep. We drove for a minute in silence and then she said, "I don't know what I'd have done if you hadn't been there. What's your name?"

"Sean O'Brien…and yours?"

"My real name's Angie Houston."

"Nice to meet you Angie."

"I heard you tell Carlos Bandini to stay away from Courtney Burke. That's the girl who's been all over the news, right?" I said nothing.

"She's the one accused of killing Tony Bandini, the brother. If Tony was anything like that man back there in the bus, I'd say that girl did the world a favor. Is she like related to you or something?"

My phone buzzed in my pocket. It was Detective Dan Grant. "Sean, wanted to let you know I got the okay to submit the DNA samples for testing. I was thinking…the day we picked Courtney Burke up at your boat. Did she eat or drink anything? Maybe smoke a cigarette and leave the butt somewhere?"

"No, she didn't smoke, and she didn't eat or drink on the boat."

"All right. Another thing, we ran the plates on that bike. It's owned by a guy named Samuel Nichols, AKA the Pirate, hence the skull and crossbones. He's got a long rap sheet. Did a dime stretch in Raiford Prison for manslaughter. Former member of the Outlaws. He's a gun for hire, no doubt. If Nick will press charges, we'll find this guy and pick him up."

"Nick can't positively ID his face. And I don't think Nick wants to go through the legal system."

"Okay, then anything he might think of doing outside of it is illegal. And that goes for you, too, Sean."

"Thanks, Dan." I disconnected. After I dropped Angie off at Big Lots, I'd head to a bar.

A place called the Lone Wolf Saloon.

FORTY-ONE

I manually set my GPS for the Lone Wolf Saloon. I didn't think any GPS voice recognition programs would recognize it as a trendy bar featuring its own craft beers. The bar was located about twenty minutes east of Daytona Beach. I drove on Highway 92 through scrub woodlands, and under canopies of live oaks, the branches stretching over the blacktop and casting the road in deep shade, the limbs interlocked like fingers laced in prayer.

I called Dave and asked about Nick. He said, "We just got back. Nick's in his boat, knocked out on Vicodin. The puncture wounds in his hand didn't require stitches. He actually didn't need a tetanus shot. He had one after he was cut diving inside that sunken German U-boat with you. So, he's on some meds, and was ordered to stay off his feet for a day or two."

"Good." I told Dave about my encounter with Carlos Bandini and what Dan Grant had let me know about the biker who goes by the name of Pirate. I added, "Bandini's a poster child for the criminal sociopath. He hires freaks of nature like Pirate to bully anyone who is in his way. I think his revenge for the death of his brother isn't so much motivated because he feels loss as it is that he feels anger, and he wants to send a message. Courtney Burke is in his crosshairs because she was in the wrong place at the wrong time."

"As was Nick when he overheard Bandini's employees in the Tiki Bar. You think you put the fear of God in him? Think he'll return?"

"You have to believe in God to fear a divine consequence. Narcissists like Bandini only fear a tangible foe more deadly than themselves. I hate having to go there—to become that adversary, and I may have to go even further to deal with Pirate."

"Sean, just dial it down, okay? You walk in a biker bar and start pulling this guy's chain and you could wind up being attacked by a pack. Maybe Bandini didn't go ballistic after you left him with his pants down, bloodied and bruised, because you managed to represent that rival—that image even more dangerous than what he can muster."

"Maybe. But I have a feeling that Bandini will keep swinging because his brain is wired that way."

"How far are you away from the Lone Wolf Saloon?"

"Seventeen miles."

"If I don't hear from you within an hour, I'm calling the national guard. You're going to war, and you're one man. Call me, damnit."

"Take care of Nick." I disconnected.

— —

THE SIGN NEXT to the road read: *Bar-B-Q Tonite–Wet T-shirt Fri Nite*. I pulled onto the gravel lot where more than twenty motorcycles were parked near the Lone Wolf Saloon, a low-slung, ramshackle bar built from cypress wood, oak, and red brick. The aged building sat among tall pines and palmetto palm trees. Neon beer signs, Budweiser, Miller, and Pabst Blue Ribbon smoldered from behind dirty windows and a large porch with sagging patched screens the color of charcoal. The wind changed and from the far left of the building, hardwood smoke drifted across the parking lot, the smoke escorting the smells of charred pork, fat dripping on hot coals, and beer.

I spotted the motorcycle—the Harley with a Robin's egg blue gas tank, the skull and crossbones on both sides. It sat further away from the other motorcycles. I walked across the lot, towards the left side of the saloon, the hot sun winking off flattened beer cans and paper pieces of exploded fireworks lodged between the gravel. Coming from the back of the building, I heard loud voices, laughter, and amiable cursing mixed in the smoke and humidity.

I rounded the corner of the building and saw two sweating cooks turning ribs and pork shoulders over pot-bellied grills as bikers sat in lawn chairs or stood in small groups talking and telling jokes. Blake Shelton sang a country song from the outdoor, all-weather speakers. A fifty-something biker, with a ZZ Top gray beard down to his belt and faded blue tats over both arms, tossed a horseshoe into a sawdust pit with a steel pole in the center.

Among those standing, I looked for the tallest man. Within a few seconds, eyes were drifting my way. I wasn't a regular. Wasn't wearing a sleeveless denim jacket or leathers. I was a different species edging myself on the perimeter of their little savanna, about to sip from their watering hole. I stepped over to a rough-hewed bar and bought an iced-down bottle of Corona from a blonde female bartender wearing short cut-off jeans and a tank shirt. I gave her a five-dollar tip. She smiled and said, "You here for the barbecue? We have some of the best in Florida, they're barbecuing gator, too. It's real good." She moistened her full bottom lip.

"Matter of fact, that's one of the reasons I'm here. My old friend Sam Nichols said I should drop by today. I was going to come by during Bike Week, but the place was a little crowded."

"Oh my God. We must have had a zillion customers that week. It's second to the Daytona 500 week." I smiled and sipped the beer.

"What'd you say's your friend's name?"

"Sam Nichols. Some folks know him as Pirate."

She grinned and wiped her hands with a small white towel. "Yep, Sammy the Pirate." She looked around. "Don't see him out here. He was inside earlier. Saw him shootin' pool when I was stocking the bar. He's so big, I can't miss him. Plus he always wears that yellow pirate's bandana, kinda like Hulk Hogan wears."

I smiled. "Got to use the toilet. Good talking with you." I picked up my bottle of beer, didn't lock eyes with any of the Vikings, stepped around the banana plants, walked back down a dirt path to the parking lot and entered the Lone Wolf Saloon.

FORTY-TWO

A rustic bar ran almost the entire length of the far wall. I quickly did inventory. Less than a dozen bikers scattered at tables. Four guys sitting at the bar. One bartender. Two waitresses, showing a lot of skin, working the tables. A Mexican cook stood in a kitchen area beyond the bar, filling tacos and grilling burgers. To the far right were three pool tables, pockets of soft light falling in sharp cones from the lamps above each table.

I watched shadows move around the tables. Fur. Ink. Denim and black motorcycle boots. Every few seconds a body leaned into the cones of light and made a shot. The orange tips of cigarettes glowed, smoke funneling through the lamps like indoor chimneys.

I stepped to the bar and waited, standing because if I sat, the Glock might show a slight bulge under my shirt. In a place like this, I wanted to lower the risks wherever and whenever possible.

"Hep you," said the bartender in a South Georgia accent. He had a scruffy sleep-deprived face and pupils expanded as large as his irises. He wore a T-shirt with an image of a red-eyed wolf and a caption that read:

Lone Wolf Saloon
Who's Afraid of the Big, Bad Wolf?

I said, "Sure, you have a Corona?"

"Comin' up."

I watched him pop the top on the bottle, and I glanced over to a discolored mirror behind the bar where I saw eyes drifting from tables over to where I stood. My guess is that they thought I was an undercover cop.

"Be three bucks," said the bartender.

I handed him a five. "Keep the change." I made small talk with him for a minute as I casually glanced around, never making eye contact with anyone, watching the pool tables each time a player leaned into the light to make a shot.

The yellow bandana.

A giant of a man wore it. He had to go at least six-six, shoulders like a water buffalo. When he lined up the cue ball to make a fresh break, I could see the muscles move like waves under his brown skin. He wore a hoop earring—arms covered in multicolored tattoos. Dirty blond hair curled and matted like grapes from where the bandana tied behind his head.

I watched him call a shot, line it up, and sink the eight ball. He grinned, playfully punching the other player on the arm. "Gotta split." I overheard him saying. "My old lady's coming back from Utah. Been gone a fuckin' week visiting her mama out West. I got the worst case of blue balls, bluer then that number two ball." He laughed, placed the stick in a rack and left. He walked past me, the smell of testosterone and body odor followed him out the door.

I gave it a few seconds, listening for the sound of a Harley engine starting. I inhaled deeply, turned and walked across the floor of the bar. He stood outside on a wooden deck elevated off the ground a foot or so. He lit a cigarette with a Zippo lighter, the smell of lighter fluid in the breeze. I walked up to him and said, "Hey, man, you got a light?"

He looked at me oddly, his bloodshot eyes searching my face. "Sure." He fished in his pants pocket for his lighter. "Where's your smoke?"

"Here." I reached inside my shirt and retrieved the icepick he used on Nick. "You left something behind. Thought I'd return it." Before he could fully register what I said, I drove the icepick into the center of his left shoulder. Between the rotator cuff. All the way in to the wooden handle. To the bone. The cigarette toppled from his mouth.

He swung at my head with a powerful right hook. I danced backward, his fist missing my chin by an inch. He yelled, "Mother fucker! You're a dead man!"

"I heard that earlier from your pal, Carlos Bandini."

He charged me—an enraged brown bear. I knew the embedded icepick was taking some of his prowess down. But to be caught in his massive arms and body slammed could lead to a broken back. I dodged his attack and kicked him in the side of his thick skull. He fell for a moment, shook it off, and stood, blood pouring down his chest and over his belly. He pulled the icepick out of his shoulder, grinned, and swiped in the air at me. "I'm gonna stick this through your neck. Shoulda done it to your pal. Next time I'm gonna skin that curly-headed bastard."

He lurched forward, the icepick barely missing my chest. He jabbed, the steel point raking down my forearm. When he thrust again, I used both hands to pull his arm hard. Pulled him off balance. He fell, dropping the icepick. I grabbed the pick and slammed it through the center of his palm, skewering him to the wooden deck. Then I drove my fist into his jaw with a hard right, a fast left and another right. His eyes rolled. I hit him again. I grabbed him by the bandana and lifted his head off the deck. I leaned into his face and said, "If you ever touch Nick again, they'll find your body parts in the same place they'll find Bandini's, that'll be on the windows of cars because after the vultures digest what's left of you, that's all you be. Bird shit on a window. You stuck the icepick into Lonnie Ebert, didn't you? Answer me!"

He grinned through blood and loose teeth. "Fuck you, dead man. He'll come huntin' you."

"Who? Bandini? I found him."

"You'll never find him 'til he wants you to."

The front screened door opened and two bikers stepped out. One slid a long, serrated knife from a sheath on his belt. I reached behind my shirt and leveled the Glock at them. "Drop the knife!" They did as ordered, both with palms facing out. I glanced over at Pirate's Harley-Davidson. The skull and crossbones, the vacant eye sockets in the skull staring at me. I looked down at Pirate, barely conscious, the dropped cigarette smoldering near his shoulder. I said, "Didn't you learn how to use an ashtray? That's a fire hazard."

I turned and shot a bullet between the eyes of the black skull painted on the gas tank. Gasoline poured out, splashing over flattened beer cans and remnants of fireworks. I picked up the burning cigarette and tossed into the puddle of gas. Then I turned and ran to my Jeep. I started the engine and roared out of the parking lot as the Pirate's motorcycle exploded in an orange ball of fire that reached higher than the brick chimney on the Lone Wolf Saloon.

— —

BLOOD DRIPPED FROM my arm as I drove fast, my thoughts bouncing from Nick to Courtney Burke. I didn't know if the damage I did to Bandini and his henchman, Pirate, would build up more fear than anger in them. But I did know that to do nothing would prevent nothing. I learned a long time ago that a douse of preventive medicine can lower the risks of disease. Bandini was a cancer walking on two legs. Maybe I'd cut it off at the knee. Maybe not.

Who had Pirate been referring to when he said, *'You'll never find him 'till he wants you to.'* If it wasn't Carlos Bandini, then who was it? Maybe Pirate was doing what cons do…conning. Deception is their reality.

I pulled into the parking lot of a strip shopping center. I went inside a drug store, bought gauze, tape, and a bottle of hydrogen-peroxide. Outside, I stood beside my Jeep in the lot and poured half the bottle over the deep wound the icepick carved into my forearm. White bubbles boiled up out of the six-inch gash. I dressed the cut and got back in my Jeep, heading for the marina.

I drove through the Florida countryside, beneath the canopies of live oaks on both sides of the road, their thick limbs arching over the highway. I had a sudden urge to pick up little Max and head back to our old cabin on the St. Johns River. To canoe down river and fish for bass hiding in the shallows around the cypress knees. To lie back in the canoe under the warm sun and simply drift in the slow current, letting the ancient river guide me, floating like a reed basket on the Nile. I wanted the St. Johns to carry me and my little dog around the mossy bends and shoals laden with bald cypress trees, honeysuckles, and weeping willows whose slender fingers scratched the back of the old river.

Maybe I could push the events of the last few days out of my mind, push Andrea Logan's appearance back into a college yearbook, into a black and white memory, a static image in alphabetical order with no biological order— no lifeline connection to the present. Maybe I could learn to not care how and why Courtney Burke knew about the birthmark on my arm—to let her find whatever eats at her soul without trying to save it for her—to somehow keep Nick from taking such a bad and humiliating beating. Maybe the old river could rock the cradle of my world and return the genies to the bottle, to lock away the time capsule of my life and allow me to live in the present, the moment, without worrying about what I do disturbing the future of others.

But I couldn't. Whoever I was, whatever gene pool my conscience floated in, I had no choice but to be engaged because it wasn't only about me. And for the good of others, I wished it was.

The buzzing of my phone lying in the center console interrupted my thoughts. I answered and Dave Collins said, "Where are you?"

I never like conversations starting with that question.

"Highway 92. Why?"

"Don't come back to the marina, at least not right now."

I figured his warning had to do with my fiery exit from the Lone Wolf Saloon. "Why shouldn't I come back there?"

"News media are everywhere. Thicker than thieves, and probably just as unsavory. They smell blood, Sean. Not so much yours as Senator Logan's."

"What happened?"

"Apparently, the DNA testing that the local constables are doing was leaked to the media. They know the cops are testing DNA samples from you and Andrea, hoping to get a sample from Courtney Burke to prove one way or the other whether she, the alleged serial killer, is the biological daughter from Andrea's former relationship with you. Problem is...nobody can find the girl. But since Senator Logan is the presumed presidential nominee, you can bet the farm that a lot people are looking for her now. And her life just might be in even greater danger."

FORTY-THREE

Boots Langley was about to drop a mouse into the snake cage when his mobile phone rang. He looked into the red eyes of the albino python coiled in the glass enclosure, its tongue tasting the rodent molecules in the air. "Bon appetite," he said, taking the top off a small Styrofoam container and setting the mouse in one corner of the cage.

Boots shuffled to the kitchen, looked at the missed call and hit the re-dial button. Isaac Solminski answered and said, "We're on the road. Next stop is near Charleston. Is Courtney still there?"

"Yes, brother. She's tucked in the trailer down by the creek. She's a good kid. Very independent, and scared. Maybe Bandini won't find her down here."

"You know them...revenge doesn't have an expiration date in their mind. But rumor has it that the guy Courtney knows, Sean O'Brien, the man who Courtney said has a unique Shamrock birthmark, supposedly gave Bandini a spanking and warned him to stay away from her."

"Really? Well maybe he will."

"He's a small threat compared to what's going on with that poor child now."

"What?"

"I'm driving and listening to it all on NPR. They're saying Courtney might be the daughter of Senator Lloyd Logan's wife, Andrea. And the father might be Sean O'Brien. Maybe that's Courtney's family connection to him. Cops and probably the Democrats, for that matter, are searching for her. If her DNA is a match, the entire presidential election could be drastically affected."

"This could get nasty."

"Boots, watch the news online or on TV. And tell Courtney what I just shared with you. I fear for her now more than ever."

— —

COURTNEY BURKE WATCHED the setting sun ignite Bullfrog Creek in a river of fire, deep crimson and orange, a breeze across the water creating a sea of winking gold coins on the surface. She sat on the seawall overlooking the creek, tearing bits of bread from a hotdog bun and tossing the pieces to a mother mallard duck and three ducklings. Courtney said, "Ya'll share. Everybody will get some bread."

She smiled and looked over her shoulder as Boots approached. He sat beside her. "That mama duck was born here on the creek a few years ago. I can tell because she has that little piece of her beak chipped. Looks like a gator tooth caused it. Anyway, this is her second brood."

"She seems to be a great mom." Courtney watched him look at the ducks and then at her. "What's going on, Boots?"

"Sean O'Brien, the good Samaritan."

"What about him?"

"Do you know a woman named Andrea Logan?"

"No. Who's she?"

"She's the wife of the man who may be the next president of the United States."

"What's that have to do with me?"

"Well, I was about to feed Sheba a morsel when my brother called." Boots told her everything Isaac told him, and then added, "There will be a lot of people trying to locate you. Isaac and I both believe this could be very dangerous for you. Your face is on all the news stations and online. You're welcome to stay here as long as you can. Maybe you could find a way to get to someplace like Costa Rica. Just disappear until this thing works its way out."

"I'm not their daughter any more than I'm a serial killer."

"I know you said your mother and father were murdered. Before his death, what was your father like?"

"A salesman. Life of the party. And then one day, before his death, it changed. Daddy was an Irish traveler, sort of like gypsies. Here today, gone tomorrow. Mama usually worked in hospitals from time to time. She was a natural healer, real good with patients. One day Daddy left Mama and me in our trailer home in South Carolina. He came back a year later. Never admitted to her where he'd been all that time, and he never seemed the same since. Said he was lookin' for work, but he always found trouble."

"I'm sorry to hear that. Do you have siblings?"

"No."

"How long were your parents together before you were born?"

"About four years. They told me they'd almost giving up trying to have a baby. Mama said her eggs didn't always drop like most women. When she became pregnant with me, she called it divine intervention, and I was supposed to be her angel." She lowered her voice to a whisper. "But I'm not so sure that I was, and that bothers me a lot now, you know?"

"This may sound like a strange question, but I'm strange, okay? Could your parents have adopted you?"

She looked at Boots, her eyes widening, face skeptical, thoughts racing. "No. I have pictures from the time I was a tiny baby."

"You might have been adopted out right after you were born. That appears to be the case of the infant girl fathered by Sean O'Brien and given up for adoption by her mother. And, as I mentioned, that woman's husband is running for president of the United States. Look, Courtney, maybe you should consider ending this hunt for your uncle. If he is the Prophet, he's more aligned with the devil than God. If you turn yourself in, it could be safer for you in the long run."

"Safer? They'd find a way to kill me in jail. One thing my uncle knows is who I am and where I come from. Maybe he'll admit it before…"

"Before what?"

"Nothing."

"If you kill him, you become him."

"No, I don't. I may be part of his blood, but I'm not part of his soul." She tossed the last of the bread to the ducks.

"My brother, Isaac, mentioned the Shamrock birthmark that you said is on this man…Sean O'Brien's shoulder. How'd you know? What does it mean for you?"

She turned towards Boots. "If my life's in danger from those powerful people, it's best I don't tell you. Because if you know, then your life might be in danger, too. And I don't want that to happen. You and Isaac have been so kind to me. I would never forgive myself if something bad happened to either of you because of me."

"No worries. Oh, I almost forgot. This package came for you."

She nodded and opened the small package. She unwrapped a slim cell phone. "This came from my grandma." She looked over his shoulder, her eyes far away.

"What is it Courtney?"

"I have to go."

"Wait until daybreak. It'll be safer to travel. You can take my old Toyota truck."

"I'm not sure I can wait that long, Boots."

FORTY-FOUR

On the way back to the Ponce Marina, I called Dave and asked him to take the Zodiac and meet me at a remote dock away from the Tiki Bar parking lot and the main entrance to the private docks. I parked my Jeep behind a boatyard storage building, away from the central public areas. I walked about one hundred feet to the dock used for hauling boats out of the water. Deep in thought, I waited for Dave to motor up to the dock. My phone buzzed in my pocket. I didn't recognize the number. I answered.

The woman said, "Sean?"

"Yes."

"It's Andrea."

"I'm almost afraid to ask you how you're doing. I can only imagine."

"It's been very difficult. I shouldn't be calling you, but I had to."

I said nothing, waiting for her to continue.

She exhaled a pent-up breath into the phone. "I overheard Lloyd and two of his top advisors talking. I was in the next room on the campaign bus and heard them say things that frightened me."

"What kind of things?"

"It's about this girl…Courtney. Do you really think she's our daughter?"

"I don't know, maybe."

"Regardless, whoever she is, she's someone's daughter. I heard Robert Cairo, the man who will be chief of staff if Lloyd wins the election, say, and I'm quoting here, *'there's no way in hell that the girl can ever be tied to us. She must be found and removed.'* Sean, he said it like he was talking about pulling weeds in a garden. And the worst part is that Lloyd said if that's the way it has to be, then for the good of the nation as a whole, we have to take certain uncomfortable risks. I had to call you. Do you know where to find her?"

"Maybe."

"Please try. I truly believe she'll be safe only if she's kept in the public eye, visible but protected by law enforcement or the courts."

"I'll do my best to find her."

"Thank you. God, I'm so very sorry this has happened. I have to go, Sean, someone's coming down the hall."

I looked across the marina, through the sea of bobbing boats. To the far right in the distance were satellite news trucks, microwave antennas rising up from other trucks, TV lights blazing. I could see reporters conducting interviews with boat owners, barflies, anyone who might shed a better theory on what he or she did or didn't know about me or even Courtney Burke. I hoped the media were leaving Kim Davis alone. I called her.

"Sean, where are you?"

"Close, but not that close."

"Stay wherever you are. I've never seen anything like this. The marina hired off-duty deputies to enforce the private property rules. Still, Dave Collins told me he ran off two of them who were taking video of your boat. Dave's been keeping an eye on Nick and Max. Wherever you are, Sean, let me help you if I can. I can take Max to my house. I can bring you guys groceries, whatever you need, okay?"

"Thank you. I might go back to my place on the river for a while."

She was quiet for a moment. "I can deliver there, too."

"I'll keep that in mind. I appreciate it."

"Before you go, all these reporters and airheads on the cable news stations are talking about is Courtney Burke and whether she's a natural born killer, and what will happen to the presidential election if she is. They're speculating how, if she's Andrea Logan's daughter, how Andrea—a mother—must feel. Nobody's saying anything about how you might be feeling as the father. I just want you to know I care, your friends care, and we're all thinking about you."

"Thank you, Kim. I have to go."

"Be careful." She disconnected. I stood there, on the dock, in deep thought. I watched three white pelicans sail over the sailboat masts, over the mangroves between the marina and the Halifax River, and turn east to Ponce Inlet and the Atlantic Ocean. I thought about what Andrea had told me. And I thought about Courtney. I closed my eyes for a moment, recalling the number I'd memorized from Isaac Solminski's phone. Then I made the call.

One ring. *Come on, Courtney, pick up. Answer the damn phone.* After the fourth ring, a man said, "Hello." His voice was high. It had some of the tonal qualities I heard in Isaac's voice.

"May I speak with Courtney?"

There was a short pause. Even through a mobile phone I could detect it—the hesitancy that comes with knowledge of a hallowed subject, but not prepared to respond to questions about it. He said, "There isn't anyone here by that name. Goodbye—"

"Wait! Before you hang up, listen, please. My name's Sean O'Brien. I'm a friend of Courtney's and—"

"I'm sorry, sir, but I must go—"

"Please…just hear me out for thirty seconds. I got your number from Isaac Solminski. Maybe you're related to him. It doesn't matter. What matters is saving Courtney's life. If she's there, please let me speak with her. If she's not, can you get a message to her?"

"We have no one here by that name."

"If you see her, please tell her to call Detective Dan Grant with the Volusia County Sheriff's department. We're getting more evidence that will clear her in the killing of Lonnie Ebert. She has to stop running because she can't be protected if she's in hiding."

"Protected from what?"

"From people who will kill her."

There was another long pause. In the background, I could hear a dog barking and a train whistle. He said, "Okay. What's her last name?"

"Burke, Courtney Burke."

"No problem. If a Courtney Burke arrives, I'll give her the message to get in touch with Detective Grant at the Volusia County Sheriff's Office. Good bye—"

"Where are you located? I can help her." He disconnected. I went online and looked up his phone number, looking for an ID. There was no public record of the number. I squeezed the mobile phone so hard I thought it would break.

I glanced up to see Dave Collins approaching in the Zodiac, the small rubber boat creating a V trail across water painted in shades of purple, cherry, and merlot reflecting off clouds drenched in the colors of a sunset.

But his face mirrored the opposite of twilight serenity. With his seasoned years in covert intelligence, even from a few yards away, I could tell the uneasy look on his face forecast a bad storm on the horizon.

FORTY-FIVE

By the time we'd crossed the marina in the Zodiac, darkness was creeping over the boats like a dark tide. The smell of sautéed garlic shrimp drifted from the deck of a Grand Banks trawler tied to the dock, while the pulse of reggae, Bob Marley's *One Love* came from a houseboat lit with multi-colored Japanese lanterns. We quietly boarded Nick's boat, *St. Michael,* keeping low, staying in the shadows, watchful of security cameras and prying eyes, neighbors and news media.

Nick greeted us with a crooked grin, his face still swollen. The swelling around his eye had gone down some. His hand was wrapped in a large, white bandage, his shirt unbuttoned, ribs supported with a flesh-colored binding. He sat on his couch and sipped a micro-brew from a bottle, Max beside him. She jumped off and trotted over to us, tail animated.

Nick lifted his bottle. "Sean, where the hell have you been? Hotdog and I were getting a little worried."

"Just trying to take care of a little business."

"Man, looks like all those reporters want to make your business everybody's business. They're like gnats around a dock light."

"How are you feeling?"

"Good. I decided to stop the meds and replace 'em with cold beer." He looked at the bandage on my arm. "What happened to you?"

"Just a scrape. I'm glad he used an icepick rather than a real knife or he'd have cut me to the bone."

Nick's eyes widened. He sat up on the couch. "Did you find the guy who did this to me?"

"Yeah, I found him."

Dave sat down at the three-stool bar and poured a Grey Goose over ice. He sipped and motioned with his head towards the media in the parking lot. "In view of all this national, even international news coverage of, shall we call it, the situation, tell us you didn't kill the guy."

"He's alive, but his motorcycle is dead." I told them about the chain of events at the Lone Wolf Saloon, and then I let them know what occurred on Carlos Bandini's bus. Nick listened in pain and disbelief. Dave started his second cocktail in the five minutes it took me to tell them what had happened. I set my Glock on the coffee table and sat in the canvas deck chair.

"Shit," Nick said, pursing his lips to whistle, but it sounded like he was trying to blow up a balloon. "Sean, I know you saved my life a couple of years back when you pulled those guys off me. Man, we're square, okay? You didn't have to walk in a biker bar, by yourself, and kick the shit out that guy and blow up his bike in the parking lot, and do it in front of his BFF's." Nick shook his head and took a long pull from the bottle. "I gave up my meds too damn early."

Dave said, "I made a simple seafood bouillabaisse with some shrimp, redfish, tomatoes, onions, garlic and clams. Nick was shouting the Greek recipe to me at the stove. I'll get you a bowl and a beer."

"Thanks." I scratched Max behind her ears, her attention on Dave in the galley. Then I set her on the floor and she made a beeline to him. My phone buzzed in my pocket.

Detective Dan Grant said, "I tried to reach you earlier."

"You didn't leave a message."

"I usually don't. I wanted to let you know that I'm not sure how the media got wind of the DNA sampling of you, Andrea Logan, and the fact that we're searching for a sample from Courtney Burke."

I said nothing. Dave set the bowl of food and a Corona on the marine coffee table in front of me, lifting Max up and carrying her to the bar with him.

Dan said, "The chain of evidence leaves me and goes through a number of people, Sean, including lab techs. You know that. Maybe someone read my report and was looking to make some money by selling the story to the media."

"That's inexcusable, Dan. The perp should be found, fired and prosecuted. The leak to the media is placing lives in danger, especially the life of Courtney Burke, the woman the media are all labeling a suspected serial killer."

"My apologies, Sean, okay? This has never happened in the department before now. It's only because of this unbelievable media coverage; someone got greedy."

"And dangerous."

"Speaking of danger, there was a report of a fight in the parking lot of the Lone Wolf Saloon, a hangout for the Outlaws and other biker types with about the same criminal IQ qualifications. The owner said someone assaulted a customer, no, he beat the living shit out of him. And then pinned him to a wooden deck with an icepick through the hand. Sounds like an eye-for-an-eye kind of retribution. And that wasn't easy to do since they report the victim is six-six, two-ninety-five. Witnesses describe the perpetrator as a man with a resemblance to you. Whoever this guy was, he blew up the vic's custom motorcycle, a bike some would kill for."

"Is the vic pressing charges?"

"No, but if he does, do you have an alibi for your time?"

"I was visiting with Carlos Bandini. You can ask him."

"Hey, Sean, let's get something straight. Because you were once a cop, the fact that we have a past together on that psycho federal agent case, I grant you slack and some professional leeway. But you don't have nine lives. Your law of averages is expiring, pal. And now you have all this shit with your former girlfriend—the wife of a presidential contender...and maybe a biological tie to a girl who could be your daughter. Every man has his breaking point."

"Can you run a phone number through your system?"

"Did you hear me?"

"Yes."

"Hearing and listening aren't the same. What's the number?"

I told him and said, "The area code, eight-one-three, covers Tampa and the surrounding area. Can you pinpoint it with a location, or a name?"

"It depends. People are using everything from throw-away phones to Internet phones. It's not as easy as it used to be when they had to always go through a carrier. I'll call you back."

FORTY-SIX

Within twenty minutes, rain began falling across the marina, an Atlantic storm moving in from the west. Lightning illuminated the marina for a second, the crack of thunder almost immediate. Nick sauntered from the couch to a side window on *St. Michael*. He said, "Maybe the rains will wash away the reporters. Looks like most of them are splitting. Lightning has a way of doing that."

Dave chuckled. "They'll be back."

I finished the plate of seafood and felt the knots between my shoulder blades begin to loosen a little. For a second, I thought of Kim Davis, her smile as I walked her in the rain to her car the other night. I sipped the Corona and said, "There are a couple of things I didn't mention."

Nick returned to the couch, Max following him. He attempted a smile and said, "Don't hold back now."

Dave nodded. "Tell us you found a DNA sample from Courtney."

"I wish, primarily for her sake, and Andrea's too."

"Unless she's your daughter, and this begins a whole new chapter that will make political history books." Dave swirled the vodka around the ice in the glass.

"Two guys, maybe federal agents, I don't know for sure, but they weren't connected to Bandini. They'd been following me for miles until I had breakfast at Denny's where a server accidently spilled ice cold soda in their laps."

Dave said, "Serendipitous, no doubt. They probably weren't federal agents, although Senator Logan has been assigned Secret Service protection. Logan and the Democrat's candidate, Governor Les Connors, are raising tens of millions of dollars from the Super Pacs, donors who have anonymity and thus no responsibility. Analogous to the lack of culpability that one might find in the collective mentality of a lynch mob. Nevertheless, there is so much concealed money going into these campaigns, what's a few hundred thou to hire mercenaries? It's the cost of doing business in an election method where the vote, the majority will of the people, doesn't always translate into a win."

"That's essentially what Andrea Logan told me earlier on the phone."

Nick's dark eyebrows arched. "Your old girlfriend has your number?"

"Yes." I looked over to Dave. "And she believes Courtney might never surface if her husband's closest advisors can prevent it. She overheard a conversation to that effect, and she's terrified."

Dave folded his brown arms over his thick chest. He leaned back on the stool and said, "So a presidential candidate could be complicit in a murder on his way to the White House. His wife is indeed terrified for a lot of reasons, perhaps first is the real possibility that the young woman whose life is in danger may be her daughter."

I told them about my call to the person who answered the number I'd memorized from Isaac Solminski's call history. "What intrigues me is not so much what he said, but what he didn't say and how he phrased some things."

"What do you mean?" Dave asked.

He said, *'Although we have no one here by that name, if someone arrives with the name, Courtney, what message would you like for me to give to her?'* That sounds like he's working in a hotel or a motel."

Nick said, "That narrows it down."

I said nothing, watching the rain against the salon window. My phone rang. Dan Grant said, "Sean, I have an approximate match for you on the number."

"What is it?"

"It pinged off a cell tower near a small town south of Tampa called Gibsonton. It's tied to an apparent fictitious name, Showtime Estates, associated with a post office box. You think the girl is somehow connected to wherever this number leads?"

"Maybe. I'm not sure."

"Where'd you get it?"

"From Isaac Solminski, the dwarf at Bandini's carnival."

"Why'd he give it to you?"

"He didn't actually provide it. I happened to see it in his call history."

I heard Dan release a long exhale. "Gibsonton or Gibtown, from what I remember, is or was the winter home for circus and carnival people. An odd place off the Tamiami Trail. Maybe Solminski's just touching base with old friends or a family member."

"Could be."

"Sounds like a long-shot to me, especially when we don't have a physical address, no location."

"You're probably right."

He was hesitant for a few seconds. "Be careful, Sean, remember what I told you about those nine lives. I personally believe you've used up eight and are working overtime on number nine.

Talk to you." He disconnected.

"Nick, where's your laptop?"

"Right here." He reached beneath the coffee table, under a stack of boating and cooking magazines, pulled out a MacBook Pro, turned it on, then handed it to me,

Dave said, "You sounded a little more civil with your detective friend. Did he come through after the DNA debacle?"

"He said the number I lifted from Isaac Solminski's phone is coming from somewhere in a town called Gibsonton."

"Where's that?"

"South of Tampa."

"You trying to find it on the map?" Nick asked.

"That's part of it. I'm also looking for a hotel near some railroad tracks. When I was talking with the guy on the phone, I heard a large dog barking and a train very close by to wherever he was at the time." I quickly found train routes on an Internet map. The nearest location of tracks, relative to Gibsonton, was close to Highway 41, over a body of water called Bullfrog Creek. I checked for motels on both the north and south sides of the waterway. I stood and reach for my Glock.

"Where you going?" Dave asked.

"Gibsonton. Should be able to make it in about four hours."

"You think Courtney's there?"

"Maybe. Somebody's there who knows Solminski. He's made too many calls to that number since Courtney ran away. He could have sent her there… to someone and someplace he feels is safe."

Dave stood and stared out the window towards the parking lot. "Looks like the storm chased the news media lads and lasses away. Storm's moving west, so you'll be traveling with it. Here's something to keep in mind, Sean: Andrea Logan is frightened. Who knows how well she can disguise it. But if there's any reason to suspect she may do or say something that will blemish her husband's electability, you can bet they'll try to catch it before it becomes a liability. That means her phone calls might be tapped. If Andrea's are, then you can bet yours are or will be, too."

Nick sat on the edge of the couch. "So that means they might know about Gibtown, and they fact that's where Sean's going to hunt for the girl."

Dave nodded. "That's exactly what it means."

I said, "Please keep an eye on Max for me."

Dave asked, "So you're still going there tonight?"

"Yes. The place I found nearest the train track is called the Show-Town Fish Camp. They rent cottages and trailers. I'm going to see if they have a big dog."

FORTY-SEVEN

Courtney Burke finished eating a bowl of tomato soup she'd heated in the microwave, washed dishes, and folded extra towels for Boots. She refused to stay in the trailer for free, and doing some extra work for him was the right thing to do. She heard the 8:00 pm freight train cross the trestle over the creek, and she looked at the clock above the control panel on the microwave.

Leaving at dawn. Better pack my stuff. She half smiled. There was no stuff to pack. Not really. Another pair of jeans, underwear, and two T-shirts. She tried to remember the last time she wore a dress. *Mama's funeral…that was the last time. God, it felt like a hundred years ago.* She thought about her grandmother, thought about what she must be going through listening to the news and all the crazy stuff about the senator's wife, Sean O'Brien, and how she might be their daughter. Then she heard Boots' falsetto voice echo in her mind. *'This may sound like a strange question, but I'm strange, okay? Could your parents have adopted you?'*

She felt hot, air difficult to get deep into her lungs. The last time she had an asthma attack she had been running, running from the carnival after Lonnie was murdered. She'd had her inhaler with her, but lost it later that night when Sean O'Brien kept those men away from her.

She opened the door to the trailer and stepped outside. The air was a little cooler, but not by much. She stood on the seawall and hugged her bare arms, sucking air into her lungs. *Just breathe, stay calm.* She looked up and saw a firefly a few feet from her face. Her breathing became easier, back to normal.

She bit her lower lip and felt a warm stream of tears roll from her eyes, down her cheeks, falling into the creek. She was so tired, and so alone. She looked up at the moon peeking through the marshes, reflecting from the dark water. There was the solitary hoot of an owl across the creek.

She turned to go back to the trailer.

A noise.

The sound of something moving near the right side of the trailer—close to the canoes. *Gun's too far away—inside.* Courtney stood there. Barely breathing. Heart racing. A shadow moved by the garbage can. Gradually, a fat raccoon looked up at her from behind a hard plastic trash can, the black mask around its eyes like a burglar in the night. Courtney smiled. "Hello, Mr. Coon. You scared the dickens outta me. Sorry, but you won't get much from that. I've been eating soup, and we recycle the cans." The raccoon stood on its hind quarters for a moment, sniffed the breeze off the water, and waddled across the yard.

Courtney saw lightning in the distance, to the east. *Maybe rain will cool things down.* She walked back to the trailer, went inside, and locked the door behind her. She undressed and crawled into bed, her mind racing, the heat in the small trailer building. The last sound she heard was the train in the distance crossing the trestle over Bullfrog Creek.

— —

SHE WAS AWAKENED by another noise. She sat up in bed, the oscillating fan on the dresser pushing hot air around her bedroom. *Darn, hardheaded coon. Go away.* Then, the sound stopped. She could hear the frogs and cicadas competing in a rousing nocturnal tug-of-war chorus. The sound of thunder rolled a few miles away. *How much time before daylight?* She tossed and turned on the hard bed, her sheets and flat pillow damp with perspiration.

How long had it been since the train rolled by, heading to some northern city? An hour? Maybe two? She lay there, wishing for the morning sunlight to slip through the cracks in the venetian blinds. But now it was dark, so dark she couldn't see her hand in front of her face. There was a whine near her ear. A mosquito. She scratched at her forearm and sat up in bed. She flipped on the light, looking around the room for the mosquito. It alighted on her left arm.

She smacked it, leaving a red stain of blood the size of a nickel. "Oh crap," she said, walking into the kitchen to wash the blood off her arm and hand.

Standing at the sink, she felt it getting harder to breathe, to fill her lungs in the hot trailer. She turned out the light, unfastened the lock on one window, slid the glass up, and put her face close to the screen. The cooler air felt good on her damp skin. She sucked air into her lungs, and closed her eyes a moment.

A dog barked.

Fast barking. Courtney recognized it as Clementine the cockatoo. But this wasn't her normal imitation of a dog bark. It was her frightened mock barking—of a dog agitated, in fear. She remembered what Boots had said: *'Clementine may be able to imitate sounds, but in her tiny bird brain she has a sixth sense about real threats. Heed her warning.'*

Courtney looked up at the Fish Camp office. The lights were coming on. One…two…lights turned on, then the side floodlights illuminated the perimeter yard. Courtney saw the silhouette of a man standing near the office. She could see a pistol in one hand. Her heart slammed in her chest. She grabbed blue jeans, shimmied into them, and pulled a T-shirt over her head. She took the Beretta out of a drawer and scooped up the keys to the truck. If there was more than one intruder, maybe she could create a diversion to save Boots' life. She lit a candle on the kitchen table, turned on the gas stove without igniting the pilot light, quietly opened the door, and stepped out into the night.

Clementine started the barking sounds again. In less than five seconds, the barks ended. Courtney ran by the canoes on blocks, keeping low. She pressed against the wooden fence that went from the trailer up to the office and the circular drive where the truck was parked. The fence was covered in blooming bougainvillea. She tried to keep the orange and tangerine trees between her and whoever had entered where Boots lived and worked. She was shaking. Breathing shallow. Adrenaline pumping into her bloodstream. A taste like ashes on her tongue. She was frightened for Boots. Was the man inside? Did Boots have his gun? Did he have time to get it?

She held the Beretta in both hands and stayed in the darkest shadows. Lightning flashed in the distance. In that second, she saw two men enter the office from two different doors. Both had guns.

Go! Run! Take the keys, jump in the truck. Leave. She fought the strong urge to flee. Run hard and fast to the truck. She remembered one thing her father had taught about hunting deer. *'You can stalk a buck all day. Maybe never get off a shot. Or you can surprise him from a stand and bring a buck to his knees with a clean shot.'*

She stayed in the long shadows cast by the royal palm trees. Moving closer to the office. She knew the layout. Bedrooms. Kitchen. Bathrooms. Screened porch that served as an aviary. The make-shift lobby. Where would Boots be at the moment? She heard noises—a man yelling. Another man said, "Where's the girl?" She couldn't hear Boot's voice. Then there was a noise that sounded like the thrust of a bottle rocket—a staccato puff sound.

Within seconds, the two men were coming out of the screened door. She ducked behind a sago palm tree. They ran right by her. Courtney stood, raised the pistol, and aimed. She could hear her father's voice, his advice about deer hunting. But these were men, not deer. She lowered the Beretta as the men went around to the front of the trailer. She heard them kick in the door. Three seconds later, the trailer exploded in a massive white and orange ball of fire that rose higher than the live oak by the creek.

Even from the distance, she could feel the heat against her face and exposed arms. She turned and ran into the aviary, stopping at the base of the T-stand. Clementine was on her back, her neck broken. Courtney held her hand to her mouth, tears forming. She ran in the office and froze as she entered the lobby. Boots lay in a pool of dark blood, a single bullet wound between his open eyes.

"Oh God!" Courtney cried out. She ran backwards, stumbled to the bathroom and vomited in the toilet. She picked herself up and ran from the building, hands shaking so much she couldn't get the key into the truck ignition. She started the engine, pulled away from the circular drive and drove off into the night. When she glanced up into the rearview mirror, the flames looked like the plume of a fiery volcano.

FORTY-EIGHT

I didn't need the GPS to tell me I'd reached my destination. A raging fire told me that. I pulled my Jeep into the circular driveway of Show Time Fish Camp. I drove past a dark SUV near the entrance. Neighbors were spilling out of nearby trailers, wearing pajamas and shocked looks on the faces of what appeared to be mostly retired people. I saw a woman in a red bathrobe hold up her phone. Maybe she'd dialed 911.

As I parked, I could hear the sound of sirens in the distance. I lifted my Glock from under the seat of the Jeep, got out, and peered in through the open door with a bronze plate on it that spelled: *Office*. I took one step inside and listened for a few seconds. All I could hear was the crackling of the fire roaring from somewhere beyond the office.

I held the Glock in both hands. Walked silently. There was a movement out of the right corner of my eye. I aimed the pistol to the floor where a large white and yellow snake crawled over the chest of man who'd been shot in the head. The entrance wound looked to be a small caliber gun, maybe a .22. His lips were blue. No sign of breathing. Open eyes staring up at a ceiling fan. He was a dwarf with some features resembling Isaac Solminski. The snake slithered off the body, through a large pool of blood near the dead man's head, leaving a bloody S pattern as it crawled across a white tile floor.

I quietly searched each room. Nothing. No sign of the perp or perps and no sign of Courtney Burke. Beyond the office was what appeared to be a screened-in aviary, filled with orchids, other flowers, and a few birds. I spotted two blue and orange lovebirds sitting on an open perch. I almost stepped on a large white cockatoo lying dead on the floor near a bushy philodendron.

I ran outside as rain began to fall over the area, the water doing little to douse a fire more than two-hundred feet away from the office. I sprinted through citrus trees towards the firestorm. It looked like a trailer or mobile home was burning. I searched for a garden hose. Nothing. The thought of Courtney Burke trapped in that incinerator made my hands feel as hot as the flames against my face. The trailer was less than twenty-five feet from a river, and no way to get water from it. Where was Courtney?

My heart hammered in my chest. I felt absolutely powerless. I assumed police would be here probably before I could leave the neighborhood. The trailer was so engulfed in a maelstrom of flames, if anyone was inside it they would be cremated. And there was nothing I could do for the dead man inside the office.

The air smelled of soot, burnt rubber and plastic—and something I smelled on the scene of a plane crash in the Everglades…charred flesh. There was not a doubt in my mind that someone died in the fire, I just didn't know who. I felt a drop of cold rain run down the back of my neck as I dialed 911.

I reported the shooting and fire, and I left them with my name. The incentive call was to ease their suspicion about me when the cavalry arrived. My thoughts raced, searching for evidence, maybe something dropped on the ground—something to connect Courtney to this place. I could see very little in the drifting smoke and pelting rain. I thought about the black Lincoln SUV near the drive. Whose was it, and where was that person or persons?

The wail of sirens and horns filled the night air now pulsating with the flash of blue and white emergency lights, radios crackling with staccato bursts, handguns drawn. They were followed by firefighters. I tucked the Glock behind my back and under my shirt as they rolled hoses from the tankers, through the side yard, down to the inferno. I looked back to the office and could see police, detectives, and paramedics working the scene. A few minutes later, a young police officer approached me. He held a long flashlight and a short pistol, a .38. "Who are you, sir?" he asked. "And what is your business standing here in these orange trees?"

"My name's Sean O'Brien. I arrived twenty minutes ago looking for a friend of mine I had reason to believe might be staying here. When I arrived, the fire was burning down there, front door open, and a man's body on the floor. I called nine-one-one."

"I need to see some ID…slowly use one hand."

I complied and used one hand to lift my wallet from my pocket. Two more officers approached, each positioning themselves strategically on opposite sides of me.

"Okay, Mr. O'Brien," the first officer said. "This person you knew, why would you be trying to find her at five a.m.?"

"Because she needed help. She's asthmatic."

"Did you find her?" He glanced at the burning trailer for a moment.

"No, and when I got here that trailer was fully involved."

A tall man dressed in a tweed sports coat and blue jeans approached. He wore no tie, badge clipped to his belt, eyes red and puffy, morning stubble on his thin face. "I'm Detective Lawrence." He glanced over my shoulder to the fire. "What'd you see?" "As I told your officers, not a lot. A dead man in the office. A snake crawling across the floor, and that trailer engulfed in flames."

"Are you armed?"

"Yes."

All three the officers pulled guns out of their holsters and pointed them at my chest.

Detective Lawrence said, "Interlock your fingers and put your hands behind your head." I did so and he motioned to one of the officers. "Search and disarm him."

The officer nodded, pulled on white cotton gloves and carefully removed the Glock from under my shirt and then patted me down. The detective said, "Why didn't you bother to let anyone know you were carrying?"

"No one asked. I have a permit to carry that gun."

"Not at an apparent homicide scene you don't."

"I'm the one who called in the shooting and the fire. And I waited for you to arrive. If I shot that vic, why would I do that?"

"Vic? Were you in law enforcement?"

"A long time ago. Homicide. Miami-Dade PD. Look, that entrance wound on the vic's forehead was caused by a much smaller caliber gun than the Glock, especially at close range. You can check my gun. It hasn't been fired, at least not today. Fully loaded."

He said nothing for a few seconds, his green eyes reflecting the orange flames. "Doesn't take but a few seconds to reload. Are you now a private investigator?"

"Nope. I'm a fisherman. I was here because a friend of the deceased thought a young woman I'm searching for might be here."

"What's her name?"

"Courtney Burke."

His jaw muscles tightened. "Courtney Burke. Is she the same person suspected in the multiple deaths near Daytona?"

"She's a person of interest."

Then he made a disdainful grin out of one side of his mouth. "Now it's coming into focus. You're the Sean O'Brien who's all over the news. The old boyfriend of Senator Logan's wife…and Courtney Burke just might be your daughter."

"In your business, you should know you can't believe everything you see on cable TV."

"Tell you what I do believe, I believe she's wanted for serial murders."

"She's presumed innocent until proven guilty in a court of law, not a court of public opinion."

He shook his head. "We'll be taking you to the sheriff's office to talk more about all of this. Swab him for gunshot residue, too, Wally."

"You might want to talk with the drivers or owners of that black SUV out front. Since it's still here, odds are the occupants could be in what's left of that trailer. Or maybe my alleged daughter's in there."

He motioned with his head and two officers escorted me across the lawn, around the side of the office, and over two fire hoses, water leaking from their connections. We rounded the building and stepped into a blaze of TV news lights and reporters behind yellow crime scene tape. I heard one reporter shout, "It's the guy who's mixed up in the affair with Andrea Logan."

More questions peppered me from behind outstretched microphones and the glare of lights. One of the officers opened the rear door to the police cruiser and motioned for me to enter. We drove off into golden sunlight just breaking through the tall bamboo and coconut palms, and I was without my Jeep, my Glock, and the girl who might be my daughter. If she had been staying in that trailer, any DNA proof of her existence on earth was gone as a new day dawned over the planet.

FORTY-NINE

I owed the lady in red a debt of gratitude. Two hours into answering the same questions from three detectives, a fourth came in from the field. He was pushing retirement, early sixties, jowls like a basset hound, and drowsy eyes with a touch of cataracts in one. He sat with me in the interrogation room and related her story. Gladys Johnston, the woman in the red bathrobe, had been shooting video on her mobile phone, video of the roaring fire near Bullfrog Creek.

And it was video that happened to capture my arrival, after the fire, and after two men had appeared at least fifteen minutes before me.

Gladys, a former trapeze artist who worked in circuses around the nation, told police that her world now was her close-knit community. As captain of her Neighborhood Watch, she knew everyone. She didn't know the two men who got out of the black Escalade. Strangers in dark clothes. Years earlier, a trapeze accident had caused damage to Gladys's back. At 5:00 a.m. today she was at the kitchen sink sipping water and taking aspirin for an old injury when she noticed a car quietly pull up to Show Time Fish Camp with its headlights off. It was hot and her window at the sink had been open, a breeze coming through the screen. Gladys told detectives that when she didn't see the dome interior light come on as the men got out of the SUV, didn't hear them slam the doors, her radar came on.

And when they started picking the lock, she went to wake up her sleeping husband.

I was glad for Gladys and me. I was getting my Glock back and Jeep returned, but I had no indication that Courtney Burke had been living in the trailer park. As I started to leave the sheriff's department, the senior detective said, "I found out about your history with Miami-Dade PD. Did you ever know Gus Mansfield?"

"I remember that he was a guy with great investigative instincts. I didn't actually work with his division, but I knew of his talents."

"We worked together in Detroit until we got tired of the cold and corruption. Came south. Gus was a bird dog 'til he got hit in a crossfire with the Colombian Cartel. Now he's in a wheelchair." His eyes drifted around the room for a few seconds. He blinked hard and stood from the chair. "We need to get you out the back entrance. Get your car from the compound and avoid all those damn reporters in the lobby and parking lot."

"I appreciate it."

"When I came in, must have been more than two dozen news media hounds out there. All of 'em got their sights set on you. C'mon, you've been here long enough." He stopped on his way to the door. "Oh, by the way. Don't know if anybody's told you this,

but the coroner pulled two bodies from that fire." I felt my pulse quicken. He shook his head. "Burned beyond any sort of recognition. Don't even know if they'll be able to get dentals."

"Can they determine gender?"

"Looks to be what's left of two men. Probably the perps who broke into the Fish Camp office. I hope the poor bastards died in the explosion and didn't burn to death. They're crispy critters now." He sighed and led me down the hallway to the rear exit.

I shook his hand asked, "Did forensics find anything near the body of the dwarf?"

"A damn big snake. Talk about weird blood trails—try tracking a snake that crawled through a bloody crime scene. The perps, though, left nothing. Vehicle they arrived in was wiped clean or they wore gloves. It was a rental—prepaid, cash. Non-traceable credit card number. Whoever they were, even if we could ID the bodies, we'd be hard-pressed to follow the bread trail to where the kill order came from." He looked at me curiously for a second. "I know you said you were hunting for the girl. Looks like somebody wanted to find her as much as you do. How did the two dead guys know or believe she was there?"

"That's what I've been thinking about since you told me the two bodies were found."

"No one we questioned at the trailer park remembers seeing the girl." He paused and undid his burgundy tie with a small coffee stain near the knot. "I hope you find her first. I got a bad feeling in these old bones that some ruthless sons-of-bitches are looking for her. Good luck to you. Here's the keys to your Jeep. It's parked in the row closest to the building."

— —

I DROVE A perimeter road around the sheriff's office and the adjacent county courthouse. I looked to my right before getting on the highway and almost did a double-take. I counted more than eight satellite news trucks anchored in front of the building, open dishes aimed to the sky, supposition aimed at the masses.

My plan was to drive back to Ponce Inlet, pick up Max and head to our river cabin and try to assess what to do next. There, at least, I could be somewhat isolated from the news media, let calm return to Ponce Marina, and have a more secure fortress to lie low in the event I was still being followed. I had no idea where Courtney was, where she'd been, or where she was going. I thought I was close to finding her before all hell broke loose, before a man was shot between the eyes, and one of his trailers became scorched earth with the charred remains of two bodies under the rubble.

The one thing I was certain of was that the two dead guys didn't follow me to the Fish Camp. They knew about it probably very close to the time that I figured out that Courtney might be hiding there. And this meant one thing: my phone was tapped. That's a good and bad thing. Bad because privacy is lost. Good because I can set a trap.

— —

A HALF HOUR later, I parked in front of the trailer where I'd seen the woman in the red bathrobe standing when I first arrived at the Fish Camp. Her small yard was cast in deep shade, red and white impatiens planted in a circle around the base of a live oak tree. I heard her talking loudly before I actually saw her. Gladys Johnston sat on a rattan couch inside a screened-in porch, fanning her face with a Japanese hand fan. I said, "I just wanted to personally thank you. My name's Sean O'Brien. Thank you for talking with police."

"Come in." I heard her say a fast goodbye to whomever was on the phone. She stood and smiled as I entered the porch. Her aged face was still attractive. Her eyes were robust and the color of blue swimming pool water. I could tell she would have been a striking woman in her prime. She said, "I've seen you on TV. Was the senator's wife really your old girlfriend?"

"That was more than twenty years ago."

"And now they're saying you two might have a daughter." She fanned and dipped her head slightly. "That's who you're hunting for, right?"

"Did you see a girl staying at the Fish Camp?"

"Most folks who rent Boots' trailers are repeats. Snowbirds who'd come down from up north every winter. They usually stay through tax time, middle of April. Mostly fishermen and their families rent here in the summer. But Boots, I can't believe what happened to him; he was such a nice man. He only had six rental units on that three-acre property. The one that blew up and burned to the ground was the most isolated."

"Do you think the girl may have been staying there?"

"Maybe. Boots, sweet as he was, was a little weird. And I don't mean in some kind of sexual deviant type of way. I come from a circus background, okay, so when I say weird, I know what I'm talking about. He was always on, as in on stage. He sort of kept to himself, though." She glanced across the street to the Fish Camp, a piece of ripped yellow crime-scene tape flapping in the breeze. Her eyes narrowed a notch. She touched her lips with two bent and swollen arthritic fingers. "Something's different and for the life of me I don't know what it is."

"Since you shot video of those men arriving, maybe I could take a look, okay?"

She cocked her head and lifted one manicured eyebrow. "I can do that." She set the hand fan down on the coffee table and picked up her iPhone. "Here it is. I'll play it for you."

I moved over and sat beside her on the couch. She tapped the stationary image and video filled the screen. Although the images were grainy, shot under the light of one street lamp, I watched as two men appeared from the shadows, one quickly picking the lock and both entering the building. The video ended at that point.

"Here's where I started again," she said, tapping a second frozen image, the video began to play.

I watched myself enter the building, the fire raging beyond the office. I saw something in the second video, something missing.

"Did you see that?" I asked.

"See what?"

"There's something gone from the second video."

"What's gone?"

"A pickup truck. In the first video, I noticed one very small portion of the tailgate. It was to the far left of the screen, which means it was parked to the left of the circular drive. It was gone in the second video, which you shot only a few minutes later, correct?"

She looked up from the phone screen to across the street. Her mouth opened, eyes unsure. "Yes. Boots always kept an old red Toyota truck parked under the live oak to the left of the front door.

It's gone."

"When did you last see it parked there?"

"Before I went to bed. Didn't notice it during all the commotion. The cops hauled that SUV away. They left Boots' Ford, and I'm pretty sure they left the truck, too." She turned her head towards the open door to the mobile home and shouted, "Ike, when's the last time you saw Boots' truck?"

I heard a man clear his throat and yell, "Yesterday I think. Can't be a hundred percent sure anymore."

She turned back to me and folded the Japanese fan, putting it on a glass coffee table next to a vase with plastic blue flowers. "If the girl was there, maybe she stole the truck."

"Maybe Boots let her borrow it." I smiled.

"That's a possibility. But whoever took the truck must have done it when I went to get my husband out of bed. I showed this video to police, they made a copy, but I don't think they noticed the small section of the truck that you saw. You're observant."

I smiled and stood up to leave. "If you don't mention it to them, they'll never know it's gone."

She reached for the fan and opened it like a peacock spreading its feathers. She fanned her face and said, "I hope you find her."

FIFTY

I was leaving Gladys Johnston's driveway when a propane gas delivery truck rolled to a stop in front of the Fish Camp. The side of the red truck with the large white propane tank read: *Paul's Propane Service.* I watched a twenty-something service tech get out of the truck, clipboard in hand, toting a small camera. He looked at the crime scene tape flapping in the breeze and made a decision to enter the property. I parked and followed him.

He was about halfway down the property line when he stopped, almost like he had paused to pay his respects to those in a funeral procession. He stared at what was left of the trailer. I walked up behind him and said, "I don't think they'll be needing gas for the immediate future."

He jumped like he'd been touch with a cattle prod. "Man! You scared the crap outta me."

"Sheriff's deputies will scare you more if they see you traipsing through a crime scene."

"I thought that yellow tape was just hanging all over the ground, like they're pretty much done."

"Not yet."

"I'll be quick, I'm just taking a couple of pictures. It's for insurance. I can see it wasn't our tanks that exploded. They're still in one piece, pretty black from the fire, but they didn't blow. Man, I just filled 'em, too. Couple of days ago. So if somebody left the gas on, they got lots of gas to ignite."

"When you filled the tanks did you see the girl living in the trailer?"

"She was feeding some ducks down there in the creek." He turned and looked closer at the remains of the trailer. "She wasn't hurt...was she? The news said two guys were killed in the fire."

"She apparently wasn't home when it happened."

He inhaled deeply, reassured, nodding. "That's good. She was real nice. This explosion and fire's bad enough, but when you know somebody involved it sort of makes it personal."

"Yes, it does. What'd she look like?"

"The girl?"

"Yes."

He looked back down to the creek as if she was standing on the bank. "She was really pretty. About five-five, I'd say. She had dark brown hair...and her eyes." He glanced back at me. "Her eyes were the prettiest I've ever seen. It's hard to describe them."

"I know what you mean."

"Well, I best take the picture and be on my route."

— —

I CAUGHT I-75 north and headed across the state of Florida back to Ponce Inlet. I watched the traffic behind me, looking for a tail. I pushed the Jeep to near one-hundred miles an hour for a minute, then pulled off the interstate at a rest stop, parking on the side of the building farther from the highway. I watched for cars pulling into the rest stop, those passing in the event a driver might hit his brakes. Three cars entered the parking lot. One had a family of five, including a grandmother. The second car had two teenagers in it. The third was pulling a small boat. Two fishermen shuffled out, faces red from the sun, and walked to the restroom. I started my Jeep, placed the Glock on the passenger seat, and made my way back to the highway.

As I drove north, I now knew that Courtney Burke had been hiding in the trailer before it exploded, she was driving a red Toyota pick-up truck, and she was probably long gone from Gibsonton. On one hand, I wanted to call Detective Dan Grant and tell him what I knew. On the other hand, not so much. If my phone was tapped, my calling Dan would alert killers hunting

Courtney. Dan and state police would issue a BOLO and set up a dragnet on major roads leading out of Tampa and Florida.

Since two men hunting Courtney had just died, and because one man giving her a safe haven was murdered, I knew that Courtney could easily be shot to death during a road-side stop. *Subject resisting arrest*, the report would read. *Armed and dangerous*. As long as the elimination was not in the immediate scope of the dashboard cameras, cross-fire shootings can be beyond accusation and reprimand.

The presidential election was coming up quickly. Somehow I had to keep Courtney safe until then, and that's if Senator Logan's opponent won. What would it mean if Logan won? Would Courtney always be a political liability? If she was found innocent of the charges, would that lessen her embarrassment factor? Andrea Logan would no longer be labeled the possible mother of a serial killer. But that would mean finding Courtney and getting a DNA sample first. That alone would clear the landscape for Logan or destroy it. Were they willing to roll the dice? The two dead guys in the fire spoke volumes. And now, under the circumstances, there was no safe jail or prison to hold her in some kind of protective custody.

I needed to buy a couple of disposable mobile phones, and then make a call to Dave or Dan Grant that would set in motion a trap that would catch hired guns and maybe free Courtney from what I now knew was a death sentence.

FIFTY-ONE

When Courtney Burke reached New Orleans, the rain that seemed to have followed her since Florida, ended. She'd driven straight through, stopping once to put gas in the truck and to use the restroom. There had been very little news on the radio stations that constantly faded in and out as she drove through the night.

She didn't know if her face was still plastered everywhere, of if she could move about with relative anonymity. She remembered what Boots had told her: *There will be a lot of people trying to locate you. Isaac and I both believe this could be very dangerous for you. Your face is on all the news stations and online. You must be very careful.'*

She turned onto Decatur Street, saw the sign for Café Du Monde, and then entered the parking lot. Tourists roamed the streets, hopping horse-drawn carriages, watching street performers and snapping pictures. With so many people about, Courtney thought she'd blend in better in a city like New Orleans.

She parked, slipped on a pair of dark glasses, and a baseball cap Boots had given her. She fixed her hair in a ponytail, and pulled it through the open spot in the back of the hat. She unfolded the piece of paper and read Boot's writing: Mariah Danford, 41 Dumaine. Courtney got out of the truck and walked towards Café Du Monde.

She could see the three towers of the old St. Louis Cathedral across the park-like setting of Jackson Square, church bells ringing in the distance, the oaks alive with birdsong. Portrait artists were setting up shop on the tree-lined street, opening beach-sized umbrellas, propping up easels. She watched a man wearing a Star Trek T-shirt and black derby twist balloons into animal caricatures. Another performer was dressed in Civil War uniform. His entire body was spray-painted in shades of Confederate gray. He stood motionless, a human statue in the park, only moving his head or arms when an unsuspecting tourist approached to take a picture.

The morning air was filled with the smell of chicory coffee, blooming camellias, and fresh-cut grass. Courtney watched the Mississippi River roll quietly by as horse-drawn carriages traveled down Decatur. She heard the trot of hooves on the pavement and carriage drivers telling riders about the history of the square, the cathedral, and Jax Brewery.

She ordered two beignets and a large café au lait at Café Du Monde. After Courtney paid for them at the counter, she asked the middle-aged woman running the cash register if she knew how to get to Dumaine Street.

"You're not far, honey," she said, counting back change. "Five blocks down Decatur and then take a right onto Dumaine."

Courtney found an empty park bench close to Jackson Square under the shade of old live oaks draped in tousled cloaks of Spanish moss. The beignets, warm and covered in powdered sugar, tasted delicious to her. The hot coffee seemed to flow into her through all her pores, warming her. For the first time since Boots' murder, she could breathe easier without her lungs feeling as empty as her heart.

"Draw a pretty picture for a pretty lady," came a voice from behind her.

Courtney turned around and saw a street artist bend in a slight bow from the waist, tipping his medieval Robin Hood-type hat. It was fern green with a red feather wedged into one side of the hatband. He stood straight and grinned, a dark black goatee on his round face, eyes the color of his hat. Courtney thought the man probably weighed close to three-hundred pounds.

He said, "Hello, me lady. You can be my first portrait of the morning. I assure you that all other portraits after you today, and tomorrow for that matter, will pale by comparison. I am Little John, and I'm at your service."

Courtney swallowed a bite of beignet and looked up at the man, the morning sunlight in his plump face, left eye squinting, the rumble of a tug-boat diesel pushing a barge up the Mississippi. "Thanks, but I really don't need my picture drawn."

"Why so serious?"

"Just tired, that's all."

"It's more than that. I can tell because I look at faces all day."

"No offense, but you don't need to be staring at mine."

"Since I draw caricatures of people, I look at how faces have certain, let's say unique qualities, and then I just use pen and ink to embellish them. And because I study faces all day here in front of Jackson square, I'm a pretty good reader."

"I have to go."

"Some people read cards, some read palms, and I try to grasp the energy of the person in the time it takes me to sketch out the crux of the face. I always begin with the eyes. Would you mind taking off your sunglasses?"

"I told you I wasn't interested in having my picture drawn. Please, just go away."

"I can't. This is my office, or studio."

"Then I'll leave."

He smiled and angled his head. "Tell you what, I'll do it for free. Your only cost is the twenty minutes of your life it takes me to capture you on canvas."

"I don't want to be captured on canvas."

"Before I started doing caricatures, I was a police sketch artist. Did thousands of sketches of bad guys and gals just from descriptions people remembered. I find now that it's hard for me to forget a face I've drawn or wanted real bad to draw." He pulled a phone out of his jean's pocket and raised it to snap a picture of Courtney.

She lifted her hand in front of her face. "No!"

"Aw, c'mon. Such a pretty face. Even with the hat and glasses, I can tell."

Courtney turned her back to the man, grabbed her bag of beignets and her coffee, and walked quickly away from him. After she'd gone farther away, she looked back for a second and saw him talking on the phone. *How'd he make such a quick call? Maybe he dialed 9-1-1. I've been spotted!* Her heart raced. How could she escape or hide in a city she didn't even know?

Think! She ran, trying to ensure that there were trees, cars, people, and objects blocking the view of the street artist to her movements towards the

Toyota truck. She ran across the parking lot, jumped in the truck and started it. She remembered the directions the cashier had given her, and Courtney drove down Decatur Street, hoping that the woman named Mariah Danford was home.

FIFTY-TWO

I bought two disposable phones and used one to make a call to Dave Collins. I told him what happened and he said, "So right now there isn't a posse on the tail of an older model red Toyota pickup truck, but it's just a matter of a short time before that changes. Courtney may still be in Florida. It's unfortunate that in her wake three more people are dead. Two probably because they were, no doubt, hired guns who stepped in the wrong trailer at the wrong time. So their SUV was wiped clean and no one has a clue who leased it, right?"

"Someone does."

"Of course. I'd love to follow the bread trail back to wherever the hit order originated. Maybe it was Bandini."

"I don't think so. Why would they shoot the dwarf? These guys took orders from bigger fish—sharks, and they smell blood. Maybe they were the two guys who followed me into the Denny's parking lot, or could be from the same litter. Somehow Courtney survived the first attack. I've got to find her before they do. If I can prove that she's not Andrea Logan's biological daughter, Courtney will no longer be a liability in the eyes of corporations and PACs funding Logan's presidential bid."

"But if you prove the opposite it will be deadly for her."

"It's already deadly. I don't have a choice."

"Yes you do. This kid's stepped into the middle of some serious defecation. And by default, she's taken you with her. We need to think this through, Sean. Every possibility, angle and probability. The irony is the more visible you are, the less likely that someone will put a bullet in your head. With your old connection to Andrea Logan, if something should happen to you, her hubby or at least those orchestrating his campaign would be more than suspect. They can't afford for that to happen. It's similar to when Giuliani was fighting the mafia in New York. The mob hated him, but he was too visible, too public to be the recipient of an organized hit. You're that way now. Courtney is not. And because she's wanted in murders, it's worse."

"I have to find her."

"You have no idea where to look. She's not going to show up at another carnival. Do you think the murdered dwarf is related to Solminski, the one working for Bandini?"

"Yes. Looked close in age. Maybe brothers. Possibly twins."

"She might try to get in touch with him, especially since they're friends and she's driving the dead man's truck. Could you convince Solminski to tell you if she does?"

"Maybe. If he is related to the dead man with the bloody snake, he might have a motive to help me find who's threatening Courtney. Maybe he'll point me toward her if he knows where she is or where she's trying to go."

"But there's still a remote chance that the guys in the fire were sent by Bandini. Since you were detained by the local constables in Hillsborough County, the media flew the coop here, most following your trail, the trail of destruction down there in Gibsonton. Courtney might be hiding out with some family member somewhere. FBI will probably find her, and let's hope it's before she becomes unfindable—no body—no proof of a murder, and certainly no result of a crime. Logan skates into the White House, and Courtney gets tucked away in the scrapbook of legacies and mysteries next to Jimmy Hoffa's grainy picture."

"I can't let that happen."

Dave lowered his voice. "I know you can't, but I have to be the voice of reason in a situation where reason can't float your lifeboat. You're my friend, and that's the least I can do."

"How's Nick?"

"Better. Moving about. He walked Max, and spent some quality time with her at the Tiki Bar. Good thing Kim is there to send them both home."

"I'll see you in less than an hour—"

"Speaking of Kim, she told me to tell you something if I heard from you. She said a woman called the marina and left a message for you. Kim said the woman had been watching all of the news coverage, saw the allegations about Courtney being the daughter of you and Andrea Logan, and then she said she knows Courtney. Apparently she gave her a ride after she found her walking in the Ocala National Forest."

I accelerated the Jeep, felt my chest tighten. *Who was this woman? Was it some kind of ploy or trap?* If I didn't get pulled over for speeding, I'd know very soon.

FIFTY-THREE

Courtney drove slowly down Dumaine Street searching for an address on the old buildings. Many were decked with shutters painted lime green or salmon pink, propped up with timeworn red brick, balconies laced in wrought-iron, hanging baskets dripping with color. One balcony was almost covered with ferns growing from clay pots. She had her window down, the breeze warm and tinged with the smell of horse droppings, stale beer, and azaleas.

A white Lincoln eased away from the curb, opening the only parking spot on the street that Courtney could see. She parked and looked for change in her bag, finding four quarters. When she started to drop a quarter in the meter, she saw that it had a full hour of time remaining. *Maybe this is a good sign. Maybe Mariah Danford would be here.*

Across the narrow one-way street was a bar with doors yawning wide, paddle fans turning in slow-motion, a woman's rippling laugh coming from the cool recesses inside where two men sat at the bar, their profiles silhouetted in a blue neon wash from an old Jaxs Beer sign.

An elderly black man sat on a swayback bench in the shade of a balcony and to the right of the bar door, his eyes closed, gnarled fingers picking the strings on a guitar, his raspy voice singing a blues song, *Rock Me* by Muddy Waters.

Courtney looked for addresses, crossed the street and stopped when she walked by the old black man, watching him sing and play the guitar for a few seconds. The four quarters she didn't have to put into the parking meter, she dropped into a rusted French Market coffee can at the man's feet.

"Much obliged, darlin' girl," he said, pausing from singing. He opened his eyes and looked somewhere above Courtney, his irises clouded with cataracts, his smile wide. A lower front tooth was missing, and the hint of gold flashed near a front incisor.

"How did you know I was a girl? Your eyes were closed when you thanked me."

"I could feel you standin' there. Been sightless long as me...o'ter senses commence to gettin' sharp as a razorblade."

Courtney studied him a moment, glad he couldn't see her. White whiskers sprouted from the old man's gaunt face. A harmonica was perched on his lap, threadbare khaki pants stained from coffee and tobacco. He held a guitar pick made from a broken plastic clothespin. "Where you be headin,' darlin' girl?"

"Just passing through."

"Passin' through what...life?"

"Sometimes."

"No times. It's too short pass through."

"I have to go."

"Go where? Maybe I can hep you get there. Been here all my life, me. I used to see with my eyes. I know the Big ol' Easy. Where you tryin' to get to?"

"The address is forty-one Dumaine."

The old man inhaled deeply, lung tissue making a wet sucking sound. "You are close to it. Don't know if'n it'd be best to get much closer than where you is right here."

"What do you mean?"

"I means to tell you that ain't no place for a girl to go."

"Why?"

"On account that folks who go there are dem peoples who don't believe in Heaven."

"What is this place?"

"Used to be what they called a hot pillow joint." "You mean a brothel?"

"Yes ma'am. I'd heard the upstairs might still be. The downstairs is a place where they sells Voodoo stuff. I ain't never seen no need for it, me. No way. No how." He shook his head and cleared his throat. "They's lots better spots in Naw'lens to see."

"Where's this place? I've found forty, forty-two, and other addresses, but no forty-one."

"It's ain't properly marked. Don't need to be. Evil don't need directions, just an invite. It's a block down Dumaine, right past Moe's Place, a bar. There's an old arched brick entranceway, ivy growing all over it, kinda like somethin' you walk through entering a graveyard. They got a wrought iron door on it. Probably ain't locked no how. Once you go in there...just follow a brick pathway down the alley 'till you come to the front door."

"Thank you. I really like your singing."

"This one's for you, darlin' girl." He cupped his hands around the worn harmonica, brought it to his mouth, and started blowing. Robert Johnson's song, *Cross Road Blues,* poured out of the harmonica. Then he picked up his guitar and started singing, eyes closing, his voice carrying the keys of emotion and compassion. Courtney walked away, towards a brick doorway that the old blues man said looked like the entrance to a cemetery. Before his words faded in the breeze, the last thing she heard him sing sounded like a prayer, *"I went to the crossroad, fell down on my knees...asked the Lord above, have mercy on me if you please..."*

FIFTY-FOUR

When I arrived at the marina, I parked my Jeep away from the main lot and even farther away from the Tiki Bar lot. I walked quickly down the central dock that was adjacent to the seawall, the dock straddling most of the marina waterfront. The captain of the *Sea Witch*, a forty-four-foot, half-day fishing boat loaded with tourists, slowly accelerated the big Cummins diesels and headed out towards Ponce Inlet and the Atlantic. A half-dozen seagulls followed in the boat's wake, the birds squawking over the drum roll of the engines.

Approaching the Tiki Bar, I turned left between the marina office and a yacht broker's small building and walked to get a clear view of the parking lot. No news satellite trucks. No microwave trucks. No hordes of reporters grazing the perimeter. Maybe a few sat at the bar. At this point, I didn't care. A woman had said she knew Courtney. And I wanted this person to speak to me before she spoke to the news media. My immediate plan was to walk into the bar, ignore any reporters who may be stalking the area, and then I'd find Kim Davis. I hoped she was there.

I entered the Tiki Bar through the rear delivery entrance. The cook, Big John, an Army veteran I knew, mid-thirties, pushing 280 pounds, sweatband over his thick eyebrows, poured fresh shrimp into a deep-fryer. He nodded and used his index finger to flick a piece of shrimp tail from the back of his hand to the floor. Then he grinned and said, "Dude, don't blame you for comin' in the back door. You doin' all right?"

"Yeah, is Kim working today?"

"Her shift ended about ten minutes ago. She might still be out there. Angie's here along with two servers." He wiped his hands on a frayed white towel and folded his arms across his big chest. "I've worked here three years and never seen biz like it's been recently. It's slacked off today, but all this political crap on TV brought out the news crews and the gawkers. Man, I hope all this shit comes out clean for you." He used a spatula to flip a burger on the grill.

"Thank you, John." I walked around him in the small kitchen and entered the Tiki Bar. Two charter deck hands and a charter boat captain tended sweating cans of beer at the bar. A half-dozen tourists sat at wooden tables eating and drinking.

Kim was headed for the door, her back to me, purse hanging from her shoulder. I caught up with her and said, "I heard you got a strange phone call."

She turned around. "Sean, how do you walk so quietly?"

"Boat shoes."

She glanced down at my shoes and smiled, her brown eyes lifting up to meet mine. She looked around and adjusted her purse strap. "Let's get out of here. Can we talk on your boat?"

"We can. Come on." We stepped out the side door leading to the docks, unlocked the gate, and walked down L-dock. A forty-foot Beneteau sailboat was motoring into its slip, the captain using bow-thrusters to maneuver the boat, two women in bikinis sitting in the cockpit with him.

Kim said, "I can see Nick's doing better. Looks like he's grilling something in that smoker on his cockpit."

Max sat in a canvas chair near the grill, Nick turning over sizzling fish, using a brush to apply olive oil and his special sauces. I said, "Max are you helping or just observing?" She jumped from her chair and ran around the cockpit, between Nick's bare feet, barking, tail flapping, watching Kim and I approach.

Nick turned to us and grinned, his bruises no longer purple, the swelling was going down. "Hot Dog knows how she likes her fish. She watches me to make sure I get it right. Ya'll hungry? Dave's comin' over to eat. I can toss another couple of pieces on the fire. Red snapper. Grilled with olive oil, lemon, salt, pepper, some paprika and a touch of garlic. Greek style, baby!"

Kim smiled and said, "No thanks, Nicky. Big John made me a lunch."

Nick looked her, one eye squinting in the sunlight. "Big John is good, but he ain't Greek."

I said, "I'll take a rain check, Nick. I can't stay long."

He shook his head. "That's 'cause shit happens, and you got some big shit happening. Did you find the girl?"

"No, not yet."

"The news said three more bodies were found, but no sign of the girl, huh?"

"Some signs. Not many."

Dave walked across the dock, a bottle of water in one hand. He said, "Kimberly, so good to see you on this side of the docks, so to speak. I'm assuming you're providing Sean with the details of the woman's call."

"I'm about to. We just didn't want to talk in the bar."

"Can't say I'd fault you two there. Media will be back when they get wind of your whereabouts, Sean. I was just following this on-going political saga on some of our esteemed cable news channels. If the pundits and pollsters are to be believed, it seems Senator Logan's popularity has slipped in the polls by fifteen points in the last couple of days. Right now Courtney Burke has the fate of the Republican Party's national agenda literally riding on her DNA. Law enforcement is speculating she may have left Florida. FBI has mounted a larger scale manhunt. So how long can a nineteen-year-old kid evade that kind of dragnet?"

I said nothing. Nick raised his shoulders in a shrug and tossed Max a small piece of bread. He said, "You think Bandini's backing off since all this publicity is goin' down with the girl?"

Dave said, "Perhaps, but it gives him a great cover, too. Assuming he even knew where to find her and take her out to avenge the death of his brother, people might suspect it had Logan's fingerprints on it. But if a body isn't found, suspicion can stay inside the public's collective consciousness, but evidence is out the proverbial window."

Kim said, "Maybe the call I received from the woman will help. Sean, she wants to speak with you. She keeps seeing your picture on the news, those images the news media shot of you and Nick that day in the marina parking lot. Anyway, she said if you're the missing girl's father, she wanted to talk with you because she feels very concerned for the girl's safety. She told me that she gave Courtney Burke a ride when she found her walking on a road through the Ocala National Forest. Said she took her into DeLand and dropped her off at a medical clinic."

Dave asked, "What's the woman's name?"

I caught the flash just over Dave's shoulder. From a rooftop. "Kim! Don't say anymore." The flash was a wink of the sun off moving glass from the roof of a boat storage warehouse one hundred yards across the marina. I could see a man crouched beside an air-conditioning unit on the roof. He was holding a pair of binoculars trained my way.

"What do you see?" Dave asked, not turning in the direction I had just looked.

"Everyone act normal. No turning around and looking. One man, visible. Eleven o'clock position over your right shoulder, Dave. Top of Johnson's warehouse."

Nick picked up Max, and cut his eyes toward the building without moving his body or head in the direction. Kim looked at me, I could hear her make a dry swallow, arms folding across her breasts.

"Dave, have you or Nick seen anyone approach *Jupiter*?"

Nick said, "I haven't seen much of anything lately."

Dave grunted, "Nothing out of the norm. I haven't observed anyone physically board your boat. I would have stopped them. A marine surveyor was crawling all over the Hatteras in the slip next to yours. Looks like that boat's on the market now."

I turned to Kim. "Let's go inside and talk."

FIFTY-FIVE

Kim and I took Max inside *Jupiter*. Dave and Nick stayed back, walking covertly in the direction of the Johnson Boatworks building. Max jumped up on my couch in the boat's salon and curled into a ball.

Kim said, "This is a lot roomier inside than what it appears outside."

"I'll show you around in a minute. First, who is this woman and how can I reach her?"

Kim sat on the couch next to Max and petted her. I found a piece of paper and a pen, and handed them to Kim. "What's this for?"

"Write down her name."

Kim's eyes opened wider. "Okay." She wrote out the name and handed the paper to me. Lois Timbers. Kim said, "She's a school teacher in DeLand, and called from the school during her break. She said after dropping Courtney off at a clinic, she never saw her again until all of this news coverage began. She told me that Courtney asked to borrow her cell phone, and she made a call to someone. She didn't hear any part of the conversation because Courtney stepped out of the car to make the call."

"Did this woman give you the number Courtney called?"

"No, there was a real hesitancy in her voice when she was talking to me. She definitely wanted to speak with you…or Andrea Logan."

"Andrea Logan?"

"Yes. She said if Andrea is the girl's mother, then she ought to know her daughter needs help."

"I hope she hasn't called the Logan campaign office. Write down her number?"

Kim reached in her purse and took out a small piece of lavender paper. "I already did that. It's on here."

I looked at the number and then reached for one of the disposable phones I'd bought. "Kim, make yourself at home. I'm going to step out on the cockpit to call."

She nodded and said, "I understand."

Lois Timbers answered her phone on the third ring. I identified myself and said, "I really appreciate you reaching out to me. Was there anything in the conversation that stood out to you, something I should know?"

"Yes, the girl said her mother is dead. Said she was raised by her grandmother. And I believe it was her grandmother who she called."

"Lois, you've been very helpful. I don't know if Courtney is my daughter. It's urgent that I find out. For Courtney's safety, it's very important that everything we talked about stays between us."

"I understand."

"Please don't call Senator Logan's campaign office and leave a message for his wife, Andrea. There's no sense in stirring the pot any more than it's been stirred already. I'd rather give Andrea the news, one way or the other, when we know something definitive."

"I understand."

"Thank you."

"You're welcome. Mr. O'Brien, I have the number on my phone that Courtney called that morning. Can I give it to you?"

"Yes, but not over the phone. I'm near Daytona right now. I can drive to DeLand to meet you. There's a coffee shop on New York Avenue. It's called the Boston Coffeehouse. Do you know of the place?"

"Yes."

"Can you meet me there in one hour?"

"I can be there. I'll certainly recognize you, Mr. O'Brien. I'll be wearing jeans and a yellow T-shirt with words across the front of it that read: *World's Greatest Grandma*. Goodbye."

She disconnected and I stepped back inside *Jupiter* to tell Kim that I was leaving. She was no longer sitting on the couch. "In here," she said, her voice coming from the galley.

I walked down three steps to the galley where Kim had a spray bottle of Windex and a roll of paper towels, cleaning the counter. I said, "Sorry about any dirt. My housecleaning duties have been more than lax these last few days."

She looked up and smiled, the sun coming through a porthole window and breaking across her face and hair. "No problem. Nick and Dave can help you with some of the more physical stuff. Me, well, I can roll my sleeves up to give you a hand on your boat. I'm not a neat freak, just a gal who's organized and can shine this sweet old boat 'til she's gleaming. It's the least I can do, Sean, while you sort all this stuff out."

"Thank you."

"Besides, maybe one day you'll take me out on *Jupiter*. I've never been seasick and I love boats. Funny thing is that although I work in a marina restaurant, hundreds of boats right out the door,

I'm land-bound."

"Not anymore. We'll go for a boat ride when this is over." "I'd like that."

"I have to drive to DeLand now. I'm meeting our school teacher friend and getting a number from her."

A text arrived on my regular phone. It was from Dave: We're heading back. Suspect fled before we could get there.

—▪—

WITHIN A FEW minutes. Dave and Nick walked down L-dock. Kim, Max, and I stood next to Dave's trawler, *Gibraltar*, waiting for them. They approached and Dave said, "He either spotted us, or he left the rooftop when you and Kim weren't visible. No one saw this guy. And Boatworks doesn't have security cameras yet. They're on order."

Nick said, "He probably saw us walking down the dock and flew the coop before we could get to the parking lot."

I glanced back at the rooftop, now vacant. "These guys keep following me on the perimeter, always in my space from a distance. I'm being tracked. It's time I become the tracker. I'm assuming my main mobile number is bugged. Don't text or call me on my regular phone with any information you don't want others to know. I'm using throw-away phones until I can pick up a new, clean one. I'll remove the sim card and battery when I drive to DeLand." I told them about my short conversation with Lois Timbers and added, "I don't want Logan's people finding this school teacher and hunting down the person on the other end of the line, the recipient of Courtney's call."

Dave squinted his eyes in the sun reflecting off the water. He said, "Since our second-term president has endorsed Senator Logan, I suspect Logan has at least some of the vast resources of the NSA at his disposal. And that means that anything you do electronically, Sean, is indeed traceable. They want desperately to find Courtney Burke."

"Not more than I do." I squatted down and petted Max. "I have to make a short trip. You hang with Dave and Nick. I'll be back soon." I stood and caught Kim looking up at me in a way I'd never seen her look before, her eyes restless, her face filled with quiet thoughts, almost as if I was a sailor on shore leave and departing her port town for a long journey. She gripped her arms, the breeze across the water moving her hair.

Dave said, "Maybe this number you get from Miss Timbers will lead you straight to Courtney Burke."

"I'll know soon."

As I turned to walk away, Kim said, "Be careful, Sean. I have a bad feeling in my heart."

FIFTY-SIX

When Courtney Burke pushed open the wrought iron gate, it made a groaning sound, and the sun went behind a dark cloud, the light sucked out of the air, shadows escaped. Ivy clung to the face of the aged brick in the archway entrance. She walked inside and followed a slate path bordered by bougainvillea dipping in purple blooms. The sound of her shoes against the stone mixed with the throb of bees in the flowers. A blackbird perched on a low-hanging branch of a mimosa tree and cocked its head, one yellow eye watching Courtney walk down the path.

She entered a small courtyard surrounded by bamboo and banana trees, the smell of hibiscus in the motionless air. A wrought iron table with two chairs was positioned in deep shade near the foliage. In the center of the enclosure was a three-tiered fountain with a winged angel perched at the top, water bubbling from its open mouth and cascading down the discolored concrete layers of the fountain.

An antique two-story brick building with vaulted doors and windows, black shutters, and ivy creeping up to the second floor, stood in the speckled light like a leftover from a bygone chapter in New Orleans. The faded brass numbers tacked over the door read: 41. And above the address was a hand-painted sign: House of Cards– Voodoo. A small blue neon sign in the lower part of one window glowed with a single word: Readings.

Courtney walked through the open door. The smell of burning incense greeted her at the threshold. She stepped inside the small shop lit by candles and dimmed lights attached to the base of a slow turning paddle fan hanging from a ceiling painted black. The walls were lined with shelves that displayed hand-labeled bottles, carved bone jewelry, peacock feathers, crystals, voodoo dolls, plastic skulls, beads, imitation shrunken heads, African masks, a freeze-dried tarantula, tarot cards, and dozens of charms, statues and potions.

A curtain of multi-colored beads hang from an arched doorway in the rear of the store. Next to it a red candle burned from a two-inch sized hole drilled through the top of a skull, hot wax dripping into the vacant eye sockets.

A large black cat came in the shop from outside. Courtney turned around when the cat jumped up onto a frayed chair in one corner next to a small table with a blue tablecloth spread across it, fragments of bones on the tablecloth.

"Welcome."

Courtney spun back around as a woman walked through the curtain of beads hanging from the rear doorway. She was a head shorter that Courtney, dressed in African attire, face furrowed and the color of dark tea. She wore a mauve bandana covering her hair, a single gold hoop earring in her left ear, and a green-print dress resembling a robe. "Welcome to our little corner of the universe. Can I help you find something?" The old woman's eyes explored Courtney's face. Her voice had a Cajun dialect with a Caribbean inflection, and she spoke just above a whisper.

Courtney smiled. "I'm really not here to buy anything."

"You are here for a reading then. I can tell. My name is Mambo Eve. You have many troubles on your mind, baby. Your eyes are not like any I've looked into before. They are captivating and powerful, but deeply troubled."

"I guess it doesn't take much of a reading to see that. I feel like I'm wearing my emotions outside my clothes." Courtney smiled.

Mambo Eve nodded. "I sense something else about you. You have a gift as well. Are you a witch?"

Courtney's eyebrows rose, and she smiled. "A witch? Oh, no. I'm not a witch, but I'm not an angel either. I'm here because I'm looking for someone."

"Someone or something?"

"Both, really. I was told that Mariah Danford was at this address. Does she work here?"

"Yes. I couldn't do it without her. Readings, at least for me, require so much energy. At my age, they're becoming more tiring. Mariah manages the front of the shop for me." Mambo Eve angled her head, looking to the right of Courtney, through the open door. "She's back from lunch."

A woman, mid-forties, entered and removed her sunglasses. She was tall and thin, face narrow, dark wavy hair pulled back into a ponytail. She wore no makeup. Her white blouse clung loosely below her long neck, revealing a sprinkling of freckles on her shoulders. "Hello," she said, dropping her straw purse behind a counter with an old cash register in the center. "You looking for anything in particular?"

"Are you Mariah Danford?"

"Who wants to know?"

FIFTY-SEVEN

*T*hree college-aged girls, all wearing Mardi Gras beads and bright sun-dresses, entered the shop, laughing, one girl ending a story about her ex-boyfriend. She pushed dark glasses up to the top of her head and asked, "Ya'll sell voodoo dolls and the pins that come with it?" She cackled. "I want to give a gift that he can feel."

Mariah smiled and pointed to the back of the store. "We have a large selection on the shelf below the skulls." The girls stepped to the rear of the store, snickering and pointing to a large bottle with a label that read: **LOVE POTION #9.**

Mariah turned back to Courtney. "Who are you?"

"My name's Courtney, and my friend Boots Langley told me to come see you."

"How's Boots?"

"Not so good. You don't know?"

"Know what? Is Boots okay? Has he been hurt?"

"I'm so sorry to have to tell you this…he was killed."

Mariah steadied herself by bracing one hand against the counter. She glanced down at the black cat dozing on the seat of the chair, her eyes search-ing the room. She turned to the old woman and said, "This is horrible. I'd like to speak with this girl outside."

Mamba Eve lowered her eyes and nodded. "Of course. Take your time."

Courtney and Mariah took seats at the wrought iron table in the court-yard. Mariah leaned in, resting her arms on the top of the table. "You bring me awful news. What happened?"

Courtney told all she knew and how she found the body. Then she added, "Boots thought that you could help me find Dillon Flanagan."

"Who?"

"God knows what he goes by now. That's the name he was born with, and he's my uncle. Boots said you might know him as the Prophet."

The color drained from Mariah's face. She pushed away from the table and leaned back in her chair, her mouth slightly parted, her thoughts far from the courtyard. There was only the sound of the water splashing in the fountain and a hummingbird darting between hibiscus blossoms.

Courtney cleared her throat. "Are you okay?"

Mariah deeply inhaled. "Yeah...I'm okay. Why do you want to find him?"

"He took something from my grandmother, and he took something from me. I might be able to return what he stole from my grandmother."

"He takes from everybody he meets, and he takes everything. If you're lucky, you still have your soul, but he'll try to claim that, too. I was fortunate to get out of there. Others, not so much. I keep thinking that he put some kind of hypnotic trance on me, and it'll be just a matter of when and where that he'll try to make me do something bad."

"But you said you got out of there. How can he make you do something against your will if he's not near you?"

"He's in my brain. At one time he was in my heart. I guess that's where the mistakes start and where they return to haunt you. I feel like I might have some kind of post traumatic syndrome. Listen, Courtney, I was your age once. I didn't listen to my mother because I thought I knew the ways of the world. I always wanted to be working as an actress in films, but I eventually wound up working in carnivals. I grew up in New Orleans. My mother used to come here to Mambo Eve's place. Eve always treated me like family."

"I didn't have much of a family. My grandmother is a little like the lady in the store, Mambo Eve—wise and kind." "Compassion was something hard to find in the carny world. Don't get me wrong, there were some sweet and good people there, guys like Boots. But by and large, it was my house of the rising sun. And it was a hard life. Men like the Bandini brothers were always there to offset the good. And now you're asking me about the very worst of the worst—the Prophet. He was calling himself Reverend John when I first met him. Wasn't long before he'd convinced some of his followers he was a prophet from God. And they believed him."

"You talked about getting out of there…where was there? Where is he?"

Mariah embraced her bare arms, the breeze blew through the bamboo, stalks rubbing together, creaking. Her eyes followed the black cat as it walked from the store and dropped to its belly, stalking a lizard warming in the sun on a brick paver. "Whatever he did to you, whatever he took from your grandmother, it's not worth going there. Nothing's worth that. He's wicked—very evil. Men like him have a special place on reserve in hell. Walk away from this, okay?"

"I can't. I don't have anything to go back to. If nothing else, he knows who I am. I just hate the fact that I'm related by blood to him. Where is he?"

"What did you mean when you said if nothing else, he knows who I am?"

"It's more complicated than I have time to explain right now. Please, if you know where he is, tell me."

"Last time I saw him he was running a small compound on twenty acres, a cult of followers, in the hills of Virginia about thirty miles west of Leesburg. I can go inside and draw a map for you. But I'm warning you, don't go there. They'll do things to you that will make your skin crawl, and if he decides to kill you, the blood won't be on his hands."

Courtney watched as the cat approached, a live lizard clutched in its mouth, the blue tail slapping the cat's whiskers. The cat dropped the lizard near the table and observed with a detached stare as its prey attempted to crawl away. Courtney turned her head from the dying animal. "The poor lizard. That cat caught and hurt it just to watch the little thing die. And I thought only humans were capable of that."

"She used to bring me baby birds. That really freaked me out. Not that it's okay to kill lizards. It's just different, you know?"

"No, I don't know." Courtney pulled the baseball cap out of her bag and slipped the dark glasses on her face. "Thanks for your help. If you can draw that map, I'll be on my way."

Mariah sat straighter in her chair. She studied Courtney's face for a few seconds. "Oh my God…you're the girl on the news, the one they say could be the daughter of Senator Logan's wife."

"I'm not her daughter."

"I had lunch at Gino's around the corner. The news was on TV, and they showed a sketch that some street artist did of you at Jackson Square. The whole world's hunting for you."

"Please, draw the map for me. I have to go."

"They say you killed two men...one was Tony Bandini."

"I was the only witness to the first man killed. And he was a friend of mine. Police didn't believe me. Then Tony Bandini slapped me and tried to stick his dick in...he tried to force me to have oral sex with him. His gun was on the table. I grabbed it and warned him, but he laughed and came for me again. I didn't have a choice."

Mariah reached across the table and touched the top of Courtney's hand. "I understand, and I believe you. I'm sure Boots did, too, and he was no fool. You just got to get all this straightened out. You can't keep running, looking over your shoulder."

Courtney heard a siren in the distance and wondered if it was safe to return to the Toyota truck.

FIFTY-EIGHT

I didn't think that I wasn't being followed as I drove from Ponce Inlet to DeLand, at least I didn't see any signs of being tailed by a car. If I was being followed by a satellite, then someone must have hidden a GPS tracker somewhere on my Jeep. I'd done a thorough search in the parking lot at the marina before I left, found nothing but road grit and mud in the undercarriage and wheel wells. Earlier, I'd left a broken piece of a toothpick wedged out of sight between the hood and the body of the Jeep. It fell to the lot after I opened the hood.

A good sign.

On my drive to Deland, I took detours, sped up and slowed down, constantly watching the rearview mirror and taking a back road into the town. DeLand is Mayberry RFD on growth steroids. The quaint town, forty miles west of Daytona Beach, oozes southern charm, a lineage of yesteryear still in its brick streets. The entire stretch of Main Street, with a slow tempo composed by birdsong from shady trees, might as well be a picture postcard of a National Historic District. The Boston Coffeehouse mixed well with the antique shops, bookstores and upscale bars.

I entered the coffee shop looking for a woman wearing a yellow T-shirt and the words: *World's Greatest Grandmother*. She wasn't there, and she didn't sound like the type of person who'd be late. I walked through the shop with its dark-wood tavern feel, the smell of ground coffee, chocolate, and fresh-squeezed orange juice followed me to a table in the far corner. I sat and waited. Three other customers, college kids with open laptops and ears closed by earbuds, occupied tables. I approached one student, twenty-something, jock build, Stetson University T-shirt, baseball cap on backwards.

He looked up and took the buds out of his ears.

I said, "How's school?"

"It's all right."

"A grandmother needs a favor."

"Whadda you mean?"

"She's coming in for coffee. She just needs a strong guy like you to escort her back to her car. Here's twenty bucks if you can walk her to her car." I dropped a twenty dollar bill on the table.

"Sure, dude. I don't mind helping little old ladies." He smiled.

"Good. I'll give you the high sign when she's ready to leave."

"Cool. Where is she?"

"She isn't here yet, but she will be."

"No problem."

"Thanks."

I turned and walked back to my table. I was on my second cup of coffee and no sign of Lois Timbers. I hoped the college kid had a lot of homework. As I waited for her, I replayed the conversation I had with Kim on my boat. I'd mentioned where I was meeting Lois, but I didn't speak her phone number aloud. If my boat, buy some remote chance was bugged, they'd know where I was meeting Lois, but they'd have no idea how to contact her. And I'd left not long after I'd spoken with her. No one, unless they lived in DeLand, could have arrived here quicker than I did.

Then where was Lois Timbers?

I thought about dialing her number on my disposable phone, and then a woman wearing a banana-yellow T-shirt strolled into the coffee shop. She paused near the front counter, her eyes adjusting from the sunlight outside to the dark interior. I stood and smiled. She nodded and walked to my table. "Mr. O'Brien. I'm so sorry to have kept you waiting."

"Please, call me Sean."

"It's good to meet you. You're bigger and even more handsome than you appeared on TV." Her voice rolled off her tongue in a southern drawl that was charming and sincere. She was barely five feet tall, skin the color of the coffee I sipped, wide smile. She sat down and said, "My daughter and her youngest, little Timmy, were at my house. He fell riding his bicycle, poor thing, and he had a few well-earned scratches on his knees."

"How old is Timmy?"

"He'll be five next month."

"Would you like some coffee?"

"Oh, yes, please. They know how to make it here."

I signaled for the waitress, and Lois ordered a cappuccino. I said, "Thank you for seeing me today. The number on your phone that Courtney dialed, did you call it?"

"I thought about it, just to let whomever answered know that I'd seen Courtney. Figured someone was worried. Then all that stuff on the news seemed to happen overnight. Those murders, and the connection between you, Andrea Logan, and maybe Courtney. When I saw that video of you on the news, you looked really concerned—not so much about the questions the reporters were asking, but maybe deep concern for the girl. That's when I called the marina and left a message with the woman who said she knew you."

"Kim."

"Yes, Kim. She was so sweet."

"May I have the number?"

"Of course. I wrote it down for you." She reached in her purse and handed me a folded piece of paper. "I did look up the area code."

"What did you find?"

"Looks like she called someplace in South Carolina, but I don't know where."

"Is the number still on your phone?"

"Yes."

"Delete it."

"Why?"

"Because if the number's gone, no one will be able to call it."

"Well, to call it, they'd have to steal my phone from me, and that means they'd have to steal my purse." She smiled. "One time a mugger in Detroit tried to do that. I have a scream that would wake the dead."

The waitress brought the cappuccino. Lois stirred sugar through the foam and sipped. "That's delicious." She held the cup in both hands, her eyes moving from the steam up to my face. "The girl, Courtney, she does favor you some. Do you think she's your daughter?"

"I don't know."

"I bet you'd make a fine father. An old grandmother like me can tell. Where's the rest of your family?"

"They're all dead. No one's left."

"I'm so sorry to hear that. Family and close friends is what life is all about, if you get right down to the real meaning of it."

"You think so?"

"Yes, yes I do. Maybe Courtney is your child, and maybe she'll be part of your life and you part of hers, too. What if that's why I saw you on the news and made the call? Something was pulling at my heart, weighing heavy on my mind."

"I'm glad you did make the call. Lois, some very bad men are frantically hunting for Courtney. The number on your phone might get them a lot closer to her. Right now only Kim and I know you have a tie to Courtney. No one can check your phone records because they don't know your name or the connection. We want to keep it that way. I'm going to leave, and I'm going to go out the back door. I'm parked two blocks away. Wait at least ten minutes before you go, okay? The young man at the table next to the bookshelf is a college student. He attends Stetson. He will walk you to your car before you drive away. It'll be just like you met him for coffee." I stood and motioned to the college kid. He nodded.

Lois looked around a second. "Sean, I'm getting a little bit frightened."

"Did you memorize the phone number?" "No."

"It's deleted from your mind. Now, delete it from your phone. No one can take something that doesn't exist. Thank you, Lois."

She smiled. "You're a kind person. I hope you find Courtney before they do. And I hope she's your daughter. I'm a teacher, and the one thing I've learned in life is people need to be needed. Courtney needs you. And I believe you need her."

FIFTY-NINE

When I opened the door to my Jeep, I took the piece of paper from my pocket. I looked at the number Lois had written on it, and I wondered where in South Carolina this number would lead me. Was it to one of Courtney's relatives? Her parents? A sister, brother, or grandparent? Maybe it was the number to one of Courtney's friends.

I sat in the Jeep, closed the door, sealing off most of the outside noise, and I lifted a mobile phone. What would I say to whomever answered? What could I say? It would depend on who answered the phone. I dialed the number.

"Hello." It was the voice of a woman. A tired voice. A soft voice that, in one word, spoke volumes. "Hi, is Courtney there?" Silence.

"Is Courtney home?"

"I'm sorry, but you must have a wrong number. There is no Courtney living here."

"Do you know Courtney?"

A two second pause. My heart raced. Would she hang up?

"There is no one here by that name. Goodbye—"

"Wait! Please, don't go. My name's Sean O'Brien. I'm trying to help Courtney. She's in a lot of trouble. None of it's her fault. Do you know where I can—"

"Please, sir, I have to go…I'm sorry."

Her breath was slightly labored. Emphysema, maybe. She disconnected. The sound of silence crushing. I lowered the phone from my ear and looked at the screen. Who was the person? What's her relationship to Courtney? Was there a relationship—a connection? I believed there was something—a modulation in her voice gave it away. It was when she said, *'There is no one here by that name...'*

She didn't answer my question. Didn't say whether she knew Courtney when I asked her a direct question. Only said there was no one here by that name. I started the Jeep, the voice of the mysterious woman from the phone call echoing in my ears like a troubled whisper imprisoned in my brain and bouncing off the inside of my skull.

— —

WHEN I DROVE into the Ponce Marina parking lot, the cracking of the oyster shells under my tires popped thoughts that had transported me as far away as South Carolina. I'd considered calling the number again. Would the woman pick up the phone? If so, what could I say differently to try to convince her to speak with me?

Nothing.

Not a damn thing. If I wanted to talk with her, I'd have to find her—have to find her before Senator Logan's black ops people found her, or before one of Bandini's hit men tried to put a .22 caliber bullet between Courtney's striking eyes.

A black Mercedes with windows tinted dark pulled into the space next to my Jeep. I instinctively reached for the Glock wedged on the right side of the seat. My hand rested on the butt of the pistol. I waited for someone to get out. I glanced around the lot. Three cars. Two out-of-state license plates. One local. A TV news truck was pulling into the lot from the far side, closer to the Tiki Bar. The last thing I wanted was to be caught on camera in a possible shootout with whoever was sitting inside the Mercedes.

The car's driver-side door slowly opened. I saw boat shoes hit the ground. The guy who got out of the car was someone I knew. I felt my pulse slow. I slipped the Glock behind my back, under the shirt, and got out of the Jeep.

It had been a few weeks since I saw the man who parked the Mercedes, but I knew he owned the sixty-foot Hatteras docked next to *Jupiter*. He was a chiropractor from Orlando. I said, "Hey, Kevin. How are you?"

He turned and grinned. Fiftyish. Cotton hair. Deep tan. Very white teeth. "Sean O'Brien. How the hell are you? Man oh man. Nobody can remember all the names of Republicans who were in the horserace for the nomination, but the voters sure know you. Ever think of running for office?"

I glanced to my far right and could see a TV news crew walking our way. "No, Kevin. Never thought about it. I hear your Hatteras is on the market. I guess you have a serious buyer, right?"

"What? My boat's not for sale. I haven't even had *Changes in Latitude* a full year. Now, ask me in another year and I might sell her. You ready to step up your game—get a bigger boat?" He grinned.

"So you had no marine surveyor on your boat?"

"No, why?"

"Thanks, Kevin. I need to check something." I turned and ran past the news crew, heading for *Jupiter*.

"Hey! Wait! Mr. O'Brien! Can we talk with you?" shouted a blonde reporter, her camera-man rolling video of me running by them.

SIXTY

I unlocked the sliding glass door between *Jupiter's* cockpit and her salon. In thirty seconds, I had music coming from satellite radio tuned to a blues station, Keb Mo singing through the Bose speakers. Then I started searching. Checked every lamp shade. Checked behind the couch. Under the smoke alarm. Worked my way through the galley, the master berths, and the other sleeping areas. Nothing. If there was a bug somewhere on *Jupiter*, it couldn't be buried in the engine room or the bilge to be effective. It had to be hidden in the open area to pick up conversations.

But where?

I sat on the couch and looked around at everything I'd touched. And I looked at places I hadn't inspected. I got down on my knees and stared up at the underside of the bar. And there it was, hanging like a barnacle under a dock. I stood and stepped to the bar, bending down to get a better look. It was no larger than a cap from a bottle of beer, but deadly as a cobra within the striking distance of its listening limit, which was most of *Jupiter*.

I assumed the bug was planted by the phony marine surveyor. What had I said, in person or on the phone, since then? I played back the conversations I'd had—conversations with Dave, Nick, and Kim...even chatting to little Max. When Kim and I talked, I made sure she wrote down the number to Lois Timbers, never speaking it.

And now that might prove to be a horrible mistake. Although they didn't have Lois Timbers name or number, they had Kim's name, and they heard her talking with me. I remembered the part of our conversation, what Kim said, that might cause them to hunt for her. '*She's a school teacher in DeLand, and called from the school during her break. She said after dropping Courtney off at a clinic, she never saw her again until all of this news coverage began. She told me that Courtney asked to borrow her cell phone, and she made a call to someone.*'

I had one of three choices to make, and I had to make it now. I could either call Dave or Nick to *Jupiter*, and unknown to them, paint a picture that would tell the eavesdroppers that the call and message Kim delivered to me turned to be a nothing but a hoax. I could say it was probably some political junkie calling to stir things up. Since Nick or Dave had no clue that I would be lying, the bluff might work.

The second option would be to speak directly into the bug and give the listeners a warning. If they even considered approaching Kim, I'd hold a news conference—tell reporters what Andrea Logan told me about her husband, show evidence of the bug, and let the voters sort it out at the polls.

But what if it was too late? What if they were at Kim's home, or heading there? What could I really say? Maybe nothing. But I could do something, and that was to find Kim immediately.

I stepped out of *Jupiter*, locking the door, jumping over the transom to the dock and running to Dave's boat. He was sitting at a teak table in the salon working a crossword puzzle, windows wide open, white drapes flapping in a breeze blowing across the marina water. Max jumped from the couch to greet me. "Hey, Kiddo," I said, scratching her head. "Dave, do you have Kim's number?"

He looked over the tops of his bifocals. "No. However, if I were twenty years younger, I'd make it a priority to get it. Why?"

"I think she's in danger." I quickly told him what I knew, including my call to the mysterious woman in South Carolina. "Is Nick on his boat?"

"I think so."

"Call him and see if he has her number or knows where she lives."

"Good idea." He made the call and asked the questions. "Thanks, Nick. Yes, he's standing here. Sure…" Dave handed the phone to me. He said, "Nick doesn't have Kim's number, and he says he thinks she rents a small home near the lighthouse."

I took the phone and Nick said, "That detective, the black guy who knows you…"

"What about him?"

"He was here about an hour ago. Said he tried to call you, but got no answer. He wants you to call him."

"Did he say what it was about?"

"No, man. Told him I'd pass it on if I saw you. Is Kim okay?"

"I don't know, Nick. I need to find her."

"Big John ought to know how to get hold of her."

"Thanks, Nick. Gotta go."

I turned to Dave. "Can you keep an eye on Max? There's some food for her in *Jupiter's* galley. You have a key."

"Go find Kim; take care of her. I can take care of Maxine."

— —

BIG JOHN, AT the Tiki Bar, gave me Kim's number and the address to her home. I stood on the dock adjacent to the bar and made the call. On the second ring I heard, "Hi, this is Kim. Please leave a message."

"Kim, it's Sean; call me." I left the number and ran hard to my Jeep. She lived less than a mile away. But I felt like it would be a long journey because I couldn't get there fast enough. I drove more than sixty through a twenty-five zone down a winding, narrow road that hugged the west side of Ponce Inlet, near the Halifax River. It was bordered on the left with cabbage palms and windswept scrub oak resembling giant bonsai trees. I swerved around bicyclists in the center of the road, golf carts crossing the road, tourists on mopeds, and cars crawling well below the speed limit.

I turned off Peninsula Drive onto Sailfish Street, a street filled with ranch-styled homes. The fourth house on the left was the address. It was a small brick home. Yard neat. Royal palms on either side of the house. Kim's car was in the drive. I spotted a white Chevy van across the street, under the shade of a large oak. Not a good sign.

I parked near the van. Made a mental note of the plate number. I got out of the Jeep, stood in the shade a moment, the ticking of the engine cooling was the only sound. I walked toward a large banyan tree, keeping the tree between me and the house, a strangler fig gripped the tree trunk with octopus tentacles. I lifted my Glock from under my belt.

On the way to the front of the house, I placed my hand on the hood of Kim's car. Very warm. I dialed her number and walked silently to the front door. I stood at the door and heard the phone ring. On the fourth ring, it went to her voice mail. *Phone's here. Car's here. Where's Kim? Napping, maybe? Not likely.* I looked at the lock on the door. There were some slight abrasions. Not worn by keys, but fresh. Picked. I gently opened the door. I held the Glock with both hands, and walked inside. I felt a drop of sweat roll down the center of my back. The cool air encircled me. I stood in the foyer and listened. There was the hush of air through the vents in the living room ceiling. The ticking of a grandfather clock in the corner to the right of a blue sofa. The floors were wood, polished. A large oriental rug in the center.

A noise.

A creak coming from the wooden floors. Somewhere in a back room. I slipped my boat shoes off and walked barefooted down a hallway, Glock extended. Adrenaline pumping. Another creak. Was Kim walking? I wanted to shout her name. To verify that she was okay. The grandfather clock started chiming. *Bong...bong...bong...*

The sound of someone walking carefully was closer. And there was the distinct sound of a gas stove ignited, burning.

I stopped in a closed doorway—maybe a bedroom. Listened. The *whoosh* of a gas burner was louder. I turned my head to the left, guarded, and peering into the kitchen. The front right burner was on high, blue flames whispering. There was a bright white flash. Next to my head, a framed glass photograph on the wall exploded. The bullet missed my ear by less than an inch. I hit the floor, rolling, and came up behind a kitchen counter, Glock firing.

Two men returned fire, bullets ripping through the kitchen, room filling with white smoke, the smell of cordite heavy. I fired again. One man screamed. I heard them running, tripping over furniture. Smashing things. They bolted out the front door. I followed, smoke in my eyes. There was blood on the floor. One of my bullets connected. I'd try for two. I stood at the open door and aimed my pistol. They ran through the yard to a waiting dark blue van. I started to squeeze the trigger. A neighborhood kid on a bicycle was less than fifty feet behind the running men, and the kid was in the line of fire.

The men jumped into the passenger side of the van and the driver sped off, the tires throwing loose gravel. I lowered my Glock and turned to go back inside. Horrified at what I might find.

SIXTY-ONE

found Kim lying on her stomach in an alcove off from the kitchen, blood oozing near her right ear and pooling on the white tile. Her hair was matted with blood. I dropped down beside her and gently touched her. She shuddered. "Kim, it's me, Sean." I checked her wounds, making sure there were no obvious neck or spinal cord injuries. Her mouth had been sealed with duct tape. She looked at me, her eyes blinking tears, pleading, nostrils flared, inhaling in fast heaves—so very frightened.

I grabbed a clean towel folded on the counter and pressed it against the open gash on her head. "You're going to be okay," I whispered, gingerly pulling the tape off her mouth.

She gasped, "Sean!"

"It's all right now. Take a deep breath and slowly release it." I used my phone to dial 911, gave the dispatcher the address and told her to send paramedics. Then I turned back to Kim. "Help's coming. We have to get you to the ER."

Kim looked at the roaring blue flames coming from the burner, eyes tearing. "They came out of nowhere as I was making a cup of tea. One man pushed me against the wall and screamed for me to tell him the name of the woman who lent Courtney Burke her phone. When I told him I didn't know, he started beating me. He kicked me in my side, and he wore those military boots. He knocked my breath out. He said he was going to hold my hand over the burner until my memory returned. Sean, if you hadn't arrived, I'd be dead. They weren't going to let me live. I know what one man looks like. The other kept watch at the front door."

"Describe him."

"He's about your height, but stocky. His hair is blond…cut short. His ears stuck out just a little. He had cleft chin and hateful green eyes. He smelled of that body spray I've smelled before. One of the deck hands uses it. I can smell it when he sits at the bar. He told me it was Axe body spray. Sean my hands are tingling. I feel like I might pass out."

"Stay where you are—don't move until we can stabilize you." I turned off the gas to the burner and knelt down beside Kim. I took the towel from her head and examined the gash. I could see the white bone of her skull. "You're going to need some stitches." I dampened a fresh towel and cleaned her wound, stopping the flow of blood. I used the thumb of my left hand to push a bloodied strand of hair from her face. She looked at me, eyes welling, biting her lower lip. "I hear the siren. Paramedics will be here in a minute." "Thank God you were here, Sean." I said nothing.

She inhaled deeply. "What do I do if he comes back?"

"One of my bullets hit him. They might not come back."

"There might be others."

"I know, but I'm going to send them a message. It'll be one that they can't ignore, and it should toss a safety net over you. It's Courtney they want."

She looked at the stove for a moment. "Dear God…does that poor girl have a prayer?" Her eyes opened wider. "Where's Thor? My dog…is he… okay?"

There was a whine and scratching at a door. I stood and walked to a closed bedroom door, opened it, and a German Shepherd darted around me, heading into the kitchen.

A barrage of sirens came around the block. I stood and looked through the front window to see six squad cars pull in a semicircle around the perimeter of the property.

A neighbor must have heard the gunshots.

The ambulance and paramedics were kept at bay until officers and a SWAT team were in position. There was only one thing I could do. I left my Glock on the table, walked to the front door, raised my hands and stepped out onto the porch. I could count no less than twenty gun barrels pointed at my chest. I yelled, "It's clear. I'm the one who called nine-one-one. We have an injured woman inside. The perps have fled."

"Keep your hands up! On your stomach! Face down!"

I complied. A half dozen police officers ran over to me, guns drawn. I was patted down, cuffed.

"He's clean," said one taller officer.

I said, "The victim's female. She's lying on the kitchen floor, bleeding from a head wound. She may have a fracture to her neck or back."

The SWAT guys ran past me, ballistics armor rattling, and assault rifles readied. I heard the sound of shoes on the sidewalk very close to me. I lifted my head and turned. The brown wingtips were less than three feet from my face. He was a silhouette in the sun over his shoulders, but his voice was no stranger. Detective Dan Grant said, "Sean O'Brien, lying on his belly, hog-tied...my, my, what's this world coming to?"

SIXTY-TWO

He squatted down, a toothpick wedged in the corner of his mouth. Dan Grant removed his sunglasses and said, "Okay. You wanna tell me what the hell happened? Neighbors said it sounded like a shootout at the OK Corral."

"Dan, the paramedics need to get in there. We're the victims, and she's injured."

"Soon as my men give the all clear, the EMT guys can have at it."

"See those drops of blood near the tip of your shoes?"

"I do."

"There's your DNA sample. More in the foyer. I hit one of the perps as they were trying to splatter my brains all over one wall. The woman inside, is Kim Davis. Employed at the marina. Runs the Tiki Bar Restaurant. Extractors—men used to get information from people, were sent here."

"Why would someone do that? What does this woman have or know that's worth this...this mess?"

One of the SWAT members stepped from the door. "Sir, it's clear. Vic needs medical attention."

Detective Grant said looked at the ambulance crew. "It's all yours, gentlemen." The paramedics hustled across the walkway, moving a gurney and medical cases inside the house. Grant signaled to an officer. "Help Mr. O'Brien up, please. And take the bracelets off."

The officer nodded. He removed the cuffs and I stood. Dan glanced at me and motioned with his head for me to follow him. He stepped in the shade of the banyan tree. "Okay, Sean, start at the top. What went down?"

I told him most of what I knew, but not everything I suspected. He tossed the toothpick into the hedges and said, "Do you think this goes all the way up to Senator Logan?"

"Yes. Maybe not every strategic move, but his handlers aren't doing this without his knowledge, and they probably have his blessing."

"And none of this would be happening if you and his current wife hadn't hooked up twenty years ago. I wouldn't be looking for a suspected serial killer, and Senator Logan could run a clean campaign, assuming that's even possible. Funny how life works out."

"Courtney is a victim, Dan—like Kim is…they just haven't found Courtney yet."

"Sorry, I'm a little fuckin' dumbfounded over all this happening in my county. I'll speak with Miss Davis. Get her description of the perps. We'll get a DNA sample from the blood and check CODIS for a possible match. We'll notify all area hospitals to be on the lookout for a gunshot victim."

"His DNA won't show up in any national database. You won't find their prints in there, and you won't find him being treated at a local hospital. You're not going to discover evidence or an ID—just like Hillsborough County Sheriff's Office couldn't find with the two bodies they pulled out of the burning trailer in Gibtown."

"So you're saying these soldiers don't officially exist in any government records system."

"Not under their real names."

Dan loosened his tie and crossed his arms. I glanced at the dozen or so neighbors milling around behind the crime scene tape and said, "She's going to need police protection until I can direct the focus off her. Can you spare the manpower?"

"It'll be easier to do if she's hospitalized."

"That may be a given."

"I'll speak with her inside the house or at the hospital." He turned to go in Kim's home, then looked back at me. "Oh, Sean. You might want to return phone calls. The reason I'd called was to tell you that the guy you wanted me to interview, Smitty. We finally located him."

"Where?"

"County morgue. Two teenagers found his body in the woods where they were riding dirt bikes. He'd been shot twice in the head. Bandini may not have found Courtney, but I'd say he sure found this guy." He turned and walked inside. The air was filled with the staccato of clipped language coming from police radios juxtaposed with the hum of honeybees darting in and out of the pink trumpet flowers.

The paramedics rolled Kim from her home, the wheels on the gurney vibrating along the sidewalk. I followed them to the back of the ambulance. Kim looked up at me and said, "Thank you for getting here when you did." She reached for my hand. "How did you know—how did you know I needed help?"

"I put some pieces together. They'd planted a bug on *Jupiter*." A wide-shouldered paramedic said, "We have to go, sir."

Kim moaned. "Be careful, Sean. I'm more afraid for you and Courtney than I am for myself."

I nodded and released her hand. They lowered the gurney, lifted it, and slid Kim effortlessly into the ambulance. Two paramedics climbed in with her. Right before they closed the door, she looked at me and tried to give a heartfelt smile, the kind that always came so naturally to her. But it was a fearful smile. She lifted her trembling hand to wave goodbye, her fingers like the wings of a young bird that had fallen from the nest, struggling to catch the wind, but lacking the physical and inner strength to get off the ground.

I thought about that, watching the ambulance growing smaller in the distance, thought about the bottomless abuse of power by the bottom feeders gorging on the feedbag of greed while plowing scars into the souls of others, justified for the purported good of the masses, when it was really all about them.

I walked back to my Jeep, passing the banyan tree, a strangler fig encircled around the tree with vines thick as a broomstick. I paused for a second, the feeling was like walking by an old portrait in an art museum, the eyes in the painting giving the illusion of movement, following the viewer. There appeared to be an image formed against the tree trunk by the pattern of the vines. They'd grown and molded into a symmetrical but aged shape of a face—the face of a very old woman alive in the sap of the vines, her hair like snakes twisted and sprouting from the head of Medusa.

SIXTY-THREE

On the way back to the Marina, I stopped in the Tiki Bar and let Big John know what happened to Kim. He picked up the phone and ordered flowers to be sent to her in Halifax Hospital. As I walked down L-Dock, I thought about what I had to do and the options for doing it. I didn't know if Courtney Burke was dead or alive. To keep her alive, I had to know her real identity. My key, I felt, was lying in the brief conversation I had with the mystery woman on the phone. *Who was she? Where was she?*

I had to find out. To protect Courtney and Kim, I had to try to reach Andrea Logan. I knew that either her phone, mine—or both of them, were monitored. I stood near the palm frond thatched roof of a fish-cleaning station and made the call. After five rings, I thought it was going to voice-mail, and then she said, "Hello, Sean. I can't talk now."

"Andrea, don't hang up, please. Even if you can't talk, you can listen for thirty seconds. The life of a close friend of mine was threatened. She's an innocent victim in this, just as Courtney—a girl who might be our daughter—is an innocent victim."

"Sean, I'm sorry, I have to go."

"Before you do, tell him to back off. All this can be worked out, but if Courtney's harmed…there's no turning around. Tell him, Andrea."

"I'm so sorry." She disconnected. I stared down at the phone in the palm of my hand, resisting the urge to throw it into the bay. I started toward *Jupiter*.

"Sean, wait up."

247

I turned around to see Dave walking down the dock with two large plastic bags of ice. He said, "I caught the news bulletin on Channel Nine. They're saying a shooting just happened on Sailfish Street. Please tell me Kim's not hurt."

"She's hurt, but she'll live." I told him what happened.

He looked across the marina, his eyes troubled. He watched a charter fishing boat, four customers in the cockpit, the crew already serving the men drinks. Dave said, "They'd better keep security posted right outside her door. The only way that this roller coaster will come to a screeching halt is to find Courtney."

"That's all I've been thinking about the last few days.

"Well, apparently, she's not in Florida anymore?"

"What do you mean?"

"She was spotted in New Orleans. A street artist, a guy who used to be a police sketch artist, said he spoke with her near the French Quarter. He said she ran away, and then he sketched her face from memory, from the brief time he talked to her. Let me put this ice away, one bag's for Nick, and I'll show you the sketch on my tablet. I downloaded it from CNN."

As we walked by *St. Michael*, Dave yelled, "Nick, get your ice before it melts."

"Where's Max?" I asked.

"After playing an intense game of tag with Ol' Joe the cat, she hit my sofa for a power nap."

Nick came out of his boat, hair tousled, eyes puffy. Dave handed him a bag of ice over the transom. He grinned and said, "A boat without ice is like a car without tires. You get nothing done. Any luck on finding the girl?"

"Not yet," I said. "Nick, Kim's been hurt." I gave him a brief explanation. He listened without interruption, the condensation from the ice dripping on top of his brown bare feet.

He shook his head, glanced at a pelican soaring over the water, and said, "Sean, I'm in good shape now. Let me join you hunting for these guys. Kim's like a sister to me. I'm coming with you."

"You're still not fully healed. Sit tight. I'm trying to come up with a plan that will remove Kim from any of this."

"How fast can you pull that off?"

"Not fast enough."

Dave said, "It's believed Courtney Burke was spotted in New Orleans. Toss your ice in the freezer and come aboard *Gibraltar*. I was about to show Sean an image of what looks a lot like Courtney."

Nick nodded, walked back inside *St. Michael*, and reappeared with a six-pack of Coronas in his hand. He followed us to *Gibraltar*, sitting on a stool at Dave's bar, popping the top off a beer. "Want one?"

I shook my head. "Not now."

Dave said, "I'll be mixing a batch of Grey Goose martinis after five-thirty."

I picked Max up and set her on my lap, scratching behind her hound dog ears. Her brown eyes began to close.

Dave picked up his tablet and found the image. He enlarged it on screen and said, "The sketch artist was interviewed. He said he'd spotted the girl eating alone on a park bench near Jackson Square close to the French Quarter. He said, even with her dark glasses and hat, he could tell she was beautiful. He told a reporter that the girl had a face of an angel—a face he had to draw, if he's to be believed."

Nick sipped his Corona and said, "To me, it sounds like a way to pick up women."

I studied the image. "It's hard to say, but from the sketch, it could be Courtney. There's a resemblance…but it could be a million other young women, too. We can't be certain it's her."

Dave nodded. "But we can be certain of one thing: whoever sent those two bounty hunters to Gibsonton, whoever intimidated and hurt Kim…you can bet they've sent their troops to New Orleans, or they may already have someone in the city."

Nick said, "Maybe that'll take the heat off Kim."

I said, "If they find Courtney in New Orleans, yes. But they still believe Kim knows the name of the woman who lent her mobile phone to Courtney. Dave, do you have anyone at your old place of employment who you can unconditionally trust?"

"There are a couple at the agency who haven't retired. I'd trust them in any situation."

"Good." I wrote down the number and handed it to him. "Here's the number to the woman I told you about—the one Courtney called. I believe it's connected to somewhere in South Carolina or across the state line near Augusta, Georgia."

Dave looked through his bifocals. "Okay, what do you need?"

"The physical location of the person who has that number. It may be a landline or a mobile phone. I need the address. Home or apartment. If it's a mobile, and the GPS is on, I'll need her location as I'm tracking her."

"That'll take minutes to find out."

"Good. It's urgent. Did any of the news stories say whether Courtney's been spotted by anyone else in New Orleans?"

"No one has come forth, but with Carlos Bandini adding money to the Crime Stoppers reward, it's now at two-hundred grand.

That'll bring out the sentinels and ghost hunters."

Nick chuckled. "The Big Easy has its share of ghost hunters."

I said, "The question is—if the girl in that sketch is Courtney, why did she go to New Orleans? What's there or who's there? Will she stay hidden in the city? Now that she's been seen, probably not. Where will she go next?"

"Good questions," Nick said. "It's too damn bad that all this is happening with your ex-girlfriend, at least with her politician husband, because if Andrea Logan gave a damn about the girl who might be her daughter, she could be in a position to help find her. But you can't even tell Andrea because it places Courtney in the cross-hairs of an assassin. Screw it, Sean. I'm worried about Kim now. Call Andrea and tell her to tell her husband to back off or you'll kick his sanctimonious ass the length of the Washington Monument."

"I did call her a half hour ago."

Nick's dark eyebrows arched. "What'd she say?"

"She listened, mostly. For half a minute. Without mentioning Senator Logan by name, I urged her to tell him to leave it alone...or there will be consequences."

Dave exhaled, set his tablet on the table and said, "You walk a fine and very dangerous line, Sean. Logan has the full protection of the Secret Service. If you even utter a threat specifically against Logan, they'll arrest you so fast your head will spin. It's a hell of an unfair advantage. He's could have access to the NSA's resources to monitor calls, emails, and any electronic communications through its PRISM program and Patriot Act. Is Logan privy to it?

I don't know. Regardless, he can be in his jet or luxury bus on the campaign stops, whisper treacherous directives for his subordinates to follow, and stay beyond reproach in the eye of the law and the public. But you,

Sean, have to play by the rules."

"Maybe," I said standing. "Maybe not." "What do you mean?" Nick asked.

"I might not be able to threaten Logan, personally. But I can send a sincere message through someone else."

Nick leaned forward on the barstool. "Sincere? Through who?"

"That will depend on who they send. The invite goes out tonight. Dave, I'm going to give you a call in a little while. Play along. They're listening on my main phone, no doubt. And now it's time to turn the tables."

SIXTY-FOUR

It's not difficult to find a sex shop in Daytona Beach. The hard part is going into one to buy something that's not about sex, but rather about life or death. I needed a blow-up doll of a woman. The shop in the heart of A1A, a block from the Atlantic Ocean, smelled of latex and bleach. Its inventory of blow-up dolls was limited to one blond and three brunettes, fully blown up, all appearing to have the same anatomical assets. I picked a brunette. The beefy clerk was unshaven, lots of tats, one earlobe stretched with a black onyx piece of jewelry the size of a quarter. He had a silver pin through his right eyebrow. "Be eighty bucks," he said.

I paid in cash.

"Have a nice night," he said, sitting back on a stool in front of the register, picking at a scab in the center of a Daffy Duck tattoo on his Popeye forearm.

I walked outside and into a wall of humid heat in the late afternoon, the sound of the breakers clashing with the bass throb of rap music coming from a low-rider car at the traffic light. Max sat in the front seat. "We have company," I said to her, setting the doll down in the Jeep's rear seats, glad my new passenger was only five feet tall. Max stuck her head between the front seats, glancing back at the naked doll, and then up at me. She cocked her head, looking at me for a brief Max moment.

I couldn't think of anything to say.

Driving to my old cabin on the St. Johns River, about forty minutes west of Daytona, I rehearsed in my mind the conversation I was about to have with Dave Collins. It had to sound real, and it had to strike a sense of urgency that could set a trap for a killer or killers.

I made the call.

Dave said, "Hello."

"I heard from Courtney."

"You did? Where is she, Sean?"

"She was in New Orleans. She's been driving back to Florida. The kid's scared. She's tired and wants this to end."

"What can she do—what can you do?"

"Hold a news conference."

"That should be an eye-opener. Where? When?"

"Soon. Maybe tomorrow. That way it's all out in the wash. Detective Grant can take her into custody, at least she'll be safer. I don't believe he has the evidence he needs to get a conviction in the death of Lonnie Ebert. In the Bandini case, I think a jury will believe Courtney's story, defending herself against a sociopathic rapist."

"But the big question, the one the nation would like to hear the answer to is this: is Courtney Burke the girl you and Andrea Logan conceived twenty years ago?"

"It's time to let the chips fall where they will. This is about the life of a young woman. It trumps political rhetoric."

"Is she coming back to Ponce Inlet?"

"No, I gave her directions to my river cabin. I expect her around midnight. She'll be coming down I-75, catching 441 over to 40. Dave, my battery's dying. I gave her your number, too. If she calls, if she gets lost, remind her my place is two hundred yards on the right past the first Ocala National Forest sign off Highway 445." I hit the *End Call* button and let out a long breath. Dave had been magnificent. All of his covert training continued to serve him well.

— —

A HALF HOUR later, I was pulling into my gravel and oyster shell driveway leading down to my river cabin, a place I wish I could retreat to and take up yoga. Not today, and certainly not tonight. I was expecting guests, unannounced guests, and I'd leave the light on for them.

I was glad the seclusion of an old cabin on the river would allow me to walk into my home with a life-size sex doll and not give the neighbors a season's worth of gossip. Although my anonymity was lost, no sense in carrying the label of a sexual pervert, too. My nearest neighbor was almost a mile away, at this moment in time, not far enough. "Max, what do you say we call our friend? How about Suzy?"

Max looked up at me and snorted.

I turned toward the always smiling doll and said, "We hope you enjoy our little place on the river. You'll have a great view of the water. More importantly, those folks who'd like to shoot a bullet through your rubber head will see you, but not too well. At least that's Plan A. I've been known to go through the alphabet with my Plan A's. Back in a second." I had a sudden recall of one of the scenes from the movie *Castaway* when the character that Tom Hanks played spoke to a soccer ball he named Wilson.

Max and I left the doll in the Jeep and walked around the perimeter of my cabin. I checked windows and doors for the slightest sign of intrusion, examined the dust and pollen on windowsills and doorknobs. I couldn't see any overt signs that someone had entered my home.

And then there it was.

Max was sniffing something near a live oak. A boot print. A combat boot. I recognized the unique pattern or tread left in the dirt next to one of the largest live oaks on my property. The print was made from what was called a Panama sole. These combat boots are excellent in tropical terrain. I spotted some abrasions to the bark on the tree, a rather slight discoloration from the surrounding area of the trunk. The intruder had climbed the tree. When he'd dropped back down, he left the single well-defined boot print and a partial of another. Why had he climbed the tree? I looked from the perspective back to my house. A clear view.

Surveillance camera.

I jumped up to the first low-hanging limb, pulled myself on top of the limb and examined the tree. Someone had mounted a small camera to the limb. The camera was no larger than the water nozzle you'd attach to a garden hose. It was fastened to a metal plate bolted onto the limb. But the wires leading to a battery and a weather-sealed laptop were not attached. The job wasn't finished.

So they already knew where I lived.

I dropped to the ground and looked at the western sky, to the horizon far beyond the oxbow in the river. It was less than a half hour before sunset, the clouds beginning to blush into pinks and soft merlot colors. I'd wait until the cover of darkness to move Suzy into the house. And then, at midnight, I'd wait for them. I walked twenty feet away from the tree, turned and fired a single shot into the lens of the camera they'd mounted, glass raining down like acorns dropping.

SIXTY-FIVE

At 8:00 pm, I set the bait. I carried Suzy into the house, turned on the television, and placed my house guest in front of the screen. I positioned her so the flickering light from the TV screen would cast the silhouetted form of a woman against the curtains in front of the bay window. I adjusted the light levels in the room, walked outside and checked. Perfect. Since Suzy was presumably watching TV, no one should notice that she wasn't moving. At least I was counting on no one noticing.

And now, the countdown. In the conversation I had with Dave, I'd told him—and whoever was listening—that Courtney Burke was expected to arrive at midnight. Would they plan to be here before that time, or could I expect them anytime between midnight and dawn? I didn't know, but I did know what I needed in my hands to stop the intruders if they came as a team—two or more. I went inside and opened the gun cabinet, removed my Remington Special Ops Tactical 12-gauge pump shotgun, and loaded the chamber and magazine with double-aught buckshot. I cleaned and reloaded my Glock. Learning to expect the unexpected, I was seldom surprised.

Max seemed anxious, pacing the floor once or twice, occasionally glancing at our silent and lifeless house guest. I didn't want her in harm's way, but I needed her uncanny sense of hearing. Her bark would be a short alarm, just the edge I'd need to have a better advantage against the intruder or intruders. I'd planned on locking Max in a back bedroom facing the western approach to my cabin. The darkest area of the property. I would be outside, hidden, waiting in the shadows or trees. My point-of-view would include a bird's eye

256

perspective of the entire property, especially the road frontage, my driveway, and the side of the house with the silhouette in the window.

I went back inside, secured Max in a bedroom, and dressed in dark jeans and black T-shirt. I sprayed insect repellent on my exposed body parts before stepping onto the screened-in front porch and reaching inside a bag of charcoal. I removed two briquettes, crushing them together in the palms of my hands. Then I rubbed the black residue all over my face, ears, arms and hands. I used a wet-wipe to keep my palms clean.

A curlew called out across the river somewhere on the edge of the national forest. The dying sunset cast the St. Johns in cavernous shade from the palms, oaks and weeping willows along the shore. The river was very still. Woven in between the saw-tooth shade was the reflection of clouds like clusters of purple grapes floating in red wine, a wiry mist frolicking off the water and painting the surface into a river of dreams.

But the illusion of tranquility was short lived. I spotted the ripple of a V formation as a massive alligator slowly swam from murky water beneath a cypress tree. It swam around cypress knees sprouting like knobby posts out of the water, the big gator's nostrils and eyes above the surface.

I was wondering how I might carry out a plan without resulting to torture. The thought of replicating the use of gas on a stove, like what was almost tried on Kim, disgusted me. I'd prefer to use Mother Nature. She could be much more convincing.

— ▪ —

I USED AN aluminum ladder to get to my lookout position—my rooftop, pulling the ladder up behind me. I'd taken a viewpoint position from behind my stone chimney, putting it between me and the road. That was three hours ago. Watching. Waiting. Mosquitoes orbited my head, whining off-key in my ears. I set the shotgun down and did twenty-five pushups, moving the blood, keeping my senses as sharp as possible.

The moon was on my side tonight. It slept late, but like an old friend, the full moon was there, rising in the east above the treeline, and its light like spun gold off the liquid face of the river. Bats did aerial stunts under the moonlight. I waited. Listened. Would they come?

To my far right, in the west, I saw the distant flash of lightning. I was hoping the soldier or soldiers would arrive before the rain. It would be much harder to spot them in a moonless night with rain falling. I heard the distinct hoot of a barred owl, the hooting coming from one of the cypress trees near my dock. Cicadas vibrated in the limbs. Then there was the mechanical sound of man.

A car was coming.

I peered from around the side of the chimney and watched the light from the headlamps travel across the treetops. Within seconds, a car rounded the bend. It moved at a speed slower than the posted forty-five-miles-per hour, but not so slow to be obvious that the driver was searching for something. When the car was near the spot where my driveway joined the road, there was a minor reduction in speed. Then it passed the driveway. Fifty feet later, a tap of the brakes. But only for a second. The driver continued.

I knew he'd be back. And he wouldn't be in his car.

SIXTY-SIX

A n hour later, I knew I wasn't going to get my wish. I'd hoped the rain would not arrive before the mercenary. It did. The clouds fanned in and the temperature fell. It was as if a black hood had dropped over the moon. Gone. The first drops were large, splattering through the branches and leaves, the rain cooling the old quarry-stone chimney that still harbored warmth generated by exposure all day in the Florida sun. Now it was cool to my touch.

I could no longer see my driveway, the road was swallowed in black. I looked just above what I thought was the end of the drive, hoping I might somehow see movement. Nothing. The rain fell harder, water rolling down my face causing the charcoal to run. My hair was drenched. I glanced up into the sky, it was like staring into a coal mine.

Lightning marbled white hot veins through the gut of the clouds. I instinctively looked toward the end of my drive. And there he was. His image caught and frozen for a second in the flash from the lightning. Dressed in military fatigues. Right down to his combat boots. I could only see one man. Maybe that's all they thought they needed. They were wrong.

I crouched down behind the chimney. I knew he'd survey the perimeter of the home, staying back, cautious of motion detectors turning on flood-lights. Often the movement of rain is enough to trigger some motion detec-tors. He'd quickly find the silhouette in the window. The falling rain would make it more difficult to see movement inside the house. And if he got close enough to peer in the window, the trap door from the roof would fall on him. I knew he had orders to kill Courtney. I assumed he had orders to kill me, too.

Max barked. Two barks. Muffled, but there.

I stayed low, squatting and moving to the side of the roof above the bay window. The light coming from the window extended about ten feet into my yard. Within seconds he'd moved to the edge of the light. I could now see his face, right down to his boots. Kim's voice ratcheted in my mind. *'He's about your height, but stocky. His hair is blond…cut short. His ears stuck out just a little. He had cleft chin and hateful green eyes.'*

And there he stood. On my property. Next to my house. Pistol in his hands. He stepped closer to the window, raising the gun up. I recognized it: a FNP .45 Tactical. Often used by Special Forces soldiers. It will fire up to fifteen rounds as fast as the shooter can pull the trigger.

I watched him. He leveled the pistol. Held it with both hands. Stepped to within three feet of the window. Pointed the .45 and fired in rapid succession: *bam—bam—bam—bam—bam.*

Five shots. At the end of the fifth round, lightning exploded in the top of a tall pine. Thunder reverberated. I dropped from the roof. All two-hundred-ten pounds landing squarely on his shoulders. He fell flat on his back, his lungs trying to suck air into them. I slammed the shotgun stock into the center of his forehead. His eyes glazed, looked at me, black streaks running down on my face, wet hair, right fist cocked. His eyes grew wide—confused, and then dull, a second before rolling back in their sockets.

I turned him over, pulled his hands behind his back, and used duct tape to bind them. Then I picked him up, lifting the dead weight over my shoulder, carrying him through the rain down to my dock. I lowered him to the very end of the dock, extending more than seventy-five feet into the river. The rain stopped and quiet settled over the river. I looped a rope around the man's belt. His eyelids flickered and then opened. He stared up at the night sky, the black clouds gone, the moon back, its light reflecting off the dark surface of the river. A cottonmouth moccasin made S movements swimming across the river.

I stood over the man and said, "I love a full moon. It really makes the river come alive. Lots of activity on the St. Johns under a full moon. What's your name, soldier?"

He cut his green eyes to my face. Silence.

"Okay. I assume you're under orders not talk about your mission. But you see, part of your mission included hurting a good friend of mine when you and your buddy broke into her home. I know you like to play with fire. You know what I like to play with? I'll tell you...alligators."

He's eyes narrowed. I could see him dry swallow. I said, "Tell me who sent you."

He shook his head. "You can't stop them. They have access to dozens of guys like me. You might stop me, but another will take my place immediately."

"I'm going to ask you one more time. Who sent you?"

"Go to hell."

"We're seventy-five feet out into the river. From this point, the current kicks to the right because it hits the jetty just before my property, and it flows faster toward the center of the river. Similar to how a billiard ball bounces from the rail of the table. So when I throw you off my dock, you'll be in the center of the river in less than half a minute. My guess is that it'll take the first gator about that amount of time to swim to you. It's mating season, and they're more hungry than usual."

"You're fucking crazy."

"When a big guy like you tortures a woman, a friend of mine, it brings that trait out in me. Guess what, there's a gator in here longer than my two-man kayak. I call him Samson. My neighbor says ol' Samson pulled down a huge deer that tried swimming the river a month ago. Who sent you?"

"Fuck you!"

I kicked him off the end of the dock. He vanished under the black water, seconds later popping up more than fifteen feet from the dock. With his hands behind his back, he kicked hard, trying to tread water. The current carried him farther away from my dock. He fought hard to keep his head above water. Splashing. Spitting water. Ringing the dinner bell.

There was the sound of a *plop* across the river, like a tree falling into the water. I said, "Hear that? That was probably Samson. He'll crush your entire chest cavity in one bite. The next gator will clamp down on your leg. It'll be a tug of war. They'll pull you apart like a wishbone."

Under the moonlight, he looked around frantically, head moving side to side. He could see a large alligator swimming from the far bank of the river. Nostrils and eyes out of the water. The tail like a big paddle.

261

TOM LOWE

"Get me outta here!" he screamed.

I rolled video on my phone. "Who sent you?"

"Pull me in!"

"Who sent you?"

"Please! I have a wife and kids!"

The gator was less than one hundred feet away. Eyes like rubies in the moonlight.

"Pull the damn rope!"

"Tell me what I want to know."

"I don't know!"

"Bullshit."

"Please!"

The gator was gaining, swimming faster.

"I can't die like this!"

"This is the last time…who sent you?"

"Orders came down from Senator Logan's camp."

"Who in his camp?"

"I don't fucking know! Swear to God!"

"Gator's about thirty seconds from you."

"I heard it was Timothy Goldberg. He runs Logan's donor campaign."

"What do they want?"

"The girl dead."

"What girl?"

"Courtney Burke. She's a huge liability for Logan. Please!"

I set the phone down, lifted my Glock and fired a shot in front of the gator to scare it. It submerged beneath the surface. I pulled the rope—fast, hand-over-hand, reeling in the terrified soldier. I grabbed his belt and lifted him up and out of the river, the gator rising to the surface less than twenty feet away. The man flopped on the dock, exhausted, breathing hard, vomiting. I played back a few seconds of his confession on video. He looked up at the video screen on the phone, his face in sheer disbelief. He closed his eyes.

I said, "Get up."

"Wha—"

"Up!" I lifted him to his feet, left his hands tied, picked up the shotgun, and chambered a shell. "Let's take a walk."

262

"Where?"

"To your car."

I followed behind him. We walked to the highway and more than one hundred yards west. He'd parked the car under some live oak trees off the road. I said, "Here's the plan. You're getting off easy tonight. You're going to drive away, meet with your contractor and tell him your confession is on video—taped under the moonlight, good sound and a clear picture. Your team is going to let Goldberg and Logan know that if they continue hunting Courtney Burke, I will upload this video to YouTube. Let's see how fast it'll go viral. And then let's see how fast Logan's presidential bid goes down in flames. Turn around."

He turned around and I used my knife to slice through the duct tape. I stepped back, tapped him between the shoulder blades with the shotgun and said, "Get out of here. Deliver the message and all of this stays buried. If you ever return, you won't walk away."

He opened the door to his car and turned back to me. "Who the hell are you and where the fuck did you train?"

I was silent, the cicadas echoing in the woods.

"The girl…is she your daughter? Is that why you're putting the crosshairs across your back?"

"I'm doing this because it's the right thing to do."

He shook his head, started the car, and drove down the road, the red wash from taillights spattering against the cabbage palms and live oaks. I watched him drive past my driveway.

This time he didn't tap the brakes.

SIXTY-SEVEN

The next morning I met Dave for breakfast at Crabby Joe's, a small restaurant plopped on the side of a fishing pier off Daytona Beach. After I told him what happened on the river, I held out a flash-drive and said, "It's all on here. I made a copy to give to you as an insurance policy of sorts."

He looked over his hot cup of black coffee. "Insurance?"

"If something happens to me, upload this video to YouTube and call a damn news conference. It's the only way Courtney, and for that matter, Kim, will be safe."

He took the drive, looked at it for a moment, and dropped it into the pocket of his Hawaiian print shirt. "So the mercenary hit man was hired by Logan's top dog, Timothy Goldberg, and ostensibly by Logan himself. The guy's got ice water in his bloodstream. Regardless, dismiss with this talk of something happening to you. All right, what we have is the seamy side of presidential politics captured on a steamy, alligator-infested river. And now, Sean, the old proverbial truism is most applicable to you: when you're up to your ass in political alligators, what happens if you drain the swamp and find the bodies?"

"Logan's people know where they're hidden. I'm hoping I bought some time for Courtney. That phone number I gave you, did you manage to find a physical address?"

"Of course. I found an address and an ID."

"What's her name?"

"Katherine O'Sullivan."

264

"I wonder who she is…and what's her relationship to Courtney Burke?"

"Could be a relative or a friend. If she's Courtney's mother, that means you certainly aren't her father. And that, my friend, is one hell of a relief. Ponce Marina might return to its former sleepy self."

I stirred my coffee and looked at the breakers rolling below us on the beach, the briny scent of the surf drifting up through quarter-inch spaces between the planks in the weathered pier. Through the enclosed screen, I watched a seagull perched on the dock railing turn to face the breeze across the Atlantic.

Dave sipped his coffee, his eyes filled with deliberations. "I know, after all is said and done, it would be nice getting to know a daughter you never knew existed. Sometimes truth is a double-edge sword, it often heals the heart by cutting the heart. It leaves scars. A magician's secret, once revealed, shows the truth behind the illusion, and in doing so, the show is never quite the same."

"I have no illusions."

"Maybe not, but you're human. You have hope or you wouldn't do what you do and you wouldn't be the man you are. Look, Courtney still faces murder charges. If she's acquitted, if the charges are dropped, life goes on. Even a president-elect Logan, should he win, can survive the backstory of his wife's decision to give up a child years ago. However, his political career won't endure a long trial in which his wife's biological daughter is found guilty of multiple murders."

"Maybe this woman, Katherine O'Sullivan, is the key. What's her address?"

Dave removed a small, folded piece of paper from his pocket. "Here you go. Maybe she's the key to Courtney's past and future. And if there's no connection to your past, that means you step out of this mental cellblock and walk away, Sean. Courtney Burke becomes someone else's concern."

"You make it sound easy. Whether she's my daughter or not, she's some-body's daughter. I don't believe she's guilty of murder—only self-defense, and that's not a crime."

"But you don't know that yet. Leave it to Detective Grant or the feds."

"To do what? Put a bullet in the back of Courtney's head? Dan Grant is just trying to do his job, but the feds—at least whoever's working for Logan, are the type of soldiers who'd roast Kim's hand over a blue flame and then go home to a family meal."

"Maybe this Katherine O'Sullivan is the link to Courtney's family."

"The only way to find out is to go there. Max is napping in the Jeep. You mind taking her back to the marina, keeping an eye on her until I get back?"

"You don't even have to ask."

"Thanks, Dave."

"You leaving now?"

"Right after I visit the hospital."

— • —

AFTER I SHOWED my ID at the reception desk at Halifax Hospital, left a thumb print, and had my picture taken, I was given clearance to visit Kim Davis, room 222, second floor. I bought a dozen red roses in the gift shop and stepped into the elevator. The odor of bleach and hand sanitizer mixed with the scent of the roses as I walked down the long hallway. Nurses darted in and out of rooms, doctors spoke quickly into portable Dictaphones, recording detailed patient medical data but often never really knowing who it was that they were treating.

A sheriff's deputy sat outside room 222 reading a *Sports Illustrated* magazine. He had a clipboard propped up on the wall behind his plastic chair. I introduced myself and had him check to see if I was on the visitors list. I was. *Chalk one up for Detective Dan Grant.*

I entered the room and stopped after the door closed behind me. Kim lay in the bed, IVs attached to both arms, her face bruised, a monitor recording her heart rate. Even through the wires, tubes, and bandages, she was beautiful—the light from the window falling on her sleeping face. I stepped next to her bed and stood there for a moment, watching her breathe. I wanted to say something, but didn't want to wake her from a tranquil sleep. I set the roses on a table next to her bed and heard, "Hello, stranger." Her voice sounded drowsy.

I turned around. Kim was awake, eyes heavy, a smile spreading. I grinned. "Stranger? Come on, you've been out like a light. You don't know how long I've been here, or how many times I've been here."

"A girl knows. It's an intuitive thing. Even in our sleep, we know if some-one special is here. Also, how could I be out like a light? If a light's out, it's no longer a light. Oh, my head feels like it's in a vice. Those roses are soooo beautiful! Thank you."

"You're welcome. What are the doctors telling you?"

"They're fairly sure I suffered a concussion. I had twenty-two stitches in the back of my head and some internal bleeding. The good news is that I can go home tomorrow. Detective Grant told me you shot one of the men. Did you...did you kill him?"

"I don't know. A body hasn't been found. I did find the other guy."

"You did?"

"Yes. He decided to pay me a visit at my cabin on the river."

"Why?"

"He wanted information."

"Did he get it?"

"He gave more than he received. He took a message back to his leader. I believe it'll be safe for you to go home tomorrow. Rest and get well, okay? I have to go now."

She lifted her hand, an IV taped to the back of it. "You just got here, Sean. Don't go."

"I wish I didn't have to. I've got to bring this thing to a stop.

I'll be back soon."

"Where are you going?"

"If you don't know, you can't say."

"I thought you said I was safe."

"Safer. You're much safer now. I don't think they'll be back."

"I'm not worried about me. I'm afraid for you. Are you still trying to find Courtney?"

"Yes."

"I have no doubt that you'll find her. But I don't know what you'll find. I only met her briefly, but she seemed like a good kid. If she's your daughter, she'd have to be."

I bent down and kissed Kim on her forehead. "Get well."

"Be careful, Sean. I don't know if it's the meds they have me on, but I've been having bad dreams, really dark stuff...and you're there...caught in the middle."

SIXTY-EIGHT

Five hours and seventeen minutes. I looked at my watch as I started to cross the Savannah River. Five hours and seventeen minutes earlier, I'd left Kim's hospital room and driven nonstop from Ponce Inlet to Augusta, Georgia. Crossing the Savannah River on Highway 25, over the James Jackson Bridge, I felt as if I was crossing a bridge over troubled waters. I'd read somewhere that the Savannah River itself was one of the most toxic rivers in the nation. The bridge spanned the river, connecting Georgia with South Carolina. I was en route to a place called Murphy Village in South Carolina, a few miles north of the Savannah River.

I continued driving up Highway 25, following a printed map in search of the address Dave Collins had given to me. I'd removed the battery and sim cards from my phones. Didn't use a portable GPS either. Didn't want to chance an eye in the sky following me. I glanced from the map in my hand to my gas gauge. Nineteen miles until empty.

I pulled off the road and stopped at a Chevron station. I stepped inside to pay the clerk cash before pumping. I bought a large coffee, black, paid and walked back outside. An older model blue pickup truck eased up to the pump opposite the one I was using. A man dressed in faded overalls and a sweat-stained John Deere green cap, got out of the truck. He was at least seventy, lanky, unshaved, face filled with white whiskers. He nodded at me and said, "We sure need some rain. My corn crop won't make it another three days if we don't get us a damn good rain."

"What's the forecast?"

"Hot, hot, and hotter. Damndest weather in the last few years than anytime I can remember. I ain't no tree hugger, but I damn sure believe we mucked up stuff so much it's affected the climate. You work the land, you can tell." He nodded and started pumping gas into the old truck. He looked back at me. "Where you from?"

"Florida."

"Ya'll got hit hard with a freeze last winter. Ruined most of the citrus."

"You're right. How far is Murphy Village?"

I saw his right eyebrow rise up. "It's about ten miles down twenty-five. Can't miss it. The place is mansions and junkyards. Industrial, residential, and even some agricultural land all rolled into one place."

"Thanks."

"Don't want to sound nosey, but why would a fella from Florida want to go there?"

"I'm looking for someone."

He nodded, glanced at the gasoline pump, and cut his eye back to me. "Lemme give you a little friendly advice. Don't hire anybody in there to do anything for you. If your car needs fixin,' go someplace else."

"Why the caution?"

"That's the largest population of Irish gypsies in the country. They call themselves travelers, not gypsies, but it's the same. Every summer the men head out, they travel all over the nation. Some use fake ID's. Fake license plates on their trucks and cars. They'll paint your house with watered-down paint. Repave your driveway with materials that don't last. Fix your roof 'til the next big cloud-buster. By then, they're long gone. They're some of the best con artists anywhere. Smooth talkers. One fella will knock at your door, with a sob story, or a deal that's too damn good to be true. His partner will be stealing your silver. The elderly, people my age, that's their prime targets."

"Sounds like an interesting bunch."

He finished pumping gas, replaced the nozzle, and said, "Don't want to mess in your business, I'm just warning you. These people are real damn clannish. They simply don't talk to outsiders. Won't answer their doors. It's trailers and mansions. All of 'em have paper covering their windows to keep prying eyes out."

"Thank you."

He removed his John Deere hat and wiped his rawboned face with a red handkerchief. "Gonna be a scorcher." Then he got back in his truck and drove away, windows down, a rifle balanced in the gun rack visible through the dirty back window.

There were no posted signs letting me know that I'd entered the town of Murphy Village. It wasn't needed. The farmer's description wasn't embellished. In truth, he'd restrained his account of what I was now seeing. The homes were a concoction of mansions and trailers tucked behind scrub pines and oaks. English Tudor, Mediterranean, all brick homes, sprouted like misplaced castles on an acreage of spotty lawns, fenced warehouses, cars on blocks, and bent mailboxes with no addresses. Every home had at least one pickup truck in the driveway, front facing the street. License plates not visible. It was a land of contrasts but not contradictions. Ostentatious symbols of wealth infused in a quilt of deficiency, a measurable history of a hardscrabble life.

I saw no signs of life. No moms pushing babies in strollers. No dogs. No one watering dry lawns. Nothing. I did see what appeared to be cream-colored construction paper inside each window in every home facing the street. I looked at the house number Dave had given me and wondered how I'd find a residence in a sprawling neighborhood barren of visible addresses.

I glanced up in my rearview mirror and saw a mail truck coming my way. The postman stopped in front of mailboxes, delivering, and moving on down his route. I pulled to the side of the road and waited. When he stopped at the box behind my Jeep, I got out, and walked to his truck. I offered my most convincing smile said, "You must be clairvoyant or you've worked this neighborhood for a long time. I'm having the hardest time finding addresses. Who would have thought that delivering a birthday gift would be such a challenge? I had an easier time finding addresses in Iraq."

He looked over the top of his bifocals, his round face red from the heat, his walrus moustache damp with perspiration. "You fought in the Gulf War?"

"Yeah, a lifetime ago."

"Thank you for your service."

"You're welcome. How do you deliver the mail out here?"

270

"Been doin' it eighteen years now. It's kind of easy because hardly any-body moves in or out. Same families for years. All Irish. Lots of Callaghan's and whatnot."

"Maybe you can help me. I'm trying to deliver a package to eight-ten Murphy Road. I can find the road, but I have no clue which house it is, and I'd hate to not deliver her birthday gift."

"I didn't know it was Miss O'Sullivan's birthday. She's one of the few people here who I've actually gotten to know some. I just delivered the mail to her box. Didn't notice any cards. Too bad. She's a nice woman. Sort of a recluse, like all of 'em. But she always has something pleasant to say if I deliver a larger box to her trailer."

"Trailer?"

"Yes. She is from an old Irish clan. Some of them in here speak ancient Gaelic and other Irish brogues. I'd heard she lost her only daughter. Murdered. They never caught the killer. News said it might even have been Miss O'Sullivan's own granddaughter—the daughter of the woman who was killed. I need to get going. I hope you can deliver the present. She strikes me as a woman who hasn't had much to smile about for a long time."

"Where's she live?"

"Oh, you passed it. Back down Murphy, about a half mile on the left. It's the poorer section, no mansion out front. She lives in a light blue trailer back up in the trees. There is a hand-painted picture of a funny looking bird on her mailbox." He nodded, took his foot off the brake, and drove down to the next mailbox.

I turned the Jeep around and drove in the direction he'd given me, hop-ing that Katherine O'Sullivan was home, hoping that what she might say could be the connection to Courtney Burke's past, and be the bridge over her troubled waters to a better future.

SIXTY-NINE

I remembered something Dave Collins said to me when Nick and I hooked an old German U-boat on our anchor rope while fishing in the Atlantic. Its cargo had been weapons-grade uranium. Dave had talked about a scene in a Hitchcock film, *Spellbound*, a dream sequence in which eyes were everywhere. The art director in the film had been Salvador Dali. Dave had said just because I couldn't see *their* eyes didn't mean I wasn't being watched.

That's what I felt like at the moment.

Watched. Followed by unseen eyes in a *Stepford Wives* illusion of idyllic calm that was a prelude to a storm. I stopped in front of a light brown mailbox, a small, hand painted image of a bird on it. I recognized the species—a puffin. It resembled a cousin to a penguin, black and white tuxedo-like feathers, yellow webbed feet, and an orange and black beak. Whoever had painted it on the mailbox was very talented.

I looked up the driveway, a trailer barely visible through the trees and low-hanging branches. As I backed up to turn into the drive, a man in a white pickup truck drove slowly by me. He braked to a crawl. Watched to see what I was doing, his eyes hard as lug nuts. Then he lifted his mobile phone and drove down the road.

I put the Jeep in gear, intuitively touching my Glock between the seat and console. After more than two-hundred feet, I came to a clearing, a trailer in the middle surrounded by trees. There were no cars. But there were signs of life. Red and white flowers filled clay pots, purple and yellow bougainvillea climbed terraces, and pink impatiens lined pine mulch beds tucked in deep shade from the trees. A bench swing sat motionless under the shade from a tall cottonwood tree. The warm air smelled of fresh-cut hay and heather. The breeze picked up and the tree released its seeds, floating through the air like white, down-feathered snowflakes.

I walked to the front door and knocked. Wind chimes tinkled and somewhere in the trees a mourning dove cooed a succession of somber cries. I could hear the subdued sounds of someone moving about the trailer, making an effort to be quiet.

I knocked again. Then I spoke up, loud enough to be heard but tactful enough to not sound threatening. "Miss O'Sullivan, my name is Sean O'Brien. The only reason I'm here, ma'am, is because of your granddaughter. Courtney's in very serious trouble, and you may be the only person left on earth who can help her now."

I waited. The mourning dove cooing, cottonwood snow falling on my shoulders. And then I heard a series of locks turning, finally the door opening a crack. Sunlight fell on the face of an old woman. She looked up at me. Her eyes reminded me of Courtney's eyes, but paler, tired eyes. Her cheek bones were prominent, and I could tell she must have been striking as a younger woman. She coughed into a handkerchief, a deep raspy sound in her lungs. She glanced down at the handkerchief and said, "Sean O'Brien." She spoke with an Irish accent.

"Yes."

"That's your name?

"Yes."

"Where's Courtney?"

"I'm not sure. She's on the run. Her life's in grave danger. Is she your biological granddaughter?"

"Why do you ask that?"

"Because if she is…it means she's not the biological daughter of the woman who may be the next first lady in the White House. Have you been following the news?"

"Mr. O'Brien, I don't have a TV, don't take the paper anymore. I'm rather isolated. Friends here drive me to the doctor now and then, but I don't get out much anymore."

"May I come in?"

She looked over my shoulder, opened the door, and stepped back. Her eyes seemed to take all of me in at once. "Come in, please."

I followed her inside the trailer. It was neat and clean, furniture at least twenty years old. Framed paintings hung on much of the wall space. There was no television in the living room, but lots of bookcases filled with books. The only photographs I could see were on an end table next to the couch. Courtney Burke, as a younger teenager, was in one picture. Next to it was a photograph of a middle-aged woman—a woman who resembled Courtney.

There were two pictures of babies, one older than the other. And there was a photograph of a man standing next to a woman. They stood by the sea, the wind in the woman's hair, a wide smile on her face. The man had his arm around her waist. He was smiling, his hair dark, eyes piercing.

She said, "Please, sit down." Then she simply stared at me, her thoughts someplace else.

"Miss O'Sullivan…"

"Yes."

"Are you Courtney's biological grandmother?"

"Yes." She cut her eyes down to the photographs, and then looked back up at me.

"Is that her mother in the picture?"

"Yes, she was my only daughter, Sarah. She was murdered."

"I'm very sorry to hear that. Where is Courtney's father?"

"He was murdered alongside Sarah. I raised Courtney the last few years of her life."

"Do you know where she is right now?"

"No." Her eyes studied my face. She asked, "Are you hungry? I made meatloaf and seasoned potatoes."

"No thank you."

"Where's your home?"

"Florida."

"Is that where your parents live, too?"

"They were killed in a car crash when I was a teenager. Miss O'Sullivan… we need to find Courtney. You'll have to let the police know her real identity."

"Yes…of course…just tell me how I can help." She looked at one of the babies in the pictures then slowly cut her eyes back up to me. Her face was suddenly reflective, private thoughts filling eyes that had grown softer. She fidgeted with a wedding ring on her left hand.

"Miss O'Sullivan, Courtney knew that I had a birthmark that resembled an Irish shamrock. How do you think she knew that?"

"Courtney has a gift. She can see things...things most others can't. When she told me that you looked similar to my husband, told me your age, the fact you wore an ancient Irish triquetra pendent from a chain on your neck...I knew. I gave that triquetra to my cousin to give to you when you turned eighteen. My cousin and her husband were childless. They raised you as their own, and they swore absolute secrecy as a condition of the adoption. I insisted that it remain that way because I couldn't have withstood the pain in my heart of seeing you and not taking you back. Courtney knew you had the birthmark because I told her." My heart hammered in my chest.

She spoke in a voice just above a whisper. "It's on your left shoulder. A perfect shamrock."

"How did you know?"

"Because I am your mother, Sean."

SEVENTY

The trailer seemed hot. I said nothing. There was nothing I could say. I could feel the blood surging through my temples, the drone of the mourning dove coming in the open window.

She said, "I used to think the little birthmark was painted on you in my womb by the very hand of God. One leaf for the Father. One for the Son, and one for the Holy Spirit. The fourth, representing temptation, to remind you always how important the first three are in your life."

"How could you be my mother?"

She lifted the framed picture of the woman and man standing by the sea and handed it to me. "That's my husband, the year we were married in Ireland. He's your father."

"What?" I stared at the man in the picture. There was no denying that I bore a strong resemblance to him. "This isn't possible."

"Yes, it is. His name was Peter Flanagan. You were born Sean Flanagan. My married name was Kate Flanagan. What seems impossible is that I have found you after all of these years. I had to give you up when you were a baby. And I've regretted it every day of my life. Please, come, sit beside me."

I moved to the couch and sat next to her. She lifted up another picture, the one of the two babies. She handed it to me and said, "This is you, Sean... the baby on the right. You were less than a year old. I'd left Ireland soon after your father died. The Catholic Church paid for my transportation. I came to South Boston because I had an aunt there. I had three little children at the time, you, your younger sister and your older brother. We lived from

276

hand-to-mouth…poverty. It was only a matter of time before the county would take my babies from me and place them in foster homes. I couldn't afford to raise you by myself." She paused, her eyes welling with tears, voice cracking.

"It's okay. Take your time. I need to hear this."

She nodded. "You were the child I chose to be raised outside of there and here, Murphy Village. I felt in my heart you had such promise, and that's why I gave you up for adoption when you were a baby. I came to South Carolina with my aunt and her husband. Her husband was born an Irish traveler. Later on, he taught your brother, Dillon, the ways of the travelers. Taught him no good, evil ways. I eventually remarried to a man named James O'Sullivan. He was part of the clan here—it's something you marry into if you're not from here. One summer my husband, James, left with rest of them, but he never came home. That's been more than twenty years. He was shot by police in a robbery."

"What happened to Dillon?"

"He left home, the first time when he was seventeen. Then he'd come back, looking for money. He'd work a summer on the road with the other men, and he'd drift away again. He worked carnivals and county fairs, always conning people. He got into drugs, pills and alcohol. One summer he came back. The drugs brought out the core of evil in him. On a Sunday night, during an awful thunderstorm, he strangled your sister and stabbed her husband with an ice pick. Police say Sarah had been raped. Poor little Courtney had seen it all, but she'd been too traumatized to tell anyone, even me, until a few years later. Dillon was long gone."

"Why did the Catholic Church pay your way over here?"

"Because I was raped by one of their priests." She lifted the photograph of the other baby boy. "This is your brother, Dillon. I became pregnant with him after the rape. I'd kept if from your father until after your sister was born. All three of you were a year apart between your births."

"How did the man in the picture die?"

She was silent for a few seconds, staring at the smiling and strong image of her husband. "He was shot in the back. He'd gone to confront the priest. I'd begged him not to go."

"How'd he find out the baby wasn't his?"

"Dillon was so different in appearance and personality—very moody and prone to viciousness. And he had a striking resemblance to the priest. I finally told your father. I had to. I loved him too much to continue hiding it from him. Your father was a quiet man until someone threatened his family."

"Did this priest kill him?"

"Police couldn't prove it. Father Garvey was an important figure in the County Kerry. He was very charismatic, had lots of friends, and the church was very powerful at the time. When I told the bishop what had happened to me, he tried to make it seem like I was at fault and it may have happened at a weak time in Father Garvey's life. All they did was transfer him to another parish." She coughed into a napkin, a wet, rasping hack coming from her lungs.

"Are you sick?"

She managed a slight smile. "I'm okay. Right now, I'm better than I've been in years. I've found my son. You're so handsome. Please, tell me about your life. Are you married? Do I have other grandchildren?" She smiled and brushed a strand of white hair behind her ear.

"I was married. Almost thirteen years. Sherri, my wife, died three years ago from ovarian cancer. When she became ill, we didn't talk about having children anymore. And that hurt her maybe more than the cancer. She really wanted kids. I have a dog."

"I am so very sorry to hear about your wife's death." She paused and asked, "What kind of dog do you have?"

"A little dachshund. Her name's Maxine. Max for short."

"I bet she's precious. Courtney said you stay on an old boat sometimes. Is that your home?"

"I have a cabin on the St. Johns River in Florida. I used to be a police detective. I did that after I left the military. Now I teach some criminology courses at a local college and do an occasional charter fishing job."

"Are you happy, Sean?"

"I'm content."

She nodded and lowered her eyes. I could tell she was in pain. She touched my hand. "I want you to know you were never not loved, Sean. It was because of my love, a mother's love so deep, so unconditional, that I did what I thought was best for you. I knew you'd receive a good education, have a good upbringing, and be loved in Celeste and Michael's home. And you were. I'm so grateful and blessed that they lived long enough to see what a fine young man you turned out to be under their loving guidance."

"They were good parents…but I wish they'd told me about you. All the missing birthdays, Mother's Days, the times we never had together."

"I believe in my heart-of-hearts it was better for you to have one set of parents. And this Irish traveler's life is no place to raise a child. Look what happened to your sister, to your niece Courtney…and to your brother."

"Where is he?"

"I don't know. I'd heard he left the carnival work and formed some kind of cult following, acting like he was a prophet. There are some people here in the village who know where he is. They follow him. They talk with him. But they don't give details. Even before you knocked on my door, I know one of them let Dillon know I had a visitor. Through the years, I discovered he stays in touch with only one person."

"Who?"

"His father, the man who raped me…Father Thomas Garvey."

SEVENTY-ONE

There was a knock at the trailer door. Three seconds later a man with a baritone voice and an Irish accent asked, "Mrs. O'Sullivan, is everything all right in there?"

She stepped to the door and opened it slightly. A slender man, long neck, ruddy face, had his nose close to the door. He said, "Just checkin' to see if you needed anything from the store." He tried peering in through the reflection on the glass.

She said, "I'm fine, John. I have plenty of groceries. Everything's okay. Thank you for asking, though." She coughed and braced her hand against the doorframe, her balance off.

He stood there for a few seconds, not quite sure what to say. He ran his tongue inside his left cheek and licked his dry, thin lips before turning to walk to his blue pickup truck.

Katherine returned to the couch. "Living in this village has its good and bad points. Sometimes the word clannish really means nosey when it comes to minding everyone else's business. But, for the most part, they mean well. John McCourt's a sweet man."

"You said that this priest, Father Thomas Garvey, the man who raped you is Dillon's father, and the person most likely to know where to find Dillon."

"He'd be the one person who'd know Dillon's whereabouts, but he'd never disclose it. To openly disclose it is to publically admit to being his father...and the rape."

"Courtney is trying to find him, isn't she?"

"There's no stopping her. God knows I've tried. Although she won't admit it, I know she's searching for him to avenge the deaths of her parents and to return something Dillon stole from me."

"What was it?"

"Are you wearing the triquetre?"

"Yes." I pulled the silver chain from under my T-shirt, the pendent hanging from it.

She slowly reached out and touched it, her lined face filled with awe. She raised her eyes up, meeting mine, and she smiled. "Sean, this is very old. It's believed to be the first metal works of the Celtic Trinity Knot. It was estimated that metal workers fashioned it two thousand years ago. Your father found it and an ancient Irish torc in a bog. He was using a metal detector, and he found it under a foot of muck. The torc is a holy bracelet, maybe worn by a prophet not long after the death of Christ. And the triquetre is one of the earliest artifacts in history unearthed that gives historians a physical indication of how long ago the Holy Trinity was part of the Celtic culture—part of its Christian religion."

"And Dillon, your son...my brother...stole the torc from you?"

"Yes."

"Do you think he sold it?"

"No, he knows of its symbolism and its connection to the time of Christ. He'd rather possess it than sell it because..."

"Why?"

"Some believe the torc, like the triquetre you wear, is made by man from a mold made by God. It's said to be a physical instrument from a higher power. Man was the blacksmith. God the designer. But it's a power that really begins in the heart of its owner...an unselfish heart. Dillon may own it, but he'll never be part of what it means. Sean, maybe you can get to Courtney before she comes close to Dillon. She's blinded by her darkened heart for blood. She needs to come home, bring her back to me." She paused, her face occupied with thoughts from an earlier time. "I used to take her to elementary school, and pick her up, too. The John Calhoun School."

"I'll do my best to find Courtney."

"She's been through so much. She kept cutting herself…self-mutilation. It got so bad I had her with at least three therapists, and she was admitted to a psychiatric hospital for two months. I was terrified she'd kill herself. And now she has turned all that anger into hunting down Dillon."

She glanced down at the image of her and the man she said was my father. "This photograph was taken on a bluff in County Kerry overlooking Puffin Island." She touched the glass with two fingers. "I so loved being there. The little puffins put on such a magnificent show, riding the air currents. They're superb fliers, it's as if they can perform ballet in the air."

I gestured to the art on the walls, paintings of the coasts of Ireland, castles, wildlife, grazing sheep in the foreground, the sea as a backdrop. "Did you paint all of these?"

"Most of them. I don't paint much anymore. Between the arthritis and my failing eyesight, I'm afraid I'm not very good. If I can't do it to the best of my abilities, I won't do it."

I pointed to a medium-sized painting of a young woman standing in a lush field of clover, pink and white heather at her feet, the blue ocean behind her, gulls and puffins in the air. She wore a wide brim hat and a sundress. "Did you paint that?"

"No, your father did. He was very gifted—a good artist and a writer, too. And sometimes a drinker. He enjoyed his Irish whiskey, but he never abused it. He painted that canvas one Sunday by the sea. He wouldn't let me see it until he was finished. Then he gave it to me for my birthday."

"Is that you in the picture?"

"Yes, so many years ago. Would you like to have it?"

"I couldn't take it."

"If you'd like to have it, the painting is yours. It's the only thing in this house I can give you that is part of your father and me."

"Where's his grave?"

"He's buried in the Old Abbey Cemetery in County Kerry. I put flowers on his grave before I left for America. I always wanted to return to place flowers on his grave, but—"

"What?"

"Too much time has slipped by, and now my health isn't what it once was. Makes travel difficult."

"What if I paid for it?"

She smiled. "My health might be failing, but I still have my Irish pride." She looked at my shoulder and asked, "May I see your birthmark? I haven't seen it since I put my last diaper on you."

I pulled up the sleeve on my T-shirt, drew it beyond the birthmark. She slowly reached out, her hand trembling, the tips of her fingers touching my skin, gently caressing the birthmark no larger than a quarter. She looked up at me, her eyes welling with tears. "Sean, I am so sorry for what I did...so very sorry." Tears spilled down her lined face.

"It's all right. You did the best you could—did what you felt was the best thing for me. I don't want you to feel bad for what happened. I had a good life as a kid, just like you'd hoped. You succeeded. I'm fine. And better now that I've found you." I reached over and hugged her, she sobbed—deep long sobs, her warm tears spilling onto my arm.

"It's okay, Mom...it's okay now."

SEVENTY-TWO

Mambo Eve wrapped Courtney's head. Courtney sat on a stool in the voodoo shop as the old woman slowly wrapped her head in a royal blue and canary yellow African head scarf. When she finished, Mambo Eve handed her a hand mirror and said, "You look lovely, child. You have the face of an Egyptian queen." She smiled.

Courtney looked into the mirror and said, "The headdress is beautiful. Thank you. Do you have any hoop earrings?"

Mariah Danford looked up from using Windex to clean the glass case and said, "We do. I have just the pair for you. You could pass a silver dollar through the hoops." She went behind the counter and removed two earrings. "Let me put them on for you." In less than a half minute, she'd attached the earrings to Courtney's ears. "What do you think?"

"Courtney held the mirror up, capturing more light entering the shop. "They're beautiful. How much are they?"

Maria glanced at Mambo Eve who closed her eyes and nodded. Mariah said, "It's my treat. I'll buy them for you."

"You don't have to do that. I can pay for—"

"Shhh…I insist. It's the least I can do for you…for someone who's got the heart to do what you're trying to do."

◆ ━

COURTNEY STOOD IN the shade of a Southern live oak and looked up and down Dumaine Street. She wore dark glasses and the African headdress.

A black mixed breed dog sauntered across the street, head low, rib bones visible under the mangy fur. There was very little traffic. She walked a half block down from where the red Toyota truck was parked, discreetly glancing at parked cars, looking for occupants. Looking for anyone who might be looking for her.

She crossed the street and walked back toward the truck. A low-rider Chevy Malibu turned the corner onto Dumaine. Courtney could see two men in the car, dark features. The driver's head was shaved, tats up his neck. The passenger wore his hair in a purple Mohawk, sleeves cut from his black T-shirt, thick silver chain around his neck. Rap music pulsated from the car. The passenger stuck his head out the open window and shouted, "Lookin' fine,

Mama. You want some scratch? Crystal. Best in the city." Courtney ignored the man.

"Talkin' to you, bitch!"

She walked straight ahead, music from an approaching ice cream truck, *Turkey in the Straw,* crossing with the rap beat. Two teenage boys on skateboards coasted by Courtney. They skated around a man standing on the corner, watching the traffic. Watching the people. He wore dark glasses, ear-bud in one ear, and a baseball cap backwards on his round head.

Courtney was within fifty feet of her Toyota truck. She walked faster, the ice cream truck coming down Dumaine. And then she spotted them. Two men in a van. The van was parked on the side of the street, a parked car in front of it and one behind it. Courtney could see the driver start the engine.

The teens on the skateboards turned around and were heading back in her direction. As they got closer, she smiled at them and said, "You guys look hot. You want some ice cream?"

One teen, silver ring through a nostril, inflamed acne on his cheeks and chin said, "Sure. Sounds good."

The other teen, a taller boy with dirty blond dreadlocks, grinned. "You buyin'?"

"Yes, I am." She handed them a ten-dollar bill. "Go back to the corner, there's a blue van parked between the white car and the black car. Stop the ice cream truck by the parked van and buy your ice cream."

"No problem," said the dreadlocked boy.

Each boy used his left foot and leg to build speed on his skateboard, kicking off the pavement, rocketing back toward the van.

Courtney watched them a moment. She could see movement in the van, the men watching her. The moment the teenagers flagged down the ice cream truck, near the front of the van, Courtney bolted and ran for the Toyota. She fumbled with the keys, unlocking the door and sliding in behind the steering wheel. She started the motor, her heart racing. She glanced in the side-view mirror pulling away from the curb.

Her stomach turned. One man had jumped from the van, pointing a pistol at the teens and the ice cream truck driver. Courtney could see that the gunman was shouting, gesturing with the pistol. She zoomed away from the curb, accelerating down Dumaine, passing the bar where the old bluesman strummed his guitar and had a stare on his face that seemed to look a thousand yards away.

SEVENTY-THREE

The setting sun was coating the tree tops in a blood red profile when I left my mother's home. I pulled to a stop at the end of her long driveway, windows in the Jeep down, and simply stared at the hand-drawn puffin on her mailbox. At that moment, the puffin lit by an enchanted light from a dying sun, the air now cooler, I felt more alive than I had in a long time. The quirky little bird on the box was like a long lost renaissance masterpiece treasure that I'd found. Even in this village of the weird, the Celtic McMansions, doublewides, warehouses, cow pasture lawns, new cars and trucks parked near abandon old cars, I felt like I'd arrived in the Promised Land.

I'd spent the last four hours trying to make up for forty-three years. Four hours of getting to know a mother—my mother, someone I never knew existed. I heard about my family on her side and my father's side, where they were raised, how they'd met, and how much they'd loved each other. My thoughts moved in a whirlwind of what was, what is, and what might have been.

If the course to your future is shaped by your past, and you discover your past is made from a lie, what does that say about the present, and how will that affect your future?

I thought hard about that. I tried to put it in some kind of perspective, to hold this moment in time up to the light, hoping for clarity, hoping for a better insight into who I was—who I'd become as a man. I thought about genetics. I reflected on the loving upbringing I had from my adoptive parents, but on the outside looking in, from a scientific viewpoint—my life could have been a psychological experiment. My identity and persona under the microscope, a petri dish specimen in the venerable controversy of nature verse nurture.

And then there was my new-found brother, Dillon. Did genetics, a brutal rape of our mother, play a role in him becoming a killer—someone who'd rape and kill a member of his own family? His sister. My sister. Our sister. Was he conceived in evil? Or is the seed of evil planted in all of us, lying dormant in some people under the loam of good, in others sprouting deep roots, luring and hanging in temptation from the tree of life? Can good be short-circuited in anyone's fuse box by the rising of a black tide under the influence of a dark moon?

My mother raped by a priest inside a church, his offspring spawned to reproduce the cycle. Uncle Dillon. No wonder Courtney was so damn confused, so angry.

What I knew now was my biological father was dead, murdered. My mother is alive, but apparently ill. Courtney Burke was my niece. Dillon Flanagan was my brother. And the daughter who Andrea Logan conceived was still out there somewhere—anonymous. Maybe that was the nugget of hope found in the mix of pebbles and mud at the bottom of a gold pan.

There were two ways to show to the media, and ultimately the voters, that Courtney wasn't Andrea's daughter—my daughter. The first was to find Courtney, do the DNA testing. The second was to prove she wasn't a serial killer, but that would mean finding the person who was the killer. The image of an army of news reporters, satellite trucks, helicopters closing in on my mother's trailer, in her condition, caused my head to throb above my left eye. I wondered if Detective Grant had made any progress. I picked up one of my disposable mobile phones and started to call him.

Then I spotted the pickup truck.

Same white truck that had moved slowly by me when I was about to drive up my mother's driveway. Same wide off-road mud tires. The truck was parked under cottonwood and oak trees across the street from my mother's mailbox. The sun set in the horizon behind the truck, framing a silhouette of a man looking at me through binoculars.

I started to turn right, head for the highway and the first decent motel I could find. But then the cross-roads of time—of forty-three years and the last four hours, added up to that single moment for me to turn left rather than right. The clarity I sought, the meaning I was searching for, immediately started down a brand new path for me. The first destination was that pickup truck and whoever I found behind the wheel.

I headed for the truck. Drove across the scraggly lawn or pasture, kicking up dust in the orange sunlight, scattering cow shit and grass, going straight for the driver's side door. I reached for my Glock stopping beside his door. The truck window was down. He turned his head toward me. Narrow face red from the sun. Thin lips. His nose had been broken and reset, leaving a white scar and slight hump on the bridge. No expression. No surprise. Nothing but a cold stare, smoky gray eyes, pupils like pewter dots. His dirty blond hair was pulled back in a ponytail.

I could smell burning weed. I held the Glock in my lap and said, "Good evening." No response.

"You must be the neighborhood watch. You watched me arrive at the house across the street, and you are watching me leave.

Why the special interest?" No response.

"I see. You're a good listener. Not much of a talker. Well, listen to this, pal. That lady in the trailer is my mother."

His eyes opened a notch, nostrils flaring. I had his attention. "Yes, my mother. Which means Dillon Flanagan is my brother."

The carotid artery on the left side of his neck throbbed. He touched the tip of his nose with his index finger and said, "Take your game elsewhere. In one minute I can have a dozen men here."

"Good. They can carry your body away, because in two seconds I can turn what's left of your brain into applesauce." I saw his right hand move. "Don't be stupid. Right now we're simply communicating. You pull a gun on me and it turns to war, turns to one body bag--yours."

He stared at me, dry swallowed, his jawline like a rock. "Tell Dillon that his younger brother, Sean, sends his regards. I'm sending something else: a warning. Tell him Courtney Burke is off limits. She's to be left alone, unharmed. If he does something to her, tell him there is nowhere on earth that he can hide. I will find him."

The man in the truck half grinned. He propped his elbow on the inside of the door. "Mister, I don't know who the fuck you are or who you think you are, but you ought to go back to fuckin' Florida. Dillon Flanagan will tear you a new asshole. You got no idea who you're messing with, okay? He's a prophet. The man can only be found when he wants to be found. You being at his mother's house won't set well with him. You won't have to find him, he'll find you, and he knows how to do it through others. The man can walk through trees."

"Give him my message."

I put the Jeep in gear and drove back across the grass to the street, turned left, and headed toward the highway and a hotel. A shower, food, and some aspirin couldn't happen fast enough. I dialed Detective Dan Grant's mobile, wondering if he'd answer an incoming number he didn't recognize. He did answer.

"Dan, it's Sean. I found Courtney Burke's grandmother. I know Courtney's story, and it's a horrific one. I know who she's hunting for and why."

"Where the hell are you?"

"I'm in the Carolinas. Lonnie Ebert was stabbed to death with an ice pick."

"Tell me something I don't know, Sean."

"How about the name of the man who probably did it because he used an ice pick when he killed his brother-in-law after raping and strangling his wife…the killer's own sister."

"Who might that be?"

"Courtney's uncle…my brother."

"Oh shit."

"Well said."

"We haven't been able to match that partial print on the ice pick. It was the only one that wasn't Courtney Burke's print. So you are related to Courtney, but you're not her father…"

"I'm her uncle."

There was a few seconds of silence. I could hear him breathing through the receiver, a dog barking in the background. He cleared his throat and said, "Sean…man…I'm not sure how to tell you this anyway but just tell it straight. They found a body of a girl. Outside of New Orleans. It looks a hell of a lot like Courtney. They'll have to use dental records if they can find any teeth. Someone just about shot her head off. News media are all over it. The New Orleans PD will be processing the DNA fast. Whatever the results, it'll have an impact on who becomes the next president of the United States."

SEVENTY-FOUR

I checked into the first motel I found off an Interstate exit near Augusta. All rooms were ground level, most overlooking the parking lot in the front or the highway out back. The room smelled of bleach, cigarette smoke, and cheap perfume. The burgundy carpet was worn, a framed print of the Augusta National Golf Course hanging unevenly on the wall.

I turned on the television and found a cable news channel. The images were of police cruisers at a crime scene, blue lights flashing, paramedics, and emergency personnel converging on a wetland dotted with swamps and cypress trees.

The video cut to a twenty-something blonde reporter standing next to an airboat. She looked into the camera and said, "Police are still out here searching for the murder weapon in this grisly killing of the young woman. Investigators say the body had no identification near it, no purse or any personal effects. The body was discovered by a guide who operates a narrated boat tour of the Barataria Swamp. He said he saw what he first thought was trash near a cypress tree, but upon closer examination he found the young woman's partially clothed body. Police don't know if she had been raped. As to the rampant speculation that this could be the body of Courtney Burke, spotted in New Orleans just days ago...no one knows until DNA testing is complete. The victim, shot more than a dozen times in the head, was believed to have been about the same age and height as Burke. Detectives say the ends of her fingers were hacked off. Senator Logan was quoted as saying his prayers go out for the victim's family, whomever they may be. His democratic challenger, Governor Les Connors, had no comment pending the completion of the police investigation. Reporting from Jefferson Parrish, this is Lisa Fisher, News Channel Four."

I shut off the TV and left the stale room to get some fresh air. I had to run. To sweat. Had to clear my mind. Excess adrenaline floated like an oil slick over my heart. I needed to pound the earth with my feet, to sweat, to focus only on the potential of clear vision at the horizon and run to the edge of the world. I sprinted across the hotel parking lot, down a street, across a field and followed a path that led to a slow-moving river. I ran hard along the riverbank.

I ran by two teenage boys who were skipping stones off the surface. Bolted around an old black man fishing with a cane pole. He sat on a milk crate, threading a fat, wriggling worm onto a hook. I jogged deeper into the woods, causing a flock of wild turkeys to take flight, the beat of their wings like thunder rising from the ground.

The temperature dropped and a light rain began falling. I ran through the rain, the drops getting larger and hitting my face. Within a minute I had arrived at an old cemetery, many of the headstones partially covered in moss. Some of the grave-markers chipped and broken, a wrought iron fence worn-out, stooping, the gate sagging from age and rust. I stopped running and stood at the perimeter of the cemetery to catch my breath. I don't know why, but I opened the unlocked gate, the hinges moaning, and I stepped inside. I walked around the graves, trying to read the inscriptions. I stood there, rain pouring, thinking about my mother, thinking about her love for art, for people—for the earth and the birds and creatures that lived among us.

There was a movement, color in a forgotten acre of aged headstones and crumbling stone captions to lives once lived. A bright red cardinal darted through the cemetery, alighting on a low-hanging limb of a pine tree. I watched the bird, its feathers damp and slightly disheveled in the rain. The bird dropped to another limb and then flew to the top of an old grave-marker. The cardinal raised its head and warbled a note. I lowered my eye and saw a lone, red fresh-cut rose resting against the headstone. I stepped over and read the inscription.

DOROTHY O'CONNELL
1860 – 1929
YOU GAVE US the gift of love
AND WE ARE forever blessed

The cardinal tilted its head at me, silent, the sound of raindrops plopping against leaves. I stood there a few minutes, listening to the rain fall, the sky a deep pewter gray, and yet there was a live rose on a very old grave. I had no idea who'd placed it there. But between the cardinal and the rose, the bookends of color framed an inscription that had meaning in a too often deceitful world.

I looked up to the heavens and let the rain fall against my face and chest, the water cool and somehow a healing tonic, a gentle spring flowing from an unseen source.

— —

AN HOUR LATER, after a change of clothes, I lay flat on the hard mattress in the motel room, the two pillows were spongy, like two loaves of bread. I closed my eyes, thinking about what I'd seen today, and what I saw on the news. Was Courtney dead? If so, I knew my would-be assassin, the guy I reeled in from the river, either didn't deliver my message to his troop leaders, or he did and they ignored it. And I now knew that Courtney was my niece, my murdered sister's daughter…my mother's granddaughter.

I tried to make sense of life's curveballs. I couldn't. But I could keep my eye on the ball and swing hard, damn hard. I remembered what Courtney said that day on my boat. *'I believe there was a reason we met on the road in that forest. I don't know what it is, but I think the reason is might be bigger than you pulling those men off me.'*

I opened and closed my fists, took a long deep breath and slowly released it. I hadn't felt this protective toward someone since my wife, Sherri, died. Three years ago I was powerless to defeat her ovarian cancer. And, at the moment, I felt just as immobilized. If Courtney had been murdered, what could I do—charge Logan at one of his rallies and get shot through the head by the Secret Service?

If it wasn't Courtney's body, if she'd somehow managed to get out of New Orleans, dodging federal agents, police, and special op mercenaries, it demonstrates her uncanny ability for survival. And it would mean she's moving closer to finding and confronting her uncle, my brother, who I now knew was a raging and deadly psychopath.

The room was very warm and dark. I walked over to a wall air-conditioning unit and punched the start button. Hot air blew out of the unit for more than a minute before beginning to cool, the air smelled like a damp and moldy basement. Even over the drone of the air conditioner, I could hear the storm building, thunder rolling, and a flash of lightning blooming beyond the thin, white curtains.

I opened the curtains and watched the rain fall through the shafts of light cast by the street lamps. The rain quickly filled potholes in the parking lot, the blue neon from the motel sign reflecting from the oily sheen across the asphalt like light off of black ice in winter. The *VACANCY* sign bleeding wavy white letters over the puddles speckled with raindrops.

I lay back in the bed, kicked my shoes off, and placed my Glock under a fold in the sheets. I watched the rain roll down the outside of the window, my eyes growing heavy.

There was a buzz and vibration from one of the disposable phones on the nightstand next to the bed. I recognized the number. I answered and Kim Davis said, "Sean, I've been thinking about you since I left the hospital. How are you?"

"I'm okay. How are you feeling?"

"Much better, thanks. My sister's spending a couple of days with me. Did you hear about the girl's body they found in a bayou near New Orleans?"

"Yes."

"I hope and pray it's not Courtney. It seems like every news station is trying to beat the others to be the first to come forth with an ID. I just wanted to call you to…to just see how you're doing. You sound tired."

"It's been a tiring day."

"Where are you?"

"In the Carolinas. In a motel that could double as the Bates Motel."

She laughed. "It's good to hear your voice. I wanted to thank you again for what you did for me." She blew out a breath. "I'll let you go. Wherever you are, I hope you get some rest tonight. Goodnight, Sean, I miss you."

As I started to say goodnight, I heard the phone disconnect, its silence lingering in the room like the illusion of an imaginary whisper in the night. I closed my eyes, the sound of the rain against the window fading. I was in a dark room in Iraq, the red light on the video camera like a Cyclops eye, non-blinking, staring. I was slapped across the face by a wide, hard hand, blood and sweat falling against my bare chest, my teeth loose.

Then I was in a stone castle, or maybe an ancient church. I saw my mother's face—the face in the photograph with my father. I saw my brother's face as a baby morph into a man who turned his head away. He wore a dark robe, and he entered a small room and closed the door. From behind a privacy screen, I heard footsteps running, the sound coming from a stone floor. And then the long, agonizing scream of a frightened woman.

I sat up in bed, sweat dripping down my face, sheets damp. The odor of incense and candles burning. I glanced at the clock on the bedside table. The bright red numbers flashing 3:07 a.m.

My head pounded, and I felt as if I was halfway through a marathon. I closed my eyes, waiting for my heart rate to slow, return to normal. Then I drifted away, like swimming in the ocean at night under a cloudless sky. The darkness returning. I had the sense of freefalling, moving through a pitch-black abyss with no internal compass, no physical perception of gravity or direction. But I knew I was moving quickly. I wanted to wake up again, to take a shower and hope for a new sunrise. But I couldn't. My body felt trapped in quicksand, unable to do anything but be a passenger on a train bound for hell. I was strapped down, sweat rolling over my ribcage, the Cyclops red eye returned, the Iraqi butcher coming through the door with sharpened knives catching the light from a single lamp. Then the dream weaver made paper doll cutouts from black paper, leaning closer, his vinegary breath in my face, his dull scissors cutting through my frontal lobes. The final snap of the clippers, a rush of white noise, the lobotomy done and the red light fading into complete darkness.

And my eyes unable to close.

SEVENTY-FIVE

The next morning's ashen-lead skies, air thick with humidity, fit my sleep-deprived mood. After I checked out of the motel, I found a diner in North Augusta with good coffee and a spotty cell phone signal. The breakfast special was shrimp 'n grits, scrambled eggs and rye toast. Why not? If I liked it, I'd tell Nick about the concoction. I wanted to turn on my smart phone and find the location to a store. But I didn't risk it.

The waitress, a slender middle-aged woman with hazel eyes and hoop earrings the size of small doughnuts, refilled my half consumed cup of black coffee. "How's breakfast, Hon?"

"Good. Do you know this area well?"

"Been here all my life. You movin' into our little town?"

"I'm looking for a place to buy art supplies."

"There's only one in town, if it isn't already out of business." She looked at me for a second, as if to decide if I was the artsy type. "It's called Ben's Arts and Crafts. You're about five blocks from it. Don't think they open 'til ten. So you got a little wait. You can hang out here. We're not busy, and we're not worried about turning over tables." She lifted a folded newspaper off her tray. "Here, you can read the paper. Last customer left it in the booth." She set the paper in front of me. If the printed word could make a sound—a noise, I felt like what I read was screaming at me. The bold headline read:

Suspected Female Serial Killer Shot Dead or Missing?

— —

AT 10:20 A.M., I was in the door at Ben's Arts and Crafts, trying not to think about what may have happened to Courtney, concentrating on what I could do right now for my mother. Some things I do well. Many things, not so well. Shopping is one of them. I'm an in-and-out kind of guy. Get it and go. But now I was shopping for my mother. For the first time in my life, and hers, I was buying a gift for her. It felt good.

I found Ben, a Mister Rogers twin who looked like he'd inhaled too many paint fumes. When I told him what I wanted to do, he snapped out of his zombie character and began to advise me on all things art, leading me down the aisles, making "must have" suggestions from paints to painting knives. "Does your mother prefer oil or acrylics?"

"Well…"

"Let's get her both." He rattled on about the differences.

We filled the cart—filled three carts, with canvases, brushes, dozens of paints—oils, watercolors, acrylics, some disposable palettes, and a "French-style" easel with a storage drawer. It took three trips from the checkout register to my Jeep to load the art supplies. Santa's sleigh all packed, and Ben—my new BFF, was my head elf. He stood in the parking lot as I drove off, grinning and waving like Mister Rogers on crystal meth.

— —

MY COMFORTABLE MOOD was short lived. Two cars were parked partially on the grass and street near my mother's driveway. I watched as a dark blue, late-model Ford cargo van drove from her house, stopping briefly at the street, turning toward me and driving away. I looked carefully at the driver. It was a scene I'd watched before in and out of law enforcement. If foul play wasn't immediately suspected in a death, when an autopsy wasn't ordered, the funeral home made the pickup. Not in a hearse, but rather a van or a station wagon type vehicle. The funeral guys used the same stretchers that ambulance personnel used. But there was no sense of urgency. Death does that.

298

The driver stared straight ahead. He wore dark glasses, tan sports coat, white button-down shirt. Face expressionless. Another day, another pickup. And I knew this pickup was my mother.

I felt my chest tighten, heart pumping, adrenaline flowing into my system. I turned into the drive and headed toward her home. There were five cars parked near the trailer. I got out and walked, the air motionless, the whirr of a bumblebee in the petunias, the barking of a pit bull tied to a dogwood tree in the backyard of the mansion next door.

I wiped a drop of sweat out of my eyebrow, the late morning growing hot. A woman, mid-twenties, dark hair pinned up, stepped from the trailer. She had a three-ring notebook and two plastic bags filled with something. The bags had come from the CVS Pharmacy. I nodded and asked, "Is everything all right?"

She stared at me a second, almost like she was trying to place my face. I thought about all of the damn news coverage. "Are you a relative?" she asked "Yes. I'm her...I'm her son...Sean..."

"I'm so sorry to tell you, but your mother passed away last night. The body was just taken away by Johnson Funeral Home. I'm Debbie Thrasher, and I've been one of the Hospice caregivers for Mrs. O'Sullivan for the last couple of months. She died from lung cancer. We think the time of death was sometime during the night. Maybe around three a.m. because her bedside clock was flashing 3:07. But that might have been be due to the storm."

I closed my eyes for a second, saw the blink of the clock in the motel last night: *3:07.* The dog behind the mansion stopped barking, the chatter from a pair of blue jays ended. Nothing seemed to move for a moment. I heard Debbie Thrasher's voice return, like a radio signal becoming stronger. "... And your mother was a remarkable lady. I learned a lot just being around her. She was such a good artist, and the stories she could tell of Ireland when she was a girl, they were just marvelous." I said nothing.

"Would you like to go inside? Some of her neighbors are there. Mr. McCourt, who checks on her regularly, was the one who found her when she didn't come to the door this morning. She didn't talk much about her family. She was private in that way, and we respected that. She did share with me the tragedy of her daughter's death, but she kept her thoughts about her sons— you and your brother, close to her chest. She talked about her granddaughter who she said was on a mission trip of some sort. I took it to mean she was doing missionary work."

I tried to smile, but could only nod while trying to wrap my head around what was happening. She added, "You said your name is Sean, right?"

"Yes."

She opened her notebook. And removed an envelope. "She wrote the name Sean O'Brien across the envelope. Is that your last name?"

"Yes."

"This is yours. It's sealed, but marked with her handwriting. She had perfect penmanship. Your mother told us she'd written and filed a will. Her attorney is Sam McCowen in North Augusta. I'll get you his contact information. She'd made all the arrangements for her death a few weeks ago. She'd bought a burial plot next to her daughter—your sister, in Hillcrest Cemetery." The woman paused and looked up at me. "I'm sorry, Mr. O'Brien, to have to present you with these details at this time. We had no contact information for any family members. The people in her home are all close friends of your mother, people who were family to her. Do you know any of them?"

"No."

"I'll take you inside and introduce you."

I followed her into my mother's trailer. The chatter, the subdued mix of conversations going on all at once, it all ended when I stepped into the room. There were seven people standing, some drinking coffee, all looking very sad. Debbie Thrasher made the introductions, people nodding—a mixture of respect, curiosity, and suspicion in their eyes. They were from the clans of the McCarthys, O'Donnells, Gallaghers, and the Fitzgeralds. Irish gypsies or travelers, and they were the only family my mother had in her home at the time of her death.

I looked into the assembly of blue and green eyes, all staring directly at me, all looking for me to say something of worth, something that might somehow explain how in the hell, after forty-three years, I walked through the door. Within a second, a lyric from a Bob Dylan song echoed through my mind: 'How does it feel to be on your own, with no direction home? Like a complete unknown...like a rolling stone.'

I said, "I want to thank you all for being friends and good neighbors with my mother. I had a chance to spend only a few hours with her before her death. But I want you to know how much those hours meant to me, and how much I hope they meant to her. I learned that my mother had to give me up for adoption as a baby. She made the best decision she could at the time. Enough said about that. Thank you for looking after her. I'll speak with the funeral director and make the arrangements for her burial. I hope you all will attend the service."

I turned and walked back outside, my mother's death now truly beginning to soak into my pores and go directly to my heart with the crushing grip of a vice constricting. I looked at all of the art equipment in my Jeep, and wished I'd found her six months earlier. I got inside the Jeep and just sat there. Not sure what to do or even where to go. I lowered the window and heard the sound of a diesel motor coming up the driveway. Within seconds, the white truck was parking in the circular drive next to my mother's home. It was the same driver.

I got out and walked toward the truck. As he opened his door, I kicked it, slamming the door shut. The man behind the wheel shouted, "What the fuck's your problem!"

"You're my problem."

"Just here to pay my respects, dude."

"Get off the property."

"What?"

"You heard me. This is private property, and you're trespassing. Leave, and do it now."

He started the diesel, sneering at me. "Dillon already knows what happened. There's five acres here. All his, now. He might be here before the funeral. Could be two funerals that day. Odds are we'll bury you soon enough right next to your mama." He laughed and drove away. I stood there and watched him leave. My mother was dead, and the vultures were circling. A hot wind blew across the dry scrub lawns. I walked to my Jeep, the puffy white cottonwood seeds floating down around me like deceptive snowflakes in the heat of a South Carolina summer.

The mourning dove cooed its lonely refrain again, and the Dylan song sounded like a lost poem in the crypt of my memory banks. *'How does it feel to be on your own, with no direction home? Like a complete unknown...like a rolling stone.'*

SEVENTY-SIX

I drove toward town, needing to separate myself from the close-knit neighbors consoling one another in Irish cant, in my mother's house. I wanted to clear my head. The Hospice representative, Debbie Thrasher, had been thorough in her explanations about "next steps," giving me necessary paperwork. I wanted to read whatever it was that my mother had written, sealed, and left for me. But I didn't want to read it in the presence of others.

I hit my brakes. The sign read: *John C. Calhoun Elementary School.* I pulled into the parking lot, stopping close to the main entrance. In less than a minute, I was standing at the reception area in the principal's office. The secretary went in the back corridors to find her boss. The principal, a balding man with dark-framed glasses, met me with a hardy handshake. After introductions, I asked, "How's your art department in the school?"

He cleared his throat. "Well, it used to be better. County went through another round of budget cuts. We're short on teachers and supplies."

"Do you have an art teacher?"

"Yes, one...why do you ask?"

"Because I have some supplies I'd like to donate to the school."

"That's very generous." He glanced through the glass window with a direct view from the office into a hallway. "As a matter of fact, there goes Miss Hill, our art teacher." He stepped into the hall and called her. After brief introductions were made, she followed me outside. I was parked in a no-parking zone next to the curb. Miss Hill was in her early thirties, thick auburn

302

hair, worn stylishly in a retro 1940's coiffure, white strand of pearls hanging just below her open blouse.

I said, "I'll off-load this stuff here if you can find someone to take it to you classroom."

"That's no problem."

I unlocked the back of my Jeep. Her blue eyes opened wide. "Oh, dear. I don't know what to say. This is fantastic. This will mean so much for our students. Thank you."

"You're welcome." I made a neat stack, piling all the supplies in a mound. Larger stuff on the bottom, lighter things on the top. She helped unload and said, "This is so kind of you, Mr. O'Brien. May I ask what made you want to donate to the school? And we're so pleased that you did."

"The person I originally bought this for can no longer paint. Her granddaughter went to this school a long time ago. It just seemed like the right thing to do."

— —

I FOUND A county park along the Savannah River, a place where I could get a good cell phone signal, be alone, and keep an eye out for any mercenaries who may have been dispatched by the Logan camp. If the body found in the Louisiana swamp was Courtney, I was glad my mother didn't have to see that. What kind of man would shoot a nineteen-year-old girl a dozen times in her head? The kind of man who wouldn't let anything stop him on his road to the White House.

I'd warned them. Sent the soldier back with a message. Left a voice-mail message on Andrea's phone. They could ignore me, but I wouldn't go away. My immediate plan was to take care of my mother's funeral. If the body of the kid in the swamps was Courtney, I'd upload the video of the hit man screaming in the river. There is a certain raw honesty coming from the mouth, the lungs, and heart of a man about to be eaten by a huge alligator. That sort of credibility can't be faked. I was betting the American voters could tell, too.

Senator Logan wouldn't pass a scratch and sniff test.

And his house of cards was about to come tumbling down.

I called Johnson Funeral Home and began making arrangements to bury my mother. When the funeral director asked me what I wanted inscribed on her headstone, I was at a loss. I didn't even know when she was born, or how old she was at her death. Then I remembered the headstone in the cemetery I'd found while jogging, the red rose, the inscription. I told him I'd think about it and call him back.

My next call was to Sam McCourt, the attorney. He told me my mother had him file her will, leaving her home and property to granddaughter, Courtney Burke. He said, "Mr. O'Brien, probate won't take long, unless you want to challenge your mother's will."

"I don't."

"Okay, well, she died with no outstanding debt, seventeen thousand dollars in her savings account. She owns five acres in Murphy Village and the trailer, all mortgage free. And one other thing, she had some land in Ireland. It apparently had been in the family a very long time. More than three hundred acres and a small farm house. All of it on the coast in County Kerry. I have an exact address for you. She was forced to sell some if to pay property taxes. But she refused to sell to a multinational hotel chain company wanting to build a time-share on the land. As her son, you can certainly act as executor."

"All I want to do is make sure that the provisions of her will are carried out the way that she wanted."

"That's no problem, Mr. O'Brien. Mrs. O'Sullivan had already compensated the firm for our services, from the writing of the will through final dispensing of probate. I'm sorry for your loss. Your mother was a fine person. Please let us know if you have further questions. Goodbye."

He disconnected. I set the phone down, looked through the pines toward the Savannah River, a trawler chugging down river, its wake plowing a wide V behind the stern. It was passed by a cigarette boat, gun metal gray, slowing a second then resuming speed.

I picked up the sealed envelope with my name on the outside. What had she written in the night? It occurred to me, as I thought about what to write on my mother's gravestone, the last thing she ever wrote in her life was my name.

SEVENTY-SEVEN

I sat in my Jeep and opened the plain, white envelope with my name written in blue ink on the outside. I lowered the windows and felt a breeze blow in from across the Savannah River, the sweet smell of gardenias in the air. The sounds of children playing, laughing, came from somewhere in the park. I opened the envelope and read the words my mother had written.

Dear Sean,

I want you to know how grateful I am to have spent time with you. I feel blessed to have seen you as a grown man. I am so very proud of you. Please try to find Courtney, bring her home for me. I so long to see her face one more time. Help her find grace. You will need to protect her from your brother, Dillon. Be cautious and fearful of him. Dillon has murdered and killed his own family. He may not display the mark of Cain, but in my heart, I believe he carries the blood of Cain. He's a wanderer who preys on others. Like his father, he's soulless. Be careful, Sean.

There are many things in life I regret; having you as a son is not one of them. I am very sorry for the circumstances, and how I wasn't able to raise you. But I want you to know that I never once stopped thinking about you, the sweet smell of your skin as a baby, the way you looked into my eyes as I nursed you. It tore my heart out to give you up for adoption. Not one day after I kissed you goodbye did I not think about you, to whisper my love for you, and pray that God would always hold you in his arms as I have held you in my heart. I wish I could have met your wife, Sherri. From what you told me, she was a remarkable woman. Take care of the little dog she gave you. Max will love you unconditionally, as do I. I have some property in Ireland I leave to you and Courtney equally. The sunsets are marvelous there.

When you see a sunset, please think of me. Because it was in the twilight of my life when I found you, Sean. I hope each sunset through the remainder of your life will be beautiful, that you will know peace and love. Maybe when you see the colors of a day's end and its fleeting beauty you'll think of me...as I will always think of you.

I love you forever,

Mom

As I finished her letter, a tear rolled down my face, splashing on the paper. I felt a sense of deep loss that wrapped itself around my heart. I played back our last four hours together—the conversations, her gentle laughter through pain, the light still in her eyes, the love bottomless in her weak heart. When Sherri died, it was different. I'd felt an unending sense of despair—a loneliness that crept into my pores like cold water and never receded. I was thankful for the thirteen years we shared together, angry at the robber—the cancer who stole time from our bottle.

The time thief had returned. I was given four hours in forty-three years, bothered by the lack of time, but yet grateful for the four hours. I had some quality time in the end with the woman who was there in my beginning. She was my mother.

And I was her son.

I raised the windows and started the Jeep. As I glanced toward the river, I caught a tiny reflection. Under a tree. In a rural place where there should be no manmade objects to reflect the sun.

The windshield exploded.

The bullet tore through my side window and the passenger window. High velocity. A rifle. I dropped as far over toward the passenger side as possible, shards of glass in my hair, my forehead and face cut, blood dripping onto my mother's letter.

I reached up to the rearview mirror, quickly adjusting to see it, then I put the Jeep in reverse. I backed down the road, in the center of the park, found a clearing and made a turn. I sat up and drove straight out, circling the perimeter, driving around trees and bushes, and heading back toward the sniper by the river.

SEVENTY-EIGHT

In less than a minute I was almost there. Driving with a lap full of broken glass, I warily pulled up near where I saw the wink from the sniper's scope. He was gone. No one in sight. I grabbed my Glock, got out, and searched the area. I knew I wouldn't find a spent cartridge, but I thought I might find something else.

And there they were. In the river mud. Boot prints. Not just any, but rather combat boot prints. I knelt down for a closer look, sampled the soil between my fingers. Panama soles. I bet they were identical to the prints I found in my yard. I snapped a picture with my phone for comparison. I could still smell the cordite in the motionless air. I stood and followed the boot prints down to the river. There were indications that a boat had come close to shore, the boot prints vanishing in the water, the mud on the bank bearing the gouge of a boat.

Now I knew why the high-speed cigarette boat was here.

Which way had they gone? To the right was Interstate 20 crossing the river a few miles north, beyond that, small river communities. To the left was the Port of Savannah a hundred-fifty miles away, and the Atlantic Ocean—and lots of marinas in between.

Also, there were bridges. I needed a map, and I needed it immediately. I put the battery back in my phone. It didn't matter anymore. They knew where I was, and they found me. As I started to look at a map of Augusta and the river, a text message arrived. It was from an unknown source. The message read: O'Brien, consider that a warning shot fired over your bow

-- provide us with all copies of the video or you'll receive the same fate as the girl ...

I keyed in a map, found what I was looking for, memorized directions, and removed the phone battery. I raced out of the park, headed in the direction of the Savannah River near the 5th Street Bridge. It was less than ten miles away. I didn't know if I could make it before the cigarette boat blew through, but I'd break every speed limit and rule to try.

Within a few minutes I was turning off Sandpit road onto East Railroad Avenue, an industrial mixture of warehouses, woods, broken fences, and clapboard homes. The hard-packed dirt and gravel road went under a railroad trestle. I pulled off the road next to a drainage ditch, got my .12 gauge shotgun out of the back seat, locked the Jeep and ran up the embankment. I turned left and ran down the tracks toward the river. I had a least a hundred yards to go. I did it flat out. Knees and legs pumping. Glock tucked under my belt. Shotgun gripped in both hands.

I came to the railroad bridge across the Savannah River. It was long, expanding the river. The trestle was painted black, the sun's heat causing the metal structure to groan, the odor of creosote thick in the air. I straddled a very narrow catwalk, running the length of the bridge. I was heading for the center, and the best spot to catch boat traffic. The cigarette boat may have beaten me. Gone. I looked to the south, all the way to the 5th Street Bridge, about a mile away. I spotted a houseboat and a Boston Whaler with one fisherman at the motor.

And then I heard the unmistakable guttural power of the cigarette boat engines. Two big V-8's cranking. The boat came around a bend in the river. A Donzi high-performance boat, close to forty feet long, spraying a large rooster-tail wake behind the stern. From the middle of the trestle, I tried to estimate exactly where the boat would pass beneath me. I had seconds to decide. I ran another fifty feet to the west.

The boat was screaming. I chambered a round of buckshot and stood on a small ledge near the tracks and overlooking the river.

The wind was picking up speed. If I was lucky, very lucky, I might get off two shots. I waited for the right second. Following the boat through the gun-sight. Both passengers were male. Both wearing wrap-around sunglasses. Neither looking up. They never do.

I fired the first shot. Directly into the bow. Fired the second smack in the center of the big engines and fuel tanks. The boat made a thrashing noise as it passed under the bridge. Then the engines sounded like they'd thrown rods. Metal against metal. A NASCAR wreck on water.

Inside of five seconds, the Donzi exploded in an enormous orange fireball. I could feel the heat from up on the bridge. As fire and smoke belched over the Savannah River, I ran back across the bridge, ran down the tracks because it was easier and faster than tiptoeing the outside catwalk.

Because of the explosion and noise, I never heard the train coming.

It was right behind me. Fifty feet and barreling down. I had a second to react. The train engineer sounded the horn as I jumped off the tracks, barely able to hold the shotgun and balance myself on the narrow gangplank. The freight train surged by me with the kinetic force of a tornado moving on steel tracks.

The wind from the passing train raked across my perspiring and bloodied face. I was breathing hard. I hoped no one in the locomotive recognized me. I continued running down the gangplank as the freight train roared by, the slight gap between the boxcars allowing the late afternoon sunlight to catch me in fast staccato bursts of light.

Then the train passed. Carrying with it cargo, wind, noise and possibly acting as a barrier to allow me a more clandestine escape from the bridge. I don't think anyone actually saw me fire the shots. It was too fast. Too unusual a place. It wasn't a school or movie theater. And with the exclusion of a few boaters down river, no one was there. No one except the two men in the boat. At least one wore the same boots that made the impressions in the dirt under an oak tree in my yard. He had his chance, but he wanted to play dirty.

The Savannah River is the fourth most polluted river in the nation. And now it just became a little more polluted. As I drove back toward North Augusta, I thought about the text message they'd sent me. I pulled over to the side of the road a moment, put the battery back in my phone and re-read the anonymous text: O'Brien, consider that a warning shot fired over your bow -- you continue and you'll receive the same fate as the girl...

I responded by writing: You chose to ignore my warning. I fired one into your bow. I did it because of the fate you chose for the girl. The girl's name was Courtney Burke…remember the name that's going to take your election to the bottom of the river, too.

I was about to remove the battery from my phone when I recognized the incoming number. It was Detective Dan Grant's cell phone. I answered and he said, "Sean, since all hell is breaking loose on a number of fronts related to Courtney Burke, I thought you'd like to know we hit pay dirt on the partial print found on the ice pick."

"What'd you find?"

"Down in your old neck of the woods, Miami-Dade PD. A guy was picked up for a B&E, assault and sexual battery. He's a carny worker with one of Bandini's franchises on a seven-day run South Florida gig. Rides motorcycles in the Cage of Death. Anyway, the detective was thinking out of the box, ran the prints on the suspect, one thumbprint matched what we retrieved from the print on the ice pick."

"Dan, tell me the guy admitted he killed Lonnie Ebert."

"Wish I could. What he did say is he doesn't remember not doing it. He was working at the carnival the same time Courtney Burke was there."

"Did he work at the two other carnivals…where the first two murders happened?"

"Thought you'd ask that. And the answer is yes. He's lawyering up. But he did say he went through hypnosis to get up the nerve to ride a motorcycle in a cage with two other guys on bikes all going different directions. And he said he remembered holding the ice pick, but swears he doesn't remember stabbing Lonnie or the other two guys."

"Who hypnotized him?"

"Don't know. Thought I'd take a ride down to Miami and question the guy."

"Who's working the case from Miami PD?"

"Hold on…a Detective Mike Roberts. You know him?"

"Yeah, I do. Thanks, Dan."

Driving back into North Augusta, I thought about what Dan just told me. I knew Detective Mike Roberts in Miami. We'd worked together on a homicide case two years before I quit the department. He was tenacious, a bulldog. And now I needed to call him.

I thought about Andrea, how much she'd changed since we were in college. If the dead girl in the swamps outside of New Orleans was Courtney, what did it mean to Andrea, believing Courtney was our daughter? Did she give a damn? Or was she intoxicated with the fringes of power she'd ride on her husband's coattails? I could leave a message on her phone and say the young woman your husband just had murdered was not our daughter, she was my niece. Would Andrea even believe me? Doubtful. All they consider is what the polls are saying. And right now they weren't saying much for Senator Lloyd Logan.

I would keep the battery out of my phone for a few hours, my mind now on Kim. I hoped she was recuperating well, hoped she and her sister could share a few laughs through this. Then, as I crossed a bridge over a wetlands, I could see the sun setting beyond the marshlands, the water drenched in ruby merlots and pinks, the cattails quivering under the nestling of the red winged blackbirds.

I glanced at the sun going down and thought about my short time with my mother. Played back in my mind her request for me to find Courtney, and the warning she'd left me about my brother, Dillon. I glanced down at the letter, my dried blood splattered across her handwriting. She'd said that Dillon carried the blood of Cain in his veins. And I remembered what she told me about his father: *"Through the years, I discovered he stays in touch with only one person."*

"Who?"

"His father, the man who raped me...Father Thomas Garvey."

In the next forty-eight hours I would bury my mother, and then I'd find a way to deliver a strong message to my brother, Dillon Flanagan. If Courtney was still alive, I'd hunt for Dillon.

And I would find him.

SEVENTY-NINE

I wasn't sure if my brother would show up for the funeral. I didn't know his adult face. Wouldn't recognize him in the crowd. More than thirty-five people came to pay their respects to my mother. We left Saint Francis Catholic Church and drove four miles to Hillcrest Cemetery through a light rain, skies dark and sinister.

At the gravesite, the rain tapered off and each of the neighbors who I'd met in my mother's home, two days earlier, stood with me and the others as she was laid to rest. Beneath the black umbrellas, and hidden in the murkiness, I looked at faces. Trying to see if any of the men, all strangers, had a genetic resemblance to me, Courtney, or some of the pictures I'd seen of my mother in her youth.

If Dillon had showed, I wanted no surprises.

I didn't see the Murphy Village resident in the white pickup with the wide off-road tires. But because he wasn't at the graveyard didn't mean he wasn't prowling in the shadows. Along the fringes of the cemetery, a willowy mist hung around the base of the pine trees like white socks that had fallen below knotty ankles. I heard gentle sobbing amid the dark clothes and umbrellas.

A fiddle player stepped forward and began playing *Amazing Grace*, a song, I was told, my mother loved. When he stopped playing, a Catholic priest, Father Joseph Duffy, early sixties, flushed face, cotton-white hair, delivered a graveside mass and that was more of a eulogy than a sermon. He'd known my mother, and his affection for her was genuine.

Within forty minutes, they were all gone. Gone back to their trailers and mansions, a dichotomy as unique as their nomadic history. Although, at home, they were known to be as insular and unreceptive as the Amish, these Irish Travelers were there when my mother needed them and they were there, today, when she did not.

I waited for the backhoe operator to scoop the dirt into the grave. Her headstone was set in place, and in a few minutes the backhoe was loaded on a flatbed truck and hauled away, the sound of the diesels fading in the drizzle. Silence revisited the cemetery. I stood there and looked at her grave. It was adjacent to the burial site of Sarah Burke, her daughter, my sister, and Courtney's mother.

I set flowers on my sister's grave, and then stepped close to my mother's headstone. I reached into my jacket pocket and took out a hand-carved piece of wood about the size of a plum. It was the figure of a little puffin, painted black, white, red beak, and matching webbed feet. The figurine was shellacked. Its wings were outstretched. "I want you to roost here for a while," I whispered, setting the little bird down on the edge of the gravestone.

I stood as the rain began to gently fall. I opened the umbrella, the sound of the raindrops popping, the smell of fresh earth and pine needles in the still air. The desolate call of a mourning dove came from the fog-shrouded trees. I looked up and thought I saw someone standing in the mist, at the edge of the woods, a man standing, looking at me. Was it my brother, Dillon? I felt for my Glock in the small of my back. I just touched the butt of the pistol, ready. But I didn't sense an immediate threat.

The image seemed to dissolve in the haze, not back off or even walk away—but rather melt away. Maybe the vision was from my lack of sleep, living on the extreme edge, stress and fatigue causing hallucinations. I blew out a breath, took my hand off the gun, and lowered my eyes to the headstone. It read:

KATHERINE O'SULLIVAN
1943 – 2013
A MOTHER, A wife, an artist

I turned away from my mother's grave and walked in the rain back to my Jeep. As I was unlocking the door, my phone rang. I looked at the caller ID: UNKNOWN. Maybe it was Andrea calling from an undisclosed number. I answered. The voice was deep, smooth as silk, exuding coolness. He said, "Hello, little brother. This is Dillon. You left your number at our mother's house. On the kitchen table, I was told. So, I assumed you wouldn't mind if I called it. Did you bury our sweet mother today?"

"Where were you?"

"I was rather indisposed. Couldn't make travel arrangements. Sean O'Brien—what a fine Irish name, although I like Sean Flanagan better. You're somewhat late to the clan, little brother. So, let me make myself very clear. You have no claim to mother's estate and property, including the land in Ireland. So, just turn around and go back to whatever world you came from."

"Where's Courtney?"

"She's none of your business as well. And she, too, has no rightful claim to mother's property. You probably didn't know Courtney was diagnosed with acute paranoid-schizophrenia. Mother tried to hide it. Unfortunately, it seems to run in the family. How's your head, Sean?"

I said nothing.

"Give me time, I will get in your head if you get in my way. Head trips are my specialty. If you're in contact with our delusional little niece, tell her to relinquish any claims on mother's property, and her allegations against me are a sad by-product of her pathetic mental state. My attorney will handle all probate proceedings. Poor thing, Courtney, when off her medication, believes I did an injustice to her and her parents. So now she has this vendetta for me. It's one that will be quite dangerous for her."

"The injustice you did to Courtney's parents—our sister and her husband, is called murder. And you raped Courtney when she was a child. In my book, there's a special place in hell for men like you. You touch Courtney, and you've just bought yourself a one-way ticket to that special place. Now, big brother, do I make myself clear?"

His voice changed. It dropped into a throaty whisper, his threat coming from someplace deep and dark where absolute evil dwelled. "Our sweet mother, the whore, might have told you she thought of me as a distant cousin to Cain. Well, the neurotic bitch was right. Like Cain, I'm a wanderer. Like Cain, who committed the first murder on earth, slaying his brother, I will do the same to you. You don't want me getting into your head, little brother. Because once I move in…I never leave."

He disconnected. I looked across the cemetery, the fog rising above the tombstones, the puffin barely visible, like a bird surfing the crest of a cloud, catching a holy wave to a better place.

EIGHTY

The thunderstorm followed me on the drive back from South Carolina to Florida and Ponce Marina. Once in Florida, I made a call to Miami-Dade PD. When I got Detective Mike Roberts on the line he said, "Sean O'Brien, it's been a long time. I'd ask how the hell you are, but I know your ass is in deep shit. You're a household name. What's all this stuff about you and Senator Logan's wife and a daughter? Is that suspect, Courtney Burke, really your daughter?"

"No, Mike, and I wish I had more time to explain. I spoke with Dan Grant, Volusia County S.O., and he told me how you ran the prints on the carny worker and you found one that matched the latent pulled from the ice pick on the carnival homicide in Volusia."

"Yeah, the homicide that's causing this political train to become a run-away-train. You don't think the girl did it, huh?"

"No, the question is do you believe the perp you're holding did the killing and maybe the other two?"

"Could be. He says he can't remember doing it, although he was working at that carnival when the homicide happened. I can't sniff out bullshit from him. My deception meter isn't reading crap coming outta the perp's mouth. It's damn weird, Sean. This guy is telling me he doesn't remember doing it... but he sort of remembers some guy telling him to do it."

"Dan Grant said the perp admitted he'd been hypnotized to deal with his fear of riding a motorcycle in the Cage of Death."

"Yeah, that's what he said."

317

"Did he say who hypnotized him?"

"Says he can't really remember. He said it was someone who'd worked the carny circuit. A guy who supposedly could mass hypnotize an entire audience. The perp said the rest of it is like bits and pieces of a dream that he can't remember the whole picture. It might not be enough to get your girl off the meat hook, but it does establish that at some time and some place the perp had his hands on that ice pick. Right now we can't prove when and where."

"How long can you hold him?"

"Bond's been set at a half mill. The guy's a habitual criminal, flight risk, plus we got him on enough stuff to send his ass to Raiford for a long damn time. Gotta go, Sean. Late for a depo."

— —

TWO HOURS LATER I arrived back at Ponce Marina, skirted around the news media in the parking lot, and made my way down L-dock. I sat in the cool salon on Dave's trawler, *Gibraltar,* the air-condition humming, Max half asleep on my lap, Dave in his canvas director's chair nursing a cocktail, and Nick sitting at the three-stool bar. They listened intently as I shared with them the events I'd gone through the last four days.

When I finished, Nick looked at me, his black eyes wet, absorbed in the story. He was speechless, which was saying a lot for Nick. Then, like coming out of a trance, he sipped from his bottle of Corona and said, "Man, I'm so damned sorry to hear about your mother."

Dave said, "That goes for all of us, your marina family."

Nick blew air out of his cheeks, his face flush. "Sean, what happened to you is so unfair. You met your mother, and you had to bury her. You find out you have or had a sister who was murdered, and the guy who did it is your freakin' brother, the brother you never even knew you had. Heavy shit, my friend. A heavy load to tote."

Dave said, "Based on what you told us your brother said, it's apparent he's as mercenary as the guy who shot through the window of your Jeep…maybe even more so because an assassin-for-hire is playing by his employer's rules. If your brother has some God complex, and he's a full blown sociopath, he believes the rules, the laws of a civil society, don't apply to him. A man like that shares many of the same mental traits associated with Hitler, and, in his own sphere of influence, can be just as deadly. The allusion to Cain and Abel isn't a stretch."

Nick drained what was left of his Corona and said, "From the day that the girl Courtney first walked on this dock…the girl we now know is your niece…I told you shit was gonna happen. I just didn't know how deep it was gonna get."

Dave grunted. "That's not exactly what you said, Nick. The Forrest Gump suggestion is well-founded, though. Sean, to say how sorry we are for your loss doesn't scratch the surface of what you just experienced—you find your mother and give her a funeral all in the same week." He shook his head and sipped his drink, gesturing toward the book on the table, and he cut his eyes back up to me. "I'm reading *Death in Venice* by Thomas Mann. Joseph Campbell was influenced by some of what Mann had to say. Campbell, of course, distilled it down to the hero's journey. And a lot of it is exactly what you went through—what you're going through. But when that journey takes you into the bowels of a dysfunctional family you never knew existed, I'm not sure how you return from a quest so intimate, so personal, without experiencing profound change akin to surviving a war."

"I haven't returned. I've made a detour to regroup. A lot of my next direction depends on the ID of the girl they pulled out of the Louisiana swamp."

Dave nodded. "Unfortunately, there are too many missing young women. Police say she's a Jane Doe until a family comes forth to connect her to a missing persons report or some kind of DNA evidence. In the case of Courtney Burke, without DNA from Courtney, there's nothing to match to the dead girl. One news commentator is calling for Andrea Logan to give a DNA sample to see if a dotted line can connect to the corpse. Hell, Sean, Logan's Democratic opponents might be coming after you for a DNA sample. With the election coming very soon, it's gone from mudslinging to throwing feces like hardballs."

Nick got up from his barstool, stepped to the port side of Gibraltar, and stared out the window toward the marina office and the Tiki Bar. "Looks like a few more TV news trucks have set up camp. Maybe something's breaking.

Sean, maybe they're linking you to blowin' up the cigarette boat in South Carolina."

"I don't think so. The closest eyewitness was a train engineer, and he saw my back as I was running for my life."

Dave said, "So you believe the sniper who shot your windows out, who came within an inch of taking your head off, was the same guy you got on camera saying Timothy Goldberg and presumably Senator Lloyd Logan had issued orders to take Courtney out?"

"I recognized the boot tread, down to a cut on the sole of his left boot."

"But yet somebody sends you a text message threat, saying that the rifle bullet through your Jeep windows was a warning shot, along with the demand about the video. Maybe the shooter just missed and they made it seem like a warning because you were still alive."

Nick said, "Just from those glass cuts on your face, you're damn lucky you didn't lose an eye."

Dave stirred the ice in his drink. "The irony is you pull this assassin out of the St. Johns River, literally, as a big gator is closing in, and then you take him out, or vaporize him, in the Savannah River. You're going to release that video, aren't you?"

"It was an insurance policy to keep Courtney safe. If they killed her…I'll release it and let Logan's handlers handle that."

Nick glanced up at the TV screen behind Dave's bar. The sound was muted, but the picture was on, images of a reporter near a wetland in New Orleans. "What's this?" Nick asked, reaching for the remote control. He turned up the sound.

I wasn't ready to hear it.

EIGHTY-ONE

Max barked, her hound dog ears following movement on the dock. Nick looked out the starboard side of *Gibraltar*. "A news cameraman is walking toward your boat, Sean. The guy decided to go around the locked gate and the no trespassing signs. I see another one following him."

Dave said, "It's the tip of the iceberg, and right now *Gibraltar* is beginning to feel a bit like *Titanic*. As long as you stay sequestered aboard, Sean, we should avoid a collision with a media mob. I'll call security and the sheriff's office. Turn up the sound on the TV, Nick. Looks like they have reason to call what I'm seeing as breaking news."

The scenes were of a Louisiana parish sheriff and two FBI agents holding a news conference in front of the sheriff's headquarters. The voice-over came from a news anchorman who said, "That was the scene minutes ago when the results of forensics tests were announced by Sheriff Ralph Perry and special agents with the FBI. Let's go to Peter Zimmer live at the crime scene where the girl's body was found. Peter…"

The camera shot cut to the field reporter, a square-jawed, dark-haired man wearing an open sports coat, standing next to an airboat. "That's right, Larry, police and FBI say they have made a positive identification in the tragic death of a young woman found here in Barateria Swamp by a tour boat operator. Investigators are saying the body is that of nineteen-year-old Gina Boudreaux, reported missing more than a week ago. Two remaining teeth in the girl's body matched with dental records. Then police got a DNA sample from the Boudreaux family in St. James Parish. Also, we're told there was an apparent match of a small tattoo, a sunflower, on the girl's left shoulder. Her distraught parents say the last time they saw their daughter was last Saturday when she came into New Orleans to visit the area voodoo shops. Gina Boudreaux's car was found abandoned three blocks from the French Quarter. Police and federal agents have few leads and apparently no suspects in this grisly murder. Reporting live from Barateria Swamp, this is Peter Zimmer, now back to you in the studio."

The image cut to a blonde news anchorwoman who said, "Thanks, Peter. On a national scale, the news of the murdered girl's identification means that the whereabouts of Courtney Burke, wanted in connection with the deaths of three carnival workers, and the young woman who may be the daughter of Andrea Logan and her college boyfriend, Sean O'Brien, is still unknown. Andrea Logan's husband, the presumed Republican presidential nominee, Senator Lloyd Logan, says he stands by his wife, and says that their long-time relationship and marriage has no bearing on what happened in the past, after Andrea Logan gave a baby up for adoption twenty years ago. More on this breaking story tonight at eleven."

Nick hit the mute button and turned toward me. "Wow, what the hell are you gonna do now?"

"Find Courtney."

"Nobody can find her, and everybody is looking."

"But they're not looking in the right place. I don't know why she went to New Orleans, but I know where she's going. She's trying to find her uncle, my brother, Dillon."

"Why?" Dave asked, turning his head from the television to me.

"Retribution, among other things. He killed her mother, his sister—our sister, and raped Courtney when she was a young woman. I have a feeling in my gut that he killed the three carny workers."

Nick's dark eyebrows lifted. "What? You said Miami cops just picked up a guy who left a thumbprint on the ice pick."

"They did. His print along with Courtney's print is on the same ice pick. No eyewitnesses. No security camera video. The suspect says he wasn't there and didn't do it. But he was there, at least working for the carnival as a motorcycle stunt rider. He'd been hypnotized to become fearless to drive a motorcycle in the Cage of Death. If hypnosis, with a guy like that, can remove his fear of death, could it eliminate his fear of capture or guilt in a killing?"

Dave said, "Killing as in murder, of course. Not self-defense."

"Exactly. What if a master hypnotist could plant a posthypnotic suggestion, or a command, to have someone killed? Maybe that order is triggered from a cell phone call or some other remote way to prompt whatever psychological tripwire that's needed to send this person into a robotic kill mode and not recall anything after it's done. The killer could beat any polygraph because he has absolutely no connection to the act. Courtney said Dillon Flanagan is a master hypnotist. He knew Courtney was going to cause trouble for him, bring in murder and rape charges. He killed her mother and father. He'd have no hesitation to kill her, or frame her for murder…especially if he could hypnotize someone else to do it."

Nick said, "This kind of brainwashing sounds like the *Manchurian Candidate* movie."

Dave nodded. "It's mind control. The CIA experimented with it for years. Began in the 1950's as something call MK-Ultra, or code name *Artichoke*. Candidates, if you will, most susceptible to it, are subjects with what's called a dissociative mental state, in other words, those who've been hurt or abused, even those with PTS…people who found detachment in creating more than one personality."

Nick popped the cap off a Corona. "But for the average Joe, you can't manipulate his personality to assassinate another human if that truly goes against the person's conscience."

Dave said, "We're talking subconscious, Nick, which means a much altered state-of-mind. To engage an unconscious action that doesn't have the rational parameters found in the conscious mind. And that, for most of us, comes with a guilty conscience if we cross the line—the scruples and morality factors found in our knowledge of right and wrong. So in mind control, to bypass that, the hypnotized person might answer his or her cell phone and hear the words *yellow-dog*, and then become an assassin, following a preprogramed post-hypnotic command."

I said, "And, in theory, they have no memory of how they were hypnotized, or who did it. This creates the ultimate mole or spy because, even under torture, they can't break since they have no source memory of the connection—the orders and who gave them."

Dave stirred his drink. "And you think Dillon, your biological brother, might be capable of this level of hypnosis?"

"I do."

"Why?"

"Because it's beginning to look like that's how he functions."

"There's no expiration date for a post-hypnotic suggestion, or in this case, command. If he's that good at entering the human subconscious and essentially derailing the ethics of the conscience, then what if he has a band of followers he's recruited. People he's met, mesmerized, and hypnotized to do his bidding at his will? Would they be his subservient drones—each person fundamentally two people in one body?"

Nick ran his fingers through his hair, glanced out the window and said, "This is getting crazier by the hour. You have a mastermind psychotic brother, with a Cain complex, and a politician with a littler pecker personality, and both of 'em have a hard on to screw you to the floor. More news types are shooting video of your boat, Sean. We got to get you the hell outta here. Someplace safe. Someplace where you aren't bothered by what amounts to a bunch of paparazzi."

Dave stood and looked out the tinted window. "Nick's right. Looks like the paparazzi bus just hit Ponce Marina. You could always just step out there on the dock and tell the media that Courtney is your niece not the daughter of you and Andrea Logan. But with all members of your family dead, none of the Irish travelers the type to go on camera to corroborate or even say they knew or knew of Courtney in Murphy Village, you will literally have to produce Courtney in person to disprove what the news media have been hammering—this forbidden love child, serial killer scenario. The question is…how can you find Courtney Burke before they do, before Logan's special ops guys find her…or God forbid, before your brother locates her?"

"I fly to Ireland."

"Ireland? You think she's there?"

"No, but the man who is my brother's biological father is there. He stays in contact with Dillon. If I find him, I'll find my brother. And just maybe before Courtney can get to Dillon…or before he can get to her."

EIGHTY-TWO

A half hour later, two Volusia County Sheriff's deputies and a rent-a-cop, hired by the marina, began to escort the news media off the private dock, back toward the Tiki Bar. In the meantime, Dave was searching online, and wherever else in the digital world where he finds data, people and places. He looked at me, over his laptop, bifocals at the tip of his nose, his probing face lit by the bluish light from the screen. "It took a little digging, but I found the current whereabouts of Father Thomas Garvey."

Nick said, "Bet the old bastard is lying six feet under in an Irish cemetery."

"No, he's still alive and kicking. And he's still a priest despite the fact that the Catholic Church relocated him to four different parishes, each time because of allegations of sex abuse. The church paid out more than six million in lawsuits filed against Father Garvey and two other Irish priests. Most of the class-action litigation filed years after the abuse. And Father Thomas Garvey was right in the thick of things. The church simply moved him around, paid hefty fines, and tried to keep a low profile."

Nick said, "Just like whack-a-mole, you whack-a-pedophilepriest and he pops up somewhere else. Hide your kids, mama. There's a new guy at the church. They rotate their pedophiles 'till the music stops, and that's a sad damn song."

I set Max down on the salon floor. "Where is he right now?"

Dave looked down, through his bifocals, his eyes searching the screen. "A church in County Cork. St. Colman's Cathedral. It's in Cohb…an Irish seaport. He's semi-retired. According to this bio, Father Garvey continues to

325

serve God and his parishioners as a teacher, healer, and a minister, following the example set by the first priest, Jesus Christ."

I thought of my mother, thought of what she endured. Thought of what might have happened had my father lived and not been shot in the back of his head. What would that have meant for me? The two people who raised me were fine, loving parents. The year of their tragic deaths, my mother died in a car accident a few months after my father was shot to death, was a life-changing year for me. I missed them then, and I miss them today. Now, I know, the only mother I'd ever known, was my biological mother's cousin. I was fortunate. I had a good upbringing, and at the end I had four hours with the woman who had given me birth.

Dave closed his laptop and pushed back in his chair. "Sean, maybe Ireland's not such a good idea. Even if you do go and find this guy, he might clamp up tighter than a clam. If he knows where Dillon Flanagan is, there's no assurance he'll tell you. And if he did, what's to keep him from warning your brother? Maybe you can track Courtney down from here."

"Time isn't on my side. If Logan's people can throw her into the trunk of a car, we'll never find her. And the bastard will probably win the election, too."

Nick said, "And don't forget about your brother."

"I can't forget about him, the cold warning he whispered to me on the phone won't leave."

Dave pushed his glasses on the top of his head, buried in his thick, white hair. He exhaled like a bear and said, "Cain killed his brother, lied to God about it, was banished and roamed the earth. We know your brother, Dillon, is migratory—working carnivals, conning the faithful in small churches. I think you're going to Ireland for an ulterior motive, too. The old priest might squawk and tell you where Dillon's holing up, but the priest is the guy who raped your mother, impregnated her with a bastard son…and he may be the killer who ended your father's life with a bullet. Since we're talking fortysome-thing years ago, way before all the public outcry over the clergy and pedo-philia, here was a heterosexual priest raping young women under the bullshit deception of a divine plan. And it's not until years later, his victims, all grown women, are finally heard. Unfortunately, your mother wasn't one of them."

I stood and stepped to the starboard window in the salon. The lone secu-rity guard paced at the end of the dock, near *Jupiter*. All of the news media were back at the public area, the head of the dock closest to the marina office and the Tiki Bar. I said, "Nick, I don't want to walk through the mob. Can you bring your Zodiac around to *Gibraltar's* stern? Max and I will hitch a ride with you to my Jeep."

"No problem." He left *Gibraltar*, hands buried in his jean pockets, looking east and west on the dock, as if there was two-way traffic. The news media on Nick's mind.

Dave said, "You can leave Max here if you want. She's no problem."

"Thanks, but since I'm traveling overseas, I don't know when I'll return. And when I do come back, I'm going to be tracking down Courtney, or Dillon, or both. My neighbors, Martha and Herb on the river, will beat me up if I don't let Max spend some time with them when I'm gone."

Dave stepped from the salon to the door leading to *Gibraltar's* cockpit, his eyes filled with concern, looking away from me, and then back. He said, "Be careful, Sean. I have an uncomfortable feeling about this one. You're too close to the source. One way or the other, you're untying family knots. Courtney. Your brother. The child you produced with Andrea Logan is presumably still out there somewhere in all of this. Make damn sure the knot you untie first is the hangman's knot. Too many people want to slip it over your head and kick the chair out from under you. Be careful. We've seen you fight battles for others, but never have you had to battle your own family. When those combat aspects change, you change. I can already see it in your eyes. Revenge does not become you, Sean…it becomes the executioner, and it digs two graves." "That's not my motivation. Courtney's safety is." "Are you sure?" His eyes searched my face.

"Yes."

"Okay then." Dave exhaled and slapped me on the back. "Stay safe."

"If you don't hear from me in three days, I want you to upload the video confession of the guy I pulled from the river."

"It's definitely your ace in this house of cards. Play it smart, Sean."

I heard Nick's small Evinrude engine sputtering on the stern of his inflatable Zodiac. I scooped up Max, walked to the dive platform on the back of *Gibraltar*, and quickly got in the Zodiac. Nick nodded at Dave, gunned the little fifteen-horsepower motor, and we cut a path across the marina.

Max stepped to the bow and stood on her hind legs, ears flapping in the wind, eyes bright. I glanced back at Nick, his hand on the throttle, his seaman's dark eyes searching the boats in the marina. He grinned and gave me the thumbs up sign. I nodded and did the same. As we glided over the water, Dave's voiced replayed back in my head like a smooth stone skipping across the surface of my thoughts. *Revenge does not become you, Sean…it becomes the executioner, and it digs two graves.*

EIGHTY-THREE

Forty minutes later, Max and I were pulling onto my driveway on the river. The acorns and shells popping under the Jeep's tires now had the soothing rhythm sound of symphonic music. And my rustic cabin by the river stood like an old friend welcoming me home after the war. I thought about the mansions and trailers, warehouses, tool and die shops, all stitched together on a commercial and residential quilt across the rolling acreage of Murphy Village.

In a way, I suppose, the last few days were not unlike a war. I'd been threatened—three times, shot at, dodged the news media posse, and spent four hours listening to stories about a life and family I never knew existed. But it was more than worth it because I got to spend time with my mother. I'd found her, lost her, and buried her in a span of a few days. I'd placed flowers on the grave of my murdered sister and learned it was my brother who'd killed her.

I tried to wrap my mind around it. And the fact that I still had a daughter I'd never met out there somewhere. Maybe I'd take Max down to the Everglades, rent a canoe, and simply vanish for a couple of weeks. But I know I'd return to another death—the murder of my niece, Courtney. And that's assuming her body was recoverable. My mother asked me to return her to safety.

And that I would do.

Before entering the cabin, Max and I checked the perimeter. She sniffed, peed, chased a squirrel and reclaimed her world by the river. I checked windows and doors for any subtle signs of entry. Everything looked as I had left it, in what felt like a lifetime ago. I glanced up at the camera they'd mounted in the old oak closest to my home, the bullet hole almost dead center in the shattered lens.

I disarmed the alarm system, entered our home, and went online to buy airline tickets. Round-trip. I didn't plan to stay long. I fixed Max dinner. Then I poured a Jameson's over ice, and the two of us followed each other down the backyard to my dock. We sat at the end of it, Max enjoying her fish and lamb nuggets, me enjoying the Irish whiskey and beginnings of a marvelous sunset over the river. The air was cool, smelling of honeysuckles and trumpet flowers.

I wanted the glow of the sun to hang over the river a little longer, to stay and let Max and I bask in its warmth, its light. I'd seen too much darkness in the last few days and I wasn't ready to say farewell to the one thing that separated us from the cloak of darkness, the stealth of the night.

Within minutes, the sun slipped below the oxbow bend in the river, stoking the bellies of low-hanging clouds with crimson embers, the light reflecting from the moving water with the heartbeat of life, the clouds like masked faces spilling blood red tears into the river.

I pulled the Glock from under my belt, set it next to me, and sipped the Irish whiskey. A gentle breeze caused the weeping willow branches to sway, the tree's narrow limbs like long fingers tickling back of the river. Trumpet vines, filled with purple flowers, mixed with the yellow blossoms of riverbank grapes and poured motionless over the embankment near the river like a frozen waterfall of color. Max and I watched an osprey catch its bass dinner from the center of the river.

It was good to be home.

I looked over to Max, her ears rising, nostrils quivering, a minor growl somewhere in her throat.

"What do you hear, girl?"

She cut her brown eyes back to me, almost asking me to be quiet so she could listen closer. She focused her attention on the road. A car drove by slowly, too slowly. The driver touched the brakes twice and continued driving. I lifted my Glock and stood from the bench. Max jumped up, huffed a subdued bark, and began trotting off the dock to the backyard.

"Max, let's take it easy." I lifted her off the ground, carried her to the screened-in back porch, and said, "Stay here. I'll be right back." I closed the door. She looked at me like I was an alien and she paced the worn cedar flooring, her ears following the unseen.

I slipped into the woods adjacent to my property, fireflies crawling out of the pine needles, from under leaves, rising up with their lanterns winking. I walked toward the road, Glock in my right hand, ready for Logan's soldiers to step over the line in the sand. And this was the last line I'd draw.

If they came at me again, I'd take no prisoners, do whatever I had to do, and then release the admission-of-guilt video, or maybe the implication-of-guilt video would be a better label. I'd let the press chew on it and see what the voters would swallow and what they'd vomit up. I'd grown tired of Senator Lloyd Logan, and I was disappointed in the woman I once knew, thought I'd loved – Andrea Logan.

I could hear the car stop, the driver finding a spot in the national forest to turn around and head back this way. The car entered my driveway, lights on. Why? Why so brazen? Maybe this was a distraction and the other team members were coming from the rear and moving toward the back of my house.

Max. She'd bark, no doubt. But what would they do to silence her on the back porch? If they'd put a dozen .45 caliber rounds into the head and face of a young woman…I didn't want to think about what they'd do to little Max. I stayed in the thicket and followed the car as the driver moved very slowly down my driveway, unhurried as a walk, like he was trying to dodge the acorns and oyster shells. That wouldn't happen. I'd placed the shells there for that reason. The oaks added their own touch.

I slipped in behind the palms and oaks, keeping the trees between me and the driver's line of sight. The driver tapped his brakes, pulled to a quiet stop, and the headlights went out. I came closer, within fifteen feet of the driver's door. The door slowly opened and the driver stepped out as I leveled the Glock, aimed for the person's spinal cord and said, "Hands up! Now, or I'll blow a hole through your backbone."

The hands shot up in the night air, and the woman's voice pleaded, "Don't kill me!"

"Turn around."

Kim Davis turned around, holding her arms straight up, eyes wide. "Sean, can I put my hands down?"

EIGHTY-FOUR

We walked around the cabin to the back porch, the full moon rising in the east over the river, fireflies hanging like holiday ornaments under the limbs of the cypress trees, Spanish moss motionless in the night air. Kim stopped, looking down toward the river, the reflection of the moon as if liquid gold shimmered over the water. She said, "This is spectacular. Sean, it's so beautiful out here. No wonder you don't spend more time in the marina. It's so peaceful here, and so quiet."

Max barked.

"Sometimes it's quiet," I said, as Kim turned toward the back porch and approached the door. Max stood on her hind legs and cocked her head, almost smiling at Kim.

"Max," she said, "what are you doing in there?"

"She's doing what watchdogs do…keeping an eye on this part of the property."

"Can she come out?"

"Sure."

Kim opened the door and Max almost jumped into her outstretched arms. "How are you girl? I've missed you." She petted Max, then stood, her eyes rising up to mine, the light of the moon in her wide pupils. "I guess you're wondering what I'm doing here."

"The thought crossed my mind. First, tell me how are you doing, how are you feeling?"

"Good as new, for the most part. My body's healed, my psyche is getting there." She smiled. "The reason I drove out is because Dave said you might be going out of town. He said a lot of stuff happened to you, but he wouldn't get into details. Anyway, I thought I'd offer to watch Max if you'd like. My sister went back to her home. Max could stay at my house until you got back. We'd do girl things. Watch sappy movies and eat popcorn out of the same bowl."

I smiled, glanced down at Max. "How about it kiddo, you want to hang with Kim? Remember, she cooks better than me." Max tilted her head and barked. "There's your answer, Kim. I'd pack her bag, but she travels light. Let me show you the river while you're here."

We walked down to the dock, the three of us, Max scampering ahead, running to the end of the dock. The bullfrogs sang baritone on the riverbank and perched on half-submerged cypress knees. The moon lit the river and the national forest with an ethereal light that appeared to hover through the tree limbs and over the surface of the river.

We sat on the wooden bench I'd built months ago, Kim looking at the stars and the silent flow of the dark water. A great horned owl hooted, its call coming from a dead cypress tree on the edge of the national forest. I pointed to three white-tailed deer standing where my backyard merged into the forest, the deer nibbling from a mulberry bush. They looked our way and then drifted back into the pockets of shadow under the trees.

Kim hugged her upper arms and said, "This is powerful…earthy…I feel it in my soul. It's like some kind of an enchanted land, the full moon off the river, the owls, deer—even the bats, and look over there, I've never see so many fireflies in one place."

"To the left of the cabin is a shell mound. It was used by the Timucua Indians for a century or two as a sacred burial ground. A friend of mine, a Seminole, his name is Joe Billie, tells me this spot above the river is hallowed ground."

Kim smiled. "You mean haunted ground?"

"No more than any cemetery, I suppose. I think the ancient mound is a place to respect and hold in a higher light."

She raised one eyebrow, her eyes feisty. "So Sean O'Brien's never seen ghosts?"

"Well…I didn't say that."

She lifted my drink from the end of the bench, sniffed, her eyes even more playful. "The good stuff, Jameson. I bet after a few of these you'd see ghosts out here."

"Would you care for a drink?"

"Looks like you barely touched yours. Will you join me? But only one. I have to drive."

We walked up to the cabin, Max following us after sniffing the spot where the deer had grazed. On the back porch I said, "This is a reversal. You're always fixing drinks for me, Dave, or Nick, and now I have a chance to reciprocate. What would you like?"

"What do you have?"

"Jameson, of course. Vodka, gin, a few craft beers, and a bottle of cabernet."

"The wine sounds nice, thank you."

"Let's go into the kitchen." I uncorked my last bottle of cab, poured it slowly in a wine glass and handed it to her.

Kim sipped, closed her eyes for a moment, savoring the taste, her lips wet, and said, "This is good." She looked around the kitchen and adjoining dining room with its knotty pine walls, ceilings, and cypress floors. "I love your cabin, which is more like a rustic home."

"I'll show you around." She followed me throughout the house, stopping in what would be called a great-room in many houses. To me, it was a cozy den, a place to make a fire in the hearthstone fireplace, read a book, or watch an NFL game during the season.

She said, "This is so you, Sean. This room, this house, this place. It's got a rough-hewn feel to it, yet the home is very comfortable. I like it."

"Glad you do. It's a little large for Max and me, but we like it here."

"How'd you ever find this grand old home?" She sipped her wine and followed me onto the back porch, Max behind us.

"After Sherri died, I needed to get out of Miami. I resigned from the department, sold our house, and began looking for someplace remote, some-place to find stillness again. I always liked the St. Johns River, fished it years ago, and I found this place in an estate sale, the surviving family members at each other's throats over ownership, sale price, you name it. No one had lived here in ten years. I made them an offer when they were in a compromising moment. They accepted, and ever since I've been replacing stuff—stuff like bathroom plumbing, wood around the house, the dock, fixed the roof twice. Please, sit down. I'll be right back."

I freshened my drink, brought the bottle of wine to the porch, and we sat on wicker chairs with overstuffed cushions. Kim curled her legs beneath her, holding the wine glass in both hands. Max jumped on the wicker couch and transformed into a reddish-brown ball, her chin resting on a toy squirrel she often carried from floor to chair.

Kim sipped from the glass of wine, the cicadas chirping in the oaks and palms, the nasal call of a nighthawk over the river. "Is that a picture of your wife?" she asked, looking at the framed picture of Sherri on the table next to the couch where Max slept.

"Yes, that's Sherri about a year before her death."

"She was beautiful."

"Inside and out." I stirred the ice in my glass and sipped the Jameson.

"She was your only family, right? At least until Courtney entered your life."

"Sherri, and of course Max, were the only family members I had on the planet, or so I thought until all of this began unfolding. And it's not unwrapped yet."

"You mean determining whether Courtney is your daughter, the daughter from your relationship twenty years ago with Andrea Logan, right?"

"Wrong. Courtney is not my daughter. If she's still alive, she's my niece."

"Niece?" Kim sipped her wine, took a long second sip, her eyes caring and confused.

"What Dave Collins didn't tell you, Kim, is I found out my life, as I knew it was…it was a lie. I just buried my biological mother—someone I never knew existed. I learned that Courtney is the only child of a sister I didn't know I had, and I discovered that a brother—my older brother…killed her." I told her what happened.

"Oh, Sean…dear God." She reached out and touched my hand. "I wish I knew what to say."

"And that's why I'm going to Ireland tomorrow."

"Ireland?"

"That's where it started when my mother was raped by the Catholic priest. I need to go back in time to alter the future, if I can."

She sipped her wine again, slowly exhaled and set the glass on the table in front of her. A look came over her eyes that I'd never before seen in Kim. She spoke without speaking, reached for me without reaching to me, touched me without touching me—and she did it with such unreserved honesty it felt as if time somehow really stopped or at least slowed in a dimension that can't be calibrated by a mechanical clock. It's attuned and measured in heartbeats, in the pendulum motion and cycles of life itself.

I said nothing.

She spoke in a voice above a whisper, never looking away, focusing with all her spirit, her life-force on me. She said, "Sean, my heart aches for what you've gone through recently. You are such a good man to have such bad—no, such evil come into your life. If what's happened from Senator Logan's people wasn't enough…you bury you mother and learn your brother would kill your niece if he could. I know you well, Sean. Call it a history…call it a connection. Just being a small part of each other's world through the good times and the bad. I hurt seeing you hurt, and I know one thing. Tonight, on the eve of you traveling to Ireland to find the man who raped your mother… maybe even killed your father…tonight you don't need to be alone. I believe we need each other, at least for one night. Can I stay the night?"

EIGHTY-FIVE

I set the house alarm, put Max in the great room, and held Kim's hand, leading her into my bedroom. The bedroom was on the east side of the cabin, and moonlight poured in through the windows. I kept the lights off as we stood at the end of the bed and undressed, Kim laying her clothes across the chair at the small desk in the room. She stepped to the edge of the bed and held out her hand. I took it. She kissed my palm, never taking her eyes off of mine. Under the light of the moon, she stood nude, no tan lines, body firm and toned, breasts and hips flawless, like a Greek goddess. Her natural beauty took my breath away.

I touched her cheek, using one finger to brush a strand of hair from near her eye. I cupped her face in my hands and leaned down to kiss her lips. She responded with a kiss soft as the moonlight, lips warm, mouth slightly open. We kissed for a few minutes, searching, probing—the heat building between us. She looked up into my eyes and then at my chest. Her fingertips tenderly tracing the beaded scars across my chest. War wounds. She said nothing. And then she saw the birthmark on my shoulder. She touched it, her index finger moving slowly over each of the four images that resembled the leaves of clover, an Irish shamrock.

"Kim…"

"Shhh…" She pressed one finger to my lips. "Lean closer," she said in a throaty whisper.

I lowered my shoulder and she stood on her toes, kissed my birthmark, her eyes never leaving mine. The last woman who'd touched the birthmark was my mother, touching a birthmark that consummated what she knew and felt—that I was her son. And now Kim pressed her full lips to my skin, like she might do if she found a four-leaf clover, picked it, and made a silent wish as she kissed it.

She used one finger to touch each spot that resembled a clover leaf and said, "This one's for faith…this one's for hope…this one's for the spirit…and the leaf closest to your heart is for love." She leaned in and kissed me again, this time her mouth searching, tongue touching mine, her passion rising.

I lifted Kim up and carried her to my bed, her brown hair fanning out over the white pillow cases. We kissed, intensely, her eyes tender, desire building, and her body arching up to meet me. As I entered her, she wrapped her legs around my hips, pulling me deeper inside her, kissing intensely, mouth voracious, moaning with each deep thrust. Our bodies fell into a perfect rhythm, slowing and building again and again. She uttered a sensuous moan, her eyes closing, her mouth slightly open, breathing fast. She looked up at me, her brown eyes expressive and caring, drawing me to her.

"Kiss me, Sean…kiss me."

I kissed her, holding deep inside her body. She shuddered, a moan coming from her throat, both of us climaxing together. We lay there, neither moving, just breathing, the bedroom filled with moonlight. I kissed her on the lips and then withdrew, lying on my back beside her. She pulled the sheet to her breasts and turned toward me. She ran her fingers through the hair on my chest, touching one of my scars. She said, "Your wounds, the scars…how did you get them?"

"In the desert. The Gulf War. I was captured for a month."

"You mean somebody did this to you. Tortured you?" "Yes."

"Sean, why haven't you shared or told anyone about this?"

"Some things are better left in the past."

"Maybe…but it can make us really appreciate the present. Maybe plan for the future a little better. You so much as said that on your porch. The reason you're going to Ireland is to learn more about your past, to try and help Courtney, to help her future."

"I don't have a choice."

"Yes you do, and that's what makes you the man you are. You do have choices and you choose to take the high road, to do what's good and right. I heard Dave Collins tell Nick at the bar one night that the meaning of life is to find meaning in life, because without it, without purpose, then what's really worth living for?"

"I think the challenge is beating or learning from the tests of pain and human suffering. Those things are inevitable. It's what we choose to do about these trials that makes conquering them rewarding. Or as Nick puts it when he's in the gym—no pain, no gain."

Kim squeezed my hand and sat up, her body a silhouette against the moonlit drapes. She looked toward the window and then back at me. "Sean, all this you've been through, whatever happened in the war, the crime on the streets you saw as a detective in Miami, losing the parents who raised you, losing your wife, finding and losing your mother...in a way you've been blessed. I know that sounds weird, but think of how you've survived—lived in spite of the dark side, the danger. Someone, maybe some*thing*—a guardian angel, is keeping you from harm because of the good you do here on earth. That doesn't mean you don't suffer, but you somehow survive to go on another day. I've never been a very religious woman in terms of traditional religion, but I have to believe there's a purpose, a connectivity, between forces in life and even death. Why did Courtney walk into your life? From that day you saved her life, pulling those two men off her, to what you're trying to do now, finding her again, righting the wrongs that happened to her, and even your mother, is a good and moral thing."

She leaned over and kissed me, pulled hair behind her right ear and said, "It goes back to what Dave and Nick were talking about at the bar, the meaning of life is finding your meaning in life."

I sat up and smiled. "You're a smart and perceptive woman. And you're a beautiful woman, on the inside and out."

"Ahhh, you know how to touch a girl's heart, Mr. O'Brien." Her wide smile suddenly melted. "After tonight, after you come back from Ireland, after you face those dragons, I don't want you to think you owe me anything, Sean. You have known the pain of finding and losing family, we're your family at the marina. I've always been close you. I don't need to be your wife, your girlfriend...anything more than a part of your family of people who care deeply about you, okay? This is important. Are you okay with that... because I am?"

"Okay."

"May you find what you're looking for in Ireland, and may that help to right a wrong. Return to us safely, Sean. That's all I ask of you. Come home safe and whole. I told you about the dark and frightening dreams I had in the hospital, what I didn't tell you was they were about you. I believe you are about to walk through the darkest chapter of your life. And it will take everything you have to endure."

EIGHTY-SIX

After I landed at Dublin International Airport, I rented a car and drove straight to County Cork and the coastal town of Cobh, Ireland. It was here, from this seaport that a ship known as *Titanic* sailed for America in 1912. It never arrived, but millions of emigrants did. The town was the gateway to the Promised Land, America, when more than six-million Irish said goodbye to their homeland between 1848 and 1950.

When I came over the crest of a hill and saw the port town, the first thing that caught my eye was the cathedral. St. Colman's Cathedral was impressive, sitting on a hill high above the business district near the water. The exterior of the old cathedral was clad in shades of gray; inside, I knew, was where the real darkness lay in waiting. My challenge would be to somehow gain access to the semi-retired senior priest whose collar was as false as his title, healer, teacher, and a minister—*'following the example set by the first priest, Jesus Christ.'*

Driving through town, I had the feeling that the place hadn't changed too much since *Titanic* set sail. Maybe the old coastal town was a bit more colorful today. It had a tourist vibe with a seaport edginess, bars for longshoreman, and pubs for holiday vacationers. Most of the two and three-story buildings that faced the harbor were painted in soft shades of blue, red, burgundy, yellows, lime greens, strawberry, and other ice cream flavors of color. I parked in front of Jack Doyle's Pub, found a pay phone, and called the main number listed for St. Colman's Cathedral

A woman answered, "Thank you for calling Saint Colman's, may I help you?"

"Yes, I'm new in town. Just getting settled, my family and me. We're looking for a Catholic church to help raise our children. I've heard good things about your church."

"Oh, yes indeed. The church has a long history with Cohb, way back when the city was called Queensland. Please come attend a Sunday mass with us. I believe you will find a new church home with Saint Colman's."

"I'll definitely take you up on the offer. However, before I bring the whole family…this is difficult to say, I'm sorry."

"Please, take your time."

"Thank you. I haven't done a confession in thirteen years. It's not right, I know, especially for a man my age. Something happened that I need to make penitence for, something for which I must seek forgiveness."

"When would you like to come in?"

"When is Father Garvey available?"

"Father Garvey? He's here part-time now. Perhaps you could see Father O'Conner—"

"Father Garvey comes highly recommended. Since I'm no longer a young man, I think a priest with Father Garvey's experience gives him the knowledge and skill to help me. When is he available?"

"Let me check his calendar."

As I waited for her to return to the phone, I looked down to the harbor, the water a sparkling cobalt blue, a huge three-masted schooner entering the port, its white sails expanded with wind. Church bells rang out in the direction of St. Colman's Cathedral. I glanced at my watch. It was exactly four o'clock.

"Father Garvey will be here tomorrow, Saturday. He comes in occasionally on Saturday. Looks like he'll be here from one 'till four o'clock. Would three o'clock work for you?"

"Yes, thank you."

"You're more than welcome. Oh, sir, what's your name?" "Taylor, Mark Taylor."

"Thank you Mr. Taylor."

"Thank you, before you go, I hear church bells. Are they coming from St. Colman's?"

"Yes. We have the largest carillon in all of Ireland, even the British Isles. Forty-nine bells, one is big as an adult elephant. Each day at four o'clock, the carillon bells play a song. It's all automated. However, on Sundays, and holidays, we have a professional carillon player climb the steps to the top of the old spire and play by hand. He uses his fists, really. It's quite remarkable. I'm afraid I must go, there's another call and I'm the only one in the office. Goodbye, Mr. Taylor, and welcome to Cohb, Ireland."

I wanted a dark and uncrowded place to eat. I didn't know whether my picture had made it into the Irish news media. I ducked in to Jack Doyle's Bar, my eyes taking a few seconds to adjust to the darkness. Sports memorabilia hung on each wall, pictures of heavyweight boxers, rugby and football players. Three people sat at the bar. Two looked like dock workers, muscular, T-shirts and tattoos. An older man, white hair, white bushy moustache, wore a tweed cap and nursed a glass of Guinness, his moustache wet with the beer foam.

I took a seat next to the older man, he nodded, sipped his beer and said, "We're seven minutes into happy hour."

I smiled. "Looks like I need to make up for lost time."

He chuckled. "When you hear the church bells ring it's time to drink a pint and get ready to sing. Name's Hugh Donovan."

"Mark Taylor."

"American?"

"How'd you tell?"

"Lucky guess."

"How's the corned beef here?"

"Best in town."

The bartender approached. I ordered a Guinness, corned beef 'n cabbage, and some Irish potatoes. Hugh sipped his beer, his blue eyes dewy. "What brings you to Cohb?"

"Holiday. I'm a history buff."

"You look more like the guy this place was named for—Jack Doyle. He was a hell of a fighter and a movie star, had the nickname of Gorgeous Gael. And he rode the legend all the way to Hollywood. Before he made movies, he fought twenty-seven pro fights, all won by knockouts, most in the first minute. He was six-three with a seventy-nine-inch reach. That's him in the photograph above the bar." He pointed to a framed black and white picture of a dark-haired man, boxing gloves raised, smiling at the camera.

"What happened to him?" I asked.

"Slow booze and fast women. He spent money like these drunken sailors that come in here when they hit the docks. Jack died a shadow of the man he once was."

The food and Guinness arrived. I ate and listened while my new-found-friend reminisced about the history of Cohb. I learned that Cohb was where the surviving victims of the sinking of the *Lusitania* were treated. The Germans sank the British ship seven miles off the coast of Ireland. As he drank and talked, I glanced down the bar and caught the lone woman staring directly at me. Her blue eyes bright as swimming pool water. I smiled and sipped the Guinness.

"Jack used to train hitting hundred pound sacks of flour. He even used his fist to pump the carillon in the cathedral, could only play one song, *The Old Rugged Cross.*"

I finished my meal, swallowed the last of the Guinness, paid the bill and got up to leave. Hugh said, "You sure you aren't Jack Doyle's son? There is a strong resemblance. Whose son are you, or as my Irish cousins say in the states, whose your daddy?"

"Good meeting you, Hugh."

He extended his hand. I shook it and he said, "Good luck to you, lad. May you discover what you came here to find."

I drove to the WatersEdge Hotel and checked in under the name Mark Taylor. I entered my second floor room, tossed my one travel bag on the bed and stepped to the sliding-glass doors leading to the balcony overlooking the Cork Harbor. I stood on there and watched the freighters and cruise ships in Cork Harbor, a moderate breeze blowing from the east, the moon above the harbor, the slight smell of salt and diesel in the night air.

I thought about the people who boarded *Titanic* from this harbor, and how their lives would forever change a few days later. I remembered what Dave had said on his boat before I left. '*It's the tip of the iceberg, and right now Gibraltar is beginning to feel a bit like Titanic.*'

I tried to picture what this harbor looked like three years after Titanic went to the floor of the Atlantic, when more than a 1,195 survivors of *Lusitania* were rescued in the Irish Channel and brought in to this harbor, most badly injured. And I tried to place myself in the shoes of the German

officer who gave the command to fire the torpedo at the ship with full knowledge it was a passenger liner.

I couldn't.

Then I stepped to the edge of the terrace and looked to my left, up the
hill. St. Colman's Cathedral stood at the top of the hill, lights pointed upward
from the ground lighting the old stone. I could see a large clock halfway up
the largest spire. The clock was big enough for me to read the time. Midnight.
In fifteen hours, I would meet Father Thomas Garvey. I tried to place myself
in my mother's shoes as she was about to be raped.

I couldn't.

EIGHTY-SEVEN

I arrived at St. Colman's Cathedral at 3:00 in the afternoon, glad it was a Saturday. Limited office staff, if any. The front doors were slightly ajar. I opened them and entered the old church. The sanctuary was cavernous, massive marble columns supporting ornate and carved marble arches, the afternoon sunlight igniting the stained-glass windows, casting rainbow colors over the marble floor and wooden pews.

The sanctuary appeared vacant. I walked toward the altar, my hard soles echoing off the marble. The air was cool and smelled of incense and candles. I could see the confessional booth in a far corner, hand carved, polished wood. There was a small red light burning above the closed door to the right. The door on the left was closed as well. I sat in a pew closest to the confessional and waited. I could hear the subdued voice of a woman speaking, weeping, and followed by a man talking in a monosyllabic, rehearsed response.

A few seconds later, the door to the right opened. A woman dressed in black exited the booth. She knelt in front of the altar, looked up at a carved statue of Christ and made the sign of the cross. She bowed her head, whispered a silent prayer, got up and left. She never saw me sitting alone in the pew.

The light above the right-side door turned green. I entered the booth. It was lit with one small wattage blub. I looked at the lattice that separated the left side of the booth from the right. Entering into full combat mode, my senses were heightened. I could hear him breathing. I could smell his aftershave lotion. He was less than three feet from me. I said, "I'm here in the name of the Father, the Son, and the Holy Spirit." I pressed the audio record button on my cell phone.

He said nothing for almost fifteen seconds. And then he spoke. "Do you wish to confess your mortal sins?"

"I do."

"Proceed."

I quietly opened the door to my side of the booth, then reached for his door—jerked it open. He was an old man, sitting in a high-back wooden chair, one elbow resting on the arm of the chair, the other hand in the folds of his white robe. His eyes had the color of a butane torch, intense, piercing, silver hair combed back. I said,

"I'll confess, but not before you do."

He looked up at me. "Who are you, son?"

"I'm Sean O'Brien, and I'm sure as hell not your son."

"Are you a member of the congregation? Do I know you?"

"No, but I know of you. You raped my mother more than forty years ago."

He pushed back in the chair, stunned, unable to maintain eye contact with me. His eyes moved from his lap to the floor, as if his contact lens had fallen out. Finally, he looked up at me. "What do you want?"

"Are you not even curious as to who my mother was? Or did you rape so many women and girls you've lost count?"

He said nothing. His eyes now smoldering, staring straight at me. Then he said, "How dare you come into our Lord's house and make these accusations. Who do you think you are? Get out!"

"I'll tell you who I am...I'm Katherine Flanagan's son. Her second son. You, you son-of-a-bitch, impregnated her when you raped her. Don't look so surprised. Where's Dillon?"

"I don't know anyone by that name."

"Didn't you learn that lying is a sin? Get up!"

He pulled his right hand out of the thick robe, and he gripped a .357 pistol. His hand like a claw, skin the color of bone. He said, "There's been a rash of crime in Ireland recently. One priest was robbed here in the confessional. So, of course, police will believe you, too, were here to rob the church—a most egregious sin." He wet his lips and smiled a crooked grin. "I do remember your mother. How do you forget a woman who enjoyed it as much as she did? Rape…hardly. She was one of my regulars. And guess what? Dillon might not be the only son I produced with her." His eyes grew wide, cruel and hard as the marble floor.

I said, "Put the gun down. You've caused enough pain."

He cocked his head, his eyes filled with loathing. "Pain? I only follow God's will. That's what I did when your father found out I'd sired the first son in the Flanagan family, Dillon. I followed God's holy directive."

"You're sick."

"And you don't understand, but your brother does."

"Where is he?"

"You'll never be the man he is. Nor was your father. So when he brought his sinful weakness to me, threatened me…threatened God's word, I destroyed him. And now I'll do the same with you; the difference is, I'll shoot you in the front of the head." I saw the white flash.

The gunshot echoed throughout the sanctuary. The bullet tore through my upper arm. I slammed the door closed. Then used my legs and back to turn the small confessional on its side. He opened the door, disoriented, like a rat flooded out of his nest. I kicked the gun from his hand. It slid across the marble. He ran to it. Picked it up and fired three shots at me, running in the opposite direction, toward a door in the far corner marked: stairs. He opened the door and vanished. He'd fired four times. Two rounds left.

I followed, holding my wounded shoulder with one hand. The door led to some marble steps, the stone worn down near the center of each step after more than 150 years of foot traffic. I quietly slipped my shoes off and followed Father Thomas Garvey. I climbed a dozen flights of narrow steps, stopping every few seconds to listen. I could hear him above me, climbing, running, panting.

The steps escalated in a spiral circle, like climbing steps in a lighthouse—leading me all the way up the center of the largest spire. As I ascended, came closer, I could hear his labored breathing above me. Within twenty feet, I came to a bell tower. Dozens of bells were mounted on massive wooden beams. Rope and strikers hung from each bell. A strong wind blew through the large arched openings in the belfry. I could see the town and the harbor below the cathedral.

Then I saw the white robe, behind one of the largest bells. I reached in my pocket and found a quarter. I tossed it at a pumpkin-sized bell on the opposite side of the tower. It rang out. Father Garvey shot in that direction, the bullet ricocheting off the bells.

One shot left.

I moved quickly, the noise from the bells dulling the sound of my approach. I kept the old wooden posts and the largest bells in my line of sight. I saw his shadow move across a far wall. I crept up slowly, holding my breath, my blood dripping onto the wood floor. I found a penny and tossed it over at the bells against the far wall. He turned and used both hands to raise the pistol. I charged, slamming him hard up against the stone wall. I grabbed his wrist and wrestled the gun from his hand. Then I backhanded him to the floor.

He fell on his back, mouth bleeding, front teeth lose, one knocked out. He grinned and said, "You don't have the balls to kill me! You piece of human shit! I screwed that whore you call your mama."

I pointed the pistol at his head. I saw my mother's face the day she told me what happened. Saw the tears spill down her wrinkled cheeks, saw the dignity in her eyes clouded with pain more than forty years later. I saw the pain in Courtney's face the day she told me her story. I played back the TV news images of the murdered girl whose body was pulled from the swamps, a white sheet draped over the coroner's gurney, blood on the sheet where her face once was. I pictured Kim in the hospital, the gas flames roaring on her stovetop.

"I'm going to ask you one last time. Where's Dillon?"

"Go to hell."

I set the gun down on the top of a smaller bell. He grinned and said, "You're just like that weak-kneed Christian daddy you had."

I removed my belt. Then I pulled him off the floor, backhanding him again across his mouth. Blood ran down the white robe. I wrapped my belt around his neck and said, "You're right about one thing I'm not going to kill you, at least not quickly. I'm going to hang you out of this bell tower for the entire town to see you for the rapist, murderer, and pedophile you really are." I pulled by mobile phone out of my pocket, the red record light on. I stopped the recording and played back the part where he admitted raping my mother and killing my father. I said, "Now, father figure, that's one hell of a confession. You'll go down as not the greatest Catholic priest in Ireland, but one of the most prolific and heinous sex offenders to hide behind that collar." I ripped the collar from his neck, shoving him against the largest bell. "Where's Dillon?"

"A place you'll never find him. Maybe the distant Aideen."

"What?"

He looked at my wound, blood seeping into my shirt. "You need balm for the wound and your soul, lad, for your feelings of grief. Dillon found it, but you, I think not. You wretched soul…you enter my confessional, my private chamber opening my door, but there's darkness there, nothing more. Are you surprised?"

He grinned and cocked his head. Then he bolted and ran ten feet, leaping through one of the wide arched openings, falling in utter silence. I heard him hit with a dull thud. I leaned over the side of the window, almost at the top of the tower. He had fallen across a wrought iron gate, landed on his back. Three long black spikes protruding through his chest, his eyes open, Father Thomas Garvey staring at the heavens.

EIGHTY-EIGHT

I didn't know if anyone had heard the gunfire from the bell tower. I slipped on my shoes and ran full bore to my rental car parked on the street in the shadow of the cathedral. Father Garvey died in a courtyard in what appeared to be the rear of the church. No cars in the lot. I saw no people. I didn't know if anyone was in the church on Saturday. I did know that I wasn't going to be here when police arrived.

I sprinted to my rental car, the pistol wedged under my blood-soaked shirt, sweat dripping from my face. My heart raced, my mind playing back what Father Garvey said before he jumped through the open window and committed suicide. I recognized parts of what he said, but from where? *Think.* I couldn't place it. Not now. Not with blood pouring out of a gunshot wound, and the sound of sirens in the distance.

As I opened the car door, I tried to remember if I'd spotted any surveillance cameras mounted on the exterior or interior of the church. It didn't mean they weren't there. If so, it was only a matter of time before they recognized me and then made the association to the U.S. presidential race and the notorious fly in the ointment for Senator Lloyd Logan. And that irritating insect would be me. Maybe the media would connect the dots—look at Courtney's last name, my last name, and begin speculation as to why I might be in Ireland.

And right now I had to get out.

I put the Toyota in gear and roared away from the cathedral. As I did so, I heard the carillon bells ringing. I looked at my watch: 4:00. I lowered my windows and couldn't help but smile because the largest collection of bells in the Republic of Ireland was playing *Amazing Grace*.

I hoped my mother was in a place where she could hear them.

— —

I DROVE WEST on Highway N22, through the small town of Macroom looking for a medical clinic. Nothing but pubs, shops, eateries, a feed and seed store, a small hotel, and picture-postcard beautiful scenery. I drove over a stone bridge crossing a fast-moving river. The sign indicated Morris Bridge was built in 1768, the river rushing under five Romanesque arches. I continued driving toward Killarney, my destination was Shannon International Airport, and home.

The pain hammered in my shoulder. My head throbbed. I pulled to the side of the road right past the Killeen Lodge, got out of the car, and removed my long-sleeved shirt. I wore a black T-shirt underneath. I ripped the sleeve off the shirt, pushed up the short sleeve on the T-shirt, and examined my wound. The bullet had entered my shoulder less than an inch from my birthmark, the round still lodged in muscle and tendons. I tied off the wound and wrapped the ripped sleeve around my shoulder, stopping the flow of blood.

I braced myself holding the roof of the car, inhaling the cool country air through my nose, trying to clear my head. I heard sheep bleating, their hooves clacking across the road. I turned around and was met with at least two dozen sheep, a border collie running, and a man walking with a cane. The dog darted around the perimeter of the herd, the man at the rear. They came to my side of the road, the sheep ignoring me and climbing a green hill to pasture land. The man wore a tweed cap, flannel shirt, and blue jeans. He was in his mid-sixties, his closely shaved cheeks flushed, green eyes like spring clover. He said, "Good day, sir. Looks like you could use some medical attention." His accent was thick as the grass on the hill. "Is there a hospital or medical clinic nearby?"

"Nearest would be Cohb to the east, Killearny to the west." He raised a bushy white eyebrow. "From the looks of things, I'd say you ought to have that examined right now."

I blew air out of my cheeks. "What do you suggest?"

"I could take a look."

"Are you a doctor?"

"Don't carry a license, but I carry the knowhow." He leaned in and pulled back the sleeve, carefully inspecting the wound.

"How'd you get in the way of a bullet? You rob a bank?"

"No. It's a long story. A deranged man tried to kill me."

"Seen plenty of those types in the service. I was a medic in the British Army. Twenty bloody years. Saw my share of combat and treated more wounded men than I want to remember. I retired to the farm, and today I administer medical care to all my animals. My house is a hundred meters down the drive. Between my wife and me—she was a nurse, we can help you. Name's Cormac Moore."

"Sean O'Brien."

"Come on, Sean, let's get you patched up."

—◆—

I LAY ON a bed in the guest room, the small county house very clean and well-kept. The man's wife introduced herself as Rebecca and told me she'd retired as an emergency room nurse from a Dublin Hospital. She was in her early sixties, a round face, kind eyes and a calm demeanor. She looked like a woman who'd seen the worst and yet the best in people.

Considering their backgrounds, generosity, and the fact that I might come out of surgery at a large hospital and look into the faces of people wanting to arrest me, this was becoming the best option I had.

Cormac Moore poured three fingers of Jameson's into a clear glass. "Here, knock this back. Best thing we have here to dull the pain."

"I usually sip this stuff."

"We need it to kick in now. No time to sip. Becky's boiling the tools. We want to keep the possibility of infection to a minimum."

"Good idea." I downed the whiskey.

Rebecca Moore brought in a tray, the surgical instruments—whatever they might be, were wrapped in white towels. She set the tray down on a bedside table, cleaned and prepped my wound, her eyes kind and confident. "Cormac, he's ready."

He came from an adjacent bathroom, flannel sleeves rolled up, hands and forearms wet from washing. He used a towel to dry them and said, "Sean, you just lie here and stare up at the bloody ceiling. This ought to be quick."

"Let's do it."

He nodded, lifted a long, thin knife up and began. I clenched my teeth and tried to block the pain, wishing I had another Jameson's. The knife and knitting-needle-like-prod he used felt like both had been heated over a scorching flame until they were glowing. I gripped the mattress, neck muscles tightening, sweat rolling down my face and onto the pillow. The room felt hot, the air thick. I glanced out the bedroom window and could see sheep grazing nearby.

Cormac said to his wife, "Hand me the retractor."

I could see her move, slightly, feel him scraping my bone, heard the bleat of sheep in the pasture. Fought back the urge to vomit. Then I heard the clank of a bullet hit the metal bowl.

"Looks like a heavier caliber," he said. "No splintering. All's intact. Very little damage done, Sean. You're a very lucky man."

His wife said, "Maybe that's why you have that unique birthmark on your shoulder. It's a perfect shamrock, and four leaves to boot. Most people have to get a tattoo to have that. You're the lucky one. You wear the mark of St. Patrick himself."

Cormac poured himself a shot of Jameson's and said, "Becky will close you up. She's better with a needle and thread. Besides, I've misplaced my glasses." He winked at me and touched me gently on the arm. "After she sews you up, you should have another whiskey. Looks like you could use it."

As his wife closed the wound, she said, "He's teasing you, Sean. You look fine. Please stay and get some rest, give the wound proper time to set."

"Thank you."

After she placed a sterile bandage on my shoulder, Cormac poured two fingers worth of Jameson's. I propped a little higher on the pillows, took the whiskey and swallowed it. Then I looked out the window for a second. Something caught my eye. Something black. I watched a raven fly from an elm tree to a clothesline just outside the window, the white sheep in the background. The bird turned its face to the sun, one yellow eye visible.

It was then I knew where I'd heard what Father Garvey had said. And if I could make the connection, it might lead me to my brother Dillon.

EIGHTY-NINE

I spent three days at the home of Cormac and Becky Moore, resting, recuperating, and planning my next move. On the fourth morning, I sat on the edge of the bed and looked out the window, two sheep staring back at me. The pistol I took from Father Garvey was on the nightstand. There was a knock at the door. I turned as Rebecca Moore entered. She smiled and said, "Good morning. How are you feeling?"

"Much better, thank you. I have to hit the road today."

"I hope it's not too soon. I have another fresh shirt for you, one of Cormac's. Might fit you. But you'll probably had to turn the sleeves up a bit. You've got longer arms. I've set out fresh towels for you. Please join us for breakfast. I made biscuits this morning.

Cormac likes to brag about my biscuits."

"Thank you."

She nodded and turned to leave. "Rebecca."

"Yes?"

"The hospitality you and your husband have shown me, what you did for me...I'm a stranger and you took me in. It's rare, and I want you to know how much I appreciate it."

"You're welcome, Sean. I believe you'd do the same for us. As matter of fact, I know you would. I can tell." She smiled and left the room.

—•—

I FINISHED ONE of the best breakfasts I've had in my life, pushed back from the table and said, "I want to thank you both. Can I pay you for all you've done for me?"

Cormac Moore looked at me curiously. "For what? Doin' what needed to be done? I think not."

"Just when I start to wonder if we're doomed as a species, people like you come along. Thank you."

Cormac nodded. "Say nothing more." He slid a full bottle of Jameson across the table, followed by a bottle of aspirin. "Wherever your journey takes you in Ireland, here's a little something for the road. I'm no doc, but a shot of whiskey and two extra-strength aspirins will ease that pain in your shoulder."

"Sounds like a good prescription." I smiled.

"Where will your journey take you?" Rebecca asked.

"That's a great question. Immediately, I'm looking for some acreage in County Kerry."

"What kind of land?"

"The old place was known as the Wind in the Willows. I hear it's abandoned. Near the coast."

Cormac's shaggy eyebrows rose. "Wind 'n the Willows, you say, lad? That's not near the coast—that's *the* coast. Maybe a half kilometer of coastline. We're familiar with it because one of those international hotel chains was trying to muscle its way in, buy the land for below market price, and build a mammoth time-share resort, and a casino with all the garish trimmings."

"What happened?"

"The woman who owned it refused to sell. It was in her family for more than three hundred years. A classic Irish estate was built there by the seventh earl of the Flanagan family. It burned to the ground in a horrific fire. Just an old caretaker's cottage on it today, but the ownership of the land predates Cromwell's invasion."

"Can you give me directions to the place?"

"Of course. Follow N22 through Killarney to N70. Turn right or east on R565 and head toward the coast, on Skellig Road. The property overlooks Puffin Island."

I said nothing. My thoughts racing.

Rebecca asked, "Are you in pain, Sean."

"I'm okay."

She smiled. "That part of Ireland is remote and so beautiful. Care for some more coffee?"

"No thank you. Cormac, I wanted to leave the pistol on the night-stand in the bedroom with you. I can't take it on the plane, the guy I took it from won't be needing it anymore, but I still might need it before I leave Ireland."

He smiled. "I can only bloody assume that you're being chased, hunted. You don't have to tell us why if you don't want to. You're obviously American. I'd wager your appearance here it has something to do with your wound, and maybe your surname, too. Sometimes people run from something, some-times they run to something. Which is if for you, Sean?"

"I'm not sure any more. I'm trying to locate a man in America, and the only person who knows, or knew where he is, lived here in Ireland."

"And he's dead, correct?"

"He committed suicide."

Rebecca sipped a hot tea and asked, "Did he tell you what you came for before he took his life?"

"Not directly. Do you have a computer with Internet access?"

Cormac said, "Yes. Laptop. I'll get it for you."

Rebecca cleared the table as he brought in a laptop computer. He turned it on and handed it to me. I searched online for key words to what Father Gravel had said before he jumped. *'A place you'll never find him. Maybe the distant Aideen…you need balm for the wound and your soul, lad, for your feelings of grief. Dillon found it, but you, I think not. You wretched soul…you enter my confessional, my private chamber opening my door, but there's darkness there, nothing more and nevermore. Are you surprised?'* "You bastard," I mumbled.

"What is it, Sean?" Cormac asked.

"The guy who jumped to his death was baiting me, cat and mouse like. He wasn't about to tell me directly what I wanted. But he did utter a clue before he died. And made a very subtle reference, an alliteration, to the words and cadence from Edgar Allen Poe's poem, *The Raven*. From the house of God to the *House of Usher*." "How's that?" Rebecca asked.

"He mentioned Aideen. That's a poetic allusion to the Garden of Eden."

"It's believed the Garden of Eden was somewhere near the Euphrates River in what today is Iraq."

"I have a feeling the reference the priest left is somewhere in America. And I have to find it."

NINETY

I drove through miles of rolling farmland, terrain in shades of avocado and olive greens, pocketed in deep shadow around old growth trees, and ancient cemeteries where many of the dead from Cromwell's conquest lay interred. More than twenty thousand died in battle, and there were tens of thousands more civilian casualties. As I drove by cemeteries, I thought of Abbey Island Cemetery, the place my mother had told me my father was buried.

Before flying out of Shannon, I'd find the cemetery.

I had the windows down on the rental car, the smell of the sea now in the wind. I followed the directions that Cormac had given me, the last turn was left onto Skellig Road. I drove up a slight hill, grass green and verdant on both sides of the narrow road. At the top of the hill, it was as if I'd opened a panoramic window into a world that might as well have been sixteenth century Ireland.

The green hills were like humpback leviathans bordering the cliffs and the sea, the lush acreage cascading down to the rock cliffs, the Atlantic Ocean a deep sapphire blue, the sounds of sea birds in the air. Less than a hundred meters off the cliffs was an island, and I knew it was Puffin Island.

A weathered hand-painted sign nailed to a slanting post read: *Wind 'n the Willows*. I got out of the car and walked past the sign, down a long gravel drive to a small, egg-white cottage. I cupped my hands to one of the sea-stained windows. The place was modestly furnished, wooden furniture, throw rugs on the floors. I could tell no one had lived here full time in years. Yet, it was fairly well preserved. No sign of vandals or broken windows or doors. Now I really felt as if I'd entered a different time period—isolated, the sound of breakers present, waves of humanity not, a barren rugged land, secluded, yet a strong feel of ancient Irish history in the soil.

I followed an old stone slab fence down the property. The rocks looked ancient as Stonehenge, set by human hand from the top of the hill all the way down to the sea. The rock fence was less than three feet high, but it was at least the length of two football fields. I walked next to it to the end, the cliffs. From there the view of Puffin Island felt primal, as if I'd been transported through time to a Jurassic era and to a place humans weren't supposed to go. It seemed only fitting that long-necked sea creatures should be breaking the surface off the island.

Although there were no plesiosaurs, there were dozens of seals. Some lying on the rocks, others diving into the indigo sea. Thousands of aquatic birds teemed over the island. I could see cormorants, razorbills, gulls, and many birds I couldn't identify—and those that I could because I first saw them on my mother's mailbox, the puffins. With their orange, red, and black bills, their tear-drop eyes, and chalky white faces, they looked like little clowns waddling on the rocks.

But it was in the air and water where their performance was anything but comical. They flew with bullet-like speeds over the ocean, diving and swimming like penguins on steroids hunting for fish. I couldn't help but smile.

And then a rock exploded below my right hand.

I rolled off the stone wall, keeping the wall between me and the shooter. I peered through an opening in the stacked stones. A man, one lone shooter, crouched on a grassy hill, his rifle on a bipod, maybe a hundred-fifty yards away. There was one round left in the .357 under my belt. But to hit a target a hundred-fifty yards away with a round from a pistol was extremely difficult. I'd done it in the military, on shooting ranges under fairly controlled circumstances.

Not here.

Not with the wind blowing off the Atlantic. Not with a human target crouched in a near prone position. I crawled on my hands and knees behind the rock wall a little closer toward the parking lot. A second shot shattered a stone right above my head.

I found a spot in the wall where I could peer through it, like looking through a rocky porthole. The shooter stood, lifting a pair of binoculars to his eyes. Now was my chance. I aimed the pistol through the opening in the wall, looked at the way the wind blew the grass and leaves, watched a puffin fly into the gust off the ocean. I knew I had to aim above the man, calculating for the pull of gravity, the long-distance drop of the bullet, the trajectory of the wind.

He held the binoculars with both hands, lowered the glass and looked with his naked eyes, holding one hand above his eyes to shield out the sun's glare.

I raised the sight at the end of the barrel to about one inch above the top of his head, calculating the distance for a torso shot. For more control, I placed a rock under the barrel. Then I held the stock with two hands. I glanced up to see a peregrine falcon call out; it rose from a tree, the bird startled from its perch. I didn't breathe. *Focus*. I had to enter a mental state of total control. Silence. I squeezed off the shot. The concussion sound blowing back from the rock was deafening. I watched, aware that the bullet would arrive at the target before the sound.

He stood there. Lifting the binoculars.

One thousand one.

One thousand two.

The shooter fell to his knees and onto his back. I could see his hand flaying at the center of his chest. I ran hard to the road.

Someone was coming.

The falcon cried out in flight to Puffin Island, and then there was the unmistakable noise of a diesel engine chugging up the gravel road. I stopped running and walked to my car on the side of the road.

A school bus was only a few feet from my car, dozens of kids getting off the bus. Two adults, probably teachers, stood near the bus instructing the kids to line up on their march down to the cliffs to view the island. Many of the kids had binoculars, and books depicting birds of the world. I walked by them and smiled, hoping I hadn't pulled the stitches in my bullet wound, hoping blood wouldn't soak through the bandage and shirt. And I hoped they wouldn't see the body of the dead assassin.

I got in my car and drove off, flying down the gravel road as fast as the rental could go, looking up into my rearview mirror. I couldn't see anyone else following me. But because I couldn't see them didn't mean a thing.

I put a battery back into my mobile phone. I waited a few seconds for it to boot up, then I called Dave Collins and said, "I need you to upload the video confession in the river."

"Are you sure?"

"It's the only way I can return massive fire." I told Dave what happened and said, "They're following me, somehow. The video, if it goes viral, will keep them in crisis control up until the election. Since my voice is on the video asking questions, if I wind up dead, if my body is recoverable, maybe a good prosecutor can indict Logan for murder."

"And if you could find Courtney Burke, all of this could be moot when you prove she's not the daughter of you and Andrea Logan."

"I think I'm getting closer."

"In Ireland?"

"No, in the states. The priest left a mocking, sardonic clue." I told Dave what he said and added, "Try to research Poe's poem, *The Raven*, and let me know if you can find a physical location to the translation of Aideen in *The Raven*—I know it means east of Eden…maybe there's a connection to a location in the states. That's where I think I'll locate my brother Dillon, and if I can get there in time—maybe I'll find Courtney."

NINETY-ONE

I t wasn't an island. Not by the real definition of the word. I reached for the bottle of Jameson's that Cormac Moore had given me, rolled my pants up to my knees, and walked from the shore of Derrynane Beach through ankle-deep water to Abbey Island. The pristine spot was about fifty miles south of Puffin Island on the western coast of County Kerry. Within five minutes of walking and climbing, I could see the ruins of an ancient stone abbey and the nearby cemetery. My heart pumped.

The wind blew across the Atlantic, gulls chortling and riding the air currents off the cliffs. Cotton-white cumulus clouds floated like small nations across a cobalt blue backdrop of the universe. I scaled to what I knew was a sacred place in the history and hearts of Ireland. Suspended on what felt like the skybox of the Atlantic, on a high cliff overlooking the sea near the ruins of the old monastery, were dozens of graves marked with iron crosses, Celtic crosses, gravestones worn thin from time and the sea. It was the Abbey Island Cemetery, a place filled with the remains of Irish sailors, farmers, and their families. All of the headstones overlooked a horseshoe-shaped deserted beach that reflected the ice blue sky.

I walked slowly through the cemetery, the smell of the sea mixed with damp moss and aged limestone. I saw the gravestone of Mary O'Connell. The inscription read that she was the wife of Daniel O'Connell, known as The Liberator–a man who fought for Catholic Emancipation in Westminster Parliament.

I continued walking, carefully scanning each headstone for the name I'd come to find. Why? Why walk through an ancient cemetery off the Coast of

County Kerry Ireland searching for the name of a person I never knew... would never know? What was the connection beyond the fact that my mother had told me about him. In the four hours I had with her, she painted a picture of a caring and kind man, a man who lived for his family, a man who eventually died for his family. I was only a baby when he was killed. I had no conscious memory of him. But my subconscious may have his whisper concealed. That was all the connection, all the bridge to the past that I needed. He was my father.

And I was his son.

I looked to my right, and there it was. A Celtic cross. For more than four decades it faced the Atlantic, faced the winds, sun and salt air. The old weathered cross was very much an old rugged cross, as was, I felt, the man buried beneath the cross—rugged and tough on the exterior, tender as a spring night on the inside. My mother had told me stories of his physical and internal strengths. How he could build a house from the ground up with plans he'd drawn and the expertise he had with his hands. And how inside his heart was at peace, and how he was her rock, her guiding light into an often too-dark world.

The inscription read:

PETER FLANAGAN
1946 - 1970
HE TRUSTED IN our Lord
HE SOARED ON the wings of eagles

There was an old and faded embossed photograph of a man, and it was bolted to the lower part of the Celtic cross. I couldn't take my eyes off the picture, almost as if it had a magnetic pull to it. He was dressed in a tweed sports coat, wide smile, angular face, thick dark hair and eyebrows. I felt as if I'd seen him before, dressed in the exact same clothes. But where? I looked at the old photo, the dark hair, the eyes, and I saw a little of myself.

And then I remembered.

It was at my mother's funeral. Across the cemetery, after the others had left, the man appeared, fog swirling around his legs. He seemed to have worn the same style—the same cut of suit, same dark hair and rawboned face. *Impossible.* I felt fatigue build behind my eyes, my shoulder burning. *Move on.*

I blew out a breath and poured a shot of Jameson in the plastic cup that Cormac had given me. I raised my cup and said, "Hello, Dad. It's been a long time coming. I want you to know that the man who put you here is no more. I didn't kill him, his evil did. Maybe it was time to collect…I don't know. You probably already know that Mom's gone, at least she's not in this world anymore. I bet she's in yours, maybe right beside you. I hope so. You have a granddaughter. Her name is Courtney…she's Sarah's only child. And right now, she's in trouble, some serious trouble. I'll do everything I can to help her, because I'm about all the family she has left on earth…and she's about all I have, too. Mom told me you enjoyed a shot of Irish whiskey. I'm going to leave this bottle next to your picture. Maybe you can sip and enjoy here overlooking the sea."

I knocked the shot back and swallowed the whiskey, the breeze kicking up over the Atlantic, the smell of shellfish in the air, gulls calling out across the cliffs. I set the bottle of Jameson down at the base of the cross, just beneath my father's picture and said, "I wish I could have known you." Then I turned and walked away, walked barefooted down the hill and across the tidal pool, the sound of shrieking cormorants over Abbey Island, waves breaking against the rocks, and the undertow of my father's voice pulling at the edge of my conscious mind.

I stopped and glanced back at the island and somewhere under the breeze, I thought I heard or maybe recalled the murmur of his voice, like the whisper from the bottom of a well. *"He doesn't resemble his brother…Sean is different…different as the shamrock mark on his shoulder."*

When I opened the door to the rental car, my phone rang. It was Dave Collins. "Sean, Logan's people are scrambling. Doing whatever damage control and denial they can. The river confession video is viral, getting a hundred thousand views an hour, globally. The news media have ID'd your voice on the video asking the questions of the guy in the river. All of it, the near attack by the big gator, the gunshots, your questions and his hysterical, but real answers are more than convincing. It's reality TV at its finest. The media are hunting for the guy you pulled out of the river and you."

"They won't find him. And I'm sure there's no public record of him in existence."

"I'm not so sure the pressure is off you. If the media can't find you, they can't corroborate this, and the Logan camp will contend it's all manufactured by democrats who are hell-bent on political chaos. So it's in Logan's best interest to make sure you never surface again, at least until he's done with a second term. Where are you?"

"A place called Abbey Island, near the Ring of Kerry, on Ireland's west coast. I found my father's grave."

"When you get home, when this settles down, we'll sip an Irish whiskey and you can tell me how you found his gravesite. Speaking of finding places, that information you gave me from the priest with the God-complex, Father Thomas Garvey...a background check reveals a lot of skeletons in the priest's closet, so to speak. Thomas Garvey was maybe the worst of the worst in the Catholic Church sex abuse scandals during the seventies and eighties in Ireland. Beyond that, he was also known as an expert, a scholar in his knowledge and appreciation of nineteenth century poets and writers. Dickenson, Cummings, Carroll, and Poe, among his specialties."

"Let's focus on Poe."

"The narrator in *The Raven* seems to get a perverse pleasure between his desire to remember and forget, like a shunned lover. Your brother Dillon, if he's a master hypnotist, he specializes in causing people to forget or remember—to recall what he wants them to remember, and ultimately, to have them carry out his desires."

"And if the desire is murder?"

"Like Nick mentioned, you might get a Manchurian Candidate, a pre-programmed assassin. Dillon could surround himself with these types."

"Maybe."

"Father Garvey used the word balm for the wound and your soul...in the Raven, Poe writes: *'On this home by horror haunted - tell me truly, I implore - is there balm in Gilead? - tell me - tell me, I implore!'* Sean, the mention of 'balm in Gilead,' is found in Jeremiah eight – twenty-one, where it asks...'is there no balm in Gilead?'"

"What's your take on that?"

"He may be referring to Mount Gilead. In biblical times, it was east of the Jordan River. Some speculate in the land of Nod, places were Cain wandered, east of Eden, if you will. There is a Mount Gilead in America, or at least there was."

"Was?"

"Yes. According to my research, it was hidden in the hills of Virginia. An eccentric herbal doctor, a spiritualist, built a health commune there in 1821. Way atop a Virginia mountain he renamed Mount Gilead. Apparently it had the right elevation, natural springs, Goose Creek in particular—the spiritual vibe and so on. Anyway, the conditions may have been right, but something else wasn't. A few serial murders happened back up in the woods, people fled, the Civil War arrived and the Goose Creek area became a blood bath. Eventually the county no longer maintained the one road leading into Mount Gilead. The settlement was literally at the end of a dead-end road, no highway to Heaven, for damn sure. The village became a ghost town. Father Garvey told you that Dillon found *it* and Aideen, but not you. What was *it?*"

"I don't know."

"We do know Aideen is east of Eden, and the reference to balm and Gilead. Although there are two other towns with the name Mount Gilead in the states, one in North Carolina and the other in Ohio, I'd wager the ghost town in the mountains of Virginia might be pay dirt."

"And that's where I'm going. Dave, rent a car at Dulles in your name. List me as one of the co-drivers. Make up a name for someone else."

"Okay."

"One thing, more."

"What's that?"

"On *Jupiter*, under the bed in the master, I have my Remington 700 there. It's packed in a travel case. Wrap it in brown shipping paper and overnight it to the Red Fox Inn in Middleburg, Virginia."

"Is that where you'll be staying?"

"For five minutes. Book a room and tell the clerk someone will be picking up a package that's being delivered to the hotel. Tell them the package is part of the accessories for a group meeting, part of visual presentation."

"Gotcha."

"Thank you."

"Be damn careful, Sean. Between the legacies of those serial murders, which were probably some kind of Hatfield and McCoy-style killings and a bloody Civil War battle, Mount Gilead has a very dark history."

NINETY-TWO

Courtney Burke tried to find something that wasn't on the map of Virginia. At least not on modern maps of the state, and it couldn't be located through satellite GPS. But it was there. Tucked away in a valley of ghosts, blurred by the lines of change and lost through the slivers in time. The remnants of the town were still there. Vine-covered buildings left standing. An old wooden post office. General merchandise store. A saloon. A half dozen ramshackle monuments to an age in Virginia of grist mills and moonshine stills. But like a faded tintype photograph of troops from the Civil War, the town of Mount Gilead, Virginia was a shadow of its former image.

Courtney needed directions, and she needed them from someone who knew the mountains well. She drove the red Toyota truck over roads winding through the Blue Ridge Mountains. It was mid-morning and she felt that she was getting close, felt the nervousness, the anxiety of seeing him again, face-to-face. Sometimes, even after the years, she could smell his sweat, the stench of his cheap cologne, feel the scratch of his beard stubble on her skin—her thighs, and she remembered his filthy jeans. He never removed them when he raped her, only pulling his pants down to his knees or ankles. His flannel shirt was always half unbuttoned. God, how she hated the pattern of those red and black colors.

She took one hand off the steering wheel, lowered it to the space between the seat and console, her right hand wrapping around the butt of the .22 pistol. She could do it, now she could. And he would never hurt another child.

She knew he'd be wearing the ancient torc when she found him because he believed that was the source of his power. He believed all the crap about the druids, the Irish people of the Iron Age—how they thought forged iron and gold and locked in powerful spirits. They also believed in reincarnation and human sacrifice. *He was just like them, the druids—the bastard.*

She eased the Toyota off the road and slowed to a stop in the potholed parking lot of a 1950's era gasoline station and country store. There was one gas pump in the center of the lot, directly in front of the entrance to the store. She parked at the pump. The only thing that didn't resemble the 1950s was the price of gas.

Courtney entered the dim store, the smell of hoop cheese and pickles in the air. In one corner, two wooden chairs were next to an aged barrel with the stenciled words *Jack Daniels* on one side, a checkerboard on top of the barrel. A single paddle fan turned slowly, the uneven blades causing a slight squeak on each turn. Jars of honey, canned okra and green beans were sold from the top of a glass counter, hunting knives sold underneath.

Courtney rang the bell on the counter. A half minute later, a slender middle-aged man appeared, using a red towel to wipe grease off his bony hands. He had a basset hound face with an Adam's apple almost the size of a golf ball. He wore his denim shirt tucked into his jeans, the jeans tucked into his boots. "Hep you?" he asked, his dark eyes almost veiled under the bill of a John Deere cap.

Courtney smiled. "I'd like to buy some gas."

"Don't accept no credit cards."

"Okay. Here's twenty dollars." She slid the money across the counter.

"Pumps on. You know how to pump it?"

"I've done it before."

"Bet you have." He swallowed, his Adam's apple rising and falling. "You from around here?"

"All my life."

"Maybe you've heard of a place called Mount Gilead."

"Maybe."

"Can you give me directions to it?"

"Ain't much left. A few old buildings. A shut down grist mill. It's a ghost town."

"I'm a photographer, and I'm documenting places like that. Where can I find whatever's left of Mount Gilead?"

"Take Highway 797 till you come to Goose Creek Road. Go left, 'bout a quarter mile down there go right when you come to Shawtock. It's dirt. Follow the road way up in the mountains. Road gets narrow, becomes one-way. You'll have to back outta there. Not a good place to be in the winter. A fella got back in there two years ago. They didn't find his body 'till the spring thaw."

"I plan to be gone long before winter."

He leaned closer, his gaunt hands splaying on the counter, the smell of pipe tobacco on his breath. "If you go, you'd be smart to be outta there before nightfall. And once the sun takes a notion to set, it sets pretty fast. Gets dark real quick up in the hollow."

— —

COURTNEY ALMOST PASSED it. An unmarked dirt road, maybe a half mile past a sign that read: Goose Creek Stone Bridge. She turned to her right, onto the unmarked road, scrub brush scraping against the side of the Toyota. She drove slowly through the winding back road, each turn gaining elevation, steep drop-offs less than three feet from the right side of her truck. She glanced down and could see a white water river hundreds of feet below her.

After another mile, the road seemed to dissolve into the thick woods. The road simply ended. There wasn't room to turn the truck around. She shut off the motor and opened the driver's side door. The air was cooler, hickory trees and pines grew high, and a hawk circled the blue sky over the ravine and the river. She could just hear the rush of the white water against the rocks far below her, the sound like holding a seashell to her ear.

Courtney lifted the pistol from between the seats and picked up her mobile phone off the console. She got out of the truck, not sure which direction to walk, or what exactly to say when she found him. She slipped a battery into her phone, waited a few seconds and then punched in the number. After two rings it went to his voicemail. "Sean, it's Courtney." She blew out a long breath. "You said if I ever needed you…if I…never mind. I shouldn't have called." She disconnected and slipped the small phone into her bra. She quietly closed the truck door and began following the overgrown trail into the woods.

She walked more than a mile down the narrow path. The farther Courtney walked, she felt, the closer she was to finding him. She stopped in her tracks when she heard pounding. With her eyes only, she followed the sound, the hammering coming from a tree. A pileated woodpecker, its tuft of bright red feathers resembling a cap on top of its head, scurried around the bark of a pine tree drilling for insects with the ferocity of a small jackhammer.

Courtney swatted at a deer fly and continued, glancing down at the path, watchful for snakes. She stopped and pulled her left pant leg up. A tick, the size of a raisin, sucked blood from the skin over her calf muscle. She pulled the swollen insect off her, felt her shoulders spasm involuntarily, and she ran through the woods, her eyes on the obscure path.

She looked up just as she ran directly into a spider's web that stretched between low-hanging tree branches, the sticky web covering her face, nose, and eyelashes. A black widow spider, large as a silver dollar, dropped from a limb, suspended by a strand of web, the spider's blood-red hourglass rocking like a pendulum within a few inches of Courtney's nose.

"Oh God!" she said, backing up and using her fingers to peel the web from her face.

"God. Do you believe you deserve divine help? My little niece, Courtney. I've been expecting you."

Dillon Flanagan stepped out from behind a hickory tree.

Courtney reached behind her back for the pistol.

NINETY-THREE

I hadn't shaved since before leaving for Ireland. And I was better off for it. Prior to flying out of Shannon, I'd bought a pair of dark framed reading glasses, and an Irish tweed hat. I wore them both as I walked through Dulles International Airport.

CNN was on the airport TV monitors, the talking heads mentioning my name and how the Logan camp could most effectively do damage control. I heard one commentator say that the river confession video had had more than 250 million views and had achieved that number faster than any video in the history of the Internet. I looked straight ahead and walked fast, quickly finding the Hertz counter. Within twenty minutes, I was driving west on Highway 50 toward Middleburg, Virginia and into the threshold of the Blue Ridge Mountains.

— —

WALKING INTO THE lobby of the Red Fox Inn was like walking across a page of American history. Constructed from fieldstone and wood, the inn has more of a tavern feel, the kind of place Jefferson might have enjoyed a drink after knocking off the first draft of the Declaration of Independence. I stepped up to the front desk. A twenty-something blonde smiled wide, her blue eyes twinkling. "Can I help you?"

"Yes, I'm here to pick up a package, a delivery for my boss, David Collins. Wherever we travel, it seems like our video and PowerPoint presentation travels with us. It's such a video centric world today."

"You've got that right. I blame it on cell phone cameras. All of them can shoot video, some in high definition. It takes a few clicks and the video can be uploaded to YouTube."

"That's good and bad." I smiled

She pushed a strand of blond hair behind one ear. "I agree. Let me see if I can find your package." She left through a side door and reappeared a few seconds later with the long box in her arms.

"The note says Mr. O'Brien is picking it up for Mr. Collins."

"Dave's the boss. I take it and tote it."

"Well, here you go." She lifted the package to the counter. "It's a little heavy."

"Thank you." I took the box and started to walk away.

She said, "You look familiar. Have you stayed with us before?"

"No." I could see her eyes scrutinizing my face, trying to place me. I nodded, smiled, and left. I placed the box in the trunk of the rental car and then inserted the battery back into my main cell phone as I drove off.

There were three messages. I played the first one, from Detective Dan Grant. *"Sean, where the hell are you? I've been trying to reach you for two days. But I guess every news outfit in the nation has been trying to do the same thing. Call me. I have some news about the perp we're holding in connection with the carny murders."*

I played the second message, and was caught off guard when I heard Courtney's voice. *"You said if I ever needed you…if I…never mind. I shouldn't have called."* I felt a lump in my throat, a tightness in my chest listening to her frightened voice. The third message was from the same number, but this time Courtney didn't leave an actual message. She inadvertently recorded a heinous scene. It was audio captured by her phone as she ran. It could hear her breathing quickly. Panting. Running. I heard her scream, followed by, *"Oh God."*

And then I heard him.

It was the same, unmistakable voice I'd heard when he called me. The voice of my older brother. Adrenaline pumped into my bloodstream when I heard him say, *"God. Do you believe you deserve divine help? My little niece, Courtney. I've been expecting you."*

Three seconds later, her phone sounded like white noise was pouring from the speaker.

374

I called Detective Dan Grant. He said, "Sean, the guy we're holding in connection with the carny murders…we have enough to go on. We spoke to his veteran's hospital shrink, some family members, even a couple of Army buddies he fought with in Afghanistan. This guy's PTS is off the charts. He said after banging the crap out of his head in one of our holding cells, he began remembering bits and pieces of things—things like killing Lonnie Ebert and two other carnies. But he said he was told to do it by someone else. Get this, Sean—he said he was under a spell from the devil."

"Are you immediately dropping charges against Courtney Burke?"

"Yes, but we haven't been able to find her to tell her that."

"Then tell the world. Hold a damn news conference before she's killed."

"We're doing that in the next hour. We just went to the DA with the stuff we have on the perp. He's a sad case. Guy's served three tours of duty—the first two in Iraq, and then two years in Afghanistan. His veteran's hospital-appointed psychiatrist says the perp believes he hears voices—voices of his dead buddies from the war. Anyway, he wound up working the carny circuit. He said in Richmond, he'd met some magician, a guy he called the Prophet who told him he could cure his PTS through hypnosis back on the farm. The guy is telling us he vaguely remembers the Prophet putting him under, as in under a damn spell. Said the Prophet was a direct descendent from an ancient Irish druid god. Listen to this, the perp said this Prophet guy has some kind of commune up in the mountains where he predicts the future by human sacrifice, apparently like the druids did. He said the Prophet orders his followers to stick an ice pick into the victim. By watching the way the vic's limbs convulse as he or she falls, along with the pattern of gushing blood, the Prophet predicts the future."

"Dan, I'm giving you a cell phone number. Last call was made at 3:47. I need to know where it originated. This is a life or death emergency."

"Give it to me."

I gave him the number of the phone that Courtney was using, and then I called Dave Collins and said, "You told me a few weeks ago that you have access to software that can track GPS mobile phone signals to with a few feet."

"I do, and I tried it with the number you gave me for Courtney Burke. She never came on the GPS radar, apparently she removed the battery and sim card."

"She's put them back in because she just called me."

"She did?"

"Could have been the case of a butt-dialed call because I could hear her running. She was panting, breathing hard, like someone was chasing her. And then I heard the voice of my brother,

Dillon."

"What'd he say?"

"It was a cold welcome that was really a threat, like the cat had caught the mouse and was smacking his perverted lips. Keep checking her phone. Maybe you'll see something."

"I saw Kim today. She brought Max by, left her with us while she works a shift. Nick and I had lunch with Miss Max. Sean, I don't know what, if anything, is going on between you and Kim. But I do know this much, she's very worried about you. More worried than I've ever seen her."

"Tell her I'm fine. Tell her I'm trying to tie up some loose ends and will be home soon."

"You need to tell her, Sean."

"I will…I have to take this call." I disconnected and spoke with Dan Grant.

He said, "That call pinged off a tower on a mountain near Linden, Virginia."

"Thanks, Dan."

"It's Courtney's number, isn't it?"

"Yeah, it is."

"Be careful, Sean. If it's the same mountain, same place where our perp had, for all practical purposes…an oral lobotomy, you might run into the guy he said is the Prophet."

"My goal is to bring Courtney to you, get the DNA test, and end the nightmare for her." I disconnected and started driving, speeding toward Linden, Virginia.

.

NINETY-FOUR

he man touched the barrel of the shotgun to Courtney's back and said, "Not on my watch, girl. Raise up your arms. Now!" She did as ordered and the man lifted the .22 from her belt and stepped to the right side. He was in his mid-twenties, unshaven, feathered dirty hair under his cap. He glanced to his left as Dillon Flanagan approached.

Dillon looked like Abe Lincoln without a beard. Rangy. Gaunt face. Piercing black eyes with a molten, swirling fervor behind the irises. He rarely blinked. He was dressed in a black coat with tails, like a maestro's jacket worn over a black T-shirt and dark jeans. His cowboy boots were narrow-toed, ostrich-skin.

"Greetings, Courtney," he said, stepping closer to her. Two additional men stood on either side of him. Both looked like they'd slept for weeks in their clothes, grimy dungarees over flannel shirts, mud-caked boots. Neither had shaved or bathed recently. Courtney took a small step backwards. Dillon grinned, leaning in some. "You don't look very pleased to see me. You tried to pull a gun on me. And all this time I thought I was your favorite uncle." He grinned, his black eyes animated. "Diviciacus sent you, didn't he? The man would cheat the gods to serve Caesar."

"You're a freak and you live in an insane world. You're even sicker than I remember." She lowered her eyes from his face to the gold bracelet he wore on his left wrist.

"I do live in an insane world, and I'm doing my part to change it." He lifted his arm. "Is this what brings you to the mountains? You want this torc and all the power that it possess?" Courtney said nothing.

He grinned, his eyes now fiery. The men stood a few feet away, each man's whiskered face as vacant as field of weeds. Dillon said, "I think not, Courtney. You forget how to speak, girl?"

"Give me what you stole from my grandmother."

"Why? Your grandmother's dead."

"No! Don't lie!" Her heart raced, palms moist.

"The old woman finally left this world. I expect her to return as a sheep. Nothing more. Since you're here, I have no doubt my brother, Sean, shall follow. Did you bond with your other uncle? Nothing like a family reunion to rock the cradle of your illusions. Let me paint a clearer picture for you, Courtney, one I'll share with Uncle Sean when he joins us. You have no claim to the property in South Carolina or Ireland. That inheritance is mine. Always was. Always will be."

"You killed her, I know it."

"I can't kill, I can only change the form of life through the act of death. It's like an elevator ride to a different place, a different floor in your progression to reach enlightenment. That's why the Celts never feared death in battle. They feared boredom in life. So when I change your life for the better, channeling through your death, you will one day praise me for having done so." He turned toward his followers. "Bring her. We will begin the ceremony in a grove of mighty oak, because to catch a hungry lion, you have to set the trap by tying a lamb to the stake."

— —

I FOLLOWED WINDING mountain roads en route to Linden, the rental car getting low on gas. I didn't want to take the time to buy gas. Every minute Courtney was being held by Dillon was a minute too long. And I knew she'd never walk out of the mountains alive. I parked in the gravel lot of a country store, dust blowing from the lot.

There was one pump. And the handwritten sign read: pay inside before pumping.

The interior of the old store was dark, some light coming from the front windows and a small wattage clear-glass bulb screwed into the base of a paddle fan. The wooden floor was made from knotty pine, worn smooth from decades of shoes and probably a lot of bare feet. I smelled barbecue pulled pork, hoop cheese, and barreled pickles as I approached the counter. A man sat motionless behind the counter, only his eyes moving under the bill of his cap, following me.

I said, "I'll take forty dollars' worth of regular."

He nodded, stood slowly. "Okay, pump's on."

I set the money in front of him on the scratched glass counter. He used two fingers, pressing down hard on the old cash register keys. The cash register was non-electric, solid, mechanical, and the color of tarnished silver. Everything in the store appeared dated, old—merchandise that could have been sold from a Sears and Roebuck catalog. It was an antique store by default avoidance of the present. Everything was old except one thing. Something I spotted when I first entered.

A video camera.

Wide-angle lens. High definition. Perched like a silent Cyclops to the immediate left of a mounted deer head behind and above the counter. I looked into the glass eyes of the dead deer and into the glass eye of the live camera, streaming real-time video to someplace.

As the clerk counted back change, I asked, "Where's Mount Gilead?"

"What's that?"

"Mount Gilead. Probably not much left. Like an old logging camp back in the mountains."

"Sounds like someplace in the Bible, not in Virginia. Never heard of it." He looked directly at me, unblinking while he tapped tobacco slivers into a pipe bowl. "Thank you."

He nodded and I left. I began filling the tank with gas, my back to the store entrance. I could see the store from the reflection in the side mirror. I saw the clerk answer the phone, his head nodding. The call was brief. I was twisting the gas cap back on the rental car when I heard the gravel crunching, someone approaching quickly. I spun around just as the clerk raised his arm, an ice pick clenched in his right fist.

I ducked, the ice pick missing me by inches. I grabbed his arm at the wrist, twisting it behind his back, shoving hard. Pushing his arm to his shoulder blades. Snapping bones and cartilage. The noise like someone stepping hard on a Styrofoam cup. He screamed, a painful howling. Then I spun him around and drove my forearm into his mouth, shattering teeth like hitting a corncob with a baseball bat. He dropped to his knees vomiting pulled pork, white bread and blood.

I grabbed him by the collar and shouted, "Where's Dillon Flanagan? Tell me!"

He tried to focus on me, his eyes drifting. I said, "Where's the Prophet?"

He attempted to smile, nerves in his smashed lips twitching, his eyes watering. He coughed and said, "Exodus."

"Look at me! Where's the Prophet?"

"*Exodus.*" Then he slumped over, his eyes dazed, and he mumbled, "Nobody finds the Prophet 'ceptin' God himself. *Exodus.* You have been set apart to the LORD today, for you were against your own sons and brothers, and he has blessed you this day. *Exodus.*"

I left him sprawled in the gravel lot, mumbling. I jumped in the rental and sped off, gravel and dust flying. My phone buzzed.

Dave Collins said, "I've got Courtney's location on GPS."

"Where?"

"Not too far from you. I have your location and Courtney's on a split-screen computer satellite grid here in my boat. Sean, she's about twenty-two miles from where you are right now. Take Highway 797 to the right. Go north to Goose Creek – to an unmarked dirt road. Looks like there's an old logging road about eighteen miles down on your left. If Dillon's got her, they could be walking because the GPS location dot is moving slowly. So she's not in a car. And it appears on a satellite topographical map of Virginia that she's in some very remote mountain country. Better hurry, Sean."

"Let me know if you can find an elevated area, a clear area, where I can spot them—someplace where I can get off a shot. That might be my fastest way to stop Dillon."

NINETY-FIVE

They led Courtney back in time. It was a small community of long-standing log cabins with river-rock chimneys, rough-hewn one-story buildings, split rail fences, a small clapboard store and a grist mill by a running stream. The big wooden wheel turned slowly as water from a trough was channeled and diverted to fall onto the blades of the timeworn wheel.

Courtney looked at the people as she was led, arms tied behind her back, like a captured prisoner into their world. The smell of wood smoke drifted over the settlement. Women looked up curiously from the creek where they washed clothes. One man, pushing a wooden wheel-barrow piled high with corn, set it down and stared. Barefoot children wearing bib overalls played by the stream.

The men and woman were dressed in Amish-style clothes—long dresses for the women, overalls for the men. None of the men wore hats. They all watched her with suspicion as Dillon Flanagan and three of his men walked into the camp. Courtney noticed that many of the women were pregnant.

Dillon turned to her and said, "You're blood related to some of those children, Courtney. They're your little cousins. All of the women swollen with child are swollen with my children." He grinned and whispered, "My seed will never be removed from the garden."

Dillon stepped up on the sawed-off stump of a tree. He shouted, "Gather about brothers and sisters. More than two dozen people formed a semi-circle around him and Courtney. He said, "This poor woman is unclean. She fornicates...prostitutes her body for the pleasure of men. She is not without redemption, but she must be isolated, taken to her knees in the dark to understand the depth of her sins. God requires it of us."

"Amen, Prophet," said one of the men.

Dillon nodded, his penetrating eyes scanning the rapt faces of his followers. "She is a descendent of Caesar, an emissary."

Courtney felt like she'd awakened in a nightmare. She screamed, "No! I'm not a descendent of Caesar and I'm not a prostitute. My grandmother was Dillon's mother. He's my uncle. Yes! It's true. And he raped me. The first time when I was eleven. He stopped when I turned fourteen. And he'll rape your children, too."

"Blasphemy!" shouted Dillon. "You're wicked. If she's released, she will tell them about us, and they'll come here. They will hang us from the cross."

Courtney shook her head. "Can't you see he's insane? What did he do? Did he hypnotize everyone here? Can't you see him for what he really is...a sick fake?"

— ∎ —

I FOLLOWED DAVE'S directions, driving up a steep, unpaved road that was carved around the perimeter of a mountain. He said, "It looks like there's an overlook—a cliff, maybe, about a half mile to the north of where I see Courtney's location. The satellite images are pretty good. But they appear to have been shot in the fall when leaves are off most of the trees. So I don't know exactly what you'll be able to see, if anything."

"How close am I to this place?"

"Maybe a quarter mile. Whatever Dillon is doing with Courtney, there is very little movement. They've stopped...looks like it's in a clearing near a large expanse of woods. Unless Dillon tossed her phone, somehow she's managed to keep it and to keep it turned on. I could lose the connection any second."

"I'll be at the overlook in less than a minute."

"You can't get there fast enough, Sean."

When I came around a bend in the road, it looked like a door had opened to hell.

"Courtney!" I yelled.

Dave was saying something as I dropped my phone in the passenger seat.

A Toyota pickup truck was burning in a ditch on the side of the road. Flames roared from the open windows, tires belching black smoke, the sounds of metal popping, glass shattering.

The hungry and ugly sound of a ravenous fire devouring prey.

Was Courtney inside the truck? Could someone have stolen her phone?

I ran to the truck, the heat like a furnace from fifty feet away. I held my arm up to shield my face from the fire, trying to see if Courtney's body was behind the melting steering wheel. I couldn't remember the last time I felt so helpless.

—■ ■—

NO ONE IN the crowd said anything. They simply stared at Courtney, collective eyes shifting over to Dillon who shouted, "Dig a hole—a grave, back up in the field of clover, beyond the grove." He turned to a tall, lanky, scarecrow of a man. "Brother William, my carpenter!"

"Yes, Prophet."

"Make me a casket. Bore a one-inch hole near the head of the box."

"Yes, Prophet."

"Brother John, my blacksmith."

"I'm here, Prophet," said a man with the shoulders of an ox.

"Make me a pipe. Five feet in length. Fit it to the hole that William bores in the box."

"Yes, Prophet."

Dillon turned to the men at his side. "Bring her, and bring me the infiltrator you caught yesterday."

Two men nodded and left. The third grabbed Courtney by her forearm and led her away, Dillon following. He paused, stopping next to a pregnant young woman. He placed his wide, open hand on her dress over her belly, looked at her, his eyes piercing, and said, "I feel the blood and spirit of a Celt warrior. You are a chosen woman, Sister April."

She lowered her eyes, a demure smile working in the corners of her small mouth. The residents drifted back to their routine tasks as Dillon caught up with Courtney and her sentry walking down the hard-packed dirt road, past a cornfield, and then coming to a small clearing bordered by a large strand of oaks. Two men brought a third, younger man, his feet and hands shackled in chains.

He was in his late twenties, wearing a University of Virginia T-shirt, red baseball cap, jeans and hiking boots. Courtney could see he was terrified, his breathing quick, eyes darting around, vein pounding in his neck.

Dillon said, "Remove the iron from the limbs of this dissident. And two of you hold his arms until I say to release them."

The man said, "Let me go. I didn't do anything. I was just up here scouting the area for a student film we're shooting. I heard about these old buildings. I didn't know anybody actually lived in this place. Please, just let me go, okay. I won't say anything about you people living here."

"You people?" Dillon cocked his head, his eyes like laser beams. "You, sir, have no idea who these people are and why they're here. This is the valley of the gods, a place of rebirth. To find a renaissance, to seek a better path to the future, death is often the key because the transference—the spirit leaving the body uses the limbs, even the blood of the body to point the way to the future." He looked at one man without moving his head. "Brother Arthur, it is your turn."

——

AFTER THE FLAMES subsided somewhat, and I could see there wasn't a body in the Toyota truck, I moved on quickly. The last two hundred yards were not accessible by car. I carried my rifle, put Dave on speaker-phone and ran, ran hard in the direction he pointed out. He said, "Another hundred feet and you should reach it. Be careful. The drop-off is damn steep, more than eleven hundred feet straight down. There's a fast-moving river at the bottom."

"Got it." I arrived in a small clearing of ancient rock and cedar trees on the edge of a mountain. Ground water seeped between the boulders making their surface slick. I looked toward a small valley to my left, maybe a quarter mile away. There were a few ramshackle buildings, wood smoke curling from a chimney attached to a rickety cabin. A few people milling around the property.

"What do you see, Sean?"

"Hold on Dave." I slipped my phone into my shirt pocket and then used an outcropping of rock to set up the bipod for my rifle, looking into the scope. I panned slowly to the right across the cleared property, spotting men, woman, and a few children. It was an agrarian, eighteenth century Appalachian farming community. I kept panning to the right, past a grist mill, past a whitewashed church.

And then I found Courtney.

And Dillon Flanagan.

It had to be him. Tall, thick black hair, cheekbones. A resemblance to the actor Daniel Day Lewis. He stood next to Courtney, her hands shackled behind her back. Standing there, next to five men, her head cutting from right to left as if she was looking for a place to run. But there was no escape, nowhere to run. One man, wearing a red baseball cap, was being held by two others. Even through the scope, I could see the man was pleading for his life.

I chambered a round, moving the cross-hair sight to the back of my brother's head.

— —

THE MAN CALLED Brother Arthur waddled like a grizzly bear walking on its hind legs. Courtney watched him, saw the vacancy in his eyes. She knew what was about to happen. He towered more than six-four, near three hundred pounds, ruddy face with a salt and pepper Van Dyke beard. He slid an ice pick from his overall pocket and slowly approached the frightened man who was held by two other men, each one gripping one of the man's forearms, stretching his arms outward.

Courtney shouted, "Leave him alone! Uncle Dillon, please, don't hurt him. Dear God, please."

"God?" Dillon turned to her, his head cocking like a cat watching a goldfish in a glass bowl. "God can't help you. Never could. Never will."

"Please, let him go. Kill me instead."

"Is that what you would desire, Courtney? Be careful what you wish for. This man before us was sent here on a mission. And now his mission is altered, he will help show us the future because the honesty of a real death cannot be false. The flailing of the limbs and blood flow speaks the truth and the future. It is the way of the Celts." He looked at the large man and said, "Proceed."

The large man gripped the ice pick, slowly raising it in the air. Courtney bit her bottom lip and closed her eyes just as the bulky man's head exploded.

He was dead before he hit the ground.

NINETY-SIX

As the big man was collapsing, I sighted the cross-hairs on the chest of another man. He was one of two gripping the outstretched arms of the captive man. I squeezed the trigger, saw a cloud of red mist erupt through the scope, and then sighted on the chest of the man on the opposite side of the prisoner. The round hit him just below the neck. Three down in less than five seconds.

And in that time, Dillon Flanagan was gone. He fled, pulling Courtney with him, vanishing in the thick woods. The younger man who had been held captive, ran the opposite direction and away from what he undoubtedly must think was the village of the damned.

"Sean, are you okay?" Dave's voice sounded synthetic, like it came from inside a lead pipe.

I fished the phone out of my pocket. "Yeah, I'm okay. Three hostiles down. He's got her, Dave. Dillon vanished with Courtney back up in the woods. He's running an eighteenth century farm here. Looks like some kind of cult following. It's definitely a compound. Don't know how well they're armed. But I've got to go in, and do it quickly."

"You can't cross the ravine, at least not fast. Walk back to your car. I see what looks like an old logging road. According to my data, International Timber logged some of the mountain before World War Two. Some of the loggers probably stayed in whatever homes or buildings that were left standing from the ghost town of Mount Gilead."

"From what I can see, there are about a dozen cabins and assorted buildings including a working grist mill. Residents may be heavily armed."

"Only one road leads into that place. You can bet it's being watched."

— • —

ONE MAN HELD a pistol on Courtney. Two others carried a wooden box as they followed Dillon Flanagan deeper into the forest, down winding logging trails. Soon they came to a low-lying area, a gorge or a large washed out gulley that had been cut at the base of the cliffs by fast moving water. Dillon pointed to a spot in the sand, turned to his men and said, "Dig."

They used two shovels to remove the soil, and within a few minutes had dug a hole—a grave. Dillon said, "Brother John…fit the pipe onto the box. We'll sink it to allow for three inches of pipe to rise up out of the soil."

The man called Brother John nodded, worked the pipe into the hole that had been cut to receive it.

Courtney bolted.

She ran hard through the gorge, her shoes slipping in the mud. Dillon watched for a moment and said, "Retrieve the runaway. Bring her back alive and put her in the box."

The men took off, running like hounds chasing a fox. With hands tied behind her back, Courtney's speed was diminished. In less than a minute, the men had caught and tackled her in the mud. They lifted her up and brought her back to Dillon, dropping her at his feet. He kicked her in the mouth, squatted down and said, "Little niece, you're gonna die, but not 'till I say how and when. Now lie down in your coffin."

She spat mud and saliva in his face. He grinned, wiped if off with one hand, wiping it on her shirt, across her left breast. He leaned in her ear and whispered. "I remember what they felt like when they were growing." Then he rose up and said, "You will cross the threshold tonight. You'll do it with my brother. A full moon is rising across the abyss." He paused and inhaled deeply through his nostrils. "Smell that? That's the promise. Lots of rain. A big nor'easter is due to arrive about midnight. You know how fast the water from the rains come down this canyon? It'll be a flashflood. Won't take long to cover up that pipe. Drowning is a bad way to go 'cause it takes so long to die. Lungs burn, you cough, spit up water, trying so hard to catch a breath of sweet air. Then you'll have nothing but water to breathe, and you'll finally begin to surrender…sort of dreamlike because in the casket you'll plainly hear your own heart beat its last thump-thump." He grinned, a rising moon trapped in his black eyes. "And you have asthma."

"You will burn in hell! You bastard!"

"Pack the witch in, brothers. Remove the rope from her wrists. I like to hear vermin scratch the wood."

The men grabbed Courtney. She kicked. "No! Don't listen to him! He's the worst kind of evil. Dillon Flanagan is no prophet. He *is* the devil himself." They used a sharp knife to slice the ropes from her wrist, shoving her in the coffin, quickly slamming the lid on, two men sitting on it, one man nailing it shut. Courtney screamed as the last nail was driven into the wood. The men set the coffin in the grave and began shoveling dirt and mud into the hole.

She kicked at the lid. Pounded with her fists. She took short breaths through her nostrils, the odor inside the coffin smelled of sawdust and mud. She lay there and listened to the sound of dirt falling against the top of the tomb. She prayed silently. Thought about her grandmother. "Sean, where are you?" Then she felt as if the walls to the tomb were closing in, her breathing labored, asthma coming on strong. She pursed her lips into the pipe that protruded inside the casket. She fought for her breath, her lungs burning.

Dillon stood over the grave and smiled, the full moon rising in the sky far beyond his shoulders. He bellowed, "I smell the promise of rain!"

Courtney screamed, used her fingernails to claw at the lid of the coffin, her mournful cry sounding as if it came from the center of the earth.

NINETY-SEVEN

A rising full moon was my only light source driving the twisting logging road around the edge of a mountain. Tree limbs and branches raked down the side of the rental car. I set my phone on the center console and listened to Dave give me random directions from satellite GPS signals that could definitely see the forests, but not the trees. "Sean, looks like you're within maybe three or four hundred yards from what appears to be the perimeter of Dillon's compound."

"What are you getting from Courtney's phone signal?"

"It's stationary, and it's weak. Hasn't moved in more than an hour. I'm worried."

"How far do you think it is from where I am right now?"

"Mile, maybe a little more."

"I'm running out of what's left of this logging trail. Got to go the rest of the way on foot."

"I'm following you. Stay off any obvious paths into the compound. You don't know if they're booby-trapped. He could even have buried a few landmines."

I saw a text message pop up on my phone. Reading it, my blood ran cold. Dillon Flanagan wrote: **I know you're here little brother - during the great flood, God murdered everyone on earth except Noah's family - He set an example for me to follow - bury your heart because Courtney**

390

will perish in the flood waters - and you're next, as was Abel-

I sat in the car and re-read the text, my thoughts racing. I shut off the engine, grabbed a flashlight from the glove box, extra rifle cartridges, and stepped out into the light of the moon. The tall cedars cast shadows across the trail. I could smell pine needles and rain in the air. I glanced up in the sky, the full moon bright, but clouds in the distance, the dark guts of the clouds streaking with veins of heat lighting.

Dave said, "What's happening? I can tell you're not moving."

"I just received a text from Dillon. I'll read it to you. He said: *I know you're here little brother - during the great flood, God murdered everyone on earth except Noah's family - He set an example for me to follow — bury your heart because Courtney will perish in the floodwaters - and you're next, as was Abel.*'"

"Is that all he wrote?"

"Yes, but it's enough. It looks like a hell of a storm is brewing over the mountains. Look on your satellite topography chart and find a low-lying area."

"There aren't many in the Blue Ridge Mountains."

"Find someplace that might be prone to flooding. A valley or gorge, maybe. Someplace that could be susceptible to flash flooding, and somewhere close to Dillon's compound."

"Give me a minute. You think he stuck her in a ravine somewhere?"

"Yes. He said to bury my heart because Courtney will perish in the floodwaters. I think he buried her somewhere, and the rain is coming."

"Sean, he's laying a trap for you."

━ ━

COURTNEY TRIED TO control her breathing. The coffin was almost airless, muggy and hot. Perspiration soaked her blouse. Her left cheek was throbbing and swollen from Dillon's kick, lower lip puffed-up, dried blood crusted in one corner of her mouth. Soft light from the moon came in through the pipe, illuminating her face damp from sweat. She forced herself to stay calm. It was the only way an asthma attack wouldn't return.

She thought about Boots, his smile and his kind encouraging words. She remembered the long talks she used to have with Isaac, and how much his dog meant to him. She remembered Sean's dachshund, Max—her big brown eyes, the way she could catch a piece of food in mid-air. Courtney smiled. She thought about her grandmother. A single tear spilled from her eye and rolled down her cheek, falling onto the wood beneath her head.

She looked through the pipe, watching the moon, watching a wisp of dark cloud floating in front of the moon. The interior of the coffin darkened for a moment, and then the cloud passed, the light returning. She lay there, staring through the pipe, the light coming from so far away. And then a large cloud seemed to devour the moon.

And the interior of the casket was the darkest black Courtney had ever seen and felt.

NINETY-EIGHT

Lightning popped in the sky above the Blue Ridge Mountains, each burst of light giving the mountains the look of dark purple dinosaurs slumbering since the ice ages. I used the light from the cracks of lightning to help me see through the woods, trying to stay off worn paths and heading in the direction of Dillon's compound.

The rain began falling in large, heavy drops coming through the gaps in the tree limbs.

I plugged an earphone into my phone and said, "Dave, I'm close to the village. I can smell wood smoke. It's raining. Can you hear me?"

"Barely. Sounds like you're in a tunnel. I think you're about a half mile from where Courtney's signal is originating. Maybe it's the interference from the rain, but her location signal is getting weaker. Head toward the two o'clock position. And hurry."

I ran, branches and limbs slapping me in the face and across my chest, the rain pouring harder. Within a minute I was entering the compound. I stayed on the fringe, working forward but staying in the perimeter near the woods. I could see light in the windows of the cabins, the light flickering like it was coming from kerosene lanterns. I heard the braying of a donkey in the night, could see farm animals standing next to one another under the limbs of an oak tree in a small pasture bordered by a split-rail fence.

I heard the rush of water, a fast moving creek. Lightning cracked and I could see a lot of water pouring from the end of a wooden trough, gushing in a torrent onto the blades of a grist mill, the wheel spinning. I had to find

393

Courtney, and I had to do it within minutes. My immediate regret was that I didn't take Dillon out when I had the chance. I'd saved a man's life, and now my niece was very close to losing hers. *Come on big bother, step out of the shadows.*

Dave said, "Sean, you're less than five hundred yards. Head toward the noon position. Go straight. Can you—"

"Dave! Can you hear me?"

Nothing. Only white noise in my earpiece. I'd lost him.

I ran, gripping my rifle. Not willing to use my flashlight yet. A hard rain fell, the drops stinging my face as I ran. *Hold on Courtney. Just hold on.*

—•—

RAIN DRIPPED INSIDE the pipe and fell onto the center of Courtney's forehead. *Drip...drip...drip.* After a few minutes, the drops felt like rocks hitting her between the eyes. She could hear water rushing outside. "Oh God," she whispered. "I don't want to drown...please...help..."

Water began seeping in the casket through the joints, a slight trickle, enough to wet the back of her hair. She felt the air go out of the coffin, pushed her mouth closer to the pipe and breathed. Rain hit her in the back of the throat. She could hear Dillon's mocking voice: *'Drowning is a bad way to go 'cause it takes so long to die. Lungs burn, you cough, spit up water, trying so hard to catch a breath of sweet air. Then you'll have nothing but water to breathe, and you'll finally begin to surrender...sort of dreamlike because in the casket you'll plainly hear your own heart beat its last thump-thump.'*

—•—

I TRIED TO run in the direction that Dave had last given me. I heard static in one ear, the waterfall of a pounding rain in the other ear. I pushed farther, knowing that the rain would smother the noise of my approach. Unless Dillon and his men could see me in one of the flashes of lightning, I didn't think I'd be ambushed. I knew I couldn't see them any better than they could see me. But they knew the land, and if Dillon had set a trap, I might trip over a wire that would detonate a shotgun blast to my chest.

As I ran, I tried to get a feel for the terrain, to see where the elevation began to fall—to find a chasm that might be a deluge of water in a hard rain.

I jogged downhill, almost stumbling into what appeared to be gorge between two mountains. It was very muddy. The ravine apparently carved from rain and storms through centuries. Water was covering my shoes. Moving faster.

"Sean, can you hear me?"

Dave was back. His voice scratchy, like it was coming over poorly insulated copper telephone wires. "Yes, I hear you."

"You're less than one hundred feet from Courtney."

"I'm in a ravine. It's filling with water. If it's been raining hard back wherever the canyon begins, there might be a flashflood any minute."

"Keep going in the three o'clock position."

"Okay." I trudged through the rising creek. Lightning flashed and I saw something odd entrenched in the side of a large oak tree adjacent to the ravine. I switched on my flashlight, panning the rushing water, looking for any sign of Courtney. I panned over to the giant tree and saw an old logger's double-blade ax embedded in the tree. It was as if someone had started to chop the tree down years ago, but walked off and forgot about the ax.

The rain pelted the surface of the rushing water with the intensity of millions of drumsticks splashing in water. I slogged through the water, shining the flashlight beam across the surface.

There it was.

The end of the pipe was less than two inches above the surface of the rising water.

NINETY-NINE

I didn't know if running over to the pipe would be the last run of my life. I pointed the flashlight beam around the creek-bed, looking for signs of tripwires or shotguns mounted in trees. Nothing but pouring rain and rising black water. I approached the exposed pipe carefully, reaching below the water and feeling for wires. It seemed clean. Then I took a deep breath, aimed the light into the pipe, and looked down the hole.

An eye stared back at me.

It was a frightened but beautiful eye, matching the captivating depth and colors I first saw in Courtney's eyes. I knelt down and shouted into the pipe. "Courtney!"

"Sean! Help me!"

"I'll get you out." I glanced around the outskirts again. There was nothing but a torrent of rain. I looked back down at the pipe. The water had risen another quarter inch. I reached under the water and felt at the base of the pipe. The rushing water had eroded loose dirt. The entire top of the wooden box was exposed. I used my hands to remove mud around the sides of the box. I needed a shovel.

I ran to the tree, propped my rifle against the trunk and grappled with the end of the ax handle. I pulled. It was deeply embedded, the old oak had a powerful hold on the blade. I didn't want to break the handle so I gripped the head of the ax, on either side of the blade and pulled. Suddenly, the hair stood up on the back of my neck. Lightning exploded somewhere at the top of the massive tree, limbs and leaves falling like confetti around me. I was

396

blinded for a moment, closing my eyes and pulling with every ounce of my strength. The tree let loose its grip, and the ax was free.

I ran back to the box that imprisoned my niece. "I'm here! Hold tight, Courtney." I used the ax blade as a trowel to shovel mud from the edges of the box, working as far down as my arms would reach. The water was now less than an half inch before covering the end of the pipe. I straddled above the box, planting one foot on either side, reaching down in the water, slowly pulling. The box came up about three inches, almost buoyant. I squatted down, planted my legs in the mud, and slowly pushed the box into a higher position, using my shoulder to give it the last heave. It stood upright in what was fast becoming a white water river.

I reached for the ax and yelled. "Courtney! Keep close to the back of the box." I raised the blade and tore through the lid, ripping away splintered wood. I used the blade to cut through a half dozen nails and tore off the remaining wood. Courtney stepped out and fell into my arms. She sobbed. I held her closely rocking her gently, stroking her wet hair. I said, "You're safe now. Everything is going to be fine."

She nodded and looked up at me, and then past me, her face melting into absolute horror.

"No, little brother. Everything is not going to be fine. At least not for you and our adorable niece. She was even sweeter at age twelve."

Dillon Flanagan stood less than six feet from me, pointing a .44 magnum pistol at my chest.

ONE HUNDRED

illon wore a black Australian bush hat, rainwater pouring off the brim. A burst of lightning nearby illuminated his face. It was a face I'd seen before—and one I hoped I'd never see again. I saw nothing of my mother in him. I did detect features of Father Thomas Garvey—the flame-blue eyes with the powerful compelling intensity. His eyes seemed to capture and hold the streaks of lightning for a few seconds after the light faded in the night sky. Arched dark eyebrows. Cleft in his chin. He wore a Van Dyke beard.

Dillon grinned and said, "But you didn't know her at twelve. As a matter of fact, you knew nothing of the family until you stumbled into us."

"Put the gun down. We can talk this out. No more need for violence."

"God often saw the need for violence. It's in our genes, inbred in us by the competing forces of nature, of good and evil. The human race is a race of disgrace—a lineage of mongrels."

"Just let Courtney, our niece, go. If there's something you feel that needs to be said, to be settled between us brothers, we can settle it."

"Our niece? You didn't know the girl existed until recently. Brothers? What does that really mean? We had the same mother. Quite different fathers. That's one of the reasons I'm standing here with a gun pointed at you. I spawned from a superior gene pool, directly linked to ancestors who were some of Ireland's most feared and respected leaders. We fought, killed, and ate the flesh of Roman soldiers. Caesar feared us."

"What do you want, Dillon?"

"Want? Nothing from you…or her. I do want the property in South Carolina and Ireland. I'm thinking of taking my extended family to the coast of Ireland. We'll live life as it was intended. But to do that, I have to eliminate you two. I'd then be the sole heir to dear mother's estate."

I noticed movement over his shoulder, under the tree where I'd found the ax. I didn't know if it was one of Dillon's followers, one of Senator Logan's hired guns, or somebody else. I had to keep Dillon distracted, keep him talking. I said, "It seems odd that you're actually holding a weapon. You're good at getting others to kill for you. You must have really wanted Courtney dead to use hypnosis to have her murdered by a deranged Army veteran with PTS." I glanced at the gold torc bracelet he wore on the wrist of the hand that held the .44 magnum. "Is it because you wanted to keep the torc you stole from our mother, or the fact that there's no statute of limitations for statutory rape and murder in South Carolina?"

"You flatter me. Do you really think I could hypnotize someone, to get him to kill, if it's against his nature?" Lightning streaked through the sky and his eyes burned with hate. "Of course I did it. Why? Let me enlighten you, Brother. It's the nature of us all. I just know how to dig deep enough to connect the tap root from the heart to the mind. The key to kill lies within us. I just help them unlock the hidden desire."

Courtney said, "You…you sick bastard, you put me in that coffin and tried to drown me. I know who and what you really are, you narcissistic, evil little man."

"Quiet! Brother, Sean, as the first born son, one who never was in favor with your father, one who was hated by his own mother, it's time I took you aside. We'll go into the woods, as Cain took Abel, and there we will split the brotherhood." He raised the pistol.

"No!" shouted Courtney.

"Follow me, Brother, or I'll shoot her in the face in three seconds. One… two…thr—"

The rifle round tore through Dillon's neck. He collapsed backwards onto the coffin. I looked over to the old oak tree. Beneath the tree, holding my rifle, was the man in the red baseball cap, the man I'd saved earlier. He stood and nodded, moving his hands in the military tactical "all clear," signal.

Courtney looked down at Dillon. "Is he dead?"

"Yeah, he's dead."

"Sean, please take the torc off his wrist."

At that moment we heard a loud noise—a noise that was growing louder. It sounded like a waterfall somewhere in the canyon. I turned to Courtney. "Run! Flashflood. It'll drown us."

"My grandmother's torc!"

She bent down to remove it from Dillon's wrist. I saw his left hand move, in and out of his pocket in a second. He gripped an ice pick. I shoved Courtney aside and grabbed his wrist. He was strong, pushing the ice pick closer to my neck. My hand and arm shook as I slowly overpowered him, turning the ice pick toward his chest. Two seconds later, I plunged the length of the pick into his heart.

He smiled and looked at me. It was the same sardonic grin I'd seen on his father's face before he committed suicide. Dillon said, "It won't end here. Not now…not ever…I am the son of Cain." He stopped breathing, a trickle of blood coming from the left corner of his mouth.

I looked up. The water was rushing down the canyon. Moving like a freight train. Less than five hundred feet from us. I pushed Courtney and yelled, "Go to high ground! Climb the big oak! Now!"

Her eyes were hot, enraged. "Don't let them bury him with my grandmother's…your mother's torc. Your father gave it to her!"

I turned around and tried to pull the torc from his wrist. It was similar to a near wrap-around bracelet. I wasn't sure how he got it on his wrist. There was less than a two-inch space between each end. I tried again. It wasn't coming off unless it was cut off. Dillon's body lay on its back, the arm with the torc supported against the coffin.

I looked up. The wall of water was rushing toward us, pushing trees, logs, and debris. I grabbed the ax, swinging it high above my head, slamming the blade hard through the wrist, directly behind the torc. It was a clean cut, severing the arm from the hand. I lifted up the torc, grabbed Courtney by the arm, and ran through waist-deep water to the other side of the ravine.

We scrambled up a steep hill, the sound of the rushing water like an approaching tornado. There was an outcropping of rock, a cliff just above us. "Up there!" I yelled to Courtney. "Climb!"

The man with the red cap leaned over the edge and shouted, "Give me your hand!"

Courtney clutched his hand and he pulled her up and over the cliff. I knew I was too big, too much dead weight for him. I squatted and jumped as high as I could, my hands grappling the edge of the rock. There were two-inch fissures in the boulders, and I had a good handhold. I pulled myself up, and swung my legs over the cliff as a deluge of churning white water slammed into the side of the canyon wall just below me.

I lay on my back for a second, breathing hard. I looked up in the sky, the dark storm clouds parting, and the light of a full moon illuminating the Blue Ridge Mountains in an ethereal midnight splendor.

ONE HUNDRED-ONE

*T*hree days after returning to Florida, there was a news media feeding frenzy on the steps of the Volusia County Courthouse. Courtney and I watched it live on television at my river cabin, where we'd been staying in relative seclusion pending the release of the DNA testing.

Over a long dinner, I managed to get her to tell me what she'd endured the last few weeks before I found her held prisoner at Dillon's compound. And now we stared at the television, at the live news conference, which was tantamount to looking at her future.

Detective Dan Grant, Volusia County Sheriff, Robert Nelson, members of the DA's office, and a half dozen other law enforcement personnel stood with the courthouse in the background and began their news conference. A wide angle shot showed dozens of satellite news trucks and a small army of reporters.

Sheriff Nelson, a broad-shouldered man with an American flag button pinned on his lapel stepped up to the podium and read from a prepared statement. "Today the investigation into what has been termed the carnival killings has officially ended with regard to Courtney Burke. There has been an arrest made, and the individual, Samuel Edward Nolan, has confessed to the murders of three carnival workers, one here in the county, two others elsewhere. Prior to their deaths, all of the workers had been employed by Bandini Brothers Amusements. Another man, said to be the mastermind behind the killings, Dillon Flanagan, has been killed. Previous to Mr. Flanagan's death, he admitted his involvement using hypnosis or mind-control to manipulate

Mr. Nolan, who was, at the time, being treated for post traumatic syndrome as an out-patient at Veterans Hospital in Orlando.

"As far as Miss Burke is concerned, DNA testing is complete and the tests confirm that Miss Burke is not—I repeat—not, the daughter of Andrea Logan, the wife of Senator Lloyd Logan. Also, Miss Burke is not the daughter of the other person alleged to be her father, Sean O'Brien. From this point, all pending criminal charges against Miss Burke have been dropped and she is free to go. Before District Attorney Henry Carlsberg speaks from his perspective, I'll take a few minutes for questions."

A CNN reporter asked, "If Andrea Logan and Sean O'Brien aren't Courtney Burke's biological parents, can you tell us who is and where they are now?"

Sheriff Nolan said, "It is my understanding that her parents are deceased. She was raised by her grandmother, who recently passed away as well."

A Fox News reporter asked, "Has this information been revealed to the Logan campaign?"

Sheriff Nolan nodded. "A brief summary was sent to them just prior to the start of this news conference."

A CBS news reporter said, "Murder by hypnosis, or mind control, sounds like something covert intelligence agencies might try. Can you tell us for certain that the person who confessed to the killings, Mr. Nolan, was really killing by a post-hypnotic order, or is this part of an insanity plea?"

The district attorney stepped forward, cleared his throat and said, "Mr. Nolan told us that he was recruited, brainwashed—if you will at Mr. Flanagan's Virginia compound, and then sent in to murder the men. And as Sheriff Nolan said, Mr. Flanagan admitted to being complicit in theses killings."

A throng of hands went up in the air, reporters talking over each other, shouting questions to the officials behind the podium.

I stood up and shut off the television, turned to Courtney and smiled. "It's behind you now."

She feigned a smile and said, "For the last couple of nights I've been having nightmares about what happened. I still see Dillon's face, the smirk, as he was about to shoot me in the head. I can feel the cold and darkness of that coffin he buried me in, and smell black mud and sawdust. Maybe I'll always be like that poor man Dillon hypnotized…maybe I'll have PTS too."

I shook my head in disagreement. "Maybe not. Maybe you'll move on with your life and have more good times than bad, more laughter than tears. Maybe have a family of your own one day. You have strength, Courtney… more than you realize right now. You'll never completely forget all the things Dillon did to you, but never…never let them define or dictate who you are or who you will become. If you let the ghost of his evil continue to eat at your heart like a cancer, your spirit dies, and Dillon wins. The way you defeat him the rest of your life is to forgive yourself. None of this, from the time you were a young girl through today, was ever your fault. He was mentally ill—a sick man who was patently evil. Those people prey on the virtuous, the good. You were a victim, and you were searching for a way to bring closure for you and for your grandmother."

"And somehow I found you in all of this. With seven billion people in the world, somehow I found you. What are the odds? I don't believe it just happened. I believe I was somehow guided here. And now you are the only family I have left." She grinned, dimples popping. "So you'd better not go anywhere."

"How about if we both go for ice cream? When was the last time you had ice cream?"

She smiled, wrinkling her brow and nose. "I can't remember. It's been a long time."

"I know a place that makes it by hand. What do you say we go there?"

"Sounds good to me."

"Let me make a quick phone call and we're on our way."

"Okay, I'll hang with Max outside 'till you're ready."

She called Max, both bolting outside, running down to the dock.

I called Kim Davis and said, "I'm spending a little more time with Courtney. She's healing, best she can considering what happened to her."

"Take the time you both need. From what you told me, she went through hell on earth…and so did you. I'm just so grateful that you both survived, that you're here. You're all the family she has left. Be there for her, and I'll be here for you if you need me,

Sean."

I said nothing for a moment. "Thank you, Kim."

"Bye…" I heard her exhale deeply and she disconnected.

I stood on the screen porch, watching Max and Courtney sitting together on the bench seat at the end of the dock. She was chatting with Max like she was her new best friend. Courtney pointed as a great blue heron sailed over the surface of the river. I glanced down at the framed picture of my wife, Sherri, wishing she could have known Courtney. Sherri would have been such a good influence—such a great role model for Courtney. It was what Courtney needed.

What did I need? I had no idea anymore. My entire life—my identity, had been changed, and changed for the rest of my life. But right now I watched my niece heal, watched her rebuild and restore.

And that was enough.

ONE HUNDRED-TWO

Courtney stayed with Max and me at the river cabin for a week. We grilled fish on the dock, watched baby alligators crawl from their nests, eyes the shade of a lemon peel, and plop into the river for the first time. I took her out in the thirteen-foot Boston Whaler and in the canoe. We explored the St Johns and all its mystery and majesty. We tagged along with a whiskered elderly fisherman in a johnboat as he worked his trotline, catching and releasing freshwater stingrays, keeping the yellow-bellied catfish.

He told her about how the tides from the Atlantic have an effect on the river and its wildlife, how crabs were found thriving two-hundred miles inland from the mouth of the river. He told her about the unique history of the river—about the Indians who used to live along its banks until the Spanish arrived. Courtney asked questions and hung on to every word the old man uttered.

I took her to an oxbow in the river where a pair of eagles had built a nest the size of a small car in a large cypress tree next to the water. We sat in the canoe, Courtney in the bow, Max in the middle, and me in the stern, watching the eagles catch and bring fish to their young. We drifted up the tea-colored water of the quiet creeks that feed the river, creeks that smelled of honeysuckles and were tunneled with arching tree branches, white and yellow butterflies erupting from the leaves and wildflowers with the flurry of a snow-globe.

She stood in the boat, next to Max, letting the butterflies hover between her outstretched arms, touching the pewter beards of Spanish moss hanging as far as the eye could see. I watched her laugh as Max barked at a fat raccoon sitting back on its hind legs and using its front paws to pry open a mollusk. It was good to hear her laugh, to watch her spirit rebuild, to nurture her the best I could. I knew that somewhere out there I had a daughter, a young woman who was about Courtney's age. I hoped my daughter was well and content with her life. But right now I had my niece. I had Courtney.

And she had me.

She turned back to me, a wide smile on her face, and said, "This is a cool place. It's like nowhere I've ever been, maybe this is God's little river. I can imagine a dinosaur around the bend."

"We can't go too far around the bend. It gets shallow."

She smiled. "Well, Uncle Sean, I have a feeling you could get us out if we got stuck."

"You do?"

She grinned. "Yeah, I do."

"And I have a feeling you would do okay on your own, too."

"You do?"

"Yeah, I do."

"Maybe it's part of who we are…family…we're survivors, you and me."

— • —

WE SAT ON the screened-in back porch and finished a dinner of buttered corn on the cob, garden salad, and grilled bass—cooked with olive oil, fresh tomatoes, garlic and basil. Courtney had a ravenous appetite. It made me smile to watch her eat and hear about her plans and dreams. We fed Max and the three of us walked down to the dock, Max leading the way, bowls of ice cream in hand, and we sat on the wooden bench seat facing west and the setting sun.

Courtney was in awe watching white pelicans and herons fly into a purple and gold sunset, the colors rolling off the surface of the water like molten rainbows, the smell of trumpet flowers and jasmine in the cool evening air. She savored a spoonful of chocolate ice cream and said, "This so beautiful here. And you've been so kind to me. I want you to know, Uncle Sean, how much I appreciate what you've done. Thank you so much."

"You're welcome. Courtney, I want you to know I've spoken with your grandmother's attorney. Paperwork has been drawn up giving you her home and property in South Carolina."

"Me? She was your mother. It's yours, not mine."

"No…no it's not. I wasn't there."

"It wasn't because you didn't choose to be. You didn't know."

"Listen to me. I'm your older and wiser uncle." I smiled. "Take the property. It's free and clear. The title will be transferred to your name."

"I can't live there. I just can't."

"I understand. You can sell it and go anywhere you want."

"Where would I go?"

"How about Ireland?"

"Ireland?"

"Yes. Your grandmother has some land there, on the west coast."

"Really? I wonder why she didn't talk about it."

"Maybe because she was afraid she'd lose it. I learned she had to sell off bits and pieces through the years to pay the taxes. But there are about fifty acres still there. It has a small cottage on it."

"How do you know that?"

"Because I was there."

"There? You went there…wow."

"Yes. If you want, you could live in the cottage. Maybe study art in school. You told me that was one of your passions. It was your grandmother's, too. She fought to keep the land, to keep it from being developed by people who'd like to have built a time-share resort on it. Maybe you could carry on the fight if they ever come back. It would make a great park or natural preserve one day."

"I would like to spend some time there, but I don't have the money to go."

"I'll help you get a realtor for your grandmother's South Carolina property. We'll get it listed and sold. The money from that will give you a good start, and should pay for college too. In the meantime, I'll buy your airfare, help you get settled. I believe, especially after everything you've been through, that place on the coast of Ireland will help you find what might still

408

be missing. It'll give you the time, the space, and the place you need. I have the number of an older couple, a farm family, that's looking forward to meeting you. They'll be there if you need them."

She looked at me, her eyes tearing, and said "I love you, Uncle Sean."

"I love you, too."

ONE HUNDRED-THREE

A few days later I drove Courtney to Orlando International Airport to catch a plane to Dublin, Ireland. Just before getting on the plane, she stood in the airport with me, reached in her purse and lifted out the torc. "I want you to have this, Uncle Sean. Please, take it."

"It's yours, keep it."

"No, it never was mine. I just tried to return it to my grandmother. Since Dillon wore it, I could never put it on my arm. Please, take it. Maybe it's worth something to someone else." She grabbed my hand and placed the torc in the center of my palm.

"Thank you for everything you did for me."

"You're welcome."

"You promise to come see me in Ireland, okay?"

"I promise."

She kissed me on the cheek, turned and walked toward the boarding area. I watched her with pride. I was going to miss her. Hell, I already did miss her, and she hadn't even left yet."

I WATCHED HER plane take off and thought about what she'd endured, how she somehow survived. And now the U.S. presidential election was three days away. Although DNA testing had definitely verified that Andrea Logan was not Courtney's birth mother, and evidence proved Courtney didn't

410

commit the murders, the American voting pool was stained by the flow of political rhetoric.

It was best for Courtney to go to a place where her image and reputation weren't so much in the public eye. The rural west coast of Ireland was such a place. A few months, a year maybe, and most people wouldn't be able to recall her name, especially if Lloyd Logan lost the election. But the most important thing for Courtney right now wasn't what the American people thought about her, it was what she thought about herself. And that would be better and easier formed for her in a new environment.

I thought about that as I drove toward Ponce Inlet and looked over to the passenger side of the Jeep where Max dozed in the seat. I thought about all of the change, the revelations that had come in my life the last few weeks. To stumble upon the remnant of a family, one that was removed from me when I was an infant. Would I have been better or worse having not been placed in adoption? Or maybe the question I would never answer is would I have made a better difference in the lives of others, my family, had I been raised by a single parent? Could I have helped my mother? Could I have helped my brother or sister? I would never know.

I turned off the I-95 and drove to Port Orange where I found a place I hadn't been to in many years. I used to come, for the first couple years on the anniversary of their deaths. But college, the military, much of my life was in remote countries, and I stopped coming to their graves. But I never stopped remembering their influence on my life.

I parked the Jeep under a moss-draped live oak near the center of Bellevue Memorial Gardens. Max and I walked around the graves, speckled light pouring through the oak branches, a mockingbird chortling in the pines. Max spotted a squirrel and went into hunter mode, ears up, eyes like heat-seeking missiles, low growl in the back of her throat. "Not here, Max. Let's leave the squirrels alone." She cut her brown eyes up at me, seemed to nod, and trotted toward a large pinecone on the ground.

I walked another fifty feet and stood before the graves of the two people who raised me—my parents.

Michael O'Brien   Celeste O'Brien

1939 - 1988   1940 - 1988

I was raised by a loving mother and father, two people tragically killed within eight months of each other as I was about to graduate from high school. As I thought about them, and thought about the close friends in my life, the more I realized the there is no line of delineation between good friends and good family, and that circle of people around you is the wheel supporting your wheelbarrow and the baggage you carry in it. Family isn't defined by blood any more than a person is defined by the color of his or her skin. Unconditional support parallels unconditional love and grace.

Fortunate is the man or woman who has a large circle of family and close friends. Too often, the family home isn't a shelter from the cold and predators, it is a castle with a drawbridge to keep others from knowing about the violence and abuse beyond the moat. Family, at least to me, especially now, is defined by love, grace, a true kinship of spirits more than a common blood type.

I felt my phone buzz in my pocket. I pulled it out. UNKNOWN. I knew the call wasn't coming from Courtney, and anything that read UNKNOWN was not, at the moment, in my wheel house of family and friends. That's why they invented voicemail.

A half minute later I played back the message: "Sean, it's Andrea…I just wanted to let you know that I'm glad the young woman…your niece…was cleared of those charges. Things, as you can imagine, have been pretty hectic this last week going into the election. I called to just say hello and wish you the best. We still had…we still have a daughter together. I have to believe what I did twenty years ago was for the best. I hope you understand that, and find it in your heart to forgive me." She paused, seemed to clear her throat, and her voice changed into a campaign patter. "I know you don't care for Lloyd, but the country needs a man like him now in these troubled times. Take care, Sean…I…" She disconnected.

I glanced down at Max and said, "The delete button is a wonderful thing. What do you say we go for a boat ride? We have a special passenger to pick up. Ready?"

She cocked her head and barked once. We left the cemetery and headed to Ponce Marina. From there our destination would be somewhere beyond the horizon of the sea.

ONE HUNDRED-FOUR

For a woman who hadn't spent much time on boats, Kim Davis was a natural on the water. We'd taken *Jupiter* south to the Florida Keys, Kim, Max and me—final destination unknown. But the stopping off point was a layover on the Caribbean side of Key Largo. It was a harbor I used to sail in an out of when I lived in Miami.

We spent four days there, anchored off Sexton Cove, a place of mesmerizing blue-green turquoise water. We snorkeled and spearfished in the gin-clear water, grilled fresh yellowtail, snapper, and lobster in the cockpit. The cove was bordered by sugar-white sand beaches dotted with leaning coconut palm trees. We took the dinghy to the beach and played like teenagers on spring break, Kim laughing, Max doing her happy bark. We took long walks, soft sand between our toes, and the sweet smell of blooming hibiscus on the gentle trade winds.

On the third day, I taught Kim how to SCUBA dive. After practicing in the shallow cove, I took *Jupiter* into Pennekamp National Park and dove the coral reefs. I held her hand underwater and guided her around the shallow water reefs. Her eyes grew wide behind the glass of her mask when she spotted a large leatherback turtle swimming by less than twenty feet from us. We swam through clouds of multi-colored fish, hovering above French Reef, the coral and sea ferns in a kaleidoscope of purple, lavender, salmon reds and pinks.

When we finally got to the surface and swam to *Jupiter*, Kim was awe-struck. We climbed on *Jupiter's* dive platform, opened the transom door and were greeted by Max. The three of us sat there, Max standing to keep her balance.

Kim pushed her mask on top of her head and looked out over water the color of a fresh-cut lime. She said, "I can't ever go back. Not after all this. When we were below, I could have caught a ride on the back of that sea turtle. I love Ponce Inlet, love our friends at the marina, but down here in the Keys…this is like another world, something I've seen in magazines and travel shows. I've never felt more alive, healthier. The sun, the fresh seafood and this special world. Are you sure we're in America?"

"When we get down to Key West it's debatable."

She looked up and smiled. "And, Sean O'Brien, I never knew sex at sea was even better than on land." She laughed. "I think it's the sea, the boat… and the man."

I smiled. "I'm not so sure about that last ingredient."

"I am."

"I'm glad you are enjoying all of this. We both needed to get away, to put some stuff in the rearview mirror and focus on the horizon."

"And what a big horizon it is. What's in that direction?" She pointed to the west.

"Mexico."

"And back the other way?"

"The Bahamas. Bimini is only about eighty miles from us."

"Really?"

"Really."

"Have you ever been there?"

"Not since Sherri died a few years ago. Max and I sailed to Bimini out of Fort Lauderdale."

"I'd love to go one day."

I heard the buzz of my phone on the cockpit table. I got up. "Don't answer it, Sean. It might destroy the magic of this world. Civilization be gone!"

"It could be Courtney." I stepped to the table. Dave was calling. "Sean, how are things?"

"Good, what's up?"

"I won't ask you where you and Kim wound up."

"Good, then I won't have to lie to you."

He laughed. "Have you been following the election?"

"No. Made a point not to bother."

"Well, Logan is about to make his concession speech. It wasn't even close. He lost by more than a twenty percent margin."

I said nothing, the call of a gull over my head, the sea lapping against *Jupiter's* hull.

"Are you still there, Sean?"

"Yeah, I'm here. Can't say I'm surprised."

"Me either. You, my old friend, are one of a few people on the planet who managed to influence the results of a presidential election."

"Only by default. The only political strategy was about staying alive." I looked over at Kim as she set Max on her lap. "And it was about keeping two women I care for alive, too."

"How's Kim?"

"Doing well."

"That torc you asked me to investigate, well I did a lot of research."

"What'd you find?"

"It's very rare and very valuable. Most of the torc is solid gold, inlaid with some silver and iron. But the history of it makes it even more valuable. More than two-thousand years old, dating back to the days the Romans invaded Ireland. Hell, Caesar could have worn it after taking it from a Celtic holy man. It has, as you may surmise, pagan religious significance as well. Collectors of this kind of ancient art will pay a lot to get it. Museums, especially those with extensive historical collections, will jump at the chance to own it. Based on my research, I'm estimating that this will command a price of near a million dollars."

"See if you can sell it."

"Sell it? Are you sure?"

"Positive. If you get a million, take five percent for yourself. Put half a mill in a trust for Courtney. I'll pay off the remaining taxes on the property in Ireland. You can wire whatever's left to my bank account."

"And which account would that be?"

Kim smiled and set Max on the cockpit. "It'll be a new account, one I open in Bimini."

"Bimini?"

"Yeah, Dave…Bimini. I'll send you the routing number. Thanks…we'll see you in a couple of weeks." I disconnected and set the phone down.

The sun was dropping in the western sky, the bulbous clouds filling with shades of blood red, mauve, copper, and flamingo feather pinks from the sky to the sea. A school of brown pelicans streaked across the horizon. Kim stepped closer to me, her hair wet from the dive, her eyes filled with the colors of the sunset. I cupped her tanned face in my hands and we kissed softly, her lips held a slight taste of sea salt, her skin warm from the sun.

Kim slowly ran the tips of her fingers across my bare chest. She tenderly touched the new scar near my birthmark. "I was so afraid for you, Sean. So afraid they'd destroy you. And now you return from your dangerous journey with another war wound." She touched my birthmark. "I think this little birthmark protects you."

"You do?"

"Yes, it was stenciled on by a higher power. That's a real tattoo, one that you never want to remove." She kissed my chest.

I said, "Let's head up to the bridge, fix cocktails, and watch the sunset."

"Sounds good."

"You said you'd love sail to Bimini. Want to go?"

"When?"

"In the morning."

"You're not kidding."

"Nope."

"You've got a first mate, captain. Let me call my sister to ask her to watch my dog for a while longer. How long should I tell her?" "Tell her you'll send a postcard." Kim grinned and raised her eyebrows.

We sat on the bench seat, the three of us, Max scouting the sea birds, Kim and I sipping rum punches, watching the sky drain into the ocean. After the sun vanished below the horizon, there was a half second green flash and then an inky purple and black smothered the candle smudge of daylight, and a much greater sea grew, a sea of darkness. It went opposite the way of the sun, sweeping high into the universe, turning on the nightlights, the stars, their ancient light falling from the heavens onto the faces, eyes, and imaginations of mortals below the vast curtain of the unknown.

THE END

We hope you've enjoyed

BLOOD OF CAIN

The following is an excerpt from the sixth novel in the Sean O'Brien series coming in 2014. Here's a preview of

BLACK RIVER

BLACK
RIVER

TOM LOWE

PROLOGUE

NORTH FLORIDA, JANUARY, 1862

Henry Hopkins looked over his shoulder and saw his wife disappear behind the mist rising above the river. The fog couldn't hide the fear on her face. If he wasn't killed in the next hour, Henry knew that Angelina would be there for him when he rowed the small fishing boat back across the river, after midnight. She would wave the lantern precisely at 1:00 a.m. for a few seconds to help guide him to the clearing on the shore, to the Confederate-controlled side of the St. Johns River. But now Henry and another man rowed toward the most famous racing sailboat in the world, and Henry felt a knot grow in his stomach.

The river was a half mile wide at Horseshoe Bend. The weather-beaten boat smelled of dried fish guts, wet burlap, and burnt pipe tobacco. A crescent moon rose over the eastern shoreline and sent a sliver of light bouncing from the surface of the black river -- a river filled with alligators, some as long as the boat. And it was filled with Union Navy gunboats.

The men rowed quietly, the only sounds coming from water dripping off the oars, and from a great horned owl, its night calls echoing across the river from the top of a large cypress tree near the shore. The moon cast the tree in silhouette, its massive branches holding shadowy beards of Spanish moss hanging straight down. The old cypress tree had been standing since before the first Seminole War with the U.S. government. The tree was a well-known landmark, a visual marker near the secluded entrance to Dunn's Creek, a deep-water tributary to the St. Johns River. It was in the creek where the Confederates were hiding *America*, the schooner that beat the British ten years earlier in a race now known as the *America's Cup*. The creek was more than seventy feet deep near the place where it flowed into the St. Johns, a few miles downriver from Jacksonville, Florida.

America was recently bought by the Confederate Navy and used as a blockade runner to outrun the Union Navy blocking southern ports. It had just made a trans-Atlantic voyage from Liverpool, England, and it sailed with a top-secret crew, cargo, and a contract to be delivered directly to the president of the Confederate States of America, Jefferson Davis, and his top general, Robert E. Lee.

Henry wore his wide brim hat pulled low over his eyes. His unshaven face was lean and rawboned. He watched the river, eyes as dark as the water, searching for Union gunboats, listening for steam-fired engines coming from down river. His nostrils tested the breeze, trying to detect burning coal, the smell of trouble. The two men rowed silently and spoke in whispers as they got closer to *America,* its mast and stern in a dark profile under the moon rising high above Dunn's Creek. Henry stopped rowing. "Did you hear that?"

"Hear what?" asked William Kramer, a bull of a man with a thick chest and powerful forearms. He stopped, lifting his paddle from the water and sat erect, listening to the sounds of the night on the river.

Henry looked south. "Sounded like a yank patrol boat."

"I didn't hear nothin.' Just an old hoot owl, that's all."

"C'mon. We gotta get into the creek and scuttle the ship before the yanks take her."

"Who'd you say we're supposed to meet?"

"Don't know. Top secret. Maybe General Lee himself. Time's a wasting. Let's row."

They entered the wide mouth of Dunn's Creek, bordered by towering cypress trees and thick hammocks of palms and live oaks older than the young nation. A weeping willow tree leaned into the creek, its tentacle-like limbs scraping the surface of black water. Bullfrogs competed in a thick chorus of mating calls. Hungry mosquitoes greeted the men with whines, orbiting their heads, biting at necks and ears.

America, 101 feet in length and more than 170 tons of wood and steel, was anchored in the center of the wide creek. As the men rowed closer to the schooner, they heard the whinny of horses in the foliage on the creek bank. Henry touched his .36 caliber revolver on his side. He said, "Who goes there?"

Two men on horseback stepped into wedge of moonlight spilling between the limbs of a cypress tree near the creek. Both men were dressed in Confederate uniforms. They dismounted and signaled for Henry and William to row to the shore. Captain John Jackson Dickinson, brown eyes hard as steel, watched the men approach. His gaunt face was unreadable. A shaggy moustache curled over his top lip. He wore a Stetson hat, gray coat and pants, and a saber at his side. A crooked, unlit cigar protruded from the corner of his mouth. He held his horse's reins and waited. The other man, a sergeant, wore similar clothes, but disheveled, as if he'd slept in them. Dickinson stepped closer and said, "Good evening, men. I'm Captain Dickinson. This is Sergeant Reese. Which one of you is Henry Hopkins?"

"I am, sir. This is my friend, Corporal William Kramer."

Dickinson nodded. "What are your plans to scuttle the ship?"

William spoke. "Sir, I have two very sharp augers. I believe I can drill half a dozen holes just below the waterline and she'll sink in no time."

Dickinson snorted, releasing a deep breath. He removed the cigar from his mouth, spit out a sliver of tobacco, and looked at the yacht, his eyes softening, following the masts skyward. "Damn shame. *America* beat fourteen of the fastest yachts in the world from the British Royal Fleet in 1851. Back then the race was called the 100 Guinea Cup. After *America* took it by finishing eight miles ahead of the nearest yacht, Queen Victoria renamed the race *America's Cup* in honor of that yacht anchored in front of us." He lit the cigar and blew smoke at the mosquitoes in front of his face. "It's just a matter of days before the yanks bring in the whole damn Union Navy to seize her. We can't let that happen. They'll outfit her with canons and aim 'em down our throats. Orders come from the very top. Commence your drillin', sir. Looks like you have the arms and shoulders to do it. There's one final matter." He looked at William and asked, "Corporal, do you need help with your task?"

"I'm just gonna lean over the edge of the rowboat and bore holes into the yacht right below the waterline. I figure it won't take too long. Three in the bow and three in the stern."

Dickinson turned to his sergeant. "Go on and sit in the boat, keep it from flipping over as Corporal Kramer cuts the holes. Lieutenant Hopkins, step ashore. I need to fill you in on your mission, and it's your mission alone. Are we clear on this?"

Henry nodded. "Yes sir."

As Henry stepped on dry land, the sergeant climbed in the boat. Within two minutes the men in the boat were at the bow of *America*, the auger chewing the first hole through wood.

Captain Dickinson watched the progress for a moment, eyes heavy, and then turned to Henry. "We removed all her cargo right after she arrived from England last week. She's made a trip over there to bring back something." He opened a haversack tied to his horse, lifting a strongbox from the sack. He also removed a leather satchel.

"What's that?" asked Henry.

"No one, not the corporal, no one is to hear what I'm about to tell you. Understand?"

"Yes sir."

"Inside this pouch is a letter of agreement between England and the Confederate States of America. It is signed by the Prime Minister and President Davis. I hear it has the blessing of the Queen. Your job is to get it this fully executed contract, and the strong box, to President Davis, and to do it traveling behind enemy lines. If you feel you are about to be captured, or worse, your last mission on earth is to make sure this agreement doesn't fall into Union hands." "I understand, sir."

"I'm told you were hand-picked by our Secret Service to carry out this job."

"What's in that box, sir?"

"A good faith payment from England. It'll go into the Confederate treasury to help the CSA sustain the cause, and to give us added financial stability to fight this damn war."

Henry nodded. "Understood, sir. I just wonder why England would do this, 'cause I heard Queen Victoria's neutral in the war."

"Maybe, at least in public. But it boils down to business. For England, it's about cotton and manufacturing. The Confederate Navy is ordering most of our ships, all being built from the shipyards in Liverpool." Dickinson glanced at his horse. "I also hear you're one of the best riders we have."

"I do all right."

"You'll be traveling great distances, mostly by night. The strongbox is fairly light. A diamond doesn't have the weight of gold."

"Diamond?"

"At least one might have come from the Crown Jewels."

"The Crown Jewels? One, sir? Which one?"

"We're under strict orders not to open the box. But I'm told one of the most valuable diamonds in the world is in there. It's here as a loan of sorts. A gamble to keep the South solvent. If this war drags on, and if the CSA treasury is drained, the diamond, if sold to the right people, might keep the cause alive. However, if the war begins to look like a losing proposition, regardless of a cash infusion, we're supposed to return the diamond to England. All to be done with the utmost confidentially. It's spelled out in this contract."

A movement caught Dickinson's eye. *America* was taking on water, slowly sinking. The men in the rowboat were now paddling back to shore. Dickinson said, "The irony tonight is that we are scuttling a ship that beat the British, and yet we might need their money to keep the Confederate states afloat. Are you prepared for what might be the most important, and most dangerous, one-man mission in this war?"

"I hope so, sir."

"Henry Hopkins, son, I do, too. I sure as hell do." Dickinson turned to watch *America* drop below the surface. Within minutes, the massive schooner vanished beneath the dark water. Only the three masts and their cross-beams protruded from the deep creek as if three crosses rose up in the moonlight to mark a watery grave.

— —

AN HOUR LATER, Henry Hopkins and William Kramer quietly began rowing back across the St. Johns River. Clouds passed slowly in front of the moon providing the cloak of darkness they needed. The breeze from the north brought the slight odor of burning coal.

Henry rowed, his eyes scanning the dark water, north to south. "Yanks are out there somewhere. I can smell them, smell the coal burning. It's got to be a gunboat."

William stopped rowing for a moment, listening, his eyes straining in the dark. "Yeah, I smell it. Can almost feel the steam on my skin. But I don't see or hear anything."

"Row. We're only halfway across." He looked toward the far western shore, the tree-line a slight silhouette in the dim moonlight. "There's the lantern! Angelina's signaling."

William nodded. "Yep, she's right on time. You got a fine woman, Henry. How'd a fella like you manage that?" William chuckled.

"I ask myself that all the time."

William glanced down at the strongbox in the center of the boat. "I guess you're not gonna tell me what's in the box, huh?"

"You guessed right. I swore an oath. I'm just the courier."

"Can you tell me what's in that haversack around your neck? I know it's important, or we wouldn't be meeting those men and sinking the most famous schooner in the world. Is it something that sailed across on *America* from England to Florida?"

"I can tell you that…yes, it is. Come on, we gotta get to the other side of this river."

The moon climbed out of the clouds like shedding dark clothes, the St. Johns now bathed in moonlight, the ripples across the black water shimmering with brushstrokes of buttery light. Henry said, "Let' move! We're sitting ducks out here."

William rowed harder, looking north for a second. A bullet hit him in his throat, the impact knocking him on his back, his dying eyes focused on Henry.

"William!" Dear God! Hold on! I'll get us to the other side."

William tried to speak, his words gurgling, blood flowing out of his mouth.

Henry rowed with all his strength, looking over his shoulder to the spot on the distant shore where his wife waved the lantern, the moving pulse of light like the glow of a firefly in the black. He glanced back at his friend just as a dozen rounds burst from the gunboat skirting an oxbow bend in the river. The heavy bullets ripped through the wooden boat, blowing the sides and bottom out.

Within seconds, the boat began sinking, William Kruger's body slipping beneath the black water, his wide eyes gazing up at the stars. Henry reached for the strongbox just as the boat split in half taking the strongbox and the body of William Kruger to the bottom of the river.

Henry clutched the haversack around his neck, trying to hold it above the surface of the cool water. A cloud slipped over the face of the moon and the river was black again. He could hear the steam engine on the patrol boat in the distance, somewhere in the inky darkness. Henry swam with all his strength toward the glow of the lantern. He swam toward the promise of a life with Angelina.

And he swam toward the hope of the South.

ONE

PONCE MARINA, FLORIDA – TODAY

Sean O'Brien turned to Max and said, "Let's pull your head back inside the Jeep. We'll park, unload groceries, and go to work. At least I'll go to work. You might find old Joe the cat to play a hard-fought game of hide 'n seek. On second thought, maybe not." O'Brien's ten-pound dachshund, Max, balanced herself, hind legs on the passenger seat, head out the open widow, hound dog ears flapping in the wind. Her nose tested the air as O'Brien drove across the parking lot adjacent to the Tiki Bar at the Ponce Marina, oyster shells cracking under the tires.

He got out of the Jeep and stretched his 200-pound, six-two frame. Max scampered across his seat, diving from the floorboard to the parking lot like a paratrooper on a mission. She could smell the scent of blackened redfish, garlic shrimp, and hushpuppies, all coming from the Tiki Bar. O'Brien laughed. "Whoa, if Kim's on duty, you'll be fed." He unloaded a bag of groceries, two cans of boat wax, and followed Max and her nose into an open-air dining experience that blended the smells of sun-block with deep-fried mullet.

The Tiki Bar was a restaurant on stilts, a place that appealed to bikers, babes, fishermen and vacationing families. Beyond the food and drinks, it evoked a 1950's picture postcard atmosphere addressed from a Florida of simpler times. Fifty percent of the customers came from the marina neighborhood of live-a-boards and transients, mariners with seafaring gypsy blood in restless genes. They were men who worked the shrimp boats for a paycheck and the distance the sea could place between them and their troubles anchored to land bound conflicts. The Tiki Bar's hardwood floors were stained into a piebald splatter of spilled beer, grease, and more than a few drops of blood. Bar art.

This Saturday morning all the isinglass windows were rolled up, the sea breeze delivering the smell of the grilled fish across the marina. One person sat at the rustic bar. A dozen sunburned tourists and charter boat deckhands were seated at the tables made from large wooden spools that, in a former life, were used to wrap telephone cables around them. The big spools were shellacked and turned on their sides. Three chairs to each spool. The hole in the center great for tossing peanut shells.

Kim Davis beamed when O'Brien and Max approached. Kim's chestnut hair was pinned up. Her caramel colored eyes were bright, like morning sunlight shining through amber stained-glass. She stood behind the bar, rinsing a beer mug and timing a slow-pour of a draft Guinness.

"Sean, you ever notice Miss Max is always leading you? She's the only female that can get away with it." Kim smiled, dimples appearing on her tanned face. She handed the Guinness to a charter boat captain who sipped it before returning to his table. "Hold on, Max" she said, picking up a piece of popcorn shrimp and walking around the end of the bar. She knelt down, Max almost jumped in her lap. "Hi, baby. Here's one of your favorites." Max took the treat, tail wagging, and sat to eat.

O'Brien said, "She'll be back for cocktail sauce." He leaned in and kissed Kim on the cheek.

Kim smiled, standing, pressing her open palms against the blue jeans that accentuated her hips. "It's about time you get back to your boat here at the marina. Were you getting a little lonely out there on the river?"

"A little." O'Brien smiled. "My old house is a lot like owning an old boat. It always needs a coat of paint or wax." He held up a tin of boat wax.

"I'm off at four, if you're still at it, I'll ice down a few Corona's for you."

"Sounds good, but you'd first have to sneak them by Nick's boat." O'Brien could feel someone staring at him. He glanced over his shoulder and locked eyes with an older man sitting by himself at the very end of the bar. The man wore his white hair neatly parted on the left, ruddy thin face, polo shirt, and khaki pants.

Kim said, "He's been waiting for you."

"Who is he, and how did he know I was coming here today?"

"I didn't get his name. He's been sipping black coffee for two hours, and guarding that folder in front of him like a hawk. He asked at the marina office whether or not you lived aboard. Nick was in the office paying his rent and overheard the man. Nick told him he knew you and that you had plans to work on your boat today. So the gent's been waiting your arrival."

"I wonder what he wants."

"Maybe you should find out. On second thought…oh what the hell, Sean. He's just a harmless, elderly gentleman, right? But what if something in that folder isn't so harmless? I'll keep an eye on Max for you."

Made in the USA
Middletown, DE
31 August 2020